THE GOD PLAYERS

A NOVEL

Phil Valentine

Oxley Durchville Publishing

Oxley Durchville Publishing, LLC
118 16th Avenue South
Suite 4-387
Nashville, TN 37203

OxleyDurchville.com

"The Man in Gray" by Madison Casein from "Weeds by the Wall" Copyright © 1901

For information about special discounts for bulk purchases, please contact Oxley Durchville Special Sales at business@oxleydurchville.com.

For foreign and subsidiary rights, contact rights@oxleydurchville.com.

The Library of Congress Cataloging-in-Publication Data is available upon request.

ISBN 978-0-9968752-0-2 (hardcover)
ISBN 978-0-9968752-1-9 (ebook)
ISBN 978-0-9968752-2-6 (audiobook)

Printed in the United States of America
15 16 17 18 19 ODP 10 9 8 7 6 5 4 3 2 1

ACKNOWLEDGEMENTS

The idea for this novel started long ago. Although I've written three non-fiction books, this was my first completed manuscript. It sat in a box for many years as career moves, movie projects, and other books nudged it aside. I always loved the premise of the story, but I fretted over its timing. However, just when I thought the issue might become passé there would be something else to propel it to the forefront of the nation's consciousness. I began to appreciate its timeless nature.

It was after the Supreme Court ruling on gay marriage that I was convinced it was time to release this book. I pulled the manuscript back out, dusted it off, and began the task of bringing every aspect of it up to date. I was surprised at how little had changed since I finished it and tucked it away in the basement. Obviously, the surface argument is over whether or not a gay gene actually exists. That's what makes this a work of science fiction. If you get hung up on that aspect of the story you're missing the deeper meaning. This is a multi-faceted human story. There are so many variables that make choosing one side or the other difficult.

Arguing the issue out in court, as the characters do in this novel, makes it easier to see all of the incredible dimensions. I'm fortunate enough to come from a family of lawyers who counseled me on the technical aspects of a jury trial. My father, Tim Valentine, and my oldest brother, Steve Valentine, were kind enough to pore over the manuscript and make helpful suggestions and I appreciate that. Thanks to Barbara Valentine and Art Shirley for their advice in the editing process as well.

Diogo Lando and the fine folks at Red Raven were invaluable in their contributions to this project. I thank you all immensely.

And I want to thank you, the reader. Readers give voice to the writers. Without you, we are silent.

— Phil Valentine

1

"GOD HATES FAGS."

The black, handwritten letters screamed from the white poster board held aloft by a wooden handle. The small crowd that gathered around it was dead silent, standing stone-faced on the sidewalk beneath a line of palm trees like the monolithic figures of Easter Island. Their solemnity made the protest all the more disturbing. After being hauled off to jail on several occasions before they could effectively disrupt even one wedding, they had decided to change tactics. The vitriolic spectacle was replaced by the mute protest. Prior to the change, they were just another fringe group gathering, marching, and protesting. Now they stood out, as did their message. The voiceless demonstration had made them famous, and they moved from town to town like an old-fashioned tent revival. Or a plague. Gothic figures in drab clothing standing with blank eyes focused on the object of their protest. Their only other placard read, "GOD IS WATCHING." To be on the receiving end was unnerving, like seeing an expressionless clown standing by a graveyard at dusk waving to passersby. They stood in defiance of what they viewed as the moral destruction of the country, undaunted by public opinion or by the people they protested against.

Congregants of the wedding across the street emerged from the church. Their gleeful smiles evaporated from their faces. Some dismissively waved the protestors off. Others were instantly enraged and unable to contain their anger. Their number grew, and they moved with a furious gait from the steps of the church across the street to the sidewalk where the stoic protestors stood motionless with only their signs as their collective voice. Some people shrieked obscenities at them. Others spat. Police in riot gear moved in a little closer, anticipating a clash. One protestor calmly wiped spittle from her face with a handkerchief, her passivity only serving to infuriate the crowd even more. The police positioned themselves between the deathlike protestors and the angry mob. The intervention incited the crowd further, and they had to be shoved back with batons, screaming over the shoulders of the cops. Television cameras captured the moment. This was not LA or New York. This was the sleepy mid-sized city of Loveport, not quite ready for the tribulations of heady social issues. But even small Southern cities could not avoid the inevitable societal changes. As much as they wanted to remain in the past, they were being dragged by the feet into the twenty-first century.

The nursery at Loveport Medical Center was abundant with new life. Sturdy plastic bassinets atop rolling stainless steel carts were lovingly lined with blankets of bright colors and happy designs. Newborn infants, scrubbed clean, were rolled tightly like fine silverware in linen napkins and placed on their sides. Name cards with the last names of the babies were set at the foot of the bassinets — blue for the boys, pink for the little girls. The sterile, brightly lit room almost took on the appearance of a baby factory. Fresh additions were rolled in as if they'd just come off the assembly line. They strained their newborn eyes to take in their surroundings, donning tiny caps of blue or pink. The only thing visible was their diminutive, rosy faces.

Dr. Clark Penrose found it therapeutic to stand on the other side of the plate glass window once in a while. As the nurses went about their tasks of changing diapers and taking temperatures, excited family and friends pressed their noses against the window, pointing and cooing at the small wonders. Like an aquarium of some exotic, colorful fish, these specimens needed simply to lie there to thrill the spectators on the other side of the glass. Dr. Penrose lingered on each small face, charmed by their precious expressions yet still amazed, after all these years, at their complexity. Some cried, while others yawned in contentment. Their scrunched-up faces so resembled one another, yet each was completely different. These young lives were starting with a clean slate. No mistakes. No bungled choices. Before too long, these little souls would be faced with adult choices. Not some inconsequential decision like which ice cream flavor to pick or which television show to watch. Real choices with real ramifications like choosing a career, a spouse, choosing when — or if — to have children of their own. Not participating wasn't an option. Not choosing was a choice by default. The choice. It decides who we are, what we are, what we will become, and what will become of us. When we don't choose, choices are made for us. The choices we make — or fail to make — lead to our loss of innocence. Once lost, innocence is impossible to retrieve. It's a door through which one passes, and it slams shut behind us. How Penrose envied those little figures sleeping and relaxing before him. No worries. No pressure. No choices to make. Everything was decided for them. How utterly liberated they were. How completely dependent.

It was the reality that these were actual lives and not just the result of another day at the office that Dr. Penrose sought to reinforce each time he paid a visit to the other side of the glass. It restored his clarity of purpose, his reason for being. The precious, bright faces seemed to burn through the thick fog of his tedious and incessant work.

He allowed his mind to wander back to his point of entry into this world he now called home, this life of medicine that seemed as second nature as breathing. Most of his formative years were spent in England, the result of an ambitious and adventurous father who dragged the family along halfway around the world on his great adventure. Penrose had lived there from the age of five and had grown accustomed to the ways of the British. He had planned to live the rest of his days there;

however, his mother had insisted on his receiving his post-secondary education stateside, one of the conditions on which she had agreed to make the move. She found the British pleasant enough. It wasn't that. She was saddened by the prospect of severing their family ties with the country she loved. It was reconnecting with her roots. Replanting her son in America would re-establish her American heritage, her *Southern* American heritage, if she were lucky.

Naturally, Penrose protested. Why would he want to leave the country he had grown to love just to fulfill some idealistic relic of a covenant his mother had made with herself long, long ago? His father sternly backed his wife's wishes. Penrose reluctantly agreed to accompany his parents as repatriated Americans.

Once back in the states, Penrose navigated his way through the labyrinth of undergrad, medical school, and residency. He chose his father's alma mater, Duke University, as his undergraduate school. He was a legacy, but that meant little to the admissions board. They appreciated his high marks in school, but what really impressed them was the fact that he was an Eton man. They tried not to have their heads turned by high society, but an American with a British upper-crust pedigree was a perfect fit for a university that fancied itself as the Ivy League of the South. Penrose's father jokingly referred to Duke as 'Rebel Yale.'

Upon graduation, he was accepted into their medical school program but sought a change of scenery instead. His boyhood recollections of America were vague and he wanted to take in as much of this new, vast continent as he could. He headed west, selecting Vanderbilt University for med school then accepting a residency at UCLA Medical Center. Once out in the real world, he found his considerable talents in demand in large metropolitan areas across the country, cities, which did not altogether agree with his temperament. He was drawn to the South, not just because of his parents' roots, but because of the people and the pace that reminded him of his beloved England. He was not content to live just anywhere south of the Mason-Dixon line. He longed to be near the sea, where he could stare out endlessly eastward toward home. He was a man torn between two continents, each like magnetic north pulling him in a constant state of tug-of-war. He would have set sail for home already were it not for an anchor stronger than the currents that tried desperately to pull him out to sea. He had met her while attending medical school in Nashville and knew if he didn't marry her soon, his obsession might force out every bit of knowledge stored up in his head and replace it entirely with images of her. They were wed six months to the day from their first date in a quaint, gentile Southern wedding in her home state of Mississippi. His parents were none too pleased with his impulsive nuptials but quickly grew to adore their new daughter-in-law. With that goal accomplished, Penrose was able to refocus his attention on the task at hand — graduating from medical school. After his residency in California, they both longed to return to the South. It was a godsend when he received the call from Loveport Medical Center, a facility of remarkable prestige but set in the near equivalent of the English countryside. It was the ideal location to raise their budding family.

The city of Loveport was a charming, historic town caught somewhere between its past and its uncertain future. Once a vibrant port town and crucial trading center, her prime was behind her. Deeper ports discovered to the south siphoned off what was, prior to the twentieth century, one of the busiest ports on the East coast. It was a slow and painful death as Loveport's majesty was chipped away little by little. Her inevitable decline was sealed years later when America's primary mode of intra-continental distribution of goods shifted from rail to trucking. The port town was overlooked for a major interstate which connected north to south, the result of a political power struggle in the state which favored the newer cities inland. Loveport was lost in the transition. The town fell back on the only source of revenue it could find, that as a tourist town intent on reliving its former glory. The tourist label only served to discourage industry from taking it seriously, thus, compounding its problems. The cobblestone streets down by the waterfront, which once bustled with bankers and sailors and traders, now depended on the charm of its historic storefronts and bed and breakfasts and small museums to drive the local economy. There was but one institution that saved Loveport from complete anonymity.

During the period in which Loveport served as a vital seaport, the need arose for qualified medical personnel. At the time, there wasn't a reputable medical institution in the area. Doctors were educated elsewhere in the country and literally shipped into Loveport. Shortly after the Civil War, a group of farsighted town elders sat down to change all that. The meeting they held in the study of one of the wealthy men's antebellum homes would forever alter the trajectory of Loveport's future. That small group of men started an institution of higher learning with a modest teaching hospital for physicians. While Loveport's reputation as a thriving center of commerce began to wane, its standing as a medical center was growing. Patients, first from around the state, then from all over the region, began flocking to Loveport for its quality medical care. By the end of World War II, Loveport University and Medical Center had built a considerable reputation for itself. So much so that the city found itself competing for its own name. By design or by happenstance, the city of Loveport finally ceded its name to its most famous industry. The name 'Loveport' would no longer be inexorably tied to the port city, but to that institution of higher learning. Still, when those Ivy League Schools of the South were mentioned, Loveport always managed to fall just shy of inclusion. Eventually, a new opportunity revealed itself. That new frontier was genetics and Loveport was determined to boost its reputation by standing out as a pioneer. Dr. Clark Penrose was an integral part of that plan. The iconoclast who sought to find his identity was the perfect cog in the wheel of an institution that sought to define its own. He spent countless meditative hours gazing off her coastline out into the farthest reaches of the horizon from a plot of ocean-front property he had purchased and upon which he had refused to build. When the pressure reached a point near boiling, Clark Penrose would drive the winding road up to his secluded hillside perch, mount himself on its windswept crest, and watch the waves crashing onto the beach below. The ocean seemed to cleanse his mind with each wave that washed ashore. The receding tide carried away his angst, and his troubles dissipated in the vast expanse of water.

It was as if Penrose were the captain and Loveport his ship. They were on a journey in search of a new world. What exactly they would find there, he had no clue. They were sailing in uncharted waters with no idea what lay ahead. The best he could hope for was to steer her safely along, to skipper her clear of treacherous weather, but dark clouds were gathering in the distance. He had battened down the hatches as best he could. He knew they were in for some choppy seas, but not even he could predict the ferocity of the impending storm.

2

Dr. Penrose glanced down at his watch. He had ten minutes to make his dinner date. He slowly wiped his hand over his face then massaged the back of his neck. He wasn't in much of a mood for it. Truthfully, he was never in much of a mood for it. Especially, tonight. His university colleagues were gathering, but he had more important things on his mind. Despite the long hours lately, he felt he was on the verge of a breakthrough after years of disappointment. This could very well turn out to be the biggest day of his professional career. He tried not to overstate its importance in his daily journal at the risk of sounding melodramatic. As important as it was, he could tell no one.

Try as he may to stay out of it, he was constantly being dragged in one direction or another by the political forces on campus. Not political forces in the conventional sense, but the politics of bureaucracy, inherent in any working environment, no matter the profession. He had neither the interest nor the patience for it. Loveport was no different from any other college campus in America. Idealistic university professors saw their role as crusaders against social injustice and attempted to enlist his support in their causes. They waged their war from behind their tenured fortresses, impenetrable by the world of capitalist reality. They recruited foot soldiers from their classrooms and sent them into real-world battles where these professors dared not tread themselves, like lofty generals who had become too valuable, too indispensable to risk their own lives in the fight upon which they pledged their soldiers' lives.

On the other side, no less detached from reality, were some of his doctor colleagues at the university hospital who sought to protect their franchise. They were in the minority, as doctors went at Loveport, but were a vocal contingent, indeed. Instead of following their Hippocratic Oath, this small cadre of self-absorbed physicians stuffed the fortifications of their own castles with copious quantities of cash, which served to muffle the shouts of the disillusioned rabble outside their walls. Too many of their kind had developed an attitude of pulling up the draw bridge and stocking the moat with crocodiles now that they were safely inside its confines, many by the skin of their teeth. Their mission had evolved to keep their profession and, more specifically, Loveport as exclusive as their expensive country clubs, letting no one through its doors unless and until they shared their aristocratic snobbery. Such is oftentimes the case with inferiority complexes. By pretending to be well-bred, they believed they made it so. The faux finishes on their faux mansions masked the ugly reality behind their faux lives. Certainly not all of Penrose's medical colleagues fell into this category. Most did not. There were enough, however, to help balance the whacked-out professors on the other side and give them fuel for their fire of income inequality.

Both forces clawed for Penrose's attention and devotion, and both got neither. The ideologues of the professorial set felt a kindred spirit in Penrose's non-conformist approach to his work. The social masqueraders were smitten by his British pedigree. He was too consumed with his projects — some argued, with himself — to pay either group much mind. Even his more level-headed peers who tried to steer clear of either group warned him he should lay his payment of appeasement at the altar of both of these polarizing forces on campus or ignore them at his own peril. He chose the latter and took his chances.

Yet, there he sat with a sampling of the yacht club set that his friend, Dr. Reed Mosser — who sat to his right — said he needed to befriend to keep from becoming a total misanthrope. Two other doctors from the university, along with their spouses, rounded out the large table in the back of the restaurant. Situated just across the street from the medical center, it was a regular hangout for Loveport Medical Center employees. Many familiar faces filled the tables and booths. Not familiar enough, however, to conjure up a name to go with a face. Dr. Penrose sat in silence, staring straight ahead, nursing his half-full glass of Diet Dr. Pepper. He was oblivious to the chatter that engulfed the table. It was just somewhere to pass the time. A place to wait. A place to be.

The talk seemed so altogether insignificant compared to what occupied his mind that he found it impossible to feign interest. The server cleared the dishes as each individual voice at the table dissolved until one became indistinguishable from the other, melting into a low, monotonous hum. The faces seemed like ventriloquist dolls, the mouths opening and closing but merely regurgitating the thoughts and beliefs of those who actually pulled their strings. He sat staring at a light that caught his eye across the room and it eventually blurred out of focus, like a kaleidoscope of meaningless luminescence turning and swirling in melding shapes and colors. He drifted back to his days at Vanderbilt. He could feel the excitement of becoming a doctor as if it were brand new to him. The exhilaration that lured him to medicine was as real and deep and sincere as the day he graduated.

Clark Penrose was born for nothing else. Since his earliest childhood memories, it was all he ever wanted to do. His was a virtuous enough calling if not a bit old-fashioned. He wanted to contribute to the world of medicine, though his motivation was not completely altruistic. He longed to leave his mark, to achieve an enduring legacy of immortality. He was not satisfied with merely participating in his profession, he was determined to transcend it. They might never admit it, but he sensed some of his classmates saw him as someone locked in another era. That suited Penrose just fine. He loathed the thought of being one of that kind, the kind that entered the profession for the trappings of wealth and the shallow wives they wore on their arms like Christmas ornaments. His was an obsession, a mission. He gave no thought to wealth. It wasn't even the prestige so much as it was the accomplishment itself. Although older, he still hadn't lost that zeal. He hadn't forsaken that drive that propelled him through medical school and on to become one of the most celebrated scientists in his chosen field of genetics. Still, the "big discovery" eluded him.

The dark brown temples were now streaked with gray. Lately, he had taken to scanning the medical journals with the aid of reading glasses, but his mind was as fertile and as keen as the day he accepted his diploma. It was obvious he inherited his gift for medicine from his father, but it was his mother from whom he acquired his sense of honor and duty. Honor he owed to his profession. Duty was to himself.

He often wondered how much genetics played in his own role as a doctor and scientist. When he was a child, his father accepted an invitation to head up the Neuroscience Consortium at the University of Birmingham in England. As the devoted wife, his mother eagerly packed up her young family and headed off for an overseas adventure. It wasn't until he was eighteen that his parents moved back to the states. He enjoyed a splendid education while in England and brought back with him an enthusiasm for medicine and a yearning for discovery. He also retained a noticeable British accent and a few of the famous English idiosyncrasies. He was a person the Yanks might term an 'oddball,' a label which served him well as the moody, cantankerous scientist. Eccentric might be a more apt description. There's little difference between the two. Eccentrics are merely oddballs with money. Even though he never chased money, it's true that Penrose enjoyed his share of financial success, but his lifestyle never betrayed his wealth. He took great care not to get caught up in his materialism; rather, he concentrated on his life's work.

He leaned back in his chair and took stock of that work with self-satisfaction. Nothing had ever excited him like this. Never had he been so totally consumed by something that it absorbed his every waking moment. Since the day of his discovery, he could think of nothing else. He pondered the future and how different things would be. He weighed the negatives against the positives and felt good in his decision. Human nature resists change. He was well aware of that, but in many cases — in this case — change was good. He had pondered the consequences of his discovery over countless sleepless nights. The moral repercussions collided with the social ramifications like two freight trains plowing full steam ahead towards one another, neither side the victor. The only certainty to emerge from the wreckage virtually unscathed in Penrose's methodical mind was the science. It was undeniable. Undoubtedly, there was the potential for misuse. The discovery of gunpowder had unquestionably contributed to an untold number of bloody wars. It had also tamed the West and reduced mountains to passable plateaus upon which endless expanses of railroad tracks had been laid connecting commerce and peoples across a vast continent. The immense power unleashed by nuclear fission enabled both its potential for evil abuse and the ability to power millions of homes and factories, not to mention its use as a deterrent to future world wars. The pros and cons had been carefully considered as the full scope of his discovery came into focus. The contribution of his discovery, Penrose rationalized, far outweighed the potential negative impact. He was thoroughly convinced that he sat on the cusp of one of the greatest scientific discoveries of all time. Whether or not it would be used for sinister purposes, he would leave to the politicians and social scientists. There was one thing he vowed to himself that must never occur. His discovery must not be snuffed out in its infancy. Regardless of future decisions relating to its applications, he was determined to see his dream to fruition. That moment was now at hand.

It was a second or two after the statement that Penrose even realized Reed Mosser was talking to him. Penrose jogged himself out of his daydream and back to reality. He looked around the table at the handful of doctors who drove the conversation and the appeasers who sought to impress them. "Hmm? What?" Penrose asked.

"Tell us about this project you're working on," Mosser repeated. He was one of Penrose's best friends, that being a relative term. Reed Mosser was as close to him as anyone could expect to get. Mosser was a bridge. He bridged the gap between Penrose and the professors, and Penrose and the doctor elites. He was the peacemaker, a man who felt in his heart that he was building relationships but, in reality, was compromising everything. Penrose had torched most of Mosser's bridges, but he kept trying. It was the very fact that Penrose was so difficult that actually drew Mosser to him.

Penrose knew Reed was just being polite, trying to include him in the conversation. "It's pretty mundane research, actually."

"Ah, come on," one of the doctors insisted. He sat there in anticipation as did the rest of the table who offered their undivided attention.

Penrose wondered if anyone at the table had even an inkling of what his 'project' would mean to the world. Did they know how much turmoil would be unleashed with the information Penrose so cunningly kept under his hat? Revealing his secret to his own associates could serve as a spot check, a microcosm of the reaction that would surely follow on a grander scale. By just ever so slightly pulling back the curtain on his work, he could get a taste right then and there of what he would face in the days and weeks ahead. Was he ready for the coming wrath? These were the same people whose very existence depended on the status quo. Penrose was the antithesis of their mundane lives, the very type of doctor they would love to take down a few notches. All eyes were on him. Those eyes were convincing. The faces appeared open to whatever wondrous discovery Penrose might impart to them. He adjusted himself in his seat, cleared his throat, and began.

He was working on an agricultural hybrid through genetic splicing, he informed them. Through his research, he hoped to develop vegetables which would stay fresher longer. The rest of the diners strained to pay attention. Their minds drifted like some rudderless ship at sea, blown off course by Penrose's hot air. Their conversation had been interrupted for *this,* they thought. Uncomfortable as it was, Penrose had launched into his standard cover story. He locked eyes with each person, gauging whether or not they were buying the lie. His gaze was met with the dull stare of a dairy cow. From the look of things, they'd most probably rather watch a pipe rust than hear another word about agricultural hybrids. Fortunately for them, Penrose's riveting tale was interrupted.

The cell phone made no sound, but the vibration brought Dr. Penrose to an abrupt halt. He asked for forgiveness and reached for his phone. "I've got a call."

The announcement was met with a sigh of relief.

"What a shame. I was absolutely fascinated," one of the Christmas ornaments stated sarcastically.

Penrose slipped out of earshot of the table. "Carol?" he asked with hushed excitement.

"Yes, doctor." Her voice overflowed with enthusiasm. "It's Lucy. She's in labor!"

The doctor's pulse raced. "I'll be right there."

Penrose dashed back to the table to apologize for his sudden departure. He took a large gulp from his glass, pulled a twenty-dollar bill from his wallet, and dropped it on the table.

"Sudden breakthrough in agricultural hybrids there, Clark?" one of the snide doctors asked with a grin.

Penrose ignored him and was out the door.

3

The ten-year-old Buick screeched to a halt in the reserved parking space next to the empty spaces belonging to other doctors' Mercedes and Lexus. Carol Boyce, a matronly woman with big brown eyes and beauty parlor-set hair, met him at the entrance with a clipboard in hand, bringing him up to speed as they briskly made their way down the long corridor.

"Her pulse is normal. She went into labor about thirty minutes ago."

"Everything ready in case we need to intercede?"

"Yes, doctor. We're ready."

Carol reached in the pocket of her white lab coat and pulled out a folded tissue which she used to mop Dr. Penrose's brow as they hurried along. Carol was from the old school. She believed strongly that her role was that of a supporting player. Dr. Penrose was the headliner. Whatever he needed, whatever he ordered, she was there to deliver. There was an unspoken mutual respect which had solidified their relationship over the twelve years they had worked together. Dr. Penrose grabbed the clipboard she offered and flipped the pages as they continued their swift pace. They passed through double doors and their stride quickened past walls lined with modern diagnostic equipment underneath sterile white lighting. The chairs, ordinarily occupied by graduate students and lab assistants, were cold and bare. Through another set of double doors, they entered the delivery area where Lucy quietly waited. The click of their heels echoed on the concrete floor.

"I can't believe this day is finally here," Penrose said.

Compassion filled Carol's face. "You've waited a long time for this, haven't you?"

Penrose glanced over at her to drink in the much needed empathy then returned his eyes straight ahead. "It's the biggest day of my life."

They reached the back of the room and slowed to almost a tip-toe. So as not to alarm his patient, Dr. Penrose's look of concern was wiped away by a smile.

"So, Lucy, how are we holding up, ole girl?" He glanced at his watch and scribbled something on the clipboard. With a smile in his voice, he said, "We were beginning to wonder if you were ever going to have this baby." He scanned the meters and noted their settings.

"I began to wonder about her when she lost her appetite for dinner," Carol Boyce said.

"She certainly appears to be ready." He looked up at Lucy with his warm eyes and comforting smile. "Everything's going to be just fine, my dear. Pretty soon you'll be holding your son in your arms. Would you like that? Hmmm?"

The inquisitive eyes of the orangutan just stared back at him through the bars of the cage.

"She started getting cranky right after you left," Carol said. "I have a feeling it's going to be soon."

"You do, do you?" he said with a half-smile. He initialed one page then flipped to the next. "Woman's intuition?"

She smiled. "If you believe in that kind of thing."

"Believe me, I do. Honestly, I've come to depend on it."

"I hope I don't ruin my reputation tonight."

"Well, I guess all we can do now is a wait." He pulled up two comfortable chairs.

Dr. Penrose had gone to great lengths to recreate the orangutan's natural habitat. A two-foot layer of dirt covered the floor of the oversized cage from which grew various small plants and flowers from her native Borneo. In the corner, Dr. Penrose provided the staple of Lucy's diet — tree bark supplemented by fruit from the durian tree. The enclosure was completely self-sufficient, save the birds' eggs which Dr. Penrose provided to Lucy's delight only when he was able to locate her favorite species. The bars on the cage stretched the entire twenty feet to the ceiling, which was painted sky blue. When it was night, tiny lights illuminated like stars. Since orangs were mostly tree-dwellers, several large pseudo-trees had been constructed. Penrose had become somewhat of an orang expert, what with two other baby orang deliveries under his belt in his makeshift zoo. Every attempt had been made to replicate Lucy's natural surroundings to ensure she was completely at ease. Time was of the essence, and Dr. Penrose couldn't afford any outside stimuli complicating or impeding conception. Her mate was only available for a limited time.

The male specimen was snagged by a stroke of luck. Dr. Penrose found a zoo that was anticipating a shipment from the island of Sumatra. He was able to persuade the zookeeper to allow the orang to make a short layover at the university while the zoo made its preparations, just long enough to get friendly with Lucy. Once the deed was done, the good doctor would send him on his way to his new home. This, too, was in keeping with the natural environment of the orangutan, since males in the wild preferred to mate then live their lives in solitude. It had been ten months and a week since the male had arrived and eight months since he continued on his merry way. Dr. Penrose figured Lucy to be just over nine months pregnant.

Hours passed as Dr. Penrose and Carol barely slept in their seats. They were jolted from their semiconscious state as Lucy screamed out. The blessed event had begun. Penrose grabbed the binoculars. He and Carol kept their distance. Penrose didn't dare interfere. Although she weighed only ninety pounds, the arboreal lifestyle had given the orang incredibly strong arms. She possessed the strength of several men. Penrose recalled in his studies the writings of nineteenth-century naturalist Alfred Russell Wallace who witnessed an orangutan killing a crocodile by, as Wallace wrote in his diary, "pulling open its jaws and ripping up its throat."

Penrose knew that orangs were naturally docile creatures, but Lucy's awesome strength, magnified by the excruciating pain of giving birth, could make assisting in the process quite hazardous. Thank goodness the other two Loveport orang births had gone off without incident.

After just a matter of minutes, it was over. Fortunately for everyone involved, the delivery was entirely uneventful and mother and son came through marvelously. Penrose almost felt like a proud papa as he watched Lucy cleaning then feeding her new creation. It would be morning before he felt comfortable with taking the newborn from Lucy for closer inspection. His curiosity was almost unbearable. In order to find out, Lucy would have to be tranquilized, and she'd been through enough for one day. The artificial stars flickered above as Lucy lay sleeping with a protective arm around her brand new offspring. Dr. Penrose lingered for a moment longer, contrasting the serenity of the moment with the firestorm that would surely follow if his tests turned out to be positive. He wasn't certain just how big his discovery was, but he knew it was destined to set a high watermark for controversy, not only throughout the scientific community, but throughout the world.

Just before dawn, Penrose and Carol went about the task of extracting the newborn from his mother's arms. A net was placed under the tree where Lucy made her home in case the tranquilizer proved too much for her and she dropped her baby. Once she was properly sedated, Dr. Penrose scaled the tree and gently relieved Lucy of her newborn. The young orang was given a complete physical exam, a blood sample was taken, and the baby returned to the tree. Now it was time for the moment of truth. Dr. Penrose had successfully completed the procedure in utero. That was an accomplishment in and of itself. Lucy was fine and her offspring was apparently healthy, but had the procedure been successful? The proof was going to be in the genetic testing. Carol brought the slide to Dr. Penrose in the lab and he nervously placed it under the microscope. He raised his reading glasses to rest atop his head. Before he brought his eyes down to the scope, he looked over at Carol who was impatiently biting her bottom lip.

"This is it." He slowly lowered his head.

To Carol, the next few seconds seemed to drag on into hours. Dr. Penrose adjusted the knobs on the side to bring everything into focus. She could only see his regal profile. His lips pursed and his eyes strained to see. Twice before, while two different orangs were still in the fetal stage, she had seen his anticipation turn to distress, all of his years of work dashed in a single instant. She couldn't stand to see that again. They had never made it this far before. A full-term orang with the gene they were looking for. The only question now was: did Dr. Penrose's procedure work? She stood with her arms crossed, her right palm rested against her cheek. Her foot tapped anxiously. She bit her bottom lip even harder. The light that backlit the specimen under the microscope illuminated Penrose's face with an eerie light. Carol could make out every distinctive line in his face. His teeth appeared whiter than usual against the bright light. He was smiling and his smile stretched nearly to his ears.

"There it is!" he said, not wanting to take his eyes off the slide. The light emanating from underneath the slide seemed to set his excited face on fire. "There it is! There it is!" He came up for air and grabbed Carol's shoulders, pushing her toward the microscope as if she were blindfolded. "Look at it! Is that not the most beautiful sight you've ever seen in your life?"

Carol moved closer to the scope and lowered her eyes to gaze upon this apparent object of splendor. He watched as she peered into the scope, hardly able to stand the wait until she saw his discovery, too. Once she had confirmed it with her own two eyes, she cried with joy as she hugged Dr. Penrose as tightly as she could.

"Congratulations! You did it!"

"*We* did it," Penrose corrected. "We actually did it!" he screamed between cackles of delight. "This is incredible! This is absolutely incredible!"

Carol covered her face with her hands, tears streaming down her cheeks. Penrose locked his arms around her waist and picked her up off her feet, spinning her around as she squealed with delight.

The commotion echoed out of the lab and into the warehouse where Lucy was roused from her induced sleep. Puzzled, she looked curiously in the direction of the noise. She clutched her newborn as the artificial sun began to rise and studied the door from where all the excitement seemed to be coming. There would be no rest for man nor beast now that Penrose's discovery literally signaled the dawning of a new day.

4

Dr. Roy Kirsch was the Director of the Human Gene Therapy Foundation at Loveport University. In his early sixties, he was still quite an imposing figure. A bear of a man, he filled a doorway nearly as completely as the door. He wasn't fat, just big, as if someone had taken a regular man and supersized him. His head was like a buffalo's. His hands were like catcher's mitts. His tailored suit contained almost enough material for two men.

Kirsch's disarming disposition and southern charm were almost contrary to his immense stature. He was a man's man but with a soft underbelly women found attractive. In his profession, he had turned diplomacy into an art form, but the years of arbitration and negotiation had grown tiresome. He could see retirement on the horizon and he was eager for it. His job was demanding, far too much so for the likes of Dr. Penrose. Not that Penrose was afraid of a little work. He, undoubtedly, worked harder than anyone. It was the politics of the job that Penrose found so distasteful. It was Dr. Kirsch's job to procure the funding to keep research at the university afloat. Every doctor or scientist in every department of the university thought his or her project was of the utmost importance to mankind, thus, deserving of top priority funding. Unfortunately, there was only so much money to go around. Part of the job of the director was to persuade those with money of the importance of each particular project. That meant Dr. Kirsch was subject to requesting, demanding, pleading, even the occasional groveling to get the funds necessary to keep his department competitive. He likened fund-raising to taming a horse. "Where I come from," he always said, "there are two kinds of horses. Ones that want to be broke but don't know it yet and those that know it but want to see you work for it." Instead of viewing that part of his job as a necessary evil, he looked at it as more of a challenge, another hill to climb, another conquest. He applied the same philosophy to women, which explained why he was on his third marriage.

Roy Kirsch was respected in medical circles for his extraordinary ability to attract funds for his department's projects. The void created by his lack of experience in the field of genetic research was filled with his power and authority. He certainly came with his own set of credentials — a graduate of Texas Tech and a medical degree from the University of Alabama-Birmingham. He went straight from UAB to the National Institutes of Health in Bethesda, Maryland, joining the National Institute of Diabetes and Digestive and Kidney Diseases. Then came the opportunity he had dreamt of, the director's position at Loveport University. His goal was to turn Loveport into one of the preeminent genetic research facilities in the country, a task he achieved with hires like Dr. Penrose. But even the allure of control and the admiration of his peers were not so attractive anymore. As he neared the end of his career, he often wondered how much more fulfilling his life might have been had he made more of an effort to contribute to medicine instead of concentrating on winning the never-ending popularity contests.

Dr. Penrose, on the other hand, with all his quirks, had chosen the path Dr. Kirsch respected but knew he could never have followed himself. Kirsch was much too ebullient and restless to sit still for the tedium of research. If he were ever honest with himself, Dr. Kirsch was a bit jealous of his prized geneticist with all of his awards and the trade publications touting his contributions to the world of medicine, but Kirsch was proud of his own calling. In the end, where would people like Penrose be were it not for him, he rationalized. It takes money, and lots of it, to transform ideas into reality. In an era of cutbacks, Loveport was thriving and Kirsch knew he was the reason why. Had he the chance to replay his career, he would change nothing. Now he hoped only to guide it to a smooth landing over the next few years.

Kirsch's mahogany-paneled office was an understatement in good taste. Subtle differences like the hardwood frames, which highlighted his career in pictures, hung in place of the usual inferior black plastic. The Mont Blanc pen rested in its original velvet-lined box on his desk, a gift from, and a singular reminder of, his first wife. The oversized antique Empire desk, which once resided in his grandfather's office, had been a gift from his grandmother upon the elder doctor's death some thirty years prior. As he shuffled a couple of papers on the immaculate desk, he lifted his eyes above his reading glasses in response to the knock on the door.

"Come in," he beckoned in his Texas drawl, anticipating Dr. Penrose's face through the opening door.

"Good morning, Roy." Dr. Penrose seemed a bit edgy as he closed the door behind him. A protocol — a proposal for the clinical study Penrose so desperately wanted — was tucked under his arm.

"Mornin', Clark. Have a seat." He did a double-take and inspected Penrose more closely. "What the hell happened to you? You look like you've been hit by a train."

Penrose had dark circles under his eyes. The two days' growth of a beard made him look less like a brilliant scientist and more like a bum. He settled into one of the leather Queen Anne chairs in front of the desk, clutching the ring-bound report. Nervously, he moved to the edge of the seat, ignoring the observations on his appearance.

Kirsch set his papers aside and gave Dr. Penrose his undivided attention. "All right, Clark. What's so all-fired important?"

"Well, first of all, Roy, I want to thank you for the leeway you've given me on my projects over the years." He gripped the protocol tightly in his hands. "I realize there are a lot of guys in your position who wouldn't be so understanding."

"Well, some folks you have to stay on and others, well, you kinda just let 'em do their thing. You know, take the bridle off. They perform better that way. You're the best damn geneticist we've got, probably the best in the country. I cain't be ridin' you like a herd of cattle. I've gotta give you some breathin' room. That's pretty much what I've done with you."

"I know that, Roy, and I really appreciate it."

Kirsch looked at him suspiciously. "You're not entertainin' the thought of leavin', now are you?"

"No, it's nothing like that."

"Well, you're as edgy as a cat in a room full of rockin' chairs. What's on your mind?"

"Roy, we've made a major breakthrough."

"Now, you're gonna have to be a little more specific. You've got a lot of irons in the fire. Which project you talkin' about?"

"Our experiments with the orangutan."

"With your sexual orientation experiments?" Kirsch asked.

"Yes."

"Hot Damn!" Kirsch leaned forward and clapped his oversized paws. He rubbed them together like a loaded sailor entering a poker game. "Talk to me, son."

"Now, you may remember that I've been building on Simon LeVay's Hypothalamic Hypothesis."

"Yeah, I remember." Kirsch searched his mind for the details. Penrose noticed that he always seemed to talk a little differently when he spoke to medical subjects, his delivery crisper and clearer, the southern accent not nearly as pronounced. "LeVay's the guy who determined that a portion of the anterior hypothalamus, on average, was two to three times greater in heterosexual men than in homosexual men, concluding there must be a biological reason for being gay. Right?"

"Very good." Penrose said. "Well, taking LeVay's conclusions as fact, the logical question is: why? Why is that part of the brain larger in heterosexual men? Or, to ask it a different way, what makes that part of the brain smaller in homosexuals?"

"And, of course, you believe it's genetic," Kirsch said.

"Naturally. I worked backwards from LeVay and tried to figure out why." He motioned to Kirsch's computer. "May I?"

"By all means," Dr. Kirsch offered, rising from his seat.

Penrose sat down in Kirsch's chair and inserted a thumb drive in his computer. Kirsch looked intently over his shoulder. Up on the screen popped a color configuration much like a family tree with various boxes and circles linked by lines. The boxes represented males on the family tree, while the circles represented females. Each blue box represented a homosexual in Dr. Penrose's study.

"As you can see from this figure, there is a distinct pattern of the transmission of male homosexuality," he observed, pointing to the blue boxes. "You see, in this family, for instance." He pointed to a specific family tree. "This pair of homosexual brothers has a maternally related gay nephew and a gay uncle. See?"

"Yes," Kirsch answered.

"Anything jump out at you from this?"

"Yes." Kirsch looked intently at each tree. "An obvious absence of transmission through the paternal line."

Penrose's eyes lit up as he touched the tip of his nose and pointed back at Kirsch. "Precisely. At first, we thought there might be an environmental cause, you know, an over-pampering mother, but there just wasn't a consistent pattern in our case study which led me to this theory. Since males receive their single X chromosome exclusively from their mothers, any trait that is influenced by the mother's side of the family will more than likely be transferred through an X-linked gene."

"Makes sense," Kirsch acknowledged.

"All right then," Penrose continued, "we ran a linkage analysis of sixty-two pairs of homosexual brothers. This included a statistical analysis of the pair-by-pair data and multipoint genetic mapping analysis of the X chromosome. Now, here's where it really gets interesting." Penrose hit the 'Page Down' key on the computer. The next screen showed a graph with a confusing configuration of points connected by lines looking much like a stock market trend chart. "What we found was the detection of linkage between homosexual orientation and X chromosome markers in the distal portion of Xq28 which is," advancing to the next page, "about right here." He pointed to the tip of one arm of the X chromosome with his pen.

Kirsch was in awe. "Amazing."

"Ah, that was the easy part," Penrose said. "We knew at that point the gene or genes we were after were somewhere within approximately four million base pairs of DNA on the tip of that long arm of the X chromosome in the region Xq28. With the help of the Human Genome Project, we mapped that region. After some intensive searching, we narrowed it down further until we found it."

"You found *it*?" Kirsch asked with anticipation.

Dr. Penrose swiveled around to face Dr. Kirsch. "Roy," he announced almost in a whisper. "We found the gay gene." It was the first time he had actually said those words out loud and they echoed in his head.

Kirsch felt a cold wave envelop his body. "Are you sure?" He could hardly believe his ears. If what Penrose was telling him was true, it would mean the eyes of the whole world would be focused on Loveport, a notion which far exceeded Kirsch's wildest dreams of success.

"You're bloody right, I'm sure. Without a doubt."

Dr. Kirsch's astonishment turned to a smile. He pulled Penrose up from the chair with his massive arms and gave him a huge bear hug.

"Son-of-a-bitch," he said, almost shaking with excitement. "My God, this is incredible! MIT, Columbia, the National Institutes of Health, they've all been lookin' for that gene. Hell, there was just some blowhard in *Science* last month who was speculatin' the whole 'gay gene' thing was a bunch of hogwash, and you found it!" He clasped Dr. Penrose's hand with his right and gripped his shoulder with his left. "Clark, you ole son-of-a-bitch! Congratu-damn-lations!" He shook his hand vigorously, quite nearly ripping Penrose's arm from its socket.

"Hold on, Roy. That's not the big news," Penrose cautioned.

"Not the *big* news?" Kirsch couldn't imagine anything bigger. This was a coup de maître. To a geneticist, this was the pinnacle. Dr. Penrose walked to the window. He stared out for just a moment then turned to face Kirsch. He took two steps toward the desk and leaned over it, resting his palms on the edge. He wanted to make sure he had Kirsch's attention.

"Roy, you better sit down."

Kirsch ignored the warning. He was too wired to sit.

Penrose took a deep breath and began. "In the process of trying to locate this gene, I developed an enzyme that will work much like the 'search and replace' function on that computer," he said, pointing to Kirsch's desktop. "Once this enzyme is introduced to the DNA, it replaces the gay gene with the normal gene."

Kirsch looked intently at Dr. Penrose, hanging on every word. "What are you telling me, Clark?"

"What I'm telling you…" Penrose swallowed hard. His mouth had gone dry. "What I'm telling you is this. We now have the technology to genetically alter a fetus predisposed to homosexuality. We can now make a homosexual a heterosexual."

Kirsch's face lost all coloring. "Mother-of-pearl," he whispered under his breath. He slowly rested his large frame in his leather chair.

Penrose paused for a moment to make sure Kirsch was OK. "We had many successful experiments with dogs but wanted to run tests on animals with a genetic makeup more like humans. Six months ago, we conducted an operation to correct a defective gene in our orangutan fetus. Early this morning, that orang gave birth to a perfectly healthy male. We ran the tests, Roy." He looked at Dr. Kirsch with grave intensity. "The corrected gene survived the pregnancy. This male orangutan which would have been born homosexual is now heterosexual."

Dr. Kirsch sat there awestruck. "Jesus, Joseph, and Mary," he said in disbelief. "Do you realize what this means?"

"Yes," Penrose answered resolutely.

"Do you really?" Kirsch's voice bordered on panic.

"I understand exactly what it means. It means we now have a cure for homosexuality."

Kirsch sputtered and stammered as the words rushed from his brain to his mouth too quickly to emerge coherently. "A cu.., a, what do you—? Damn, man. A *cure* for homosexuality? Is that what I hear you saying?" Kirsch was annoyed at Penrose's lack of emotion. "What the hell makes you think homosexuals want to be cured?"

"OK, maybe 'cure' is the wrong choice of words," Penrose conceded. "Let's just say that we can now *prevent* homosexuality for those who are genetically predisposed to it."

Kirsch's mood quickly changed from elation to a man slighted by deceit. "Why the hell have you taken so long to come to me with this?" he erupted.

"I wanted to make sure of what we had, quite honestly, before the university stopped me."

"Stopped you? You think this university would've stopped you?"

"It's politics, Roy. We're not talking about some high school biology experiment. This is a political hot potato. Just look at the way *you're* reacting. It's one thing to *discover* the gay gene. It's quite another to develop a procedure to change it."

Dr. Kirsch rubbed his face as he contemplated the consequences of this revolutionary discovery. Penrose sought to answer all of his questions before they were ever raised.

"Roy, look at this scientifically. Are you listening?"

Kirsch continued to rub his face. "Hell, yes, I'm listenin'. I'm all ears."

"What is the basic function of sexuality?"

"Procreation. Look, Clark, I know where you're goin' with this and—"

"Now wait a minute," Penrose interrupted, "let me finish. From a scientific standpoint — I mean, cutting through all the politically correct rubbish and getting down to basic science — the logical conclusion is homosexuality is a freak of nature. It's counter to the basic sexual function, correct?"

"I think you'll find some scientists who disagree," Kirsch said, "but, please, go on."

"God made sex so we would reproduce. It's that simple. The logical conclusion is homosexuality is an abnormality, a, uh, a disease, if you will." He thought for a second then jumped in before Kirsch could correct him. "OK, maybe disease is too strong. A *condition*."

"A condition," Dr. Kirsch said noncommittally.

"Now, if one were to have a condition which was contrary to nature, wouldn't we be obligated to find a way to correct that condition?"

Kirsch stared at Penrose. He had to admit his argument was convincingly logical. "Ah, yes," Kirsch countered, "but in this case, those afflicted with this, um, *condition* are quite content with it, even proud of it."

"Some are, some aren't, but they're not the ones we're talking about helping," Penrose explained. "There's nothing we can do about them. It's the unborn, the potential homosexuals that we can help."

Kirsch leaned back in his seat, his head shaking from side to side.

"Come on, Roy! I see that wall of yours going up. This is sound science. If you think about it logically, you *know* I'm right!"

Kirsch popped up out of his chair. "Listen to me!" he demanded. "You're talkin' about a procedure that'll wipe out about two percent of the population."

Kirsch had hit a hot button. Penrose's eyes were on fire. He held sacred the sanctity of life and he didn't appreciate anyone, even Kirsch, accusing him of *wiping out* anyone. "That's a bloody lie and you know it! We're not talking about killing anyone, for God's sake! What we're talking about is correcting a genetic defect, plain and simple, in order to give that two percent of the population, who wouldn't ordinarily have it, the chance to have children and fit into society. This is no different from our work on Down syndrome and other genetic disorders. The only difference is, unlike a Down patient, these patients are well organized and carry political clout. Does that give them the right to force that on some unborn child just because they can't change themselves?"

"You don't get it, do you?" Kirsch fired back. "In effect, what you're sayin' is homosexuals are deformed, not normal, uh…freaks!"

"Come on, Roy. You're not looking at this as a doctor; you're looking at it as someone who's scared to rock the boat, to swim against the current." He pointed to his temples. "Think like a scientist. If you believe in the purpose and function of basic sexuality, and if you believe that anything that prevents that function or purpose is abnormal, then you have to see that what I'm doing is right!"

Kirsch looked sternly at Penrose as he digested everything he'd heard. The issue was so complicated. Admittedly, from a scientific standpoint, what Penrose was saying made a lot of sense, but, still, it just didn't feel right and something deep inside him wanted to fight it. Kirsch sat down at his desk with his head in his hands, rubbing his face as he thought about this bombshell which had just been dropped on him. Penrose moved from behind the chair and closer to Kirsch to keep his attention.

"I'm talking about human beings who have never been born, Roy," Penrose's tone was more measured. "If you could correct spina bifida or MS before the child was born, wouldn't you do it?"

"Of course I would, but this is not the same."

Penrose slapped the desk. "Like hell it's not! It's *exactly* the same! They're all genetic disorders! Why is that so hard for you to understand?" Penrose was tired of arguing. He turned belligerent. "I want to go forward with this project, Roy. I want support from this university, or, so help me God, I'll find it somewhere else."

"You wouldn't dare," Kirsch said. "Not after all I've done for you."

Penrose leaned across the desk. "Damn it, Roy, I deserve it!"

Kirsch bolted upright from his chair and rounded the desk toward Penrose. For a moment, Penrose feared for his own safety. Kirsch was up in his face and wagging his finger.

"Wait just a damn minute," Kirsch demanded. "First of all, it's not always about you. This university has a reputation to uphold, and there are plenty of other people and careers to consider. Second, you head off on an unapproved wild goose chase on probably the most controversial subject in scientific history. In the meantime, you keep your boss and the people who fund your projects completely in the dark while you pursue this unauthorized project. And now you have the balls to waltz in here and say, 'Hey Roy. I just came up with a little procedure that's gonna eradicate every future homosexual from the planet. How about layin' your ass on the line, risk your reputation and your retirement, and see if you can get me some money.' Is that all you want?" he asked sarcastically. "You don't want me to see if I can get the chancellor to stand on his head and whistle *Dixie* out his ass?"

Dr. Penrose tried to maintain a serious face then said dryly, "Could you see if he knows *God Save The Queen* instead?"

Kirsch stared at him for a moment then his glare dissolved into a chuckle. "Damn, Clark. I don't believe you." It was hard to stay mad at the man who had just put Loveport University in the history books.

Penrose walked back toward the window as Kirsch tried to assimilate everything. Penrose turned, leaned back against the window sill, and crossed his arms over his chest. "Would you agree this project has merit?"

Dr. Kirsch slowly walked back to his seat, running a hand over what was left of his gray and black hair. "Of course, it has merit." He plopped down in the big leather chair. "It's a major breakthrough. Nobody's arguin' that. It's just so damn controversial."

"Progress can be that way sometimes, Roy. The pioneers always take the arrows. Part of it is fear. Part of it is pure jealously. Part of it is ignorance. There are always those who cannot grasp what it is we do in medicine and, instead, simply choose to ridicule it instead of embracing it. Sure, the response to this will most assuredly be strong, but we must look at our science and know that we're right. There will be those who resist because they are gay and they want to preserve their kind. We cannot be swayed by them. Homosexuals, by and large, have a shorter life expectancy, are generally unhappier than the population as a whole, and have a higher incidence of suicide. Were this any other medical condition with those facts, there would be no argument that we should find a solution to it. In fact, people would be *demanding* that we spend millions of dollars on a cure. The opposition will be fierce because the forces opposed to this will demagogue the issue and try to whip the rest into a frenzy. I will be compared to Hitler. I will be vilified, maligned, and impugned. I'm prepared for it all. I'm willing to take those arrows. Because I'm right. And the truth should always prevail."

Kirsch looked at Dr. Penrose then leaned back in his seat and crossed his arms, resting his chin on his bent index finger. He contemplated the full ramifications of the Penrose Project and swiveled the chair until he was looking out the window. Penrose leaned forward over the shoulder of the Queen Anne chair and stared at the back of Kirsch's head. He felt the momentum beginning to shift. Kirsch slowly swiveled back around to face him.

"OK, let's say you're right," Kirsch conceded. "Let's say this is the thing to do, medically, morally, across the board. I'm not sayin' I totally agree with you, but, for argument's sake, let's just say you're right. What do you want?"

"I want funding for this project," Penrose quickly answered.

"Right, I know that. And?"

"And I want approval from the university for clinical testing of this procedure and—"

"Whoa, wait a minute," Kirsch interrupted. "Don't you think more lab testin' is needed before I request a clinical?"

Penrose ignored the comment. "And—"

Kirsch tried again. "Cain't this wait a little while longer?"

"*And* I want this thing kept completely under wraps. Only on a need-to-know basis," Penrose insisted.

Kirsch leaned back in his chair, throwing his hands to the heavens. "A need-to-know basis? Do you know how hard that's gonna be?" He let out an exasperated laugh. "Once the Internal Board reviews the protocol, whether they approve the clinical or not, it's gonna go public. You can bank on that, Bob."

Penrose let go with a sigh of disgust.

"Now think about it for a minute, Clark," Kirsch pleaded. "You've got a project as controversial as this, then it comes out that the university was sittin' on it tryin' to keep it quiet. Don't think there won't be plenty of folks yellin' conspiracy. The press'd be all over us like a fat lady on a moped."

"I'm telling you, Roy. I know exactly how this is going to play out," Penrose said in frustration. "We're going to go before the Internal Board with a request for a clinical and, just as sure as we're sitting here, they're going to get cold feet and squash this thing where it stands. A big chunk of our budget comes from federal funding. Don't you know there'll be some congressmen getting pressure to put the skids on this? The Internal Board has got to keep this quiet. Once they've approved a clinical, all I need is a few weeks to find a willing couple. Once we've done the procedure, they'll have to let us see it through. Not even the U.S. Congress is going to force a couple to abort their child. Come on, Roy, just a few more weeks."

"Oh, is that all you want?" Kirsch asked sarcastically.

"Roy," Penrose pleaded. "It's only a matter of time before someone else makes this same discovery. Maybe Northwestern or Boston. A lot people believe the gay gene is out there and sooner or later someone else is going to stumble across it."

"You're askin' too much, Clark, and you know it."

Penrose just stared at him, his eyebrows raised, his head slightly cocked, waiting for an answer.

Kirsch stared back for a long moment, tapping his fingers on the desk. Finally, he stretched out his open hand. "Give me the damn protocol. Let me sleep on it. I'll have an answer for you first thing in the morning."

5

Penrose lazily walked through the lab, mindlessly tidying up. Carol had been sent home hours ago. There was really nothing for either of them to do. His life was on hold until Roy Kirsch gave the word. This was the intersection of his dreams and his reality. Kirsch would decide if the two would collide or merge seamlessly in a single precise movement. If there were a collision, Penrose feared, he would most likely not crawl out of the wreckage. He pondered the irony of it all. He was the single individual capable of granting Kirsch a retirement send-off he could only dream of, yet Kirsch, himself, could be standing in the way. He pushed the idea of defeat aside and tried to bring the prospect of success front and center in his mind. Worrying would do him no good. He knew that. But worry was what he did. Like a dark cloud, it crept in, slowly blocking out the light of optimism.

It always started like this. Try as he may, he could not stop it. His rational mind told him it was all a manifestation of his worst fears. It was not real, but it felt as real as the cotton sheet pulled tightly about his neck. The dead of night was when it came, when his mind was unoccupied by the daily tasks that kept him busy. He glanced over at his wife, Lauren. He could see her silhouette lying next to him in the dark. The blanket gently rose and fell with the steady rhythm of her breathing. Penrose's head turned back toward the ceiling. He braced himself for the inevitable onslaught.

He was a medical man, a man who knew better, a man who could comfort any patient through a similar experience, but he was unable to console himself. He had tried before on many occasions, but he had never been able to stop it from coming. Like a runaway team of horses, it galloped toward him at full speed. He had relegated himself to the fact that the best he could do was hold on. Its severity depended upon how successfully he managed it, how well he resisted it, how good he was at beating it back.

It began as it usually began, almost like a wave, an indescribable sensation, like an icy hot flood that began slowly somewhere around his torso then flooded up toward his head like a rising tide of terror. His mind raced. Staccato images — fragments of his memory and dreams — flew past his mind like the landscape whizzing past the window of a speeding train. No matter which direction he turned, the images in bits and pieces seemed to come in rapid succession. He closed his eyes, but it only worsened his condition, making him dizzy as if he were on a wild roller coaster ride. He quickly opened his eyes in order to locate a point of reference to quell the vertiginous whirl. His heart began to palpitate. He held his index and middle fingers to his neck, just below his right ear. He could feel the blood pulsating through his veins like a raging river. He didn't even notice that his foot had already begun to nervously move. An overwhelming feeling of dread and foreboding accompanied the physical wave that now swept over his chest and up into his head. He became so lightheaded that he fought to remain conscious. His heart beat so rapidly that the soft sounds of the bedroom, which were normally crisp and clear, became muffled. He had never lost consciousness before, but he was not entirely sure he wouldn't, nor did he have any idea what would happen if he did. Part of him thought whatever happened might be preferable to enduring this hell a moment longer, but he feared if he allowed himself to slip away, he might never come back. His rational, medical mind was quickly supplanted by his basic instincts of survival and he fought to hold on, gripped with fear.

He felt certain he was going to die, but those terrifying thoughts played tug-of-war with his intellect, which tried desperately to regain control. It was as if he had been raced up the side of a mountain by some vicious, invisible force and now stood at the sharp summit, teetering on the edge of insanity. He peered over the side of the precipice, struggling not to lose his balance and tumble over. The storm raged in his head, blowing his mind from side to side while he constantly readjusted his footing to keep from falling. If he didn't get his mind on something — anything — he might completely lose his grip on sanity.

He eased the sweat-drenched sheet from his body and turned his feet toward the floor, glancing back over his shoulder at Lauren, taking great care not to wake her. He took stealthy steps toward the bathroom and quietly shut the door behind him. He tip-toed over to the shower, removed his underwear on the way, and turned on the water. As he waited for the shower to heat up, he shifted back and forth on the tile floor, shivering uncontrollably. He ran his hands rapidly up and down across his biceps, trying to create warmth with the friction. He felt like crying out but knew it would probably make matters worse. He feared what his own voice might sound like out loud, not knowing if it would be a sound he recognized or some hideous, unnatural utterance.

Once steam began rising from the shower, he stepped into the tub and gently pulled the shower curtain closed. The water cascaded over his chest and stung as it connected with the goose bumps on his body. He tried to concentrate on the water streaming from the shower head, but the feeling of fighting back insanity refused to recede. He frantically looked around the shower and grabbed the soap. He turned his back to the shower and lathered the soap all over his body in a peculiarly frenzied motion, like a man hurrying through a shower because he had overslept.

Then he heard the voice and froze. The water continued to beat down on his back. "Clark?" the voice inquired softly. Although subdued, the tone matched the panic that griped his entire being. It came from just on the other side of the shower curtain.

"I'll be fine."

Lauren stood with one hand holding her chin, the other clutching a piece of her nightgown at her side. "Do you think you should go to the hospital?"

He became agitated. This was why he took such great care not to wake her. The anxiety that poured from her voice was like gasoline on the raging wildfire that burned in his head.

"I said I'll be fine!" he almost yelled but regretted as soon as the words passed his lips. "Please," he said, this time more measured, "just go back to bed."

Lauren stood for a long moment then turned and left the room. Penrose sighed, his shoulders slumping, as he heard the door close behind her.

He spent the next ten minutes mindlessly soaping and re-soaping his body then washing his hair. A glimmer of hope flashed in front of him and he tried to latch onto it. That glimmer was like a lifeline thrown to him by an unseen ship in the fog. He wrapped it around his mind and held on for dear life. He seemed to be slowly pulled away from the cliff. Once he was clear of the danger, he let go of the line, and the tension drained from his body.

He finished rinsing the shampoo from his head then shut the shower off. Hesitating, like an actor just before he takes the stage, not wanting to move from his safe spot, he pulled the curtain back and exited onto the bathroom floor. Once there, the flood of anxiety began to recede as quickly as it had come over him. He grabbed a towel from the towel rack and quickly dried his body. He approached the vanity and used the towel to wipe the steam from the mirror. He stared at his face in the oval clearing and slowly reconnected with normalcy. He felt like he was looking out the window after a horrendous thunderstorm. The image he saw in the mirror told him it was now safe to go outside. Exhausted, he let the towel drop to the floor, retrieved his underwear, and headed back to bed.

The telephone by Penrose's bed rang only once. He grabbed it instinctively in his sleep as if catching it on the first ring wouldn't wake his wife. Pulling the phone to his ear, he rubbed the sleep from his eyes. "Hello?"

"You've got three weeks to find a couple, not a day longer," Kirsch announced. "Then I go to the Board."

Penrose sat straight up in bed. He was wide awake. "Roy, you won't regret this."

"On day twenty-two," Kirsch warned, "I go to the Internal Board with or without your couple. You know, there's still no guarantee they'll approve the clinical even if you have a willin' couple."

"I know, I know."

"Twenty-one days," Kirsch reiterated. The phone went dead.

6

Finding the perfect primate for his experiments had been a tedious task. Homosexuality among orangutans was even less common than among humans. To narrow the field, Penrose had to do a little genealogical leg work. He subscribed to the same theory for orangs that he did for humans, that homosexuality was passed through the mother's genes. Using a modified version of the Kinsey scale, Penrose began searching the globe for homosexual orangs in hopes of locating one with a sister. He started his search for a suitable candidate even before he had located the gay gene. He knew he would need the lag time to find the right orang on which to experiment. After two years and two pregnancies with two other subjects, he found Lucy, an orang that finally produced the fetus Penrose had been looking for. Another tremendous hurdle had been cleared, but the biggest test of all still lay ahead. Altering the gay gene in an animal was one thing. Having the same success in a human was another. Keeping the university in the dark had afforded him the luxury of time. Now the clock was ticking.

Twenty-one days was not a tremendous amount of time to find a willing couple for a clinical study, but Dr. Penrose didn't blame Kirsch. He was in a different world with different pressures and demands. He was just thankful Kirsch had decided in his favor. Once Kirsch decided to join the team, things got done. There wasn't anyone Penrose would rather have at bat.

Penrose detested what Roy Kirsch had to put up with. The pompous society fund-raisers filled with leftover fraternity rush chairmen with spurious plans, more intent on networking or making the newspaper's social column than aiding a worthy cause. The painted-on smiles of pathetic social climbers in overly expensive clothes whose filed-down teeth would look like sharks' teeth were it not for the unnaturally white caps. The pretentious ladies with over-applied makeup filling in the crevices the plastic surgeon couldn't correct. How Penrose loathed excess. How he despised owing *anything* to the conspicuous consumers of the wine and cheese crowd, but, in the end, Penrose knew these events served their purpose. Married couples flirted and flitted about the room, their every move a conscious, deliberate act — all the way down to their walk — designed to impress the unimpressible. They seemed oblivious to the fact that the artificial aristocracy that passed for society would rip each other to shreds once out of earshot and safely on their way home in their luxury automobiles.

As for the singles, freshly divorced predators cruised the crowd for plastic society sycophants who arrived at the party with the foregone conclusion that they would share a bed — or a backseat — with someone, anyone. It was just a matter of which shallow miscreant they would choose. They all paid their money and ended the night like so many gigolos and whores with the charity as the pimp. Everyone came away happy.

The thought of having to endure even one of those nights made Penrose cringe, as did his memory of his heated conversation with his old friend, Roy Kirsch. Maybe he had been too heavy handed. It had accomplished the desired result, however. Perhaps it was all somehow necessary. As necessary as Kirsch's glad-handing the money-brokers to squeeze a little more juice from the fruit. Although it sometimes came across as contempt, Penrose held a deep respect for what Kirsch did for a living. Few people could have done as much as Kirsch had for the university. Penrose counted his blessings that his own talents lay elsewhere. His forte was the front line, the trenches — the thankless long hours and disappointing dead ends. But major breakthroughs such as this latest genetic discovery made up for all the disillusionment ten-fold.

Kirsch had studied Penrose as closely as Penrose had inspected him. Fortune was not what Penrose sought and Kirsch knew it. Dr. Clark Penrose was certainly comfortable. Kirsch had seen to that, even though Penrose didn't come close to living his life to the lavish extent of many of his colleagues. He had no interest in the money or the easy life.

As Kirsch struggled to understand him, he came to realize that fame wasn't really the motivation either. Those who were driven by fame sought the limelight, the television cameras, the write-ups in the newspapers. Penrose would be lying if he said he didn't get a charge out of seeing his works published in *Science*, but it was a means to an end. It was not what drove him to excellence. What mattered to Penrose was his legacy. The yearning for a legacy was different from a quest to be famous in that one would not be around to enjoy a legacy. Many a great painter never witnessed the fruits of his labor in the form of public adoration or acceptance. It was posthumous gratitude for the eventual realization that their life held worth. He idolized the Pasteurs, the Salks, the Jarvics, not because they contributed so greatly to humanity, but because they were still talked about long after their contributions. Penrose had no problem with humanitarianism. If what he did was of benefit to anyone at all, he would certainly find gratification in that, but it would not, in and of itself, satisfy his thirst for preeminence. His ultimate goal was to leave something behind which proved to make his life worthwhile: immortality. He believed any benefit to society was simply the byproduct of a brilliant mind, not the primary focus. Brilliance pines for long-term recognition. One gains recognition by turning that brilliance into something bold and new and innovative. If brilliance is channeled properly, there will be enough crumbs left for humanity. Those who professed to be altruists in science and medicine, Penrose believed, were liars. They did what they did to feed their egos, to leave behind a legacy, and he found nothing at all objectionable about that.

In this search for preeminence, he placed extraordinary demands on himself. No one gained immortality by being second. His self-imposed competitiveness drove Penrose to be first at something and now he had his chance. He was well aware of his intensity and constantly tried to keep it in check. He would periodically take a step back and examine his overzealousness to ensure his research was anchored in hard, cold facts. He wanted to be first, but he didn't want to go off half-cocked, especially at the risk of ruining, or possibly, taking someone's life.

For this project, all data had been checked, rechecked, and checked again. He fully understood the ramifications. He was the catalyst for the most controversial subject since abortion, and he left absolutely nothing to chance. Now the proof was in the pudding and the principal ingredient was yet to be found — a willing guinea pig couple. But, it wasn't that simple. It wasn't just one willing couple that must be tested. It was, perhaps, hundreds, maybe even thousands, before the gay gene showed up. Each couple had to agree to an amniocentesis, a procedure in which he would insert a needle into the womb in order to analyze the amniotic fluid. It was a procedure with minimal risk but some risk, nonetheless. For each couple who agreed to the testing, there would be far more who would refuse even the test, not to mention the actual gene-altering procedure. Was three weeks enough time? It had to be. It was all he had.

Dr. Penrose hired on every available qualified person for the project. Time was of the essence. Six teams worked around the clock, three culling qualified couples from the mountain of potentials, the other three teams performing the amnios during the day then analyzing the data. Penrose calculated their chance of finding a suitable couple within the allotted time at around 32%. Not very good odds if you're predicting snow, as Roy Kirsch said, but not bad if you're in a crap shoot, which is more or less what this was.

With Kirsch's help, Penrose had used the prestige of Loveport as well as his own reputation to assemble the best and brightest genetic research team in the country. In the interest of security, Penrose had background checks run and contracts of confidentiality signed by the entire staff. Given the short timetable, the staffers were sequestered in dorm rooms on the university campus. Dr. Kirsch joked that it was the most closely guarded secret since the Manhattan Project. They were not allowed contact with the outside world other than television. No cell phones. No Internet. Penrose wasn't taking any chances. With such a short time frame, each member was able to throw him or herself totally into the project. Each seemed as excited and dedicated as Penrose in beating the odds and finding that couple.

If Freud was right when he theorized that men want to marry women like their own mothers, Lauren Penrose was, most certainly, a textbook example. Like Penrose's own mum, who dutifully uprooted her life to follow her husband overseas, Lauren was the embodiment of the doting wife. She had given up a successful teacher's career to follow the dreams of a young scientist with whom she had fallen hopelessly in love. Her beauty was striking. Her long, dark hair and olive complexion helped keep the secret of her age. She immersed herself in the role of wife and mother, a job she referred to as the 'ultimate teaching assignment.' Lauren shared her husband's old-fashioned values and was vigilant in maintaining structure and tradition.

On their arrival in Loveport, Lauren Penrose had wanted to settle in the suburbs in a fresh, new home. Dr. Penrose preferred an older home, far away from the trappings of the social cliques and closer to his office. Lauren resisted, but once he showed her the 1835 antebellum home on Chaucer Street, she fell in love. It was in serious need of repair. In fact, the whole neighborhood was in a state of decay since the suburbs had lured the well-heeled to its safe confines. Consequently, the huge home was being offered for a fraction of its beauty and charm. Lauren could visualize the old place restored to its former glory. The fact that it was not the 'in' thing to do further drove Dr. Penrose to pursue it. Several years later, everyone was clamoring to buy up and restore the old homes near the waterfront. Prices had more than tripled since the Penroses moved in. Their neighborhood was now in vogue. Dr. Penrose found himself in one of the trendiest areas in the state, a point which irritated him to no end.

The wrap-around porch lent itself to large pots overflowing with red geraniums and over-sized porch swings of sturdy wood painted white. The Penroses had spared no expense on landscaping with beautiful boxwoods and flowers of yellow, blue, and white. It was one of the few monetary indulgences allowed by Penrose, only because it reminded him so of his boyhood home in England. The old house seemed to complete his persona. He once remarked to Lauren as they swung gently on the porch swing one mild spring afternoon, examining the grain in the planks on the outside wall, that there was just something soothing about old wood. Such an ordinarily vulnerable substance, with proper care, could last throughout the ages. It seemed to defy the elements and stand as a testament to those who recognized and appreciated its beauty and saved it from the faddish whims of myopic tastes wielding wrecking balls.

Family dinners were an evening ritual around the Penrose home. Lauren Penrose saw to it. Even when the patriarch couldn't make it, which was often as of late, she made sure the rest of the family got together and shared the events of their day. With two teenagers, Karen, a senior in high school, and Brandon, a junior, there was always lots to talk about. This was one of those occasions when the whole clan was assembled. The two younger Penroses recounted their day's experiences. Mom listened attentively. Their father seemed detached, offering only the occasional half-hearted chuckle as a response, which seemed impersonal and indifferent. He was obviously miles away, lost in his own world. It was only when the conversation turned to his world that he seemed to focus on the people around him.

"Dad, how's the 'secret project' going?" Karen queried, making quotation marks in the air with her fingers.

Dr. Penrose spooned a healthy portion of green bean casserole on his plate. "It's going very well," he said. Karen was the inquisitive one, and Penrose enjoyed playing it surreptitiously.

Brandon and Lauren smiled at each other over this little game Clark liked to play with his daughter. Karen stared at her father as he proceeded with his meal.

"Ah, come on, Dad. Can't you tell us *anything* about what you're working on? You're up at that lab day and night. It *must* be something important."

"I've told you all I can," he said between bites. "It's a genetic breakthrough."

"Yeah, I know, but what kind of breakthrough? Are you, like, working on a secret weapon for the Pentagon or something?"

Penrose leaned back in his chair and covered his mouth with his napkin as he laughed out loud. "No, honey. It's nothing like that. I've had this genetic theory for years and now I'm close to bearing that theory out. It's awfully boring stuff, really." He went back to his dinner.

"Boring, huh? That proper English facade of yours, I hate it," she joked in frustration. Penrose was unresponsive. Karen continued her interrogation. "All right then." She pointed at him accusingly with her fork. "Why all the secrecy?" She smiled slyly at Brandon hoping this question might get her closer to the buried treasure.

"Because genetic research is very competitive," Penrose explained. "It's like, say, if a genetic engineer were on the brink of engineering a hybrid of two different types of tomatoes that would result in a single tomato that would stay fresh longer in the market, he wouldn't want the whole world to know until he had perfected the technique because someone else might beat him to the punch."

"Oh, it's *that* kind of boring," she said.

"Well, I think my experiments have a little more pizzazz than hybrid tomatoes."

"Tomatoes," Karen grunted, directing her attention to her plate.

Penrose smiled across the table at Lauren. She knew every nuance of his little secret, but she could be trusted far more than a gossipy teenager. He hurried through his dinner, eager to get to some case files he had brought home. Karen laid out her schedule for the next day so Lauren could make plans. Karen was the active, athletic one. There was a track meet after school then a thirty minute window to get her to karate class. She pleaded with Lauren that she needed her own car, but they both knew the rule. No car until graduation. In Karen's junior year, she had become the first girl in the history of her high school to make the boys' baseball team. Brandon, on the other hand, showed some athletic ability in tennis but was more like his father, studious and introverted. While Karen took life as it came, Brandon had formulated a plan at an early age and followed it to the letter. He was determined to follow his dad's footsteps into medicine, a plan which made his father very proud.

Each day that Penrose returned to the lab proved to be another exercise in disappointment. He tried to keep his staff's confidence bolstered, but it was like looking for the proverbial needle in a haystack. They were checking amnios as fast as was humanly possible. Finding enough women who were having amnios proved to be problematic. It certainly wasn't routine with each pregnancy and there was a degree of risk involved. Enough risk that asking someone to have an amnio just for his purposes was difficult. The chance of a male being a homosexual was somewhere around two percent. The chance of something going wrong during an amnio stood at about one percent. Most of the subjects given the option took their chances on having a gay child rather than take an undue risk of losing their baby. Penrose figured out quickly that what they had to work with wasn't enough. He broadened his search by bringing every ob/gyn in the area into the project without compromising its secrecy. Amnios for women over 35 were routine. Penrose offered to perform the tests at no charge, which pulled in considerably more patients, but after a week, they still hadn't found a suitable subject.

Week one evaporated before his eyes. Week two was a blur. By week three, Penrose had lost all track of time in the conventional sense. He had no idea what day of the week it was only that it was day twenty-one and he was running out of time. Except for a quick cat nap, he'd been on his feet for two days straight. His colleagues finally talked him into going home for a few hours of sleep and get out of their hair. Roy Kirsch was going to call first thing in the morning, and they would have nothing. He could see it all unfolding like a bad dream. Once something as controversial as this hit, the line would begin to form for those who wanted to crush it. Without a willing couple waiting in the wings, the university would be far less likely to support the idea of genetic engineering. Abstractly, it sounded too scary. With a real couple and a real fetus, their chances of success increased exponentially. Dr. Penrose began formulating Plan B in his mind. Without an actual couple to show the board, he would have to persuade them without one. He lined up the details in his head on the way home. First, he would emphasize the gravity of his discovery, something no other scientist had been able to do and plenty had tried. He would highlight what such a discovery would mean to Loveport Medical Center in terms of exposure. Then would come the daunting task of convincing them the gay gene was something worthy of correcting. His success would depend on the individual prejudices each member brought to the table. He had no way of knowing what those prejudices would be nor could he predict his chances of overcoming them.

By the time he reached his bedroom, he was no longer capable of worry. Like a zombie, he sat on the edge of the bed and slowly removed his shoes while Lauren lowered the shades. He took a moment to appreciate her slender frame as she stretched to reach for another pull. Her shoulder-length raven hair danced back and forth as she attempted to snag the pull on her tiptoes. Not even her shapely form could redirect his mind from the much needed sleep. He flopped backwards, his head sinking into the fluffy down pillow. Almost instantly, he drifted toward unconsciousness.

The telephone on the bedside table clanged to life. Lauren, frustrated by the disturbance, grabbed it before the second ring.

"It's the lab," she announced excitedly.

Penrose's mouth became dry as the adrenaline pumped through his veins like oil through a pipeline. He snatched the phone from Lauren's hand and jammed it to his ear. They had struck pay dirt. He slammed the phone back down on its cradle. He threw on his shoes, not even bothering to lace them, kissed Lauren goodbye, and dashed out the door.

The disheveled Dr. Penrose excitedly burst into the lab to double check the test results. The lab assistants gathered around, clutching each other's hands like contestants waiting to hear which one of them would be the next Miss America. They were confident of their discovery, but it would not be official until "the man" gave it his stamp of approval. Penrose, with glasses on the end of his nose, thumbed through the chart, painstakingly at first, then quickly turned back to the first page and rapidly flipped through the same material. His anticipation turned into a grin then a full, open-mouth laugh. He yanked the glasses from his face and let out a triumphant roar. His excitement was contagious as the entire team erupted into cheers. He was haggard, running on fumes, but not even exhaustion could curb his enthusiasm. He rushed to the refrigerator and broke out a waiting bottle of champagne and poured a taste in each of their small plastic cups, paying tribute to the team with a short but eloquent toast. "To the best damn team science has ever assembled." He then downed his portion with a gulp and his team followed. They slammed down their cups, and the rejoicing began. They continued to celebrate, hugging each other and reliving the previous three weeks like old veterans recounting war stories.

The joviality continued around him when the chart resting on the counter once again caught his eye. Penrose approached it, hesitantly, this time. The noise level increased, but he blocked it out. He picked up the chart and checked the name at the top of the test sheet. Andrews, Sabrina. Married. He took a seat with the file while the rest of the staff continued to blow off three weeks of accumulated steam. Penrose pulled out his reading glasses and studied the contents. Then it hit him like an anvil. This was a *real* person, not just a name on a case file. How could he make this woman — this couple — fathom what was about to take place? How could he make them understand that, if they agreed to the procedure, they would become part of the most controversial undertaking of the last hundred years? Then another reality check. Dr. Penrose would have the unenviable task of informing this very real, very human couple that their unborn child was homosexual. Penrose looked around the room at the jubilant faces. The celebration struck him as unseemly. Their reveling in someone else's pain left him ashamed, even angry. He snatched the reading glasses from his head and closed the folder.

"All right, listen up," Penrose announced. The murmur in the lab tapered off. "We're not through here." His mood was decidedly darker. "What if these folks turn us down cold and we're back to square one? You ever thought of that?" His staffers stared back at him in silence. "Let's get back to work!"

7

Sabrina and Tom Andrews had two teenage children already. At almost forty years of age, an amniocentesis was standard procedure, since the risk of genetic disorders increases with the age of the mother. This particular pregnancy was unplanned which, in Dr. Penrose's mind, increased the chances of the couple being willing to participate. First time parents were often much more apprehensive about medical procedures and would be less likely to agree to something as new and controversial as a gene-altering operation. Dr. Kirsch had been generous enough to hold the dogs at bay for a couple more days while Penrose saw the Andrews' case to a decision. Once that decision was made, either way, he was going to the Internal Board.

Mr. and Mrs. Andrews fought the discomfort of butterflies in their stomachs as the nurse showed them into Dr. Penrose's office. They had no way of knowing why they had been asked to come in. They had been emotional wrecks since they first got the call. Getting a call from the lab telling you that there was a concern with the amniocentesis is every pregnant couple's nightmare. Something was wrong with their baby, of that they were sure, but the exact nature of the problem they had no way of knowing. The prospect preyed on their worst fears. Every malady imaginable had been discussed between them as they weighed their own emotional ability to handle each one. A sort of psychological triage had been performed to determine what kind of news would be worse than another. By the time they reached the lab, the Andrews had prepared themselves for the worst.

Dr. Penrose could read the pain in their faces. He, too, had butterflies. They seated themselves in front of Dr. Penrose's desk. The desk looked like every other doctor's desk they had ever seen with one small exception. The box of tissues which sat well within their reach was ominously foreboding. Sabrina reached for Tom's hand and squeezed it tightly. The nurse left, quietly closing the door behind her, and Dr. Penrose gently began.

"I'm Dr. Penrose. I'm a geneticist here at Loveport. I'm also an ob/gyn and I've delivered many babies right here at this hospital. I know you were told that we needed to discuss your amnio, and I can imagine your anguish, so I'll get right to the point. First of all, because of the nature of this situation, I need to tell you the sex of your child. I hope that's OK."

The Andrews looked at each other briefly then nodded.

"It's a boy."

The words fell with a thud. The usually joyous occasion of hearing such news had been stolen from them. They stared straight ahead, still bracing themselves for the bad news.

"I also want to tell you that there's nothing physically or mentally wrong with your boy. He doesn't have Down syndrome or spina bifida or anything like that."

The Andrews felt a limited sense of relief but knew there was bound to be more to come.

"The problem he *does* have can possibly be corrected by a brand new prenatal procedure. I wanted to ease your minds to that extent. Now, understand that detecting this problem wasn't even available until we tested your child. In other words, medicine has just advanced to the point that we can detect this problem and you are the very first couple."

Dr. Penrose directed their attention to a sheet of paper on his desk. The Andrews leaned forward. Pointing with his pen, Dr. Penrose explained the problem. "This is the X chromosome. Girls are born with two of them, boys have one X and one Y chromosome. The X comes from the mother, the Y from the father. On the tip of the long arm of the

X chromosome, there is a section we call Xq28. In the distal portion of Xq28, we have discovered a gene that is present in about 2 percent of all males. This particular gene causes the person to be homosexual. We've found that gene in your son."

The Andrews stared back at Dr. Penrose in shock. "You mean you can determine at this early stage that our son is going to be gay?" she asked in disbelief. "I've never heard of such a thing."

"The 'gay gene' theory has been circulating in the medical community for quite some time," Dr. Penrose explained. "The theory goes that since the X chromosome is passed along by the mother that if her brother were gay there was a much higher likelihood that her son would be gay. It's only been recently that we located that gene."

Sabrina Andrews looked at her husband. "Oh, my God. Robert."

"Who's Robert?" Dr. Penrose asked.

"Robert's her brother," Tom Andrews said.

"He's gay," she added, still in shock. "You don't know the torture he's been through." She started to cry. "And now my own baby's going to have to go through the same thing and it's my fault. Tom, I don't think I can take that." She covered her face with her hands.

"It's not your fault, Mrs. Andrews, and I'm sorry if I made you feel that way. We pass all kinds of things along to our children. We have no choice. It's nobody's fault. It's just in our genetic makeup. But there's more. There is an option for the two of you that has never before been available to parents. We have not only discovered the gay gene, but we have developed a procedure to correct it."

Mrs. Andrews looked up from her hands and wiped her tears with the tissue. She asked with a nervous laugh through her sobs, "You can fix our baby?"

"Wait a minute. Didn't you say we're the first couple you've been able to tell about this gay gene?" Tom Andrews asked.

"That's correct," Penrose said.

"So, you've never actually performed this procedure before."

"Not on humans, that's correct. That's why we need to explore your options. Let me first say that we have successfully corrected this gene in lab animals, specifically dogs and most recently an orangutan, which has a genetic makeup most similar to ours. But you're right, we've never performed this procedure on a human fetus before. That's something to consider. I *will* tell you that it's our belief that it can be done safely, of course, or I wouldn't be discussing this option with you today. There are two other options. One: we terminate the pregnancy, or two: we do nothing."

"How risky is this procedure?" Sabrina asked.

"If you mean in terms of deforming the child, the risk is minimal. There is, of course, the risk of losing the child during the procedure as is the case with the amnio. With the amnio, there's about a one in two-hundred chance of losing the baby. With this procedure, the risk is about the same. The big question of concern is what are the odds of success and, to be honest, we don't fully know. In our early lab tests where we weren't successful in changing the gene, the result was the animal was born as if we tried nothing. The particular genetic locus on which we concentrate controls sexual orientation and nothing else, so there's no chance of producing some malformed person. Anyway, we know pretty quickly if the procedure has been successful and there's still time to take other action."

"By 'other action' you mean abortion," Tom Andrews suggested.

"Yes."

"We discussed that when Sabrina first got pregnant," he explained, glancing over at his wife. "As you know, we have older children, and this certainly wasn't planned. We've decided that abortion is not an option."

"That, undoubtedly, is your decision," Penrose affirmed. "So, now you're faced with the choice of two options. You must decide whether this child will be born homosexual or heterosexual. There's always a remote chance that, environmentally, you can overcome his homosexual tendencies, but I wouldn't count on that avenue being successful. Genetic predisposition, especially homosexual predisposition, is quite tough to overcome." Penrose paused to allow the options to sink in. "I want you to know that I realize what a difficult decision this is. I have two kids of my own." He looked at each of the parents individually. "Do you have any questions for me?"

The Andrews looked at each other. They were sure they had a million questions but couldn't think of even one at the moment. Their minds were racing to process the data thus far provided by Dr. Penrose.

"Here's my cell phone number." He scribbled it on the back of his business card. "Once you've had time to discuss everything, you'll probably have plenty you want to ask me. Call me any time, day or night."

"How long do we have to make a decision?" Tom asked.

Penrose knew they wouldn't like his answer. "We're in a critical window here," he explained. "Technically, the window is approximately twelve weeks. After that, the child's immune system is developed to a point that it might fight off the procedure. But the political reality is we have much less time. The university has given me a grace period to find a couple before they make our discoveries public. As you can imagine, after that happens, there might be any number of people who want to stop the procedure. Naturally, your anonymity will be protected."

"Then how much time do we really have if we want to take action?" Tom gave him an anxious look.

"I need to know within the next two days."

The Andrews looked at each other and grimaced. Two days was not nearly enough time to make such an important decision but it was all the time they had. They rose, and Tom Andrews extended a hand to Dr. Penrose and thanked him for his compassion. Penrose felt them leaning toward the procedure. His adrenaline started to flow. His excitement mounted. Then he caught himself. He had to make it absolutely clear that the decision was theirs and theirs alone.

"One more thing," Penrose offered as they turned to leave. "I want you to understand that this is groundbreaking medicine we're talking about. This is also quite controversial. If you decide in favor of the procedure, you can expect an avalanche of media attention. We, of course, will keep your identities confidential, but you won't be able to avoid the furor that such a decision will certainly cause. Each time you turn on the radio or the television, they'll be talking about *your* baby. I just want to make sure you're fully aware."

"Thank you, Dr. Penrose," Mrs. Andrews replied. She sensed his concern for them was genuine.

Penrose watched them walk away wondering if they could really appreciate what their decision would mean. Did they — or could they — fully understand what an impact they would have on society? If they decided to go along with the procedure, and the procedure was successful, it would change the world. No small burden for a couple who merely expected the normal angst associated with having another child. Penrose had done all he could in providing them with sufficient information. The decision was now between them and God.

8

Dr. Reed Mosser's curiosity had the best of him. He hadn't seen his friend Clark Penrose in weeks, and rumors were starting to circulate. Penrose stood by the desk in his home study with the telephone in his hand.

"Nothing to tell," he said. "Just working on a project."

"Right. And don't feed me that hybrid tomatoes story again," Mosser said. "Somebody spotted a researcher from MIT coming out of your lab. That kind of talent does fly down here for tomatoes."

"Yeah, well, we hired out for some extra eyes. You know, just to check our work."

"Expensive eyes."

"We were working on basically the same problem. I thought it the courteous thing to invite her into the fold."

"Come on, Clark. Clue me in. Your secret's safe with me."

Penrose's cell phone rang. He pulled it from his pocket and looked down at it. "Hey, I'm going to have to take this call."

"Get back to me," Mosser insisted.

"Yeah, sure… Hello."

"Dr. Penrose? This is Tom Andrews."

"Mr. Andrews." Penrose took a deep breath. "Have you reached a decision?"

"Yes, we have. I want you to understand something. I know what this means to you. I know what this means to medicine. But you have to understand that our only concern is for our child. That's enough of a burden by itself."

Penrose felt his stomach muscles tighten. "I understand."

"We know that our decision is going to make a lot of people unhappy, but, quite frankly, I can't be concerned about them." Tom Andrews' voice was shaking with emotion. "All I'm concerned about right now is my wife and my son."

"As you should be."

There was a pause on the other end of the line. Penrose knew he dared not rush him. Whatever came from his lips must also come from his heart. It shouldn't be dragged out by anyone. Penrose knew he had no right to force it.

"All we want is the best life possible for our son," Andrews said. "That's all we want."

"Of course, you do."

"We've spent the last two days agonizing over what role we can play in that at this early stage. We kept going back to one point. We have an opportunity that no other parents in history have ever had. Many parents have thought they wanted this power, but I can tell you, it would be much easier if we didn't know what we know."

"I thought you both deserved to know because—"

"I'm not blaming you, Dr. Penrose. Don't get me wrong. You knew and it was your duty to tell us. I'm just saying it's an awesome burden to place on the shoulders of two parents."

"Yes, of course."

"The basic question came down to this. If you learned that your unborn child was going to be born homosexual and you had a chance to change that, would you?"

Penrose closed his eyes. He realized he had lost all control. They were in charge. Not Kirsch. Not the Internal Board. Not even Penrose himself. Tom and Sabrina Andrews held his fate in their hands.

"We could very well regret our decision down the road, but that's a chance we'll have to take. We have decided that if we have the chance to change this baby…"

Penrose felt his knees weaken and he sat down.

"…we have to take it."

Dr. Penrose's excited eyes welled with tears. He covered his mouth momentarily with his free hand and tried to constrict the elation that was screaming to explode like a volcano. He swallowed the exuberance back down below the surface. "I appreciate your thoughtful deliberation in this matter, Mr. Andrews. I respect your decision and we will move forward with it."

Tom said, "We've never been through anything like this, Dr. Penrose." A panic washed across his face now that the decision had been stated out loud.

"None of us has, Mr. Andrews, but we're all in this together. Our primary concern is the health and safety of this child and his mother. Always know that."

"Thank you, Dr. Penrose."

"We'll be in touch."

"Goodbye," Tom said.

Penrose hit the off button several times more than was necessary then looked down to make sure the call was terminated. The emotions surfaced like steam from a boiling teapot. "Yes!"

Now that the first major hurdle had been jumped, Penrose needed to move the whole project into an even higher gear. He set up another appointment to run through various scenarios which might play themselves out once the story hit the news media. This was not going to be a routine tonsillectomy, and the Andrews deserved to know what to expect. Penrose punched the contact and put the phone to his ear. The voice on the other end answered.

"Dr. Kirsch."

"Roy, this is Clark. The Andrews said yes," he announced excitedly.

"And not a moment too soon. I thought I was gonna have to go to the Internal Board without 'em."

"Set it up and let me know," Penrose urged. "I'll put together a little presentation and—"

"Whoa, hold your horses, cowboy," Kirsch said. "The Lone Ranger rides alone."

"Now, wait a minute, Roy."

"No, *you* wait a minute," Kirsch responded lightheartedly. "You're the brains of this outfit, but you're not the most tactful son-of-a-bitch I've ever known. The last thing we need is for you to lose your temper in there. I'm used to persuadin' folks," Kirsch assured him. "I'll leave 'em thinkin' it was all *their* idea."

Penrose laughed. He was hesitant to relinquish control, but he felt good about Roy Kirsch. He knew Kirsch's art of influence was legendary. "I'll wait to hear from you."

"Clark." Kirsch turned serious. "If they go for this, all hell's gonna break loose. You realize that, dontcha?"

"I know. I think the Andrews are ready for it."

"Yeah, but are *you* ready for it?"

"Roy, what we're doing is right. I can't worry about the public debate."

"All right, partner. I'll remind you of that when the defecation hits the rotisserie."

The paneled study of Dr. Penrose's house was scattered with files and articles. On a Saturday, when most of his colleagues were on the golf course, he studiously sat at his desk with reading glasses at the tip of his nose. A soft knock on the door and he looked up to see Lauren standing in the doorway with hot tea on a tray. He looked at his watch.

"Tea time already," he muttered under his breath. He removed his glasses and rubbed his eyes. He welcomed a break.

"How's it going?" Lauren asked. She cleared back some papers and set the tray down.

"Great," he answered softly, massaging the bridge of his nose. "I'm just worried about the Andrews."

Lauren dropped two cubes of sugar in his cup, stirred, and listened as she sat on the edge of the desk.

"I want this so much," Penrose fretted. "I've worked so long and I've been so excited about our discovery that I really haven't stopped long enough to take them into full consideration. Am I overlooking what's best for them in all of this? Am I thinking too much about myself and not enough about them?

"How long have I known you?" Lauren asked. She handed him his cup.

"Well, let's see, six months dating and, um, twenty-two years of marriage. We're bearing down on a quarter of a century," he said with a smile. He took a sip of tea.

"You're a good man, Clark. You're working in probably the most demanding field in science and here you are with a major breakthrough. You've dedicated your life to something and now you're reaping the rewards."

"So, you're saying I should just worry about me?"

"That's not what I'm saying at all. I'm saying that you have nothing to feel guilty about. I know you're concerned about the Andrews but look at what you're offering them. You're giving them a choice that no parent has ever had before."

Penrose rested his hand on Lauren's and squeezed it gently. He could always count on her to say the right thing, regardless of whether there was a shred of truth in it. He hoped there was.

"Look, you need to take a break from all of this," she said. "It's like you're at work all the time these days. Let's get out of the house tonight." She eased into his lap and slid her arms around his neck. "Maybe that new Chinese restaurant. Maybe a movie."

Lauren's smile was incredibly inviting. Penrose placed his cup back in the saucer and took a moment to absorb her optimism. The ring of the telephone broke his concentration. Lauren got up and answered it.

"Hello…Oh, hi, Roy…Sure. He's right here." She handed the phone to Penrose.

"Roy, how'd it go?"

"Well, it went fine. The Board was excited about the project."

Penrose detected something was wrong. "But?"

"Well, given the controversial nature of the project, they felt it necessary to hold a press conference right away."

"What?" Penrose couldn't believe it. Publicity at this stage could stop the project in its tracks. He was up out of his seat. "I haven't even had a chance to meet with the Andrews!"

"I'm sorry, Clark. Baxten was afraid this thing would leak out. The Board agreed. If the press was going to hear about it, he wanted them to hear about it first from Loveport. You understand, don't you?"

"Damn, Roy." Penrose nervously ran his free hand through his hair and grabbed the back of his head. "Don't you think it's best if I attend?"

"Baxten's the dean. He flies solo, Clark. You know that. Besides, he just got through about a half hour ago."

"He's already held the press conference?" Penrose was incredulous.

"I'm afraid so, but hey, he did one helluva job."

"But if the Andrews see this media circus, it could jeopardize the entire project!"

"Hell, I know that. I wanted to call you earlier but I had to hold Baxten's hand through the conference." Kirsch said.

Penrose knew the real reason the phone call was so late. Kirsch didn't trust him at a press conference, which, he had to admit to himself, was probably a wise decision. He was too close to the project and it would be easy to take any criticism too personally.

"Flip on the noise box there," Kirsch suggested. "It should hit the national news."

"Dammit!" Penrose glanced at the clock on the wall. He motioned for Lauren to hand him the remote control. All his thoughts were on damage control. How was he going to bring the Andrews back within his trust?

"You're welcome," Kirsch said sarcastically.

Penrose caught himself. "Look, Roy, I really appreciate what you've done. I'm just a little upset about this."

"Hey, I understand. I feel the same damn way."

"I mean, you obviously put on quite a show if you persuaded them to go with the project."

"Aw, you shoulda seen me," Kirsch boasted. "I had that group mesmerized. You coulda heard a gnat fart at fifty paces in that room."

Penrose chuckled. "Wish I could've been there."

The slide beside the news anchor caught his eye. It was the Loveport logo. "There it is, Roy." Penrose's index finger fumbled for the volume control. "I'll call you back."

Lauren and Clark stood there in silence, their eyes glued to the television.

"A major medical breakthrough was announced this afternoon at Loveport University Medical Center," the anchor began. "During a hastily called press conference, Dr. Samuel Baxten, Dean of Medicine, made public a revolutionary discovery. Patricia Meeks has more from Loveport."

Meeks was doing a live stand-up report in front of Loveport's main entrance.

"Just a little over an hour ago," she reported, "Dr. Sam Baxten announced that Loveport had made medical history. Dr. Clark Penrose, the university's foremost geneticist, has positively identified what has been termed in the medical community as the 'gay gene.'" Lauren looked at Clark and smiled. He was still fixated on the screen. "This is the gene scientists claim determines a person's sexual orientation. This is a theory that numerous members of the gay community have been espousing for many years and they've been very much looking forward to this day. The twist, however, came in the second part of Dr. Baxten's briefing."

The report cut to videotape of the news conference. Cameras flashed as Dr. Baxten, his white lab coat covering everything except a red Wembly tie with small blue dots, stood in front of a wooden podium. The curtain behind him was solid blue except for the Loveport University Medical Center logo which was positioned just above his head. Dr. Baxten was a crusty, old, no-nonsense kind of doctor. One got the impression that he had probably flunked 'Bedside Manner 101.' Penrose's heart raced at the thought of what he might say, how he might portray the whole matter. His right palm sweat beneath the tight clutch of the remote. His left squeezed Lauren's hand firmly. The sound bite picked up Dr. Baxten in mid-sentence.

"…which is why Dr. Penrose decided to experiment on an orangutan. Once he had located an animal subject with the gay gene, he attempted to correct the gene before the offspring was born. He was quite successful in his experiments with dogs, and a few weeks ago the orangutan I spoke of gave birth to a perfectly healthy heterosexual offspring. The next logical step is to try this procedure on a human subject, which is where we are now."

Cameras clicked as reporters clamored for the doctor's attention. Dr. Baxten pointed to the first one who caught his eye.

"Doctor, are you saying that you're prepared to perform this gene-altering operation on a human, a female human, today?"

"Yes," he answered matter-of-factly and pointed to another reporter.

"Dr. Baxten, do you already have a couple chosen for this procedure and, if so, will their names be released?"

"We have a couple, yes, but we are not releasing their identity, at least not at this time. This has been a hard decision for them to make and we don't want to make them uncomfortable with having made that decision."

"Dr. Baxten! Dr. Baxten!"

"Our policy on that is it'll be up to the couple as to whether or not their identity is released," he added.

"Dr. Baxten! Dr. Baxten!"

"Yes, ma'am." He pointed to a young female reporter on the second row.

"Dr. Baxten, has the hospital thought through the full ramifications of altering a gene? I guess what I mean is: has the hospital considered what the gay community might think of this breakthrough and have you consulted with anyone in the gay community, you know, to get their feelings on the procedure?"

Dr. Baxten paused for a moment. "Um…yes. Ah…yes. And no. I believe you were next." He pointed to a network reporter on the first row.

"Dr. Baxten, how long before this operation will take place?"

"I couldn't tell you at this point. Dr. Penrose is the man on this project. It's his baby, so to speak." He chuckled at the pun which sparked a smattering of laughter from the press corps. "Dr. Penrose has full latitude to proceed at a comfortable pace with the full blessing of this medical center."

"If I could follow up, sir. What will be your response to those who will say that you have no right to make the decision as to whether or not a child is born gay?"

"My response to them will be the same one I'm going to give you. *I* don't have any right to decide whether or not a child is born gay or straight but the child's parents do. I fully believe that decision is theirs and theirs alone to make. It's the responsibility of the parents to make decisions when confronted with a genetic problem. What we do here at Loveport, and what's done at any medical facility for that matter, is we inform parents about genetic defects and list for them a host of options. This is just one more option we can offer but the decision rests squarely on their shoulders."

9

He slammed his fist down on the metal desk. "Genetic *defect*?" he shouted at the television. "Who the hell do you think you are?" Muting the anchor's voice, he sat on the edge of his desk and dialed the telephone. After only a half ring, the phone picked up.

"You got the TV on?" he asked indignantly. "You're watching? Who does this asshole think he is? I mean, damn, we thought the Family Research Council was dangerous. This is all out war! Round up the troops. Let's powwow up here at the office in one hour. Oh, and make sure Kelly's here. We need to know our legal options." He slammed down the phone.

Greg Wently had spent the better part of his life denying who he was. He first noticed he was different at around the age of twelve. As other boys started losing interest in trapping frogs and climbing trees and started shifting their attention to girls, Greg felt out of the loop. Somehow something wasn't quite right.

That pivotal point from his pre-teen years was etched in his mind forever. It was a warm, humid summer night from what seemed to be another life. The cicadas were singing, and the aroma of freshly mowed grass drifted on a light evening breeze. Neighborhood get-togethers like these were a summer ritual. Just as the sun fell below the trees, the neighborhood kids filtered out of their houses for the nightly game of hide-and-seek. The usual company of kids scrambled as the little girl who was 'it' began to count to one-hundred. Greg had three or four favorite hiding places. This time he chose the huge boxwoods below the side porch of the Franklins' house next door. As he settled in behind the bushes, he discovered that someone had beaten him to the spot. It was the cousin of one of the kids down the street. Greg had met the stranger for the first time just thirty minutes prior. He was an older boy of fourteen. A little shy, he didn't say a lot, but Greg had felt a connection to him he didn't quite understand. Not wanting to share a hiding place, he started to leave, but the young boy reached out and firmly grabbed his hand as if to say it was all right to stay. As Greg settled back down under the bushes, the young boy continued to clutch his hand. Not a word was spoken. As they sat in silence, Greg was overcome with a cascade of emotions. His heart was pounding. His hands were sweating. He was frightened yet somehow comforted by the young boy who still held his hand tightly. Then in an instant, the stranger leaned over and kissed him gently on the lips. Greg was petrified by the kiss but even more frightened by the fact that he didn't want to leave. The surge of blood in his veins was nearly blinding. An almost utopian warmth enveloped him. Still, no one said a word.

The commotion of the seeker finding one of the hiders cracked the moment like a clap of thunder. Greg was consumed with the horror of being found in such a compromising position. He bolted upright and parted the bushes with all his might making a B-line for home.

He never again saw the young stranger. He never even knew his name. All he knew was that boy was responsible. He had opened a door which could never be closed, no matter how hard Greg tried. That stranger was to blame for the turmoil which now raged within him. For the next twenty years, he mustered all of his inner strength to suppress the monster that desperately and ceaselessly yearned to escape. He dated girls in the beginning, trying to spark a fire which would never burn. Later he would escort ladies to social functions merely for appearances, all the while futilely searching for a way to extinguish the forbidden desire he held inside.

Finally, at the age of thirty-three, he succumbed to the beast which that young boy long ago had awakened. He could no longer mask his bachelorhood with fabricated stories of sexual conquests and excuses for never being able to find the right girl to marry. He closed his eyes, held his nose, and finally admitted to himself his true feelings. Much to his surprise, the beast didn't consume him. The beast didn't make him his slave. The beast simply vanished. Immediately, there was calm. There was no longer a conflict raging inside. The battle was over. The guns were silent. The real person was now one with his projected persona. For the first time in twenty years, he actually liked himself. For the first time in twenty years, he actually *was* himself.

This near miraculous transformation inspired Greg to spread the word, to give others the courage to touch their innermost selves. After working with a handful of gay activist organizations for several years with only marginal satisfaction, Greg decided to start one of his own. A nucleus of like-minded homosexuals pooled their money and solicited enough funds from gay businessmen to rent a modest office with startup equipment. With that, they created an organization called Gay And Lesbian Liberation And National Tolerance or GALLANT. The acronym was a bit of a double entendre. The most recognized definition of the word was 'brave and noble.' However, Webster's first definition of the word was 'showy and gay in dress or appearance,' an irony that was not lost on its founders. Although most of the gay organizations of which he had been a part were located in New York or San Francisco, Greg Wently wanted a fresh start for GALLANT. He chose Atlanta for its cosmopolitan yet small town feel and its considerable gay population. Being born and raised in the South, he felt comfortable there. The facilities weren't what Greg was used to in the other organizations, but the camaraderie and excitement of launching something new and different in a new town gave him the fulfillment he'd been looking for.

Jon Carroll was the cofounder of GALLANT. He and Greg had been together through some of the toughest demonstrations and the most exhilarating victories of the past six years. They had started out as lovers, Jon the more effeminate of the two, but soon found they were both too headstrong to be compatible. What threw them together was a like-mindedness and determination. It wasn't enough glue to hold a love affair together, but it was the perfect bond for a business relationship. They both desperately wanted to see change in the gay rights movement. The National LGBTQ Task Force was too fainthearted for their tastes. Act Up, too immature. Both organizations, they felt, were too ineffective, too slow. These were guerrilla fighters with a 'take no prisoners' attitude. GALLANT wanted immediate action and there wasn't a gay rights organization on the landscape that could do what they felt needed to be done. Greg and Jon envisioned an organization that hit America where it lived, in the pocketbook. Not only by boycotting, but also by uniting the money forces within the gay community. Gays, by and large, are better educated and wealthier than the average American. Greg and Jon sought to tap into those strengths to bring the combined wealth and influence of gay Americans to bear on the country's psyche. They encouraged gays to pool their money to buy media outlets, high-profile businesses, financial institutions, the conventional instruments of influence, and GALLANT would act as the conduit. They wanted to take the gay rights movement to a new level, shift it into overdrive. Their efforts were met with general indifference among the established gay rights organizations who largely ignored them. They wrote them off as too small and too radical, even by left-wing standards. The truth was GALLANT wasn't capturing the headlines like the more vocal organizations. Their efforts were concentrated behind the scenes, trying to get a toehold on conventional establishments of power. If the general public didn't know them, their activities most assuredly didn't go unnoticed by the conservative watchdogs. One of their office walls sported a framed article about GALLANT written by a prominent conservative columnist. One sentence was highlighted which read, 'GALLANT makes Act Up look like a bunch of Boy Scouts. If the gay rights crowd ever had a macho wing, this is it.' Greg had bigger plans for GALLANT than just the stealth arm of the gay rights movement. He aspired to household name status for his organization but achieving that goal was something altogether different.

The gay rights movement had faced obstacles before but nothing like what the world had just witnessed on television. As president of GALLANT, Greg needed to rally the troops like they'd never been rallied before, but if ever there were an issue to galvanize the organization, this would surely be it. It made the fight for gay marriage look silly by comparison. What Greg Wently had just witnessed on television was the biggest threat ever to their very survival. If Dr. Baxten was to be believed, in another generation, for homosexuals, it would mean their utter extinction.

By the time Dr. Penrose got them on the phone, it was too late. The Andrews were already distressed to learn about their case going public. They felt they were losing control of the situation. Penrose didn't dare admit it to them, but they had *already* lost control. The floodgate had been opened and there was no closing it. Understandably, they didn't trust the hospital and were unnerved that word about them might leak out. Penrose knew he was on shaky ground but gave them his personal word that their identities would be protected at all cost. For the moment, he seemed to have allayed their fears. There was no way to overstate the importance of keeping them happy. If they pulled out, it could take weeks, even months, to find another suitable couple. In that time, the entire project might collapse under the weight of the enormous political pressure which would surely follow Dr. Baxten's revelation to the press. Penrose could ill-afford to have them upset. He reinforced their belief that they were doing the right thing, not only for science, but for their son.

The cameraman was busy coiling up the microphone cord attached to the podium. A dozen other camera crews were doing the same, breaking down equipment after one of the most historic press conferences in medicine. Don Bissette, a seasoned reporter, a bit on the pudgy side with a seriously receding hairline, chatted with the press secretary from Loveport to mop up every drop of information available. He'd been a reporter for WPCV for twenty years. Not by his own choice. He'd longed for greener pastures for years, but the opportunity to move up to a major market had eluded him. At forty-eight, he knew his chance of making that move was becoming less likely with each passing day. The TV news business anymore was about white teeth and a full head of hair, not good, solid news reporting. Don enjoyed the daily beat of a street reporter but knew the anchor desk meant more security and more money. Yet with each vacancy that came and went, the excuse was always the same. Don had been through six news directors and each one had given him the same line. "You don't have the 'look' we're after for an anchor. Besides, you're a damn good reporter. You're too valuable on the street." There was probably some truth to it. He was the best reporter in his market, but that hardly paid the bills.

The news business had taken its toll on his private life, too. In his futile search for the Holy Grail of news, he had lost two wives who got tired of playing second-fiddle to the latest murder story or three-alarm fire. It wouldn't be fair to say he was bitter. After all, he had chosen this life for himself. Desperate was almost too strong a description, but pushing fifty and still stuck in the rut, Bissette was at least strongly concerned that he might never grasp the brass ring and leave 'this godforsaken town.' He peered into his future and saw an old washed-up reporter all alone with no one to share in his misery. The image depressed him.

He wasn't completely blameless for his failure to move up to a larger city. He was abrasive and pushy, downright rude if need be to get the story. And he made no apologies. That's what got you where you wanted to be. The Rathers, the Donaldsons, they'd all stepped on a few toes on their way to the top. He also had a somewhat inflated opinion of himself. So much so that he had dropped his family's pedestrian pronunciation of his last name for a more urbane flavor with the accent on the last syllable.

In spite of himself, it was Don Bissette's good fortune that he happened to be in the right place at the right time when the assignment came down to cover the Loveport news conference. No one in that newsroom, not even Don Bissette, could possibly have known just how big this story would become.

10

Lauren called Brandon and Clark to the table for dinner. Penrose told them that as soon as Karen got home he had an announcement to make. She was due any moment, so the rest of the Penrose family took their usual places around the table. They were settling into their seats when they heard Karen enter through the front door followed by a loud slam. The rest of the family sat silently as Karen huffed her way into the room and sat down.

After a moment, Penrose asked the obvious question. "Anything wrong?"

Karen glared up from her plate. "Not a thing."

Lauren gave it a try. "Anything you want to talk about?"

"Nope," Karen heaped a forkful of roast into her mouth.

"Well," Penrose continued, determined not to let anything rain on his parade, "I have an announcement to make."

"I know about your little announcement," Karen shot back caustically.

"Karen!" Lauren scolded. This was Clark's big day and she would not see it ruined.

"Well, I don't," Brandon responded in his father's defense. He had been studying all afternoon and hadn't seen the news. He gave Penrose his undivided attention.

"Since you know about my announcement, Karen, maybe you'd like to share it with the rest of the family," Penrose suggested.

Karen sensed the tension she was causing. She lowered her tone. "I heard the news on the car radio," she began.

"Dad, wow, you made the news! All right!" Brandon was excited over his father's newfound fame.

"The 'secret project' our dear father has been working on oh these long years," Karen continued, "is a plan to get rid of all the homosexuals."

Brandon looked stunned. Lauren too, not at the news, but at Karen's portrayal of the project.

"Now hold on just one minute," Penrose rebutted. "I don't know what you heard on the radio, but let me set you straight. What I've been looking for 'oh these long years,'" he mocked, "is something referred to as the gay gene. I've not only discovered it but have developed a procedure, which I hope to make available to all parents in the near future, to correct this gene so that the baby can be born heterosexual."

"Just like I said," Karen fired back.

"Obviously you have a problem with this. Would you care to discuss it or have you made up your mind that your father is another Dr. Mengele?"

Karen looked down at her plate for a moment. When she looked up, there were tears in her eyes. Penrose felt a pain in the pit of his stomach. The first casualty of the controversy was his very own daughter.

"How could you do this," Karen said, fighting back the tears. "Gay people are caring, feeling people."

"This has nothing to do with gay people," Penrose argued. "I'm not talking about killing anybody. This won't affect one single living human being. It has to do with a parent's right to choose what—"

"Don't you realize how these people are going to look at you…at us?" she screamed.

"Look, Karen, I know at first glance this might seem anti-gay to you, but really it's not," Penrose pleaded. "Let me give you my rationale behind this whole project."

"I don't want to hear your damned rationale!" she screamed back at him, throwing her napkin on her plate. "I don't want to hear your excuses! I don't want to hear your explanations!" She pushed herself away from the table and headed for the door. She paused in the doorway to add one final thought. "The scary part is I can't believe I never really knew you before today." She ran from the room as Penrose called after her. His pleas fell on deaf ears.

He turned back to Lauren and Brandon at the table. Brandon looked shocked. Lauren's eyes revealed her empathetic pain for what her husband must be feeling. Brandon and Lauren pretended to continue with the meal. Penrose rubbed his face.

"She's got it all wrong, you know," Penrose said to the two of them, but it was more for his own benefit than theirs. "She's heard one news report. She's gauged her reaction by what she thinks everyone will think of her because of me." The two continued to eat without responding. "It's not fair. It's a knee-jerk reaction and it's not fair." He paused for a moment. "I'm not a bad person."

"No one thinks you are, Clark," Lauren assured him.

He pointed up at the ceiling. "She does!"

"Give her a little time to digest everything. I might have reacted the same way if I hadn't known about the project all along."

"I don't think you would've reacted like *that*. It's irrational."

"She's a teenager."

"Teenager or not, it's bloody irrational," he announced in disgust, taking his napkin from his lap and throwing it on the placemat. He rested his elbow on the table and his head against his fist. He felt his son staring at him and slowly turned to meet his eyes. "So, how do you feel about my announcement, Brandon?" he asked cautiously with a dash of sarcasm.

Brandon was fully unprepared for questioning. "Um." His voice cracked and he cleared his throat. "Uh, Dad, I know you've worked long and hard on this project." He attempted to muster a smile in light of the current climate in the room. "I don't quite understand everything about it. All I picked up were bits and pieces from your, uh, *conversation* with Karen. I know that you're the best geneticist in the country, maybe in the world, and I'm very proud of you."

Penrose could not detect whether Brandon was being sincere or just placating him. Neither could Brandon.

"I appreciate that, son. Let me try to explain exactly what this project is. You see—"

Lauren interrupted, "Uh, Clark, maybe now's not the best time to get into all that. Let's wait until everybody's calmed down, OK?"

Any chance of turning the evening into a positive was lost. Penrose looked down at his plate of food. He had lost his appetite.

"Give Karen a little time," she said. "She'll get used to it."

Get used to it? Penrose thought. He wondered if any of them would ever really get used to it.

The set of the television issues show *The Pulse* was bare and intentionally so. The black backdrop focused attention on the two hosts who sat in front of a nondescript desk and battled it out over the issues of the day. What separated this show from other confrontational news shows was the choice of topics. While others concentrated on politics almost exclusively, *The Pulse* hit the hot button issue of the day, no matter what it was, and devoted the entire hour to that one issue. It might be a high-profile murder case or a controversial piece of legislation. It could just as easily be a celebrity scandal. *The Pulse* was the highest rated nightly syndicated show in its time slot, and its stars were now household names. Whatever America was talking about, they were talking about, and the whole country was buzzing about the news out of Loveport.

Betty Duvall came with a resume packed with liberal credentials. A member of NOW, NARAL, and a card-carrying member of the National Civil Rights Alliance. She had a law degree from Yale and, up until the overnight success of the show, practiced law at one of Manhattan's most prestigious firms. The diminutive host was scrappy, tenacious, and given to monopolizing the conversation if she were allowed. The gray streaks in her brown hair gave her a seasoned, distinguished look. She was the darling of the liberal left and she relished every second of it.

On the other side of the table sat Duncan Reynolds. He was young and affable yet a barracuda when he had to be. He was definitely conservative but was shunned by some on the right for not kissing the collective rings of the conservative hierarchy. Many on the right felt he too often made himself a human door mat on which Betty Duvall wiped her feet. They would've chosen someone a bit more bombastic, but they had no such choice. Somewhat of a rebel, Reynolds had gained more of their respect of late because of his success on the show. He wasn't a joiner; he had no official conservative credentials to bring to the table. What he was, in fact, was genuine, real, and in touch with the everyday American. He was also apparently attractive, at least to females. Nielsen showed that his strongest audience was women ages 25-34, not the typical issues program's demo, and a large ingredient in the program's extraordinary success.

Betty and Duncan sat patiently, just moments before the show opened, making small talk. They might have gone at each other on screen, but off screen, they were the best of friends. It was that chemistry that made the show such a ratings winner.

The two hosts waited in the dim light. "Mic check, please Duncan," came the disembodied voice of the director in their hidden earpieces.

"Hello, hello, this is Duncan Reynolds. Hello, hello. "

"That's good. Thanks. Betty?"

"Hello, hello. Testing one, two, three. Hello."

"OK, thanks. Stand by for show open coming in fifteen."

Duncan smiled at Betty. "This is gonna be one helluva show tonight."

She nodded excitedly, afraid to say anything too close to going on.

"In five," the director warned, "four, three, two." A pause and then the graphics of the show came up simultaneously with the energizing show theme. An announcer, whose baritone voice almost rattled the fillings out of one's teeth, introduced the guests individually as images of each flashed on the screen. The lights on the set came up, and Betty Duvall smiled into the camera.

"Good evening and welcome to *The Pulse*. A bombshell was dropped today at one of the foremost medical facilities in the country. Loveport University announced today that one of its brightest geneticists had discovered the much ballyhooed 'gay gene.'"

"But that was only half the story," Duncan Reynolds picked up from there. "Not only have they discovered the gay gene, but they claim they've developed a procedure to alter it, and the gay rights crowd is up in arms." He turned to Betty for her response.

"As well they should be, Duncan. What gives this guy, I believe his name is Penrose—"

"*Doctor* Penrose," Duncan added.

"*Doctor* Penrose, excuse me. What gives him the right to change something as integral to who a person is as his sexual orientation?"

"Integral to who a person is?"

"Yes!"

"All right, what if a guy likes young boys? Is that integral to who he is, so we shouldn't want to change it?"

"Oh, please. You're not equating child molesters with homosexuals, are you?"

"No, but what I'm saying is they're both defects. Sure, a child molester has innocent victims, but they're both sexual deviants."

"Sexual deviants? Are you serious? You think every gay and lesbian person out there is a pervert?"

The phone lines were lit up like Times Square. The call screener feverishly screened the calls and began assigning them a place in the show. The national debate was officially on.

11

Kelly Morris was not only GALLANT's attorney, she was someone Greg Wently knew he could trust. Someone who not only talked the talk but walked the walk. She'd been selected as one of the '100 Most Outstanding African Americans' by the NAACP. With an undergraduate degree from Brown and a law degree from Georgetown — finishing in the top five percent of her class — she had received offers from some of the biggest law firms in Washington. She turned them all down to return to her hometown of Atlanta and open her own practice, taking only civil rights cases for a fraction of what she could be making with a large firm.

She had been inspired to choose the law profession by her grandparents. Although they never directly encouraged her to become an attorney, it was their tales of growing up as sharecroppers which inspired her to dedicate her life to fighting injustice. Her grandmother would sit for hours weaving stories of her tending the crops alongside the other field hands since the age of four. Life offered few options for a Negro of her era. Everyone pitched in to bring in the crops or they not only lost their livelihood, they lost their home. In spite of the immense challenges her grandparents faced, few of their stories were filled with despair or bitterness. Most were of the good times with friends and family and church. Most were of how they were so thankful for what appeared to be so little. Despite the obvious disadvantage they faced, Kelly's grandparents held no grudge.

Kelly was not so forgiving. She had dedicated her life to "the struggle." From her vantage point, there was but one primary beneficiary of the gross maltreatment of her people — the white male. More times than not, he was the target of her wrath. Heaven help him when he found himself in her crosshairs.

Kelly Morris' reputation among the disenfranchised was legendary. She was a champion of the underdog, and she thrived on the challenge. Greg Wently never had to wonder why she represented GALLANT. She did it because it was the right thing to do.

Kelly took a seat beside Greg Wently, saying nothing. She didn't have to. Her eyes said it all. She was nervous. She was scared. In spite of the dangerous prospect unveiled at Loveport Medical Center just a few hours prior, she was also excited. GALLANT needed a high-profile confrontation to put them on the map. This was a *real* fight, not some insignificant protest against some even more insignificant politician. This was a bloody conflict in the making. This was a clash with repercussions that would echo for generations to come and it was absolutely exhilarating. Greg sensed her excitement. Not only did he sense it, he shared it. He reveled in it as much as she did. He gently gripped her arm just before he stood and called the meeting to order.

"I appreciate all of you coming on such short notice," Greg began. He gazed out at his troops. Most wore buttons with the organization's logo, a pink knight on a purple horse. All twenty-two pairs of eyes were glued to their leader. "I'm sure you were just as shocked as I was when you heard what Loveport was up to. We haven't fully assessed the ramifications of such a medical breakthrough. Let me just say we haven't found much positive in Dr. Penrose's experiments."

A light chuckle sprinkled across the crowd at the understatement.

"We have been in brief contact with other gay, lesbian, and transgender organizations. Believe me, they're as upset about this as we are. However, the general consensus among these other organizations is that they're going to sift through the medical data and make a decision on what steps to take in the next few days. I've talked this over with Jon and Kelly, and they both agree with me. As president, I believe that this is the opportunity GALLANT has been waiting for. The reason most of you are a part of this organization stems from a dissatisfaction with the way in which these other groups have conducted themselves in times like this. We've all been a part of other gay rights efforts and it seems to me there's been too much compromising and not enough action!"

The room roared in strong affirmation as Greg brushed a lock of hair out of his eyes.

"We have decided on a course of action that will begin first thing tomorrow morning. We not only believe this is the right thing to do, but we believe it will thrust GALLANT into the forefront of the gay, lesbian, and transgender rights movement.

"I spoke with my friend, Rex Randle. Most of you are familiar with him. If you're not, Rex is one of the National Civil Rights Alliance's top attorneys. He represented the Ku Klux Klan in Florida versus Templeton and won over unbelievable odds. Now, I understand that none of us here tonight condones the KKK and what it stands for, but in Florida versus Templeton, the authorities took some major liberties with the Klan's civil rights. Like the Templeton case and many others, the NCRA isn't concerned about popular opinion. They're concerned about right and wrong under the Constitution. They don't lightly enter into a civil matter such as this unless they're sure someone's rights have been violated. I talked with Rex at length about this matter, and the NCRA has agreed to back us in our decision." Again he was interrupted by applause. "We're not waiting a few weeks. We're not waiting a few days. In just a few hours, our attorney, Kelly Morris, along with Rex Randle, will file for a temporary restraining order to block the actions of Loveport Hospital!" The crowd cheered and applauded. Wently continued over their enthusiasm. "Let me assure you, my friends, this is war and we will win this one and we will win it at *any* cost!"

The excited assembly rose to its feet in exuberant applause. Greg Wently smiled. This was what it was all about, he thought. It had the exhilaration of a political campaign but with far more personal meaning. This was a cause into which he had poured his entire being. It was going to be one hell of a battle, but he was up for the fight.

Jon and Kelly joined him at his side as the applause evolved into a cadence. "GAL-LANT! GAL-LANT! GAL-LANT!" the crowd chanted in unison. The battle cry had been sounded. The troops were rallied.

"They can't do this!"

"They can and they did," Roy Kirsch explained to Dr. Penrose from behind his large desk. He had invited Penrose up to his office to break the bad news about the restraining order in person, hoping that would soften the blow. It hadn't.

"Dammit!" Penrose leaned on the back of the wingback chair and buried his head between his arms. "Dammit! I *knew* this was going to happen!" He popped his head up and leered at Kirsch. "That's why I *begged* you, please let me find a couple *and* perform the procedure before we went public!"

"Hold on, Clark. You know damn well I couldn't do that. Baxten and I discussed all this before we held the press conference. We *expected* this legal challenge. But I tell ya what, it's better we fight this out in court now. If we'd gone your way, it might've done irreparable damage to the reputation of this institution."

"Who do you think *built* that reputation?!" Penrose turned and walked to the window.

Kirsch recognized a bruised ego when he saw one. He had danced this dance enough times to know all the steps. He tried not to do any more damage than had already been done. "Now, look," Kirsch consoled, "the university's committed to backin' you on this one-hundred percent. Baxten's got the lawyers downtown fightin' for us as we speak, but I don't think you quite realize what we have here. This is the biggest thing to hit the medical world since Hippocrates wrote the Oath. Brace yourself, son, the water's fixin' to get real choppy."

Penrose turned from the window. The expression on his face had turned from anger to concern. He thought he'd prepared himself for any eventuality. It was quite apparent to the both of them that he had not.

Ever since his days at Wake Forest Law School, Rex Randle had harbored a dream. Some thought that dream might be to pursue a career in the NBA. After all, he had attended undergrad at Wake on a basketball scholarship. In reality, he had little use for basketball. It was a means to an end. That end was to become an attorney. The dream was to champion the civil liberties of ordinary Americans. He couldn't care less about divorce cases. He viewed that type of practice as seedy, beneath his dignity. Likewise, he had little interest in being a trial lawyer. There was too much compromise, too many cases settled out of court for fear of confronting the truth. Rex liked the truth. He liked absolutes, clear distinctions between right and wrong. What did the Constitution say about a particular issue? That was where the rubber really met the road. That was the basic philosophy of the National Civil Rights Alliance. Rex Randle and the NCRA were a perfect fit.

Constitutional law doesn't always favor the good guys: consequently, Rex found himself working for some pretty unpopular groups from time to time. The Ku Klux Klan, for instance. He certainly had no love for the Klan. In fact, he loathed them. Yet, there was something he loathed even more and that was the trampling of basic civil liberties by authority. After the Klan trial, Rex gained national attention as one of the attorneys for the Aryan Freemen, a white supremacist group whose members were convicted of bank fraud, theft, robbery, firearms violations, and making threats against a federal judge. Certainly another 'lunatic fringe group,' as Rex referred to his former clients, but not so nuts, in his eyes, that the law enforcement agencies should be able to ignore the law and bring them in at any cost.

He was thrilled to get away from the right-wing fringe, lest he be pegged as some "solicitor to the segregationists" and work for the other side, for a change. Even before Rex got the call from Greg Wently, he was planning strategy in the Loveport case. His natural concern in every case was the underdog. To his mind, it was unthinkable that someone would develop a procedure that would wipe out homosexuals. It was a frightening prospect. Their cause was well deserving of the kind of representation he could provide. If it was controversial, all the better. The NCRA had built its reputation on controversy and this case was right up their alley. The sooner they put a stop to this procedure, the better, and Rex Randle was determined to do just that.

12

Kelly Morris sat motionless in a wooden chair in the nearly empty courtroom. The sunlight from the large courtroom window glistened off her closely cropped hair. It was only on occasions such as court appearances that she added a touch of makeup to her coffee-and-cream complexion. She could hear her heart pounding in her ears, so loudly that she thought Greg Wently and Rex Randle, who sat on either side, must surely be able to hear it too. She sucked deep breaths of air through her slender nose in an effort to calm herself.

This hearing was the first battle in what she hoped would be a short war. If they could get the judge to stop Penrose's procedure in its tracks, they could claim an early victory. Rex Randle told her from personal experience that it probably wouldn't be that simple. The silence of the wait only compounded her anxiety.

Jonathan Sagar, the attorney for Loveport Medical Center, and Dr. Sam Baxten were a little more relaxed, whispering back and forth to one another, Sagar taking the occasional note. From the time Roy Kirsch first made Penrose's stunning discoveries known, Jonathan Sagar had been by Dr. Baxten's side. If he could nip this thing in the bud, he could save his client and old friend a great deal of time and money.

The presiding judge was the Honorable Seamus Kincaid, a fiery Irishman with red, thinning hair, rosy cheeks, and a short fuse. The eldest of six children, he was proud of how far he had taken the family name since its humble beginnings in this country when the first Kincaid arrived at Ellis Island with empty pockets and a head full of dreams. He was kidded about his name which most pronounced SEE-mus, but it was pure Irish — pronounced SHAME-us — taken from that first-generation Kincaid, and he wore it with dignity. His enemies, both inside and outside the courtroom, referred to him as Shameless Kincaid, though none would dare utter it to his face. He was the first Kincaid to graduate from college, not to mention law school. He was a self-made man in every sense of the phrase, and he took pride in his duties.

Judge Kincaid painstakingly reviewed the pleadings. With thirty-three years of experience on the bench he thought he'd seen it all. He had made the tough decisions before, but this hearing was like nothing he had ever experienced before. He pored over the documents submitted by both sides, making sure of the decision he was about to hand down. The courtroom had been barred of reporters and spectators by his order. He had no intention of having any distractions in this important decision.

Because of the diversity of citizenship among the parties — the NCRA and GALLANT being from out of state — Judge Kincaid deemed the case to be in the proper jurisdiction of federal district court. He conferred with the court clerk in hushed tones, looking at her over his reading glasses then redirecting his attention back to the mound of papers. Kelly Morris fidgeted nervously. Jonathan Sagar sat relaxed with his arms crossed, squinting at the bench. Judge Kincaid ended his discussion with the clerk, removed the reading glasses, placed them on the papers before him, and addressed the courtroom.

"This court has made a decision regarding the temporary restraining order filed by GALLANT and the NCRA. Given the time-sensitive nature of this case, I believe it would be prudent for this court to order a preliminary injunction to delay this medical procedure until a time when all sides have had a chance to present their arguments."

Kelly Morris smiled at Rex Randle. Greg Wently took comfort in their obvious pleasure in the announcement but didn't quite understand exactly what the judge meant.

"It is also the opinion of this court that there is a need for a resolution of this issue regardless of whether that resolution takes place inside the normal 266-day human gestation period. In other words, even if time runs out on the couple in question, this matter is important enough that it must be decided."

Judge Kincaid cited a 1911 case, Southern Pacific Terminal Co. v. ICC. The Supreme Court referred to the case in determining that such cases involving pregnancy be decided regardless of whether the decision came after the child was brought to term. The justices reasoned that if gestational restraints were placed on the case, it could be "capable of repetition, yet evading review." Judge Kincaid wanted to make sure the issue was thoroughly argued before they opened "Pandora's Box." He did note, however, that the consequences for the couple involved dictated the court act expediently.

"This is how we will proceed with this case. There are two questions of fact that must be decided," Kincaid informed the attorneys. "The first is whether the present accepted condition of this fetus — that being he is homosexual — is one deemed necessary of correcting. That is the central and crucial issue that must be resolved," he stressed. "If it's decided the current condition of the fetus warrants correcting, then a decision will have to be made on the second question of fact. That question is whether the outcome of this procedure justifies the risk. Now, before *that* question can be answered," Kincaid instructed, "a determination must be made regarding the *degree* of risk to the fetus in Dr. Penrose's procedure."

The two parties differed greatly on that point. Sagar argued the risk was minimal. Kelly Morris, on the other hand, argued the chances were high for a spontaneous abortion. This argument would hinge on the expert testimony presented in court. Because of the two questions of fact, Judge Kincaid decided a trial jury would be selected.

Jonathan Sagar protested. "Your Honor, as you can imagine, my clients are on a limited time schedule. There's a window of opportunity of about twelve weeks here. A jury trial would just be too time-consuming.

The defense feels this court would be more qualified and better suited to decide this case."

Judge Kincaid smiled at the defense attorney's obvious effort to score some brownie points with the bench. "Mr. Sagar, this trial can be over and done within plenty of time," he responded decisively.

Jonathan Sagar returned to his seat.

"My next concern is the guardian ad litem," Kincaid said, referring to representation for the unborn child.

Rex Randle popped up. "Your Honor, the NCRA requests that we be named the legal guardian."

Before Jonathan Sagar could raise his hand in protest, Judge Kincaid handed down his decision. "Request denied," Kincaid said curtly. "It is the opinion of this court that the best interest of the unborn child is not represented by either party in this hearing. Therefore, I will be appointing a third party to act as guardian ad litem for the child. Once a legal guardian has been chosen, the court, in a timely manner, will confer with counsel from all sides and a mutually acceptable trial date will be set."

With that, Judge Kincaid closed the proceedings with the slam of his gavel and retired to his chambers.

The back doors of the courtroom flew open and Kelly Morris, Rex Randle, and Greg Wently hurried down the corridor.

"What exactly does this mean?" Greg asked, trying to keep pace with Kelly.

"Well, there's good news and bad news," Kelly explained. "We got the preliminary injunction, which means they can't do anything until the case is decided."

"Which means we'll get our day in court," Rex added.

Kelly nodded. "The big problem now is the guardian ad litem."

"What's that?" Greg wanted desperately to cut through all the legal mumbo-jumbo.

"The guardian ad litem is the legal term for a court-appointed guardian or legal representative for the unborn child," Kelly explained.

"We wanted to represent him, but the judge feels we won't act purely in his interest."

"Which we kind of expected," Rex said.

"The guardian," Kelly said as her mind raced. "That's the wild card."

"Who's that going to be?" Greg asked.

"That's just it," Rex answered, "we won't know until the judge makes a decision."

"Well, maybe the ole judge needs a little help making the decision," Kelly said as they exited the courthouse.

"You got somebody in mind?" Rex asked.

"Oh, yeah. I've got somebody in mind. Convincing them to come on board is another matter."

13

Clark Penrose arrived at work just as he did any other day, only this was no ordinary day. He was now at the center of the biggest controversy in the nation. Some saw him as a brilliant scientist, even a humanitarian, out to save homosexuals from a life of misery. Others saw him as the devil incarnate. Whether good or bad, everyone had an opinion of Dr. Penrose. He rolled past the main entrance to the medical center witnessing a crowd of protesters on the sidewalk out front. They were peaceful, yet the sheer number of them took Penrose completely by surprise. Ordinarily with a crowd that large one would expect an appropriate level of noise, but they were perfectly quiet. Penrose blanched. They were there in support of him. The stark silence of that mass of humanity was so surreal it sent a chill down his spine. Expressionless, the core of the mass slowly moved in a circle carrying their placards as the rest looked on. The soft shuffling of the soles of their feet on the concrete was the only sound. Television cameras trying to capture the moment only added to the bizarre nature of the scene. A rowdier crowd could be heard in the distance and had been sequestered on the same side of the medical center but across the entrance street from the silent mob. They chanted slogans against Loveport. A young man wearing a Guy Fawkes mask led the chants through a bullhorn.

Penrose made the turn into the entrance and drove the block to the back. He pulled his Buick into his reserved space and 'the swarm' was upon him all at once. Media from all over the world clawed and clamored for a statement. Cameras with bright lights were on top of him. Boom microphones loomed over his head trying to catch every morsel that dripped from his mouth. Reporters screamed his name followed by an incomprehensible stream of questions. Penrose was overwhelmed, almost terrified. His immediate concern was to make it the twenty yards or so to the front door. He tried to bulldoze his way forward, but the swarm had him surrounded. He lowered his head and cut through the jungle of humanity with his arms, all the while the shouting and shoving increased, reaching the point of hysteria. At last, he made it to the door where Carol was waiting to let him in. She quickly opened the door and half pulled her boss through the small slit as the mob called after him. She closed the door behind him and locked it. Penrose leaned up against it to make sure it was secured and breathed a sigh of relief.

"What in the bloody hell was that?" Penrose asked.

"Your adoring public," Carol joked. "You're quite a hot commodity these days. Come here. Let me show you something."

She led Penrose into his office. On his desk lay a huge, gray denim sack.

Penrose looked at her curiously with a raised eyebrow.

"Your morning mail," Carol announced.

"You're kidding." He walked over, pulled open the drawstrings and dumped a chunk of it on the desk. "Let's take a sample of the American psyche, shall we?" He tore open one of the letters and read it out loud.

"'Dear Dr. Penrose. I want to applaud you for your courage. You've ignored the current political climate and pursued a cure for homosexuality in spite of the immense pressures under which you must be working. As a gay man, I'm happy to know my condition will not be forced on another generation.' That's very nice," Penrose said. He set the letter aside and proceeded to open another.

Carol held another in her hand. "Dr. Penrose," she read, "your callous and malicious attempt to eradicate homosexuals is an atrocity surpassing the evil deeds of Nazi Germany. May the jaws of Hell swallow you whole.'"

"We'll put him down as uncommitted," Penrose joked.

"Dr. Penrose, this is scary," Carol said.

"Aw, come on, Carol. These are the nuts, the flakes. These are the same folks who write their congressman every week. Don't let them bother you."

Carol was not convinced.

"Look, if it'll make you feel better, I'll call Dr. Kirsch and get security beefed up over here. While I'm at it, I'll get him to do something about that media mob out there." He put a consoling arm around her. "We'll be fine."

The law firm of Carr, Campbell, & Douglas was one of the oldest and most respected in the state. The modest practice started by Marcus Douglas, Stephen Campbell, and Timothy Carr in the early nineteen-hundreds had grown to a staff of twenty-four attorneys. The original partners had all long since passed away. Several senior partners had come and gone. Many more successful attorneys had called the firm home since its humble beginnings but none dared add their own name to the shingle. CC&D was a franchise, a household name throughout the state and much of the South. Although the famed firm had enjoyed much success over the years, its true affluence had been fairly recent. Jonathan Sagar was now senior partner and the person responsible for the firm's phenomenal growth. His high profile clients included some of the most enterprising and successful businesses in the state. One of their oldest clients was Loveport University and Medical Center. Jonathan Sagar himself had personally handled a landmark malpractice suit against the hospital which would have cost it a tremendous amount of money and severely damaged its reputation.

In the suit filed against the hospital, the plaintiff charged that Loveport was negligent when two different staff physicians specializing in different areas of expertise prescribed medicines which were incompatible and potentially lethal when taken together. The patient, a fifty-year-old man, died as a result of the mix up. Although the patient never told either doctor about the other's prescription, the plaintiff's family charged that electronic record-keeping at the hospital should have caught the contraindication. Although the hospital admitted the error, Sagar argued the patient was not without culpability. He was able to obtain the patient's grocery receipts and discovered he purchased an over-the-counter drug, which was strictly in violation of the warning label on his prescription medication. An autopsy turned up the forbidden drug in his system. Having proved contributory negligence on the part of the deceased man, the lawsuit was decided in favor of Loveport. Thanks to his tireless research and adept courtroom maneuvers, Sagar saved the hospital considerable embarrassment, not to mention a hefty sum of money. Jonathan Sagar had been a trusted friend and adviser to Samuel Baxten for over twenty years. It was a friendship and business association he had carefully cultivated.

The law offices were abuzz with the preliminary injunction obtained by GALLANT and the National Civil Rights Alliance. It was this kind of high profile case that could make or break the career of a hotshot attorney. Each of the attorneys on staff was chomping at the bit to be a part of the action.

Kurt Ford had been with the firm only four years. Although his research skills were superb, his experience in the courtroom was minimal. Association with a landmark case like this, especially if they won, could propel him to where he wanted to be. There was one small problem that might affect his ability to try this particular case. Kurt Ford was gay. He had never made a big deal about it, but he had never denied it either. He didn't go so far as to bring boyfriends to company functions, still everyone knew about his homosexuality. A few on staff had a problem with it — Bill Dumaine in particular.

Bill had played football at Michigan State. He was the quintessential jock. He would probably have already made partner if it weren't for his attitude. A brilliant legal mind, he was the epitome of negativity. Combative, abrasive, arrogant, he had little tolerance for those things he didn't like or didn't understand. Being gay went against every fiber of his being. Not only did he not understand it, he didn't even *try* to understand it. He hated homosexuals and everything they stood for. Protests on television by gay activists made his blood boil. To him, being gay was a lifestyle choice as perverse and repulsive as any choice any human being could possibly make.

At six-foot-five, Bill was a towering presence over his co-workers. As Kurt Ford poured himself a cup of coffee, Bill leaned against the counter.

"What do your 'friends' think about the big news out of Loveport?" Dumaine took a calm sip from his cup.

Ford stared at the wall in front of him as he set the coffee pot down. He knew exactly what Dumaine meant by the comment. Several co-workers stopped to watch the confrontation. Ford said nothing and took a sip from his own cup.

"I'd say you've become quite a liability around here," Dumaine asserted. "After all, Loveport's one of our biggest clients. Wouldn't look right if word got out that one of you was on the defense team."

Kurt turned to face him, quickly trying to size up the situation. Surely Dumaine wouldn't start a fight right there in the office. After careful consideration, Kurt felt it safe to engage in a little debate. "Can't see how it could hurt. It would certainly look better than a pathetic homophobic ex-jock out there gay bashing in front of a jury and the press."

As soon as the words left his lips, Kurt wished he could have them back. Bill Dumaine's face turned red with rage. He took two steps toward Kurt and opened his mouth to speak. Kurt was petrified. Perhaps he had miscalculated his opponent. Jonathan Sagar appeared in the doorway. Sensing the tension, he paused as he entered the room. Each and every nervous eye was on him. Bill softened his stance and tried to act as if nothing were going on. Sagar poured himself a cup of coffee. The silence in the room made the tension palpable. He looked at Bill and Kurt then headed down the long hallway toward his office.

"Ford, I want to see you in my office," Sagar barked back over his shoulder.

Bill Dumaine smiled a victor's smile at Kurt who set his coffee on the counter and followed Sagar down the hallway. Kurt reached in his pocket and pulled out a half-used roll of Tums. He popped one in his mouth and quickly chewed it up.

Jonathan Sagar had hardly slept a wink and he was in no mood for Dumaine's shenanigans. He had a difficult decision to make and had really only made up his mind completely on the drive in. The Loveport case was too important to simply dish off to an experienced attorney and then forget about it. In this case, especially, strategy would play a major role. This was no ordinary civil case. The eyes of the world would be watching to see what came of it. Sagar had to take each step carefully. He had to cover every angle to ensure his client was taken care of. In the process, it would mean some bruised egos, but so be it. No one at the firm was indispensable. They were a team and he aimed to drive that point home. Their reputation, and the Loveport case, would depend on it.

Sagar's office was one befitting a senior partner. It measured approximately 20 feet by 30 feet. The off-white, deep-pile carpet was partially covered with a huge, expensive oriental rug. The bookshelves housed the obligatory law books along with framed pictures of Sagar and a varied array of famous people. A detailed model of a clipper ship took up several feet of the far-right cabinet top. His matted and framed Harvard law degree hung prominently on the wall to Kurt's left. Family pictures, mostly of the Sagar clan deep sea fishing on his fifty-three-foot yacht, filled the wall to the right.

"Have a seat, Kurt." Sagar gestured to one of the chairs in front of the desk. "I suppose you're aware of Judge Kincaid's ruling yesterday afternoon?"

"Yes, sir. I read about it in the paper this morning."

"How do you feel about this case?"

Kurt paused for a moment. His response must be judicious. Careful but honest. "Well, I think it's an important case for this law firm. I mean, the legal challenge is one I think we can handle."

"Let's cut through the crap, son. How do you feel about this case as a homosexual?"

Kurt was stunned. He had never even discussed his sexuality with Mr. Sagar and he was uncomfortable doing so now. He had no idea his boss even knew. Now any pretense he thought there might have been evaporated with Sagar's straightforward and candid question.

"Honestly?"

"Honestly," Sagar replied. He leaned back in his leather chair, hands clasped behind his head.

"As a homosexual, it's a little scary to think there's someone out there with a procedure to prevent the proliferation of your own kind. I mean, it's like being left-handed and finding out they've found a cure. You never thought it needed curing. However, growing up gay, I can certainly understand a parent's desire not to have a gay child. Dr. Penrose's assertion that homosexuality is a genetic disorder may be unpopular but, scientifically, it can be backed up with sufficient data, and I believe his actions can be upheld by the law."

"You have no problem separating Kurt the lawyer from Kurt the homosexual?"

Kurt frowned slightly. To be sure Sagar wasn't thinking of letting him do research for this case, he thought. Not someone with his inexperience on a case this big. "No, I don't," Kurt said after a short pause. "In fact, I really believe there are a lot of gay people who will welcome his discovery."

"Grand," Sagar said with a wide smile. He sat upright and clapped his hands on his knees. "I'm assigning the Loveport case to you."

Kurt's heart dropped to his stomach. "You're what?" Kurt was flabbergasted. "But Mr. Sagar, there are plenty of attorneys in this firm with far more courtroom experience."

Sagar pushed himself away from the desk and stood. "That may be true, but they don't have your tenacity and your attention to detail and," he paused a moment, "they aren't gay." He made his way over to the small office refrigerator. He reached inside for the champagne to pour the traditional celebration drink offered up when attorneys were assigned to cases of that magnitude.

"Wait just a minute." Kurt rose and followed him, his face filled with concern. He positioned himself in Sagar's view. "You're telling me you're giving me this case just because I'm gay?"

Sagar popped the cork. "No. I'm telling you I'm giving you this case because you're good. But your being gay gives you an added advantage."

"I won't be used," Kurt protested indignantly.

Sagar finished pouring the champagne, set the bottle down, picked up the glasses, and looked Kurt directly in the eyes. "Son, we're all being used. Don't you think if this were a race case I'd put Roberts or Turner in, not just because they're fine lawyers, but because they're black? You use every bit of ammunition you've got. Sure there are more experienced attorneys in this firm, but when that jury sees a gay man arguing our case, it makes it that much stronger. All this crap about justice being blind is just that. Justice is what that jury will see, hear, smell, feel, perceive. It's everything from a witness' accent to the defense attorney's tie, and you can bet your ass our opponent is throwing in every trick he's got too. This is too strong a card we have here. I've *got* to play it."

Kurt looked down at the patterns on the oriental rug then back up at Sagar. "What if I can't cut it?"

"Oh, you can cut it," Sagar assured him as he handed him a glass. "I've been watching you. You do good work. You're very thorough. Anyway, you're gonna have one of the best legal minds in the firm helping you. Dumaine's gonna be ridin' shotgun."

Kurt froze in shock for a few seconds, clinked his glass with Sagar's, then downed the glass of champagne in a single gulp.

"Congratulations, son," Sagar said, shaking his hand.

"Mr. Sagar, I can't work with Dumaine," Kurt announced.

"Look, I'm fully aware of Dumaine's problem. I can assure you of one thing: I won't tolerate his attitude, but you let me worry about that. You're the lead attorney." Sagar placed a reassuring hand on Kurt's shoulder. "You concern yourself with winning this case. Now, send Dumaine in here, would you?"

Kurt exited the room with both euphoria and trepidation. What a break the Loveport case could be for his career, but having to work alongside Bill Dumaine, was anything worth that? By the time Kurt reached Dumaine's office, the dread had displaced the excitement. Dumaine surmised by the look on Kurt's face he'd just received bad news. That could only mean good news for him, Dumaine thought, now that Kurt had passed along Sagar's wish to see him. Dumaine straightened his tie as he rounded his desk.

Sagar set the two champagne glasses back on the tray next to the bottle then took his seat behind the desk. Bill Dumaine knocked twice on the door.

"Come," Sagar responded.

Dumaine entered the room as Sagar read over a deposition on his desk. Dumaine noticed the champagne bottle and glasses and his heart raced with anticipation. Although he had never personally had the experience, he knew their meaning. Everyone in the firm did. He also knew this could be the big break he needed to propel his career to the next level. He sat down in the same seat Kurt Ford had used. It was still warm. Dumaine cringed.

"You're aware of the lawsuit against Loveport, I take it," Sagar asked without looking up.

"Yes, sir," Dumaine answered. "I read the article in the paper. Some of the guys and I were already plotting strategy."

Sagar looked up from the desk. "Good," he smiled. "Good. That's what I like is a little initiative. I don't need to tell you how big this case is. It'll probably shake out to be the biggest case we've ever taken in terms of publicity for this firm. It's going to take everything we've got, every trick in the book."

"Yes, sir," Dumaine agreed. He was anxious with nervous anticipation.

"That's why I've assigned Ford to head up this case."

There must be some mistakes. Kurt Ford? Dumaine was incredulous. "Ford? But he's…he's—"

"He's what, Mr. Dumaine? He's gay?" Sagar finished the sentence for him.

Dumaine shifted in his seat. "Yes, sir, he is."

"I assume from your tone you have a problem with gay people?"

"You want my honest opinion?"

"I insist on it," Sagar replied.

"I do have a problem with gay people. Personally, I find their lifestyle disgusting."

"Well, so there's no misunderstanding about where I stand on this subject, let me make myself clear. I don't care who Kurt Ford is sleeping with. I don't care who you're sleeping with. I don't care who anybody in this firm is sleeping with as long as it's not happening at my law offices. Now, as long as Mr. Ford is not hitting on you, which I assume he isn't, I expect you to afford him the same courtesy you would anyone else in this law firm. Am I making myself clear enough for you, Mr. Dumaine?"

"Yes, sir. Crystal clear," Dumaine answered.

"Now, I don't know what that little dispute was over when I came through a little while ago, but I can guess who instigated it. If I hear of anything like that happening again you'll be out on the street so fast it'll make your head spin." Sagar stopped a moment to cool his temper. "You're a damn good lawyer, son, but your attitude is going to land you in a lot of hot water. I will not tolerate unprofessional behavior from anyone. Understood?"

"Yes, sir," Dumaine answered.

"Good. With that settled, I assume there won't be any problem between you two on the Loveport case."

"Sir?" Dumaine was confused. "I thought Kurt was heading up that case?"

"He is," Sagar explained, "and you're going to be assisting him."

Sagar leaned back in his chair with his eyes burning into Dumaine, enjoying every second of discomfort Dumaine was experiencing. He loved a little personality conflict on a case. It made for greater competition and, hopefully, a better effort out of each person. Aside from the sheer pleasure it gave him, Sagar knew he had assembled the best team in the firm for this particular case and, with his supervision, he was confident they could win.

14

Jack Hawkins entered the three-story office building, carrying a cup of coffee in one hand and a donut in the other. He dropped by the front office to pick up his messages from the pool receptionist, stuffing the donut in his mouth in order to free his right hand. He hopped aboard the elevator to the top floor and thumbed through the four pink sheets. Once off, he balled up two of the messages and tossed them into the ashtray by the elevator. He folded the other two and filed them away in his coat pocket. He took the last bite of the donut, and the sound of sliding paper met the turn of his office door knob. His door pushed back the mail that had been delivered through the mail slot. He leaned down, grunting as he did, picked up the mail, and began to size it up without opening it. Bills, mostly, and several pieces of junk mail which he deposited in the waste can without opening. There was one interesting looking envelope with no return address. The only clue to its origin was the Washington, DC postmark. It was local. He almost tossed it with the junk mail, but the lack of return address suggested it wasn't junk. He walked around behind his desk, wiping dried sugar on the side of his pants, then packed the contents of the envelope down to one end and tore open the other. One nudge and a small silver key dropped out and clanged onto the top of the desk. He pulled out the accompanying note and unfolded it. 'Important job. Big money. Key fits locker #458-Union Station. Further instructions there.' No signature. Weird, he thought. Was this some of his former buddies on the force trying to play a game? Would they be waiting at locker #458 with cameras in hand ready to spring the joke?

Hawkins had spent twelve years as a Capitol Hill police officer. During that time, he got to know a lot of high-powered people. He was on a first-name basis with some of the most influential people in the country, perhaps the world. Three years prior, he decided to parlay those connections into a successful private investigation business, but it hadn't been nearly as easy as he thought. He wasn't bad at it. In fact, he was pretty good. The problem was this was Washington, DC. The best of the best were working this town. The competition was stiff. Still, he had managed to scratch out a living, something just a trifle better than his policeman's salary. If his old friends up on the Hill were having a laugh at his expense, so be it. He wasn't making enough yet to ignore an anonymous proposition for big money, no matter how odd it might seem.

Jonathan Sagar was eager to introduce his legal team to his clients. Because of the doctors' busy schedules, it was easier to assemble at Loveport than at the law offices. Sagar, Ford, and Dumaine filed into a small study adjacent to Dr. Baxten's office. Penrose and Kirsch were already there. The attorneys were introduced to the doctors and the guests were offered refreshments, which they all declined.

"We have a long-term strategy to win this case," Sagar began, "and keep Dr. Penrose's project alive. In addition to Mr. Ford and Mr. Dumaine here, I've assigned a couple of associates to assist with the case, not to mention several paralegals and all of the resources of the firm. I, of course, will be overseeing the case, but Mr. Ford will be handling your case in court. This case is our top priority."

Dr. Penrose was quick with a question. "Mr. Ford, how long have you practiced law?" Kirsch and Baxten were almost embarrassed by his candor, though they were thinking the exact same thing.

"I've been with the firm four years, Dr. Penrose."

"Have you actually tried a case like this before?"

Sagar jumped in. "Dr. Penrose, nobody's actually tried a case like this before because, quite frankly, there's never *been* a case like this."

Kurt was quick to defend himself. "If you're worried about my experience, Dr. Penrose, don't be. I've had plenty of experience in and out of the courtroom. In fact, many of the cases I've worked on involved defending doctors in malpractice suits."

Penrose bristled at the comparison of his project to malpractice. "This is *not* a bloody malpractice case, Mr. Ford," Penrose shot back.

"I didn't mean to insinuate that it was, Dr. Penrose. I was merely pointing out my experience with medical cases."

Jonathan Sagar jumped back in to cool the conversation before it escalated. "Dr. Penrose, our entire firm has a lot of experience representing medical cases. I believe Dr. Baxten can attest to that."

Penrose backed off and leaned back in his seat. Sagar took the opportunity to steer the conversation back to the business at hand. He spent the next half hour going over the nuts and bolts of the case, avoiding any language which might reopen the wound of Penrose's fixation. The doctors spent the remainder of the meeting providing their attorneys with as much pertinent information as possible. After a little more than an hour, Jonathan Sagar ended the meeting and prepared to leave. Dr. Baxten asked to speak with him alone. Sagar sent Ford and Dumaine down to wait for him as he stayed behind to face the fire. Jonathan knew Dr. Penrose was eager to voice his outrage.

"Is that all your firm has to offer?" Penrose complained once Dumaine and Ford had hardly cleared the room. "That one kid's barely out of high school!" Sagar knew he was referring to Ford. "This case is too important to be used as a training session for a bunch of interns!"

"All right, Clark," Baxten interceded, "that's enough." He turned to Sagar. "Jonathan, you understand our concern. This case is very important to this facility. We feel it's very important to medicine in general."

"Make no mistake about it, Sam. We understand the gravity of this case and take it just as seriously as you do. I also understand your concern over your lead attorney. Let me assure you that Kurt Ford is one of the brightest attorneys we have."

"He's a kid!" Penrose insisted.

"He isn't one of our older attorneys, Dr. Penrose, that's true but he has other attributes that make him perfect for this case."

"Attributes? Such as?" Dr. Kirsch asked.

"Well, for starters he's quite competitive. He wants to win this case as much for his own career as he does for the firm. He's a stickler for detail and he'll eat, drink, and breathe this case until the very end."

Kirsch wasn't satisfied with the answer. "But aren't there attorneys in your firm that are just as driven who have more experience?"

"Experience? I suppose there are, Dr. Kirsch, but none more driven. Also, Mr. Ford has one more attribute that makes him perfect for this case."

"And that is?" Kirsch said.

Sagar dropped the bomb. "He's gay."

The three doctors looked back at him dumbstruck for a moment.

"He's gay?" Penrose asked in amazement. "And you're putting him in charge of *this* case?"

"I understand your concern, Dr. Penrose, but he's totally committed to your cause and to winning this case."

Baxten said, "Jonathan, I don't really understand why you think his being gay is a plus."

"Sam, let me put it to you this way. You have a procedure here that will, in essence, cure homosexuality in unborn children. The last thing we want is a panel of macho, male attorneys who the jury may see as a bunch of homophobes frothing at the mouth to see this procedure performed. The jury needs to know that there are homosexuals who are very much in favor of this procedure. What better way to subtly convey that message than to have a homosexual as the lead attorney."

Kirsch and Baxten seemed to be satisfied with Sagar's explanation. Not

Penrose. To his mind, they were sacrificing substance for appearances, something they could ill afford.

"I'm just a researcher, Mr. Sagar. I don't have the power to make a decision here, but you can bet I wouldn't have made the decision you made. You're rolling the dice with the very reputation of this institution. For both our sakes, I hope you don't crap out."

Penrose turned and walked away.

Kelly Morris hurried into the closed offices of GALLANT. Greg Wently and Jon Carroll were waiting for her in the reception area. Greg locked the door behind her. They had been called back to work for some important news. Some good news, Kelly insisted, but she wanted to tell them in person. She was apprehensive about the way they would react, but she was positive it was the right thing to do.

"So, what's the big deal?" Jon asked.

She directed her answer to Greg. "I've got a proposition for you."

"Well, come on in. Make yourself comfortable. Tell us all about it," Greg ushered the two of them into his modest office.

Greg took a seat behind the metal and wood desk. Kelly and Jon pulled up two ladder-back chairs close in front. Greg and Jon had their eyes affixed to Kelly.

"As you know, our case might very well hinge on who the judge appoints as the guardian ad litem," she began. "Whoever that is, we hope it's someone who will strengthen our position, you know, bring something to the table that we don't have. Right?"

"OK," Greg said cautiously.

"I propose that we set up a meeting with Norm Woodruff, the attorney for the Christian Way Organization."

Greg and Jon looked stunned. One did not enter into a decision to team up with Norm Woodruff lightly. Teaming up with Woodruff was akin to slow dancing with a cobra. He was slick. He was charming. He was dangerous. He was a take-no-prisoners attorney who had parlayed his association with the CWO into a career as a talking-head on the major networks, ever careful not to overshadow the founder of the CWO and his biggest client, Lucius Gaylord. Kelly knew that dealing with Norm was like handling nitro glycerin and it could very well blow up in her face. She also knew that the road to victory could be greased with the CWO on their side.

"You're joking, of course," Greg said.

"I'm dead serious."

"The CWO? That bunch of bigots?" Jon curled his upper lip in disgust and expelled a rush of air through his teeth.

"That's what's so beautiful," Kelly explained with cunning delight. "The CWO is really upset about the Penrose Project. Enough so that they've been putting some pressure on Loveport to cancel it."

"Wait a minute," Jon interjected. "You're telling us the very group that has called us godless demons and has been out there trying to block us at every turn now has a chance to destroy us and they're on *our* side?"

"A-ha, but you see, that's what's so ironic," Kelly said gleefully. "Basically, the Christian Way Organization doesn't believe in anyone playing God, whether it's abortion doctors or genetic engineers. They oppose any genetic tampering for a variety of reasons. Today it could be changing the sexual orientation of the fetus. Tomorrow it could be changing the eye color or hair color or even the sex."

"That is, indeed, very interesting." Greg rubbed his chin then leaned back in his chair. "Go on, Kel."

"As your attorney, here's my advice to you. It's my professional opinion that we should extend an olive branch to the CWO in an effort to bring a party sympathetic to us on board in this lawsuit."

"Sympathetic to *us*?" Jon asked cynically. "These are the people who are out to destroy us. We don't need them and we surely can't trust them.

Plus, we've got the NCRA in our corner. What do we need with these people?"

"Plenty," Kelly argued. "If they file a friend of the court petition, Judge Kincaid just might appoint them as legal guardians. They carry a lot of legal muscle. We may be right about this issue, but if we get a guardian who sides with the Penrose Project we're finished. We're dead in the water before we ever start this trial."

"You're suggesting we scrap our principles for more fire power in the courtroom," Jon said.

"No, I'm suggesting that two groups with like goals forget their differences for the moment," she countered. "Two groups who oppose something should band together to strengthen their fight."

Jon felt Kelly was trying to hammer a wedge between Greg and him. He knew he could count on his old friend to put down this insane scheme. Jon turned to Greg. "This is a ridiculous idea."

Greg leaned forward with his wrists on the desk. "I think Kel's exactly right."

Jon scoffed under his breath and turned away, waving both of them off as he flung his right leg over his left.

"Look," Greg said, "I don't like these bastards any more than you do, but when you're fighting a battle with a shotgun and someone offers you a tank, you don't turn your back on them. This isn't some test to see if GALLANT has principles. This is all out war. This could mean the absolute end of people like you and me, and we can't be too particular about who's on our team. Don't you agree?"

Jon tried to hide the jealousy. He sought to maintain his status as the number two in the organization but felt less significant any time Kelly was near. "No, I don't," Jon said, "but you two are obviously in agreement, so I'm outnumbered." He folded his arms across his chest.

"Then it's settled," Kelly said. Her outstretched palms slapped the top of her thighs. She took the opportunity of Jon's momentary immature pout to forward her own agenda. "Tomorrow I approach Norman Woodruff with the proposal."

The Reverend Lucius Gaylord checked his watch for the seventh time in five minutes. He had a speaking engagement in forty-five minutes, but his attorney had insisted on a quick but important meeting before he left. He had a reputation for promptness and he dared not damage it today. He was speaking to a conference of 2,000 kindred spirits who looked to him as the moral compass of the country. A pretty lofty perch for a small-town preacher's son who was self-taught and equally self-determined.

People often asked him how he 'found God.' Lucius Gaylord didn't much care for the term. In order to 'find God,' one has to come to the erroneous conclusion that *God* is the one who's lost, Lucius always said. He was born with a healthy exposure to the Holy Spirit, but exposure alone is not enough. One has to have an open heart before that Spirit starts to work in his life. It wasn't so much his father who lit the fire under him but the revivals he attended as a boy. They were two parts religion and three parts show business. Not that he was some unscrupulous evangelist. Much to the contrary. He had cut his teeth at the knee of some of the foremost Christian organizations in the country for more than twenty years before starting the Christian Way Organization. He understood the importance and the power of the medium of television. Billy Graham brought thousands to Christ each year through his stadium revivals, but he brought millions to Christ through television. Gaylord was certain that if Christ were walking the earth today, he would be using this marvelous tool to its fullest potential.

He was quite aware of the damage done by charlatans like Jim and Tammy Faye Baker. He was always careful not to ride around in limousines and dine at fancy restaurants, even if the CWO wasn't footing the bill. All it takes is one person witnessing such excesses and the story spreads like wildfire. He recalled seeing Ralph Reed, at the time the head of the Christian Coalition, on one occasion as their plane pulled to the gate in Washington. As the plane came to a stop, Reed popped up out of his plush seat and was handed his coat by the first class attendant as Gaylord struggled to pull his carry-on from the overhead compartment back in tourist class. He overheard several of his fellow passengers gripe with disgust that a man who collected money in the name of the Lord was living the life of luxury, while those who coughed up the cash flew in the cramped quarters of economy class.

He learned many things by watching Reverend Graham, but one of the basics was appearances matter. Like Graham, he never allowed himself to be alone with a woman other than his wife. Even when he dictated letters to his secretary, he made sure the door to his office was wide open lest someone get the wrong idea about their relationship. He was a man of principle and that's why the Penrose Project bothered him so. He picked up the telephone on his desk and rang the receptionist one more time.

"Anne, still no sign of Mr. Woodruff?" he asked with a hint of panic in his voice.

"No, sir. I'm sorry."

"If he doesn't hurry up, I'm going to be late for the luncheon. Please, send him right in when he gets here."

"Yes, sir," she answered. "Oh, Dr. Gaylord, he just walked in."

"Thank goodness. Send him on back."

Norm Woodruff knew the way very well. He had been the attorney for the Christian Way Organization since its inception twelve years earlier. He had stood by Lucius Gaylord through each and every tumultuous turn of the CWO's controversial history. Through it all, he and Dr. Gaylord had become quite close. Gaylord trusted Norm Woodruff like a brother and knew if his old friend called for an emergency meeting it must be important.

Dr. Gaylord didn't wait for the knock on the door. He headed around the desk to greet Woodruff as he came in. Although certainly not a fashion plate, Dr. Gaylord was a conservative but smart dresser. More a product of his wife's tastes than his own, his suits and sport coats were always in style but in keeping with his sixty years of age. He adjusted the wire rim glasses on his nose and extended a hand to Woodruff.

"Sorry, I'm late," Woodruff offered. "I got held up in a meeting. I know you have a luncheon to attend, so I'll be brief. How strongly do you feel about the Penrose Project?"

Dr. Gaylord took his seat behind the desk and pondered the question. "Meaning?"

"How badly do you want that project stopped?" Woodruff clarified.

"Well, I think this could be the single most important issue facing our society in our lifetime." His delivery sounded like a stump speech. "If this project goes forward, I fear we'll be crossing over a threshold into a degree of medical technology we may not be able to control."

"How does this compare to, say, the issue of abortion?" Woodruff probed.

Dr. Gaylord ran his fingers through his salt-and-pepper hair. "That's a tough one, Norm. I mean, abortion is actually taking an innocent life. In that respect, it's hard to say that anything's more important. However, having the ability to pick and choose character traits I believe is the ultimate in amoral arrogance and I feel very, very strongly that it's as wrong as wrong gets."

"OK," Norm replied, satisfied with the answer. "The reason I ask is I got a call this morning with a very unusual proposition. As you know, GALLANT got the judge to issue a temporary restraining order which he has now converted to a preliminary injunction, but he's looking for a guardian ad litem, a legal guardian, for the unborn child. They've asked us to petition the court to become the court-appointed guardians."

"They want *us* to be the legal guardians?" He paused for a moment. "Why?"

"Because they know we're against the procedure and having us join them in this suit will bolster their case. I know it's short notice, but if we're going to climb aboard, we've got to do it today."

"But they're one of the most militant gay groups out there, Norm. How's that going to look to my congregation when we're in cahoots with such a group of people?"

"I understand your concern. I just felt it was my responsibility to make you aware of the situation."

"Well, what do you recommend we do?" Dr. Gaylord asked.

"If you want my honest opinion, I say we take them up on their offer. We've tried asking Loveport to cancel the project, but they've refused. We could file a similar lawsuit, but it would take days to get the paperwork together. We'd just have to get in line. And how their case is decided will have a very strong bearing on how ours goes. If they mess it up, they possibly decide the issue forever. If the judge names us as the guardian, we have legitimate standing in the case. At least that gives us some influence in deciding how this whole thing plays out. If you're worried about how your congregation will react, weigh that against how you'll feel if this project is approved to go forward."

Norm had made a strong argument. Dr. Gaylord was looking at short-term heat versus long-term, irreversible damage. Still, crawling in the wagon with GALLANT went against his basic nature. Gaylord looked at his watch. "Goodness gracious, I *have* to get going," he fretted. "I'll have an answer for you right after lunch."

"Fine," Norm said.

Dr. Gaylord's assistant dropped him at the front door of Atlanta's World Congress Center. Gaylord checked his watch as he boarded the first of three escalators which would take him to his destination in the belly of the massive building. Two organizers from the CWO paced by the entrance wondering what in the world could be keeping the always punctual Dr. Lucius Gaylord. Dr. Gaylord hurried down the steps of the third escalator then rounded the corner toward the huge meeting room. The two organizers let out a sigh of relief at the sight of him. Gaylord made his apologies and was led to his place at the head table. The rubber chicken meal had just been served. He gave the server his drink order — iced tea, unsweetened — and took his seat. He gazed out over the audience, seeing many familiar faces. Many of those eyes met his and he gave them a 'how do you do' nod. They were each eager to hear what Dr. Gaylord had to say, particularly on this day. He pulled the index cards from his coat pocket and reviewed the outline of his speech. He had chosen his words carefully, each meant to hit its mark.

The master of ceremonies recounted for the audience Dr. Gaylord's lengthy and illustrious career. He recapped his decades-long efforts on behalf of other Christian organizations then reminded them of the fine work he had been doing for the Lord since he founded the Christian Way Organization. Millions of dollars raised and dispersed throughout the world to fight hunger and poverty. Millions of souls saved through his TV ministry which originated from Peachtree Grove Baptist Church in Atlanta. Then there were the countless social issues on which Dr. Gaylord had taken courageous stands, each one detailed for the assembled multitude. The 2,000 applauded as Lucius Gaylord rose to the podium.

"Ladies and gentlemen, thank you for that warm welcome. I had a prepared text all ready for this occasion, one that I had hoped would inspire, uplift, and motivate you to go forth and spread the word of our Lord. But in recent days, a task has been laid at our feet which requires us to set aside everything else in our lives and focus on its completion. By now, I'm certain each of you is familiar with the infamous Penrose Project, a project so dangerous it could literally change the face of this planet. Now, wait a minute, Dr. Gaylord, you're saying. What's so dangerous about a chance to prevent a person from becoming a homosexual? On the surface, it appears to be quite attractive, I agree. But today it's homosexuality we're changing, tomorrow it could be any other physical or mental attribute including the very sex of the person! Imagine a day when parents will sit down with their physician and order up children like choosing options on an automobile. Imagine where this technology will lead. The differences between us would no longer be celebrated but, instead, would be pitied. Those who couldn't afford the most desirable attributes would be shunned by society. These doctors would control every aspect of our very being from the color of our eyes to our appreciation for Mozart. They would usurp the natural order of God!" He pounded the podium. "And listen to me when I say this. No one has the right to play God!"

The entire body of 2,000 rose to its feet in deafening applause.

15

The members of the defense team quietly entered the conference room of CC&D. The beautiful solid cherry conference table reflected the light of a magnificent chandelier which hung from the twelve-foot ceiling. The table seated twenty comfortably in top-grain leather chairs. The head seat was the only highback in the room.

Bill Dumaine took the seat to the right of the head of the table. Kurt Ford waited for Jonathan Sagar to take the head seat, but Sagar gestured for him to take it instead. Ford sat down with Sagar to his left. Two other attorneys took seats to Ford's right. A handful of paralegals — Jonathan referred to them affectionately as 'the diggers' — filled in the remaining seats. Jonathan Sagar cleared his throat and began.

"Good morning, ladies and gentlemen. As you know, I've just returned from a hearing in Judge Kincaid's courtroom. I'm sad to have to announce that today we suffered the first casualty in our battle with the plaintiffs. Judge Kincaid appointed the Christian Way Organization as guardians of the unborn Loveport Baby." The announcement was met with murmurs of disbelief. "The CWO had requested that Loveport suspend the Penrose Project and they, of course, refused. We should have known we were vulnerable because of that and taken the appropriate precautions by approaching them before GALLANT got to them, but we did not. I take full responsibility for not covering our collective behinds, and I can assure you I will not underestimate our adversaries again. Now it's time to move forward. This is a critical case for this law firm. I'm sure I don't have to remind you of that. I've made the decision on the lead attorney and let me add that I don't take that responsibility lightly. All of you know Kurt. Most of you have worked with him in the past. I have complete confidence in his ability to get the job done. With that said, I'll turn this meeting over to him."

Kurt Ford took control. He rose and pushed his seat against the table. He knew it would be an uphill battle to gain their confidence. His blonde hair gave him a boyish quality making him seem even younger than his twenty-nine years. His appearance was immaculate. His white shirt was so crisp it looked as though it might cut him. His suit was pressed and neat.

"I want to welcome all of you to what I believe will be one of the most exciting cases of your career," Kurt greeted the room. "Before I get into the details of the case, there's a little housekeeping that I need to take care of," he stated casually as he walked behind his chair. It was almost as if he were using the highback as a shield. He took a deep breath through his nose then began his confession. "There have been a lot of rumors circulating around this office over the years regarding my sexuality. I want to, at this point, lay those rumors to rest. I am a homosexual." He paused and assessed the room. Blank faces stared back at him. "That probably won't come as any surprise to most of you. You've more than likely suspected that for quite some time. What may surprise you is the fact that this firm has entrusted me with this particular case. Let me say that, as an attorney, I have no problem separating my personal from my professional life. There are black and white facts to this case that I have no trouble distinguishing from my emotions, but my dedication to this case goes far beyond that.

"I've had to live with my sexuality all my life. I don't want to paint a depressing picture. I've had great joy in my life. I've also lived a life of fear and confusion. I don't say that in an attempt to garner your sympathy. I say that to illustrate why I believe what Loveport University is doing is right. If one child is spared the humiliation and rejection and suffering I have endured, then this will all be worth it. Now, some of you may not like homosexuals. Some of you may be homosexuals yourselves. Frankly,

I don't care. We're here to do a job. We're here to defend a client against a lawsuit. It's that simple. I want every ounce of your energy going toward a successful resolution of this case. The reputation of this law firm depends on it, and our success or failure may very well determine your future."

Ford looked at the faces in the room. What he saw was the genesis of respect. Now it was up to him to earn it.

"Very well said," Sagar complimented. "Let me just add that I will be involved in the case every step of the way, in and out of the courtroom, but Kurt will be the lead attorney on this case, plain and simple. Every aspect of this case should be coordinated through him. He will be directing the research and conducting our case in court. Make no mistake about it. Kurt Ford is in charge."

"Thank you, Mr. Sagar." Ford took his seat and got down to the business of the case. "There's going to be a lot of cramming in this case. You're going to feel like you're back in law school. Genetics is no easy subject, but each and every one of us has to have a complete understanding of genetics and gene therapy before we can argue this case. Unfortunately because of the short window in which this particular procedure can be performed, we're not looking at a long time. We'll know better what we're up against when the judge sets the trial date."

"What's your best guess?" one of the associates asked.

"A few weeks, maybe a little longer."

There was a rumble of astonishment across the conference room.

"Dr. Penrose has agreed to meet with us for a crash course in genetics and the science behind his procedure. In the meantime, I have dissected this case into several important areas and divided these areas of research among you."

He turned his attention to a digger at the other end of the conference room. "Linda, if you would, please. What Linda is handing out is a folder with your personal instructions for this case. It's a lot like 'Mission: Impossible' now that I think about it. You each have a specific area you'll need to concentrate on. Read over the information very carefully and research your area as completely as possible. I'll expect your report in our morning meeting in three days." Everyone was busy thumbing through their respective folders. Kurt walked slowly around the room, looking down at each individual as they looked over their material. "Don't worry if you don't understand what your research has to do with this case. You're going to have to trust me when I tell you it's important. The problem is this case is so complicated that giving you the big picture on our strategy now will only serve to weigh you down. I want to make the most efficient use of our human resources. Time is not on our side. We have to make sure knowledge is."

The lights went up on the set. Betty Duvall greeted the mounting national audience. "Good evening and welcome to *The Pulse.* Today an odd alliance was forged when the Christian Way Organization announced that it had petitioned the court in the Loveport Baby case to serve as the baby's legal guardian. The judge approved the request which now aligns the CWO with the very radical and very liberal GALLANT, a grass-roots gay rights organization based in Atlanta which filed suit against Loveport University to stop their procedure to alter the gay gene." She smiled broadly. "I can hardly wait to hear what Duncan has to say about this."

Duncan laughed with her at the irony of the coalition. "I've got to say that I disagree with my friends at the CWO. I understand their fear, but I think it's unfounded. I mean, there are many procedures down through the annals of medicine that, I'm sure, scared the people of the day into thinking the procedure could be used in some sinister way. Can you imagine the reaction the first time someone actually cut somebody open to operate?" He laughed at the thought of it. "And remember, it wasn't that long ago that Cambridge, Massachusetts, home to Harvard, that bastion of liberal thinking, banned research into something called recombinant DNA. Now, I won't bore you with the details of what that is, but suffice it to say, twenty years later, recombinant DNA-produced drugs were saving lives around the world and now the economy of Cambridge is dependent on the recombinant DNA-based biotech industry. I would urge the CWO to look at this as a legitimate cure for homosexuality and not the boogie man of medicine."

Tom Andrews brushed his teeth and stared into the mirror. He stared as if he were trying to look deep into his own soul. Perhaps he was. Perhaps it was there he could find the truth, the answer to his nagging question. Were they doing the right thing? He felt they were, but was it the right thing for the child or just the expedient thing for him as a father? He had to admit to himself that raising a homosexual son would be an embarrassment, an attack on his masculinity. Was he homophobic or just a normal heterosexual male? For whatever reason they were doing it, they *were*, in fact, doing it. It was too late to second guess now. The issue was no longer in their control. The court battle was on and it would be decided now whether they stayed in or not. There was some consolation in that.

He rinsed his mouth out and hit the light switch on his way into the bedroom. Sabrina was sitting up in the bed reading, or at least trying to. She'd been on the same page of the magazine for the last ten minutes. She couldn't read anyway. The tears blurred her vision. They filled her eyes and overflowed down her cheeks. Tom gently nestled in next to her.

"What's wrong, honey?" he asked tenderly.

"I'm just worried about our baby," she sighed.

"Yeah. Me too."

"Tom, what if we're not doing the right thing? What if changing our son's sexual orientation changes who he is? What if something goes wrong?"

Tom gently rubbed her stomach. It was hard knowing just what to say. Oftentimes Sabrina just wanted a shoulder to cry on. On those occasions, Tom knew there was a time and a place for a husband's vulnerability. A time to display a softer side, a side that didn't have all the answers. Tom also sensed that this was *not* one of those times. Sabrina needed a rock. She needed a harbor in this stormy sea of controversy. "We made the right decision," he assured her. "Anyway, it's out of our hands. We'll let the jury hear all the evidence and decide. Let's take this burden off of our shoulders and let the court carry the load. If they say it's right, then it's right. If they decide otherwise, we live with that decision. Fair enough?"

She smiled down at him. "Fair enough." She didn't mean it. She and the jury would have to come to a decision on parallel tracks. She just hoped they arrived at the same decision.

16

The Atlanta offices of Clemens & Woodruff were spacious but, by any standard, conservative. After all, their largest client was the Christian Way Organization. They felt it good business to conform to the CWO style. Kelly Morris was the antithesis. Liberal in her thinking, liberal in her dress, in Norm Woodruff's mind, a disconnected idealist whose convictions were steeped in emotion bearing little resemblance to reality. He saw in her a naive little girl yet knew that her appearance was misleading. Her seemingly serene temperament could immediately turn tornadic. In her young career, several of Norm's less prudent colleagues had crossed swords with her only to be blind-sided by this walking land mine. As the attorney for the CWO, Norm had one goal in mind and that was to win. He had his way of doing things. Kelly Morris had hers. Although he couldn't fully conform to her way, he did try to bridle himself. He tended to be a bit overbearing, and Kelly was just insecure enough to go ballistic at any perceived challenge to her authority. Norm wanted to avoid the proverbial tempest in a teapot.

Rex Randle's slender frame towered over the other two attorneys. He used his height to his advantage whenever possible. Despite having a good six inches on Norm Woodruff, it was as if they were the same size. The three lawyers greeted each other pleasantly.

"Norm, I believe you know Rex Randle," Kelly introduced.

"Indeed I do," Norm acknowledged. "Nice to see you again, Mr. Randle."

"The pleasure's mine," Randle replied as he shook his hand. "And please, it's Rex," he smiled, trying to be as cordial as possible. It was difficult to get past Norm's reputation which was embedded in his brain. Rex tried to stay focused on their common goal, but the CWO's implacable position on religious and moral issues had, in Rex's opinion, encroached on the rights of private citizens. The strategy man behind the CWO's agenda stood before them and Rex felt none too comfortable about it.

Norm looked like a typical southern attorney. His classic navy blue suit was accented with a light blue Hermès tie. That gave Rex an idea of his politics. Strike one. The white all-cotton shirt was heavily starched. Norm looked like he'd be just as at home running a congressional office in Washington as practicing law in Atlanta. For someone in his early fifties, he had surprisingly little gray hair. Rex figured he must dye it black but wondered how he got the slight gray streaks to look so natural. He reminded Rex so much of the rich frat boys he tried to avoid at Wake Forest. Strike two.

Everyone took their seats at the conference table. It was round, so there was no awkward moment deciding who got to sit at the head. Norm held the chair for Kelly. She took the one next to it. Norm smiled to himself. Rex Randle took the seat next to her. A couple of Norm's secretaries were present to take notes and hand out materials.

Norm Woodruff smiled and got down to business. "We better get started. I know we have planes to catch for the meeting in Loveport tomorrow. I'm sure we all have cases in mind that will set a precedent for us in this case, but I think there's one that sticks out more than any other that may completely destroy us. As the saying goes, the best defense is a good offense, and we have to be prepared. Now, whether any of us agrees or disagrees with Roe v. Wade, it's the law of the land. That case has set the legal precedent they need to destroy our case. We're fighting for the life of that child. The Supreme Court says it's not a life. The mother has the right to terminate even though she's killing a baby."

Rex Randle dropped his pen on his pad. Strike three. "Don't go there, Norm," he warned defensively.

"No. Wait a minute," Kelly urged. "Let him finish his thought."

"Well," Norm continued, "it would stand to reason that if the mother can take the baby's life, she can certainly opt to change it."

"Not necessarily," Rex interjected. "There's the case of Talitha Renee Garrick."

"Talitha who?" Norm asked.

"Talitha Renee Garrick," Rex explained, "was a South Carolina woman who was charged with killing her fetus by smoking crack. The South Carolina Supreme Court became the first appellate court in the nation to allow prosecutions of pregnant women who take drugs. They ruled in July of 1996 that a pregnant woman could be criminally liable for actions that endanger the health of a viable fetus. The woman admitted to smoking crack a little more than an hour before her baby was delivered stillborn. She pleaded guilty to involuntary manslaughter. If we can prove that Penrose's procedure could endanger the health of this fetus, we just might persuade the jury to stop the procedure."

Norm said, "I'm not opposed to citing that case, but I don't think we should build our entire argument around a state supreme court decision. This is federal court, remember. Anyway, they could cite court cases from other states that have gone the other way. For example, a 19-year-old by the name of Gerardo Flores in Texas was convicted in 2005 of causing the death of his girlfriend's twin fetuses. He repeatedly stepped on her stomach, at her request. Although she had asked him to do it and she, herself, had beat her own stomach to try to kill the babies, the court ruled that she could not be prosecuted because of her right to an abortion. She got nothing. He, on the other hand, got life in prison. The court apparently considers the fetus a human being if *he* kills it, but not if *she* does. That inconsistency could damage our cause. I still maintain that the precedent on this type of case so far has to be Roe v. Wade. You know they're going to come at us with that and we've got to be ready. Another point is, in the first case you cited, the baby was close to term. In this case, he's not."

"Well, you've obviously given this some thought," Kelly offered. "Any ideas?"

"Glad you asked," Norm said with a smile. "Since we don't have legal precedence on our side, or at best limited legal precedence, we have to use the age-old tool that's moved masses and mountains for years."

"And what tool is that?" Rex asked.

"Fear," Norm stated emphatically. "Fear that Dr. Penrose is opening Pandora's box. Fear that once this technology is put in motion, there will be no stopping science. Once this is used on the Loveport Baby, it's just a matter of time before parents start preselecting their kids like ordering a pizza. We fashion Penrose into a megalomaniacal Dr. Frankenstein and we win."

"Sounds like high drama to me," Rex said. "I don't think the jury's going to fall for that kind of theatrics. Why not a straightforward approach? Why not hammer home the notion that being gay is as normal as being straight and no one has a right to change it."

"Wow, talk about something dangerous," Norm exclaimed. "Most heterosexuals have a natural aversion to homosexuals."

"A natural aversion?" Rex said.

"Yeah, most straight people find homosexual activity repulsive." Norm wore that forced half grin one wears in an uncomfortable, almost heated discussion.

"They may have a 'natural aversion' to gays, as you put it," Rex conceded, "but that doesn't make it right. People have a natural aversion to snakes, but they're a crucial part of nature. People have a natural aversion to liver but there's no doubt that it's one of the healthiest foods you can eat."

"Look, whether it's right or wrong, there are things that naturally turn people off," Norm said. "I guarantee if I shake a snake at that jury, they're going to draw back in horror. Whether that's fair or not is immaterial. It's a fact and you better get used to it."

Kelly was eager to jump in and move beyond this sideshow argument and on to the meat of the case. "I tend to agree with Norm," she said. "We don't know what kind of jury we're dealing with. We're taking a huge chance if we assume that they're sympathetic to gays. If they're not, trying to convert them to our way of thinking is too risky. We have to appeal to their fear that this will lead to selective breeding. In other words, we have to convince them that this procedure hits close to home for them, too. That's one of the reasons the AIDS scare has been so successful. The gay lobbyists in Washington were able to convince Congress that the disease had moved beyond the gay community and was beginning to decimate the straight community. Once that fear took hold, it was a lot easier to get federal money to fight the disease."

"Great point," Norm interjected. "They did manage to scare Congress into believing heterosexuals were at risk, but the fact is straights have never been at any great risk of getting AIDS in this country. The facts didn't matter. If they hadn't been able to convince Congress, the money would not have been nearly as plentiful. As it was, the government ended up funding AIDS research at several times the rate of even cancer research when cancer was killing many times more people. The lesson is it's important that we take this case out of the realm of homosexuality and put it in a context everyone can relate to and that's a fear of someone abusing this technology."

Kelly thought for a fleeting moment about entering into an AIDS debate with Norm, but they were pressed for time. She moved to her next point. "Now, backing off a notch on what Rex just said about homosexuality being normal, I would add, Norm, that it would be beneficial to point out the accomplishments of homosexuals. I think that would be effective while not negating the fear aspect and not requiring full agreement with the theory that being gay is normal."

"I wouldn't disagree with that," Norm said. "And let me just add that it's refreshing to hear you speak with such candor. I hope we can all lower our shields and combine our talents to win this case." He smiled a conciliatory smile at Rex. Rex chose not to return it.

"Agreed," Rex said to Kelly. "On your point about homosexual accomplishments. Another angle to consider is intertwining the creativity of someone like, say, Michelangelo, with his homosexuality. We need to get some hard numbers on the percentage of gays in the general population compared with their numbers in terms of their contributions to society."

"Excellent," Kelly said. "We can tie the two together and, in essence, convince the jury that Penrose will not only deprive the world of homosexuals, but he'll deprive the world of some of its most brilliant minds."

"Now we're talking." Norm turned to one of the secretaries. "Make a note for the research department to track down those figures, would you? We also want to see the records from Dr. Penrose's experiments on his lab animals."

"Definitely," Rex echoed.

"Make a note to contact a Dr. Evan Proctor." Norm turned to Kelly and Rex. "We've used him before. He's good. He can go over those records with a fine-tooth comb." Norm paused for a moment.

"What is it?" Kelly asked.

"Nothing. I, uh, I just thought this was going to be rather awkward," Norm said. "It's actually quite exhilarating."

What Jonathan Sagar referred to as 'The Core' huddled around the large conference room at CC&D. The Core consisted of Kurt Ford, Bill Dumaine, and two associates assigned to the case. They were two of the rising stars at the firm. The first, Sandra Spence, was thin, and painfully so. She still carried with her some of the embarrassment of growing up the awkward, gangly introvert who hid behind her glasses. She still wore the glasses but had evolved into a rather alluring woman. The fact that she had not yet realized it added to the attraction. Her long, thin hair was parted in the middle and often fell in front of her eyes creating a veil behind which she retreated in her moments of insecurity.

Vince Tordella, Jonathan's other rising star, was short and hairy with an Italian charm that made him one of the favorites around the office. His bluntness was legendary. He was not one to sugar-coat anything. Nobody from his blue-collar neighborhood in Philadelphia ever did. If he thought your tie was ugly, he said so. If he didn't like his meal at a restaurant, he said so. If he thought the judge was out of line, he said so. He could be a liability in the courtroom, but he was dynamite with strategy.

Vince and Sandra, along with the paralegals, had eked out a small amount of personal space on the table. The remainder of the surface was obscured by dozens of files piled high and Styrofoam coffee cups which littered the table. Vince sat distracted by Sandra's legs while Kurt barked out the game plan. A knock on the door and Vince jumped up to answer it, anticipating the guest. He gleefully relieved the pizza delivery boy of three large boxes and cleared a space for them on the table. Kurt stepped forward with his wallet, part of the luxury of being the lead attorney. He paid the boy, tipped him handsomely, then asked for a receipt. By the time he returned to the table, his co-workers were tearing into their lunch. Kurt looked at his watch, chose a slice, then continued the session.

"All right, a couple more things and we'll wrap it up. I've got a meeting in the judge's chambers. Let's talk legal precedent for a minute." He took a bite then a gulp of Coke to cool off the pizza. "You've all had a chance to visit the law library. Have any of you come up with a case we can use to build ours on?" Blank faces stared back at him. "Come on folks. A little help here."

Dumaine had just taken a bite of his pizza but grunted as if he had some information to share. "There's the obvious," he offered as he chewed. "Roe v. Wade."

"Yeah, I thought about that, but does it really apply to our case?"

"What do you mean?"

"Well in Roe, the issue was the viability of the fetus. In our case, the issue is not so much the fetus but what the fetus becomes. You follow what I'm saying?"

"Yes, but it also involved parental rights," Dumaine countered. "Does the mother have the right to terminate the pregnancy?"

"That's true," Sandra Spence added. She was the only one in the room who hadn't touched the pizza. "But the Supreme Court ruled that she only had that right for a limited period of time. After the fetus is deemed to be viable, the state has an obligation to protect it."

"That's the point I'm making," Kurt said. "We can fight for parental rights, sure, but the issue of viability is not an issue in this case. No matter who wins, this fetus will be brought to term. That means arguing the parents have a right to alter it is not the same as arguing the right the Supreme Court has given them to kill it, which is an intriguing notion."

"Kill it?" Sandra was offended by his characterization.

Kurt laughed. "You see. That's the problem. We bring up Roe and try to build on it and we have to wade through years of those jurors' emotions and opinions on the abortion issue, which is just going to muddy the waters. This case is complicated enough without confusing them further."

"If not Roe, then what do we build on?" Dumaine asked.

"Jeez, that's the problem," Vince said. "There *is* no legal precedent for this case. We're plowin' new ground here." He waved a slice of pizza about with his left hand. "What we have to do is argue the parents' right to do what's best for their child. You know, that's somethin' every parent can relate to, huh? Parents sometimes have to make difficult decisions for their children. Am I right? This is one of 'em." He took another bite of pizza, satisfied he had sufficiently distilled the case down to its very essence.

"OK, let's take it from that angle," Kurt said, running with Vince's hypothesis. "Spence, check into parental rights cases. See if there's anything we can use there. In the meantime, we need to load up the guns for the questions that jury's gonna have to answer. How much risk is involved in the procedure and does the outcome outweigh the risk? Bill, I'm putting you in charge of tracking down some comparative figures for the risk part. We'll also have to find someone who will testify that growing up straight is preferable to growing up gay."

"Shouldn't be too hard," Dumaine muttered.

Kurt ignored him and grabbed his jacket. He wasn't about to let himself get dragged into a fight with Dumaine, no matter how provocative he became. His sole focus for the moment was getting the Christian Way Organization thrown out as the Loveport Baby's legal guardian.

17

Judge Kincaid understood fully the ramifications of a trial such as this. He decided a pre-emptive strike was in order. There were a few ground rules he wanted to make sure everyone understood. The judge issued an order for all lead attorneys in the Loveport case to meet him in his chambers at "thirteen-hundred hours." Norm Woodruff, Rex Randle, and Kelly Morris had been warned of the judge's military penchant for punctuality. They were there at exactly one o'clock. Eleanor Henson, a schoolmarmish court reporter, had arrived a few minutes early to go over some details with Judge Kincaid. Norm, Rex, and Kelly shook hands with His Honor and Eleanor, took their seats, and exchanged small talk while they waited for the attorney for Loveport to show. After a brief moment, the room fell silent. Judge Kincaid was not much for chitchat. Trying to engage him in conversation when he was already irritated by the delay of the meeting would only aggravate the problem. The judge reached for a piece of paper on the desk and a pen in the drawer simultaneously. He began reading over the document and making notations as if he were alone in the room. Rex Randle cleared his throat and shifted in his seat. Kelly Morris closely examined her nails. The antique wall clock, which normally went virtually unnoticed, seemed inordinately loud. The ticking of the second hand made time itself almost tactile. Norm Woodruff re-crossed his legs and brushed a piece of lint from his pants.

At last, Kurt Ford came stumbling in at one-oh-five complaining about the traffic and lack of parking spaces. Everyone rose to their feet except Eleanor and Kelly. And the judge, of course. There were still some facets of male chauvinism which even Kelly enjoyed.

"I'm Kurt Ford, Your Honor, from CC&D," he said between breaths.

"I thought Jonathan Sagar was lead attorney on this case," Judge Kincaid remarked suspiciously.

"Mr. Sagar has named me lead attorney, sir."

Norm, Kelly, and Rex glanced at each other in disbelief.

Judge Kincaid looked at him with a skeptical eye. "Very well." He introduced everyone to Kurt. Kurt shook each hand, a Supreme Court tradition Judge Kincaid insisted on borrowing. Each justice on the high court shakes each other justice's hand. The "Conference handshake," as it's called, was started by Chief Justice Melville Fuller in the nineteenth century to foster an atmosphere of harmony. Ford took his seat as the men all sat down.

"Preliminary matters?" the judge asked.

"None," Kelly said.

"None," echoed Norm.

"Yes, Your Honor," Kurt said. Eleanor Henson prepared to type. "The Defense moves for a new guardian ad litem."

"What?" Norm exclaimed.

"Denied," Kincaid snapped. "Anything else?"

"Your Honor, the Christian Way Organization has no tie to the parents in this case. In fact, the parents don't particularly care for the CWO and certainly don't want them representing their son."

Judge Kincaid looked over his reading glasses with a scowl. "The feelings of the parents are of no concern to the court in this matter, Mr. Ford. The guardian ad litem is here to represent the interests of the child, even if those interests run contrary to the wishes of the parents. Motion denied. Is there anything else?"

"No, sir."

"Now then," Kincaid said, moving on to other business, "given the time constraints we're under, I'm going to set a few ground rules. According to the medical testimony in the preliminary injunction hearing, we're looking at a window of about three months from today during which this procedure may be safely performed. I want to give all parties as much time as possible to prepare, but I don't want to push us right up to the deadline. I estimate that the trial itself shouldn't take more than two weeks, a week if we move swiftly. Agreed?"

Each of the attorneys nodded.

"All right. I'm going to set a court date exactly seven weeks from today, if that's agreeable with everyone."

The attorneys checked their calendars.

"Ms. Morris?"

She conferred with Norm and Rex. "That's fine, Your Honor."

"Mr. Ford?"

"Yes, Your Honor. That's good for me, too."

Judge Kincaid made a notation on his calendar.

"I'm estimating jury selection at a couple of days, three max."

He got no argument from either side.

"Now, as far as witnesses go. I don't want anybody to feel restricted as to the number of witnesses you can call in this case, but we're working against the clock. How many witnesses do you think you'll need?"

"We estimate no more than twenty," Kurt answered.

"Twenty?" Judge Kincaid was irritated again. "We're talking about a two-week trial, not two months. I believe each side can easily do what they need to get done with a maximum of five witnesses. These are to be expert witnesses as prescribed under Rule 702. Any objections?"

Nobody said a word, especially Kurt. He already had enough strikes against him. Still, he was concerned. They all understood the time constraints, but limiting the number of witnesses at this early stage could be a potential problem. It was Rex who chose to protest, in his diplomatic way. Kurt breathed a sigh of relief.

"Your Honor," Rex said, "if, for some unseen reason, we need to call more than five, I'd like to reserve the right to ask for special consideration. If the need arises, of course."

"I have no problem with that, Mr. Randle, just as long as everyone understands that I will be in no mood for abuse of that privilege. Are we in agreement?"

"Yes, Your Honor," they said collectively.

"Very well. By five p.m. one week from today I want a complete witness list with names, addresses, phone numbers, and a brief synopsis of their testimony submitted to this court and to opposing counselor or counselors so that each side has time to take depositions and adequately prepare their case."

The attorneys made notations in their calendars.

"Now then, on this next order of business, I want each of you to listen to me and listen good." He had witnessed the wagging tongues on television and was determined to prevent those involved in the trial from adding to the stupidity. "There's already a media storm brewing over this trial and I want to try and keep this dispute contained to my courtroom as best I can. I'm issuing a gag order in effect immediately for all attorneys, employees of attorneys, clients, and anyone else associated with this case. No interviews, no statements to the press, no leaks, nothing. I've seen this kind of thing before. One side tries to get the upper hand by leaking something about the case or a witness. I'm telling all of you right now, I will not tolerate that kind of conduct."

"But, Your Honor," Kurt protested, "this is going to be a very high profile case. There's no telling what's going to be said about my client in the media. Don't we have the right, even the obligation, to set the record straight?"

Kincaid's patience with young Kurt Ford was growing thin. "Put the horse blinders on, Mr. Ford. This is a trial, not a beauty contest. The jury will be sequestered. They won't hear a word of what's being said about your client. Your responsibility is to keep yourself focused on what happens in that courtroom, not what's said in the media. You would do your client a service if you'd remember that."

"Yes, sir." Ford said.

"Furthermore, I'm issuing a gag order for the media in the matter of the parents of the Loveport Baby. Their identities are to remain anonymous. You will refer to them in court and in any papers you prepare for this court as John and Jane Doe. The child will be referred to as Baby Doe. Under no circumstances do I want the identity of that family compromised. Anyone violating the gag order will find themselves in contempt of this court and will answer to me. Any questions?"

"Yes," Kelly Morris responded, raising her pen. "Are cameras going to be allowed in the courtroom?"

Judge Kincaid leaned back in his seat. "I hadn't planned on any, although the law does not prohibit them. I would prefer not to turn this into a three-ring circus. My feeling is they're not necessary unless you have an objection."

"I do, Your Honor," Kelly pressed. "This is going to be of enormous public interest. I think we need to allow as much sunshine in as possible."

Judge Kincaid nodded as he pondered the question. "I'm assuming you're of one mind on this?" he asked, directing his question to Norm and Rex.

They both nodded.

"Mr. Ford," Kincaid inquired of the defense attorney, "what's your position on this?"

Of all the aspects of the trial covered by 'The Core,' television cameras in the courtroom hadn't come up. Kurt had no idea how Jonathan Sagar felt about the subject. Was it a major issue with his boss? His stomach was in knots as all eyes focused on him. If he delayed his answer until he checked with his colleagues, they'd conclude he really wasn't in charge of the case. If he answered contrary to Sagar's wishes, Jonathan might doubt his judgment. His mouth went dry. "The defense has no problem with cameras, Your Honor," Kurt said.

The eyes abated. Kurt felt his muscles relax.

"I see," Kincaid said. He thought about the proposition. "The court will take the matter under advisement. Any other questions?"

There were none.

"Good." With no more business, Judge Kincaid adjourned the meeting.

"What's up with that Ford guy?" Norm said while he, Kelly, and Rex descended the steps of the courthouse. "Why on earth would Jonathan Sagar put a kid like that in charge of a case this big?"

Kelly's deliberate stride indicated her aggravation. "He's gay," Kelly responded curtly. She was irritated that a heterosexual man would so blatantly use a gay subordinate.

"What?" Norm was confused.

"He's gay," Rex repeated disgustedly. "That's why he got the gig. Apparently, Sagar thinks it'll keep Loveport from looking like a bunch of homophobes."

"It's probably a damn smart move on Sagar's part," Kelly admitted, "but it's just dirty pool."

Rex Randle nodded in agreement.

Norm thought about it a moment then chuckled. "Well, you guys always wanted affirmative action. Now it's come back to bite you in the ass."

Kelly stopped in her tracks and turned on Norm with all the wrath her five-foot-two frame could muster. "Although you might find it amusing, the struggle for equality is nothing to joke about. I know the CWO. I've watched you Christians work for years and, let me tell you, I don't want any part of your intolerance. I don't want any part of your prejudice. You're associated with this case only because we have a common goal, but that's where the association ends. We don't need your smug observations on the status of society."

Norm's facade of conciliation had vanished. He bit down on his bottom lip to keep himself from exploding. "Intolerance? Let me ask you something. How tolerant was the Sudanese government in Khartoum when they killed hundreds of thousands of innocent people just because they were Christian? How tolerant is the Chinese government that's tortured and killed millions of Chinese Christians just because they dare hold a prayer meeting or read the Bible? Or the countless numbers whose tongues were burned with electric batons to prevent them from invoking God's help out loud as they were tortured for their beliefs."

Kelly was in no mood to hear Norm's sermon, but he was far from finished.

"You people sit in your politically correct ivory towers," Norm continued, "making subjective determinations about which intolerance is worthy of your attention while millions of people die waiting in vain for your help. While you've been posturing and preaching to the rest of us about tolerance, the CWO has distributed over a billion dollars from its so-called intolerant membership to feed the starving, to minister to the hopeless, and to protect the persecuted in places you couldn't even pronounce, much less find on a map. If that's your definition of intolerance, then we're guilty as charged."

Norm turned and continued down the marble steps.

Kurt Ford left the judge's chambers and walked down the hall toward the front of the federal building. On his way, he passed the leather-padded doors of the federal courtroom. He hesitated, stopped, and walked back over, peeking through one of the two round portholes. Seeing that no one was there, he eased the door open and stepped inside. As he slowly walked down the center aisle, his footsteps echoed off the tall walls. This courtroom didn't have the sterile, prefab look of the more modern courtrooms. It was more Perry Masonesque, expansive with excessively high ceilings trimmed with thick, ornate dentil molding. The huge windows were accented by decorative cornicing with heavy velvet curtains. Large silver radiators rested below the thick window sills. The broad, solid mahogany railing in the forward section encircled the courtroom action and kept nonofficial personnel in their place. Bigger-than-life paintings of deceased judges hung on the walls with brass lamps attached to their tops. The seating for the gallery consisted of long, wooden pews with padded velvet covers designed to make the endless hours of testimony tolerable. Brass spittoons, never-used icons of an earlier time, were attached to the floor beside the plaintiff and defense tables. Thick, dark-brown paneling outlined the courtroom halfway up the wall, stopping at the oversized chair railing. The remainder of the wall was painted in standard municipal off-white. The judge's bench and the area behind it was all paneling stretching to the ceiling.

Kurt took the single step up to the railing and pushed the wooden gate open. The creak echoed throughout the large room. Stepping inside was like stepping into an arena. It felt like a stage and very soon, for all intents and purposes, it would be. It was an awesome responsibility, this load Jonathan Sagar had heaped upon his shoulders. He ran his finger along the edge of the defense table made of thick, dark wood to match the paneling. He could envision himself there. He could also envision how the whole drama would unfold, where all the players would be. He looked up at the jury box and tried to imagine the jurors staring back at him. He could feel the powerful gaze of Judge Kincaid. A bead of sweat broke out on his forehead. He imagined Kelly Morris, Norm Woodruff, and Rex Randle at the plaintiff's table. There was more experience between any two of them than he'd spent on Earth. Did Jonathan really know what he was doing throwing him into this lion's den? The glare of the center stage lights seemed to bore into the pit of his stomach. He reached for the roll of Tums in his pocket.

He had been so utterly consumed with stopping Dr. Penrose's procedure that Lucius Gaylord hadn't stopped to think what the whole discovery of the gay gene really meant. Could it be he had been wrong about homosexuals all these years? If, in fact, homosexuality was caused by a genetic defect, how could Dr. Gaylord hold them responsible for their actions? How could the Bible condemn them? Perplexing questions that this man of the cloth, this pillar of the Christian community, was ill-prepared to answer. As he did on secular matters, he turned to his old friend and counsel, Norm Woodruff. Norm had just flown back in from Loveport and sat on the other side of Gaylord's desk being debriefed by his client on the day's events.

"Jonathan Sagar's outfit is playing the gay card," Norm said.

"What do you mean?"

"The lead attorney on the Loveport case is some young kid named Kurt Ford. His only qualification seems to be that he's gay."

"Heavens!" Gaylord exclaimed. "Is that going to hurt us?"

"Well, it's hard to tell. If they've sacrificed experience and talent just to play that card, they're in serious trouble. But I don't think Jonathan Sagar is that careless."

"I see," Dr. Gaylord replied, looking down at his desk and gently tapping the thumbs of his locked hands together.

Norm had known Dr. Gaylord long enough to tell when he was preoccupied. "Anything you want to talk about?"

"Hmm?" Gaylord looked up from his trance. "Oh, I'm sorry, Norm. There *is* something I can't seem to get off my mind."

Norm set his notes down on his lap and gave Gaylord his undivided attention.

"Norm, have you thought about this whole gay gene thing?"

"I'm not sure I follow you."

Dr. Gaylord struggled to express his feelings. "Let me put it this way. If Dr. Penrose is right and homosexuality is determined by genes, then is being gay wrong?"

Norm frowned as he thought about Gaylord's question. He hadn't stopped to think about it that way. His focus had been on seeing to it that Dr. Penrose's project was stopped in its tracks. As much as Norm wanted to comfort his old friend, he had to admit to Gaylord that he had no ready answer, which only served to exacerbate Dr. Gaylord's discomfort.

Norm finished his debriefing and headed back to his office. Dr. Gaylord sat alone, staring out the window. His distress only intensified. He leaned forward with his elbows resting on top of his desk. He bowed his head and prayed.

18

Penrose pulled his car into the driveway and under the side portico of his home. He hopped out then completely ignored the throng of reporters at the curb as they screamed out questions. The shouting ended when he closed the front door behind him. As he did, he heard his own name emanating from somewhere inside the house. Lauren emerged from the kitchen with a kiss. His focus was directed to the racket coming from the TV set.

"How was your day?" she asked in her usual comforting way.

"What?" Her question broke his concentration. "Oh, yeah, that. Well, it's hard to get much of anything done with this kind of distraction. I just heard my name. What's on the telly?"

"It's a panel discussion about, what else, your discovery."

Penrose walked into the kitchen. On the counter Lauren had the small TV set tuned to Fox News. The moderator was leading a discussion with a geneticist who was in studio with him along with a lawyer and a gay rights advocate on split screen from separate remote locations. They were discussing the pros and cons of the Penrose Project.

"Irresponsible is how I'd term it," the geneticist stated. "You know, in the scientific community, we all knew it was inevitable that the gay gene would be found."

"Inevitable? Yeah, right," Penrose muttered. "That's Evan Proctor," he announced to Lauren, pointing at the TV. "Last year in *Science* he said there was a good chance the whole theory was bunk." He poured himself a glass of orange juice from the fridge.

"Irresponsible, you say?" asked the moderator. "How so?"

"Well, because with science comes responsibility," Proctor replied. "We, as scientists, have a responsibility to protect humankind from something that can obviously be used in a more sinister way."

"Let me jump in if I may, John" the lawyer interjected. "Saddam Hussein built biological weapons to destroy his enemies, but biological weapons are only bad if they're used in a bad way."

Penrose almost spit his orange juice across the room. "What? And this guy is *defending* me? Hey, fella, don't help me anymore!" he shouted at the television.

"Mr. Gordon, how, pray tell, can biological weapons be used in a *good* way?" Proctor inquired.

"Oh, you knew that was coming," Penrose said to Lauren, motioning to the TV with his glass.

The lawyer attempted a reply. "Well, uh…you know,"

The moderator jumped in, "Let's bring Judith Marx back in here from Gay America. Judith, do you think Dr. Penrose is a homophobe?"

"Oh, John, without a doubt. I mean, look at this experiment. And that's what it is, an experiment. We don't know what's going to happen to this child. But look at this experiment and—"

Penrose turned the TV off. "What the hell kind of panel discussion is that? Nobody there has any idea what they're talking about, yet America sees these boobs as experts. And why? Just because they're on the bloody telly!"

"Clark, why don't you do some interviews? Set the record straight. Defend yourself."

"You know I can't do that. That would violate the judge's precious gag order. It's *that* kind of garbage that makes *me* gag. I've just got to trust that someone somewhere will emerge with some sense and tell the truth."

The front door opened and slammed and was followed by footsteps up the stairs then another door slamming.

"Karen?" Penrose asked.

Lauren nodded.

"How long is she going to keep this up? She's got to talk to me eventually. She never eats with us anymore. She stays gone all day then comes in and locks herself in her room." He was getting irritated just talking about it. "This is utter rubbish. I'm going up there right now. It's time we cleared the air." He started toward the door.

"Whoa," Lauren said, grabbing him by the arm. "Give her some time, Clark. She'll come around when she's ready."

"But I don't get it! She's taking this whole thing personally. How about a little support for Dad? Doesn't she understand what I'm going through over this?"

"I'm sure she's too busy worrying about what she's going through."

"What *she's* going through?"

"Come on, Clark. Think about what it must be like for her and Brandon at school. They're probably getting it with both barrels from their friends. They're probably embarrassed, confused. Then they have to endure the reporters, as we all do." Lauren's mood turned sour. She pulled back the curtain and leered out the window. "Those people are driving me crazy. Every time I leave the house, there they are. Every time I come home, they're still there. Don't they ever sleep?"

"I know it's tough." Penrose slid his arm around his wife's waist. "I wish they weren't there either, but it looks like they're going to be a regular fixture until this whole thing is settled. That shouldn't be too long. In just a few weeks, it'll all be over."

Lauren held him close. For the moment, she tried to take comfort in his words, but a few weeks under these conditions would seem like an eternity.

Kurt Ford ran his sessions like a drill sergeant. He wasn't there to make friends. He was there to win. Jonathan Sagar had put him in charge and he planned to make the most of it, much to the disdain of Bill Dumaine.

Dumaine bucked him at every turn. He questioned his every move. Dumaine hated things he didn't understand. That's why he hated 'faggots' and that's why he hated this whole situation. He was working for one. What in the hell was Jonathan Sagar thinking putting this lightweight in charge of the biggest case in the firm's history. Dumaine was convinced he was the superior attorney, yet he had to just sit there and take orders from this 'fairy.' It was almost more than he could bear.

"Bill, track down that psychologist in the article Mindy found. She'd make great ammunition when it comes to the emotional phase of the trial."

"I'm not your 'boy,' Ford," he announced irately. "I've got a full plate. Find somebody else."

The others in the room sat nervously, trying to act as if they didn't notice the confrontation. Exasperated, Kurt looked down at his pad, closed his eyes, and took a deep breath. Not again, he thought.

"I'm not asking you, Bill." Kurt stared him straight in the eyes. "I'm telling you."

"Kiss my ass, Kurt!" Dumaine exploded. "Or would you like that?"

Kurt clinched his teeth as the veins in his temple bulged. "Everybody, get the hell out, please. I want a word with Bill."

The other associates, paralegals, and secretaries quickly pushed themselves away from the table and exited. Holding the door for them, Kurt Ford slammed it as the last person left. The rumble of raised voices could be heard outside the conference room. The exiled staff gathered close to the door, straining to catch every word. Vince Tordella pressed his ear against the door as the others waited for him to pass along the information he was gathering.

"I can't make out a damn thing," he fretted.

"Let me try," Sandra Spencer exclaimed in uncharacteristic curiosity.

She pushed her way to the door. Vince and the others made way for her. She pulled back her long hair, exposing her right ear, and placed it against the door. The hair on her left side fell in front of her face, obscuring her expression and any hint of what she might be hearing.

"What the hell's your problem?" Kurt shouted across the conference room table.

"You don't know what the problem is? What are you, blind? You know why Sagar put you in charge of this case. Because you're gay!"

"How the hell did you get to be so damned homophobic?" Kurt said.

"Homophobic? What an absurd term. I'm not *afraid* of queers, I just can't stand 'em. I don't like the lifestyle they've chosen. I think it's sick!"

"Chosen?" Kurt held up his hands in disbelief. "You think I *chose* to be this way? Get your head out of your ass, Bill. What kind of fool would choose to be ridiculed? What kind of idiot would choose to get the hell beat out of him in high school? You think I chose not to fit in, to be ostracized? Do you *really* believe that?"

"Hear anything?" Vince asked, frustrated with the lack of information.

"Sh-h-h!" Spence scolded, straining to hear.

Jonathan Sagar rounded the corner behind the group to find them all silently leaning close to the door. He couldn't quite make out what was going on since Vince and a couple of others blocked his view of Spence. One of the diggers saw him first and tapped Vince on the shoulder. Sagar was still a good twenty yards away. There was still time to save themselves from complete humiliation. Vince kept his eyes on Sagar but reached behind him and tapped Spence on the back.

"Spence," he whispered over his shoulder, almost in a panic.

"Sh-h-h!" she shot back, pushing his hand away.

As Jonathan Sagar walked closer to the conference room, he peered around Vince with a puzzled look, trying to get a glimpse at whoever or whatever commanded their attention at the door. The staffers parted to reveal Spence leaning against the conference room door. Nervously, the others smoothed their hair, adjusted their ties, anything to appear normal.

"Spence, get up," Vince warned under his breath through smiling, clinched teeth.

"Will you please shut up!" Spence whispered firmly, tilting her head even more toward the door in an attempt to block out Vince's distraction.

Jonathan Sagar stood just inches behind Sandra Spencer. Spence still crouched in front of the door.

"What seems to be the problem?" Sagar asked.

Spence froze at the sound of Sagar's voice. She couldn't bring herself to look away from the door. The rest of the staff shifted in place hoping Spence would fill the awkward silence.

"I said, what seems to be the problem?" Sagar asked. This time, his tone was more serious.

Spence slowly slid the side of her head up the door until she was standing erect. Her face, hidden behind her thin hair, was beet red. Vince Tordella cleared his throat and offered up the truth. "Kur, uh, Kurt and Bill are going at it."

"Really?" Sagar remarked. Spence closed her eyes. The rest waited for Sagar to burst in and break it up or, at least, bark at them for their eavesdropping. Much to their surprise, he smiled, grunted, and continued on past to his office. Spence slid her back from the door over to the wall. Her head was tilted downward. Her hair still covered her face. She crossed her arms and proceeded to bite the fingernails of her right hand. Vince covered his mouth trying to contain his laughter as he looked at Spence.

Dumaine stood in the conference room opposite Kurt, steaming in silence. Kurt turned his back to him and paced for a moment, pulling on his bottom lip. He then turned back to face him.

"You want to know something?" Kurt continued, this time more composed. "I *hate* being gay. Why do you think I agreed to take this case? It's not just for the prestige. It's not just for the power. It's also because I believe in what Penrose is doing. God forbid this child should have to go through what I've gone through. And you know what?" He pointed across the table at Dumaine who stood there with his hands on his hips. "I'm going to do everything I can to see that he doesn't and I'll do that either with or without you. It's your choice."

Kurt stood there for a moment as if waiting for an answer. Dumaine clinched his teeth, worked his jaw muscle, and stared at the floor. Kurt turned and opened the door to find all of his colleagues hovered in front of it. All except Spence who held her position on the wall. The rest meekly backed away from the doorway as Kurt glared at them.

"Lunch break. One hour," Kurt snapped and exited the conference room.

Dumaine didn't stick around to be interrogated.

19

Greg Wently arrived at the offices of GALLANT just about thirty seconds before Jon Carroll. Jon unbuckled his seat belt and exited his car. Greg was pulling his briefcase from the back seat. He closed the door, and the two partners scaled the steps together. They entered the door to the hallway when they both saw it at the same time. The office door of GALLANT commanded their attention at the far end of the hallway. Spray-painted in neon pink letters were the words 'DEATH TO FAGS!'

Jon cried out and ran to the door. "Those bastards!" He beat on the door with his fist.

Greg examined the damage, running his fingers over the letters, then calmly pulled the keys from his pocket and unlocked the door.

Jon was incredulous. "What's the matter with you? Doesn't this bother you?"

Greg placed his briefcase on the desk. "Hell, yes, it bothers me, but it's not like I didn't expect it." Greg reached for the telephone and dialed 411.

"Who are you calling?"

"You've got to learn how to turn negatives into positives, Jon. All you see is homophobic, hateful graffiti. I see an opportunity."

Jon stood there steaming as Greg waited patiently on the phone.

"Atlanta," Greg replied to the automated directory assistance. "CNN. The newsroom."

Jon's glare turned into a smile.

Penrose loved talking about his work with those who could understand and appreciate it. He absolutely despised talking to laymen about it, much less a roomful of attorneys. He parked his car in the underground parking garage and pressed the button for the eleventh floor in the elevator. Kurt Ford had been warned of the doctor's distaste for such exercises. He was also well aware of the doctor's lack of faith in Kurt's talents. He waited in the lobby hoping to soften him up.

"Dr. Penrose, it's good to see you again." He eagerly shook the doctor's hand. They walked down the long corridor toward the conference room. "I know the last thing you want to do today is baby-sit a bunch of lawyers, but I understand you're an inspirational speaker and a superb teacher. I'm sure you'll have no trouble conveying the essence of your work to us today."

Penrose glanced over at Ford then returned his eyes to the front. "Please don't patronize me, Mr. Ford. I despise lawyers and I especially despise having to hold their hands. The last thing I need right now is one fawning all over me. If this trial goes balls-up I'll be holding you personally responsible."

They continued the rest of their walk in silence. They entered the crowded room and Kurt announced their guest. The associates and paralegals sat attentively, pens in hand, like freshmen undergrads at their first big lecture. Dr. Penrose plopped his overstuffed pilot's case on the table and plugged his computer into the overhead projector.

"I'm going under the assumption that none of you is a doctor or scientist. Can I see a show of hands if you're a scientist or a doctor?" he asked sarcastically.

The 'students' snickered as they craned their heads looking to see if any of their co-workers had a secret profession they didn't know about. With no hands going up, Dr. Penrose continued.

"All right, then. We're all starting from the same point. Now, without boring you with a lot of scientific phrases and technical-speak, I'll try to put what I do and what I've done in a nutshell. The mystery of sexual orientation has long been pondered. Many, many different theories have abounded, yet little real research was ever done in this area until the last few years. Conventional wisdom for many years was that homosexuality was a mental illness. Others deemed that theory rubbish and said it was an emotional rebellion. Freud blamed the parents of homosexuals for what he termed the 'castration complex' or a pathological state of arrested psychological development. His belief was that some men developed this when they realized their mother didn't have a penis, and the fear of losing their own drove them to have sex with other men. You see, to Freud, everything revolved around his penis."

The assembly chuckled nervously.

"I preferred to look at it all from a more logical point," Dr. Penrose explained. "Setting political correctness aside, I was convinced that many homosexuals exhibit effeminate qualities. Conversely, I observed that many lesbians exhibit masculine qualities. So, thinking logically now, I asked myself, do all of these gay men get together at some secret convention and decide they're going to talk with a slight lisp, make their wrists limp, become incredibly neat people, and listen to show tunes?"

The room erupted into laughter. Most everyone stole a glance at Kurt Ford who was laughing harder than anyone.

"The answer was, of course, no. I was quite intrigued by the research done by Simon LeVay. Most of you have never heard of Simon LeVay but in 1991, he made an intriguing discovery." Penrose clicked to reveal a full-color illustration of the human brain on the screen. "He discovered that part of the hypothalamus, a small area at the base of the brain about right here," he pointed out with his laser, "was larger in men than, not only women, which had been discovered sometime before, but, interestingly enough, in gay men. I know I promised no big medical phrases, but please forgive me just this once. A small group of cells, he determined, called the third interstitial nucleus of the anterior hypothalamus, or better known as INAH-3, were the key to sexual orientation. Now, building on LeVay's work, I asked the question: why? Why is the INAH-3 in homosexual men smaller than in straight men? Being a geneticist, I theorized that genetics might play a part. Do understand the theory of a 'gay gene' is nothing new. That theory has been floating around for years, but no one was ever able to prove it. I put together a study of sixty-two homosexual men, the largest study of its kind ever. We asked them a lot of in-depth questions about when they believed they became gay, were there any other gays in their family, etcetera, until a pattern began to emerge. We noticed that many of these gay men had gay uncles on their mothers' side and had gay nephews through their sisters. 'A-ha,' I said. Possibly this gene, or genes, is being transmitted by the mother. Which sex chromosome do we males get from our mothers?" he asked the group.

"The X chromosome," Sandra Spencer chimed in.

"That is correct, my dear," Penrose praised. "You folks aren't nearly as ignorant as you look."

The group laughed.

Penrose clicked to the next display, this one an illustration of the X chromosome. "Logic would dictate that if there were a gay gene, we would find it in the X chromosome and, indeed, we did. First we narrowed it down to the distal portion of Xq28, X being the chromosome, q being the arm of the chromosome, and 28 being the position on the arm, which is right about here," he said, pointing with his laser. "With the help of the Human Genome Project, we narrowed it down to GABRA 6." He clicked to the next slide. "And there it is, folks. The illusive gay gene."

Kurt's blood went cold. He looked pensively at the screen. For the first time, he was face to face with the very reason why he was as he was. The gay gene was, all at once, not just a theory but something very real.

Dr. Penrose continued. "So, the question then became: what do we do with this information? And that's where it really gets controversial. My belief is that anything that goes against nature is, essentially, defective.

Birth defects hinder the natural use of the body. Muscular dystrophy inhibits the way we walk and the way our muscles function. Down syndrome inhibits the way our brains function. Homosexuality inhibits procreation. If we found the gene that causes MS or Down, what would be the next step? Anyone?"

Vince Tordella was eager to answer. "Correct it?"

"Precisely what I thought, too. Oh my God, I'm thinking like a lawyer," Penrose joked. "Yes. We should correct the gene. But how? Well, without getting too technical, I developed an enzyme that works much like the search and replace function on a word processor. It seeks out only the defective gene and replaces it with a corrected gene. We tried the experiment first on dogs with great success then moved on to an orangutan because their genetic makeup is quite similar to our own. Once we had achieved success with the orang, the next logical step was to put this into practice on humans and that's why we're here today. Any questions?"

Kurt Ford was first with a question. "Yes, Dr. Penrose, what are the chances this enzyme you've created will go crazy and totally screw up a fetus?"

"Zero," Penrose was quick to answer. "You see, like the word processor that's instructed to change the word 'item' to the word 'thing' this enzyme can only do that one function. It's not capable of changing any other genes. It doesn't even recognize any other genes. All it knows is that if it detects one that it's designed to change, then it will change it. You could introduce this enzyme into a heterosexual male fetus and there would be no effect. If it doesn't see the gene it's looking for, it does nothing."

Another hand went up from one of the research staff. "Why does this procedure have to be performed on a fetus? Why not use it on fully developed, grown homosexuals?"

"Excellent question." Penrose was pleasantly surprised by these 'laymen.' "That would certainly be preferable. If we were able to do that, the procedure probably wouldn't be nearly as controversial. The fact is, at this point, we can't, and the reason is quite simple. The immune system. Once the immune system is developed, it sees this enzyme as the enemy. The walls of defense go up and the enzyme can't penetrate it. That's why we have such a narrow window to detect and then change the gene. The hard part is going to be developing a stronger enzyme that can make it through without doing irreparable damage to the immune system. We're working on that right now, but it's impossible to tell how long before that will be developed. Anymore questions?"

Dr. Penrose looked around the room. There were no more hands going up. Kurt Ford jumped up to take the floor.

"This was certainly quite helpful, Dr. Penrose. Thanks for your time." He led the group in applause.

"Remember, if you have any questions," Penrose added, "I'll be at work every day just like normal, as normal as it gets these days. If you have any, feel free to pick up the phone and ask."

With that, Dr. Penrose turned the dirty work of defense over to the attorneys and headed back to his own little world across town.

Bill Dumaine nervously paused in front of Kurt Ford as Kurt handed a secretary some notes to be typed.

"That was very interesting," Dumaine said.

"Yes, it was," Kurt confirmed cautiously, his attention still on his instructions to the secretary.

"Look, I never really realized…I guess what I'm saying is I never really believed…" Dumaine was running out of words. "We'll talk later. I'll see you in the conference room."

"Right." He watched Dumaine walk away.

20

Kelly Morris apprehensively entered the offices of Clemens & Woodruff, nodding to the receptionist who was on the phone. She had purposely arrived a few minutes late hoping to avoid a confrontation with Norm Woodruff after their unpleasant parting at the federal courthouse in Loveport. She had managed to evade him on the plane back to Atlanta but she knew she couldn't hide from him forever. Perhaps if she conducted the meeting as usual, with the usual participants as buffers, all would be forgotten. Much to her surprise, the conference room was empty. She laid her briefcase on the table and her purse in a chair and paced the carpet anxiously. Seconds later, Norm Woodruff walked through the doorway reading an open file. He was startled to find Kelly already there.

"Didn't Rex get you on your cell?" Norm asked.

"I, uh, I didn't have it on," Kelly answered.

"He's running a little late," Norm informed her.

There was awkward silence. Both tried to overlook it. Finally, the tension was too thick to ignore.

"Norm, about the other day," Kelly began.

Before she had a chance to finish her thought, Rex Randle bounded into the room.

"Seen CNN this morning?" Rex asked with a grin.

Norm and Kelly looked at one another and shook their heads. Rex grabbed the remote from the conference table and switched on the TV in the entertainment center at the far end of the room. A reporter was doing a stand-up in front of GALLANT headquarters then cut to a videotaped piece. The crudely drawn graffiti jumped out at them thanks to the glare of the television camera's light.

"Oh, my God," Kelly said as she inched toward the screen, never taking her eyes off of it.

"When did this happen?" Norm asked.

"Just this morning," Rex replied. "Isn't it great?! This is exactly what we need to shift public opinion our way." He turned his attention back to the TV. "Those stupid homophobic bastards," Rex added under his breath.

"This is good?" Norm asked.

"Absolutely," Kelly answered. "Now we're in a sympathetic position. That's somewhere we very rarely find ourselves. This kind of publicity will be great for the cause."

"You *do* realize we're trying this case in court, not on CNN," Norm said.

"The court of public opinion, Norm," Rex said. "Never underestimate how important it is."

"Is that what this is to you two? A PR war? Look, it doesn't mean a damn thing if everybody in the country is on our side if we lose in that courtroom. And if you don't understand that simple premise, that's exactly what's going to happen."

The Core assembled in the conference room, a place that had now been dubbed the 'war room.' General Kurt Ford recapped where they were and outlined the latest developments in the case. He plotted strategy on the big easel then began the daily ritual of delegating tasks.

"Vince, check with Penrose's people. We need to improve on those visuals we saw at his presentation."

Vince Tordella jotted a note to himself on his legal pad.

"Better yet, get our legal exhibits guy on the line. We'll get him on those visuals. He'll make 'em sing."

"For the jury or for the cameras?" Vince asked.

"Both. Make 'em big enough to see from the back of the courtroom. Bill, you got somebody lined up to convince that jury there's very little risk in Penrose's procedure?"

"Yeah, a…" He looked at his notes. "Dr. Garcia," Dumaine said. "He heads up the Human Genome Project. He's a big fan of Penrose. He'll not only testify about the feasibility and safety of his project, he'll tell them about Penrose's contribution to the Genome Project."

"Great. Any negatives? Anything we need to be aware of?"

"Not that I can tell so far. We're checking him from head to toe just to make sure."

"Great. Vince, is Dr. Glasco a go?"

"She's a go, but lemme tell ya somethin'. This broad ain't gonna be cheap. We've gotta fly her in from San Fran. That's expensive enough, but she wants first class. No coach."

"Damn prima donnas. All right, book it," Kurt ordered. "Man, these expert witnesses have bigger egos than the lawyers."

"Yeah, and they cost about as much, too," Vince added.

"Tomorrow's the deadline for the witness list," Kurt announced. "Everybody feel comfortable with ours?"

The Core all gave a collective nod.

"Great. It goes out FedEx at three o'clock. In the meantime, let's keep cramming on our people. I want to know any negatives about them before the other side does. If I find out in court, it's going to be too late. As soon as we get their list tomorrow, we'll start picking it apart."

The morning rain began to pick up. Dr. Penrose headed down the broad boulevard on his way to the office. The Spanish moss clung to the trees like a toddler to his mother's apron. The streets were lined with historic homes on oversized lots which had been tenderly and painstakingly restored. A few of the houses were reproductions, designed to fit into the motif of the quaint neighborhood. Penrose never tired of the short drive to work. Usually he let the morning pass in silence, but he was curious how his project was playing in the media. He switched on the windshield wipers as the radio news announcer finished the newscast which gave way to the musical opening of the nationally syndicated Jan Freeman Show.

"Welcome back in. This is Jan Freeman. Of course, the subject that's on everyone's lips is this horrific Frankenstenian project going on down at Loveport Medical Center."

Penrose reached for the volume control and turned it up good and loud.

"The city's getting ready for what's being called the 'Trial of the Century.' How many times have we heard that, huh? But I tell ya, folks, this one just might live up to the hype. I mean, think about this. How many cases have we seen where parents get to turn their homophobic dreams into a nightmarish reality? Can you imagine Billy Bob and Betty Lou from the trailer park getting the news, 'Mr. & Mrs. Low IQ, your baby is going to be homosexual,'" she said in the clinical voice of a doctor. "'Ain't no faggot gonna live in my trailer,'" she mocked in a hillbilly accent. "'Get Dr. Penrose in here and defaggotize that boy for me. And while you're in there can you make him a gun lover and a stock car fan?'" She laughed at her own joke. "I mean, really, what in the world has this society come to? Tony from Chicago, you're on the Jan Freeman Show."

"Jan, I wish you'd stop making light of this issue. There are a lot of us parents out here who think Dr. Penrose is doing the right thing. The last thing we want is for our child to be homosexual."

"All right, let me ask you something, Tony. If you could make your child, say, right-handed instead of left-handed, would you do it?"

"Come on, Jan, you're not being realistic. Choosing whether or not your son will be homosexual is much more important than which hand he writes with."

"So, I'm assuming you'd jump at the Dr. Penrose's procedure if you had the chance."

"Absolutely."

"Tony, are you calling from a trailer?"

"What?"

She hung up the phone. "Obviously over his head. I tell you what. For all you Tonys out there, let's make all the kids right-handed. And while we're at it, we'll make them all blonde-headed and blue-eyed. That's got a nice Nazi feel to it, doesn't it?"

Penrose could stand it no longer. He snapped the radio off just as he pulled into his reserved spot in front of the research center. The rain turned to mist. He pressed down hard on the parking brake of his Buick with his left foot. Grabbing his briefcase from the passenger seat, he pulled the door lever, opening the heavy door. Before his feet hit the ground, he heard his name.

"Dr. Penrose! Got a moment?"

Penrose looked up to see Don Bissette hurrying across the parking lot followed by a heavyset, bearded man with a large camera slung over his shoulder. Another camera crew had slipped past security. Penrose didn't bother locking the car door instead, he sighed insufferably, shook his head, and made his way quickly to the front door of the research center.

"Dr. Penrose, I just want to ask you a couple of questions," Bissette pleaded.

"You're not allowed back here. You'll have to talk with our press office for a statement," Penrose instructed curtly and headed up the three steps to the door.

"Cut it off," Bissette instructed the cameraman. The cameraman lowered the camera as if lowering his weapon for a cease-fire. "Dr. Penrose, how about a moment without the camera? Completely off the record. I give you my word. I just want to talk man-to-man."

Penrose paused at the door and looked suspiciously over his shoulder. Instinctively, he didn't trust reporters, but there was something in Bissette's voice that kept him from turning the knob and walking away. It was a momentary pause that hung in the air. It wasn't a commitment to stay nor was it a complete dismissal of Bissette. Penrose's indecision was Bissette's foot in the door. He took it as an offer to talk and stood at the bottom of the steps being very careful not to invade Penrose's space.

"Don Bissette, WPCV News 3." He offered his hand.

"Yes, I'm familiar with you, Mr. Bissette," Penrose answered in his button-down British manner, casually ignoring the reporter's hand. The flaws in Bissette's face are much more apparent in person, Penrose thought.

"Boy, this thing has really taken off, hasn't it?" Bissette said with a nervous chuckle in his voice, reeling in his awkward hand.

"It *is* a rather major medical breakthrough," Penrose replied proudly. "We figured it would get some attention."

"Yeah, but now the injunction by GALLANT and the NCRA. And the CWO joining in. You *couldn't* have expected that. I mean, nobody saw that coming."

"Lawsuits, like politics, make for strange bedfellows." Penrose chose his words carefully. "I'm a very busy man, Mr. Bissette. What is it you want?"

"Look, Dr. Penrose. I want to ask a favor of you. The national press is gonna be crawling all over you like bees on honey. Those bastards are ruthless."

"And you're not?"

Bissette paused a beat then continued as if he hadn't heard him. "They don't care who they hurt as long as they get their story. As soon as this story's over, they'll pack up the satellite trucks and head off into the sunset. It's different with me. I live here. I'm a local boy. I mean, I played first base at the Loveport Hospital Celebrity Softball Tournament last year, for heaven's sake. The point is, I'm not out to screw you over to get the story."

"Who *are* you out to screw over, Mr. Bissette?"

"Nobody."

"Nobody? Come now, Mr. Bissette. You're an ambitious reporter. I know your kind. You'd sell your bloody mother for a scoop."

"I'm not like that, Dr. Penrose. I'm really not." He said it almost more to convince himself than Penrose. "Look, I'm not going to lie to you. I'd love to have that scoop. You want to know the truth? I'm dying to break into the majors. Any reporter who tells you anything different is full of crap. This could be that story, but I won't do it at the expense of someone else. I have a better plan, a different way."

Penrose studied his face looking for any indication at all that he could trust him. He saw a slight twitch in Bissette's smile. He couldn't discern whether it was the exposed seam of the deceptive mask he wore or the natural nervousness of an honest man. "What's your plan, Mr. Bissette?"

"I want the scoop. An exclusive."

"Oh, that's all," Penrose said snidely.

Bissette ignored the tone. "But not on my terms. On yours."

Penrose raised an eyebrow.

"The big boys will twist and turn your story until you don't even recognize it. They'll manipulate your comments, take them out of context. They'll have you saying things you never dreamed you'd ever say. They have the power. They have the power and they have the agenda. It's not just getting the story, it's telling the story *their* way, from *their* point of view. Media bias isn't what they tell you. It's what they don't. Minor, off-handed comments become lead stories and front page news. They derive some journalist pleasure from advancing a cause. They think they're doing us all a favor. They call it journalistic integrity, but all it amounts to is telling the story with their spin while *pretending* to be objective. In the end, they scorch the earth with their agenda, leaving behind a wreckage of misinformation and disinformation and twisted, mangled reputations all in the name of changing the world."

"I don't need a lecture from you on the so-called left-wing media and their perceived bias, Mr. Bissette."

"It's both sides, Dr. Penrose. They all come with agendas. This is activist journalism. It's how most of these major media outlets play it and I just wanted you to know that I'm not that kind of reporter. I've been in this town a long time and I have a strong reputation. A lot of people are gonna be clamoring for the limelight in this case. You don't strike me as that kind. You strike me as somebody who wants to do the right thing. In a way, we kind of need each other. I need you to get the story, and you need me to tell the truth." Bissette held out his business card. "My cell number's on there. Anytime you feel you're not getting a fair shake from the media, and believe me that won't be too long from now, you call that number, day or night. I'll be glad to tell the story your way."

Penrose looked down at the card in Bissette's hand. "You know I'm not allowed to talk to you people."

"Hold on to this card, Dr. Penrose. Just in case, through all of this, you need a friend in the media."

Penrose stood there looking at the card as if taking it would bind him to a contract. He wondered how many other folks had heard that same speech. Don Bissette looked up at him with a steady smile on his face. Penrose slowly reached down and accepted the card.

21

Kelly Morris made herself at home in Norm Woodruff's conference room as she directed the discussion. The FedEx from the defense attorneys in Loveport had arrived an hour earlier. After Kelly had taken a look at the witness list, she passed it along to Norm. Norm instructed one of the secretaries to make copies for everyone at the table. By the time they all had copies, Norm had conducted a search for the first witness on his laptop, which provided little more illumination than what the defense lawyers had already given them. Rex Randle studied the bio. Minutes passed. Norm tapped the eraser end of a pencil on the bottom teeth of his open mouth and thought about the witness under discussion. Ginny Dunn, one of Norm's paralegals, looked bored. They had gone over and over this witness, but they were coming up dry.

Dr. Kent Garcia had impeccable credentials. He headed up the Human Genome Project for the government and could be considered not only an expert witness, but an unbiased one at that. He would testify to Dr. Penrose's contributions in the field of genetics. He would also maintain that the Penrose Project was quite feasible and, in fact, a welcomed move to many in genetic research. There must be a hole, some way to at least damage his testimony.

"All right, let's go over this again," Kelly snapped. "Garcia's going to say that the procedure is safe. Any way we can refute that?"

"That's the angle I've been concentrating on," Norm said. "I guess it's all relative. It *is* pretty safe compared to other risks of dying."

"You got any numbers?" Rex asked.

"Just what I pulled up here on the Internet." Norm looked down at the computer screen. "For instance, the chance of miscarriage with this procedure is estimated by Dr. Penrose and other experts at about one in two-hundred.

"That sounds pretty high."

"Well, according to these numbers, your chance of dying of heart disease is about one in six."

"Damn. I better lay off the burgers," Rex said.

"There's about a one in two-hundred-forty-two chance you'll die in an automobile accident. We're talking about the same risk for Penrose's procedure that there is in the initial amniocentesis that discovered the gay gene in the first place."

"Wouldn't that mean the risk would double?" Kelly asked. "It's a one in two-hundred risk for *each* procedure, right?"

"Yeah, but I think we're missing a central point," Norm said. "We have to maintain that the procedure is unnecessary to begin with. We can get lost in all the odds talk and we'll lose that jury, too. We can't lose focus of our main point and that is this isn't some horrible condition that needs to be cured. Some people are gay. You may not like it. You may think it's sinful. You may not ever want it for yourself. That doesn't mean you go around tampering with someone else's genes. Even your own child's."

"Norm," Kelly said with a smile, "we just might make a believer out of you yet."

"It's for the cause, my dear," Norm joked. "Just make sure I don't have to say it in court."

Kelly and Rex laughed.

"OK, let's build on that theme for a moment," Rex said. "What's normal to everyday Jane and Joe American is not normal in other parts of the world. Without asking the jurors to accept homosexuality as normal," he smiled at Norm, "we need to show them that, in some quarters, people are different, for better or for worse, and we shouldn't be hell-bent on changing everyone who's different from us. If we could demonstrate *that* somehow, I think it would go a long way with the jury."

"That's good. That's real good." Kelly moved closer. Her eyes danced with excitement. They were out of the mud. Her mind was turning again. "We need some stats to put this into perspective." She walked over to where Norm sat in front of the computer and leaned down to look at the screen. He caught the scent of her perfume. "Norm, how about you surf the net and get me some web addresses for the NFL, the NHL, and the NBA."

"You got something?" Rex asked.

"I don't know, but I have a theory."

One of the secretaries for CC&D entered the conference room and handed Kurt Ford the overnight package that had just been delivered from Kelly Morris' office.

"I hope it's the witness list," Vince said, rubbing his hands together.

"Yes, indeed," Kurt tore open the envelope. "All right, let's see." He scanned the first of three pages and then read out loud, "Dr. Evan Proctor. Harvard Biological Labs. American Society of Genetic Ethicists, board member."

"Oh, I saw that guy on Fox News the other night," Bill Dumaine said. "Man, he savaged Penrose. Said he was unethical, had an agenda. Called him everything but a mad scientist. He was brutal."

"Sounds like you've already started your research," Kurt replied. "Proctor's yours."

Dumaine made a note of it.

He read on, "Dr. Stanley Bernstein. President of the American Psychiatric Association."

"Whoa, callin' out the big guns," Vince said.

Kurt continued reading, "Graduate of Yale. Med school at Penn, yadda, yadda, yadda." He skipped the biographical information and went straight to the synopsis of testimony. "Dr. Stan's going to tell us about a study he's done that says homosexuality is not a mental disorder.

Boy, now there's a doc who's on the cutting edge, isn't he?" Kurt added sarcastically. "Spence."

"Yo," Sandra Spencer answered.

"Dr. Bernstein's yours."

"Check." She jotted down his name.

"And Vince, your man is Dr. Frank Bomar, pediatric surgeon at CHOP," Kurt read on the next page.

"What the hell's CHOP?" Dumaine asked.

"Children's Hospital Of Philadelphia. Come on, it's one of the best pediatric care units in the country," Vince said proudly, as if Dumaine were an idiot for even asking.

"That leaves Dr. Martin Whitaker."

"Martin Whitaker, the author?" Spence asked.

"That's the one," Kurt said.

"I've read his work. I wouldn't mind taking him."

"He's yours. OK, we'll get copies of the complete witness list to you guys," Kurt informed the group. "Remember, these witnesses are your responsibility. Don't be shy in asking the diggers to help you. We need to know all there is to know about these people. I want to know everything from where they went to school to how many parking tickets they've had to what they had for dinner last night. Everything. You get the picture. If there's a crack in their credibility, I want you to find it."

Jury selection was the one part of a trial Kurt Ford despised. It was tedious and frustrating and, regrettably, the most important aspect of the whole process. Important enough that Jonathan Sagar had hired Voir Dire, Inc., a jury consultant firm out of Los Angeles. Sagar and The Core met at length with four consultants from VDI to help formulate the profile of 'the perfect juror,' a near impossible task, but a worthwhile exercise. Sagar conducted the meeting. He began by writing the words

'Perfect Juror' at the top of the large paper tablet on the easel.

"Let's start with the sex," he said, tapping the marker on his fingers. "Is our juror a male or a female, or does it even matter?"

"I think it's a female," Kurt said.

"Why so?"

"Well, because I think she'll relate to the couple making this decision more than a man would. You know, the mother instinct."

"What if she's not a mother?" Gloria Fisher, the lead consultant for VDI, played devil's advocate. "What if she's a lesbian?"

Kurt hadn't thought of that, but he wasn't going to let Jonathan Sagar know it. "The questionnaire will weed them out." Kurt tried to sell the line like he meant it.

It was obvious Gloria was in charge of the other consultants. Every time she spoke, they wrote. "Maybe. Maybe not." She rose from her seat and glided, almost effortlessly, until she was beside the easel. "You really want to take a chance that everybody on that jury answered that particular question honestly?"

"All right, then," Sagar said, "if a woman's not our choice, it must be a man."

Gloria Fisher was confident. "Yes. Think about it. If you ask the average man, heterosexual, mind you, if he had a gay son, would he change it, he's gonna say yes. Women are more sympathetic to gays. Many of them hang out with gays. Gays cut their hair. Gays help them pick out their clothes at department stores. Gays decorate their homes."

"That's stereotyping a bit, isn't it?" Kurt asked defensively.

Gloria walked deliberately toward Kurt Ford until her face was uncomfortably close to his. "Stereotypes are what make our business work, Mr. Ford. We count on them. We *live* for them. Remember, every stereotype is based on truth. That's how it got to be a stereotype. The fact is more women are sympathetic to gays than men."

"Ah, but you said these people couldn't be trusted to come clean on the questionnaire. What if *he's* gay?" He had her now.

"If he's gay," she countered without bothering to look back at him, "we'll know it. Gay men are much easier to detect than gay women."

"Another stereotype?" Kurt asked.

Gloria glanced back over her slim shoulder.

Sagar didn't wait for her response. This was what he paid VDI six figures for. "A male," he said as he wrote it on the tablet. "Black, white, Hispanic?"

No one said a word after the blistering Kurt had just taken. After enough silence had elapsed, Gloria came to the rescue. Ironically, she would probably have failed her own profile test. She certainly was not the stereotypical dumb blonde. "White," she said without hesitation. "Everyone else is a minority. Gays are a minority. Minorities relate to gays because they feel a kindred spirit of discrimination. Not always, but many times. Why take that chance?"

"We've got a white male," Sagar said as he wrote.

After an hour or so, they had assembled a profile. Actually, Gloria assembled a profile. Jonathan Sagar had merely transferred her thoughts to the easel. A white male. Blue-collar. Low to moderate income. High school education. Preferably the father of a son. Semi-religious but not a Holy Roller. The only other kind of person they would accept in addition to their archetype was a doctor. A doctor, Gloria reasoned, would sympathize with Dr. Penrose, but the likelihood of finding one in the area who had never had any dealings with a facility the size of Loveport Medical Center was slim. As the meeting broke up, she tore the profile sheet from the tablet, handed it to one of her aides, and directed her to find the shredder. She'd been around the block. Gloria Fisher left nothing to chance.

22

Jury summonses went out to 112 citizens. All but four showed up at the federal building on the first day of the trial. The crowd outside was large but manageable. Spectators and press gawked at each person who made it through the police barricade, jury summons in hand, and was cleared through the metal detector. Once inside, Monica Lawrence, the clerk, checked each one, assigned them a number, handed them a questionnaire and a pen, then pointed them in the direction of the courtroom.

The questionnaire was a four-page survey that started out with the standard questions like name, address, occupation, amount of education, employment status. Do you have any mental or physical disability? Have you ever been convicted of, or pleaded no contest to, a crime? Have you ever served as a juror?

Page two went into more detail about the issues related to the case. Are you heterosexual or homosexual? 'Optional,' in parenthesis. The defense wanted to know if you were familiar with the issue of the gay gene? Do you have an ethical problem with gene therapy (the practice of altering genes to correct genetic disorders)? The plaintiffs' jury consultants had thrown in a few of their own. Do you have any bias against homosexuals? Would you consider yourself a religious person? If so, how many times per month do you attend your place of worship?

Page three quizzed the prospective juror on the principals involved in the trial, listing the attorneys for both sides and all of their associates. Do you know, or have you ever been represented by, any of these attorneys? Are you or any family members employed by Loveport University and Medical Center? Have you ever had medical services provided by Loveport Hospital? If so, were you satisfied with your service? If answering no, please explain in the space provided. Do you have a positive or negative impression of the NCRA? What's your impression of the Christian Way Organization? How do you feel about GALLANT?

The final page listed the witnesses and asked if the potential juror knew any of them personally. Have you ever heard of any of these people? If so, who? Please write your impression of this person in the space provided.

The prospective jurors had strict instructions not to converse with one another during the questionnaire phase. Each person sat quietly in the pew, balancing the clipboard on their knee, checking off and answering in detail when necessary. Courtroom personnel, the only ones allowed in during the process, whispered small talk to pass the time. There was no limit to how long a juror could take. As long as they needed, they were told. Just raise your hand when you're through. As hands were raised, clerk's assistants quietly collected the papers.

When the last survey was taken up, the deputies opened the back doors and allowed a handful of press to trickle in and take their seats. Lawyers for both sides emerged from the front of the courtroom and took their seats at their tables. The jury consultants for each side were allowed space on the front row behind their respective clients, four in place for the defense, two for the plaintiffs. They began sizing up the jurors.

The bailiff stepped forward and startled the courtroom with, "All Rise! Oyez, oyez, oyez. Court is now in session. The Honorable Seamus Kincaid presiding!" The judge, black robe flowing as he made his way, ascended the bench, the hint of Old Spice and pipe tobacco in his wake. He took his seat, placing his reading glasses on his nose.

Kincaid thanked the 108 for coming, like they had a choice. He launched into a small oration, stressing the importance of their duty as citizens. He then moved on to the finer points of the trial like what would be expected of them if they ended up as one of the twelve jurors. While the judge gave his speech, Monica Lawrence and her assistant clerks were busy making copies of the questionnaires for both sides then conducting a cursory examination of each one to determine which jurors would be dismissed immediately. Kincaid sought to narrow the field by asking for a show of hands of anyone over age sixty-five. Three people raised their hands. Kincaid gave them the option of being excused. All three chose to stay.

"All right, ladies and gentlemen," Kincaid said. "Before I ask this next question, I want you to understand that your answer will be kept confidential, if you so choose. I'd like to see a show of hands of any of you with a physical condition that would prevent you from serving."

Fifteen hands went up. Kincaid called each of the fifteen to the bench one at a time. The rest of the jurors were impressed with his courtesy as the judge stepped down from the bench and conferred with each juror in whispered tones. In the end, all 15 were dismissed. Ms. Lawrence announced their numbers and each side made notes on their copies. That left 93 jurors.

The judge looked at his watch and decided to break for lunch to allow Ms. Lawrence and her assistant clerks to further cull the field. He announced a two-hour recess, banged the gavel, and retreated to his chambers.

The Core wolfed down sandwiches at a deli just a few blocks from the courthouse. Kurt had split the juror surveys four ways. Each of the four poured over their share looking for red flags.

"I saw quite a few that fit our profile in there," Kurt said.

"Jury consultants," Vince Tordella muttered between bites.

"I gather you don't like them."

"Let me tell you somethin'," Vince said, not bothering to cover his mouth while he ate. He swallowed then put his sandwich on the plate and pointed with his index finger. "A wise, old man once gave me the perfect description of a consultant. He said a consultant is a guy who knows a lot of positions but doesn't know any women."

Kurt and Dumaine laughed out loud. Spence managed to muster a smile.

"If this Gloria broad from VD was so—"

"VD*I*," Spence corrected.

"Yeah, whatever. If this chick was so damn good, she'd be trying cases in court instead of traipsing all over the country trying to tell other lawyers how to try theirs. She's tryin' to buffalo us. You know what I'm sayin'?"

Jonathan Sagar swore by jury consultants. Kurt had no intention of challenging that authority. Vince had no compunction in challenging anyone. Neither did Dumaine.

"He's right," Dumaine said. "She's trying to bully us. Look, it's *our* asses on the line in there. You really wanna relinquish such an important aspect of this trial to Fisher and her three henchmen?"

Vince and Dumaine were the resident recusants at the firm. Kurt knew that and proceeded with caution. "What do you suggest?"

"I suggest you take control of this process," Dumaine said. Vince nodded in agreement. "They're consultants, Kurt. You're the lead attorney. You accept their advice with a smile and do what you think's best. Don't let that woman steamroll right over you."

Kurt sought a third opinion. "Spence, you've been mighty quiet. What do you think?"

"God forbid I agree with these two male chauvinists pigs, but they're right. A consultant is just what the word implies. You consult with them, but the ultimate decision is yours. Ole Buffalo Gal is going to get away with as much as you let her."

Kurt sat back and thought about all that had been said while the other three hashed and rehashed the subject. They were right. Courtroom savvy was more than just juror profiles and formulas. If that's all you had, you were lost. Numbers and stats and odds and stereotypes didn't mean a thing when you were interacting one-on-one with a potential juror. You got a feeling, something that couldn't be quantified. Something that couldn't be learned. Something innate. Sure, there were clear warnings you could acquire from questionnaires, and jury consultants had their place, but what distinguished true courtroom virtuosity from the Gloria Fishers of the world was instinct, pure and simple.

Jury selection reconvened at exactly two o'clock. Monica Lawrence handed Judge Kincaid a handful of surveys. Kincaid attached the reading glasses to his face and studied each one while the jurors fidgeted. All seemed in order.

"The following jurors please stand when I call your number and remain standing," Kincaid instructed. "Numbers 5, 16, 32, 33, 46, 52, 59, 66, 68, 73, 75, and 79."

The twelve jurors stood.

"Thank you for your time, ladies and gentlemen. You are excused."

Those jurors were let go because they knew someone connected with the trial.

The number was down to 81. The rest of the afternoon was spent hearing jurors make their cases for being excused from duty. Kincaid heard everything from a lady who had to take care of her sick mother to a young man who insisted he had to walk his dog three times a day or the dog would have to be treated for depression. In all, twenty-three folks made the attempt. Some were more convincing than others. By the close of the day's session, they were down to 69.

Judge Kincaid instructed the lucky 69 to return the next morning at nine. He warned them not to talk about the case in the event they became one of the final twelve. He was pleased with how quickly the selection process moved along and confided in the attorneys that he hoped to finish up the next day.

Gloria Fisher was already in the conference room with Jonathan Sagar when The Core returned to the law office. She was busily writing on the paper tablet. She had written the heading 'First String' and listed twelve numbers. Under that, she wrote 'Second String' and listed twelve more. She was in the process of finishing up when Kurt interrupted.

"What's that?"

"That's your jury," she answered confidently. "Each side's going to get ten strikes. If they strike ten of our first string, we look to our second string."

"Don't you think we should discuss the selection?"

Gloria looked to Jonathan as if asking him to keep this thorn from her side. Jonathan remained quiet. She looked back at Kurt. "What's to discuss? You have the profile. We've taken that profile and assigned a value to each attribute. We've scored each individual juror and added their numbers to determine their JQ."

"JQ?" Dumaine asked.

"Juror Quotient. The first twelve have the highest JQs. The second dozen are the next best thing. I've also listed our ten worst prospects, the ones we want to blow out with our ten strikes if the other side doesn't pull the trigger first."

Kurt glanced at Dumaine who rolled his eyes. Buffalo Gal was at it again.

"It looks very scientific," Kurt said diplomatically, "but what if there's a flaw in the profile?"

Gloria Fisher straightened her body and pursed her lips. "There's not a flaw. I can assure you."

Vince smiled. Kurt was challenging her and she didn't take too kindly to it.

"I've got some work to take care of," Jonathan said. "I'll let you two work this out." Jonathan Sagar excused himself and closed the door behind him. He had hired both of these people to speak their minds. The last thing he wanted was to hinder them from doing so. They would work things out, one way or another. He was convinced of that.

Gloria Fisher watched Jonathan leave the room then redirected her attention to Kurt. "Mr. Ford, I assume you have a better idea?" Her question was laced with sarcasm.

"As a matter of fact, Ms. Fisher, I do."

"I'd love to hear it." She tossed the marker on the conference table and took a seat. She crossed her legs and rested her hands in her lap, feigning interest.

"It's an old-fashioned notion of talking with the jurors one on one. See how they react to the plaintiffs' lawyers, see how they react to me. Ask some probing questions and see how they handle themselves. You see, you get a feeling when you're out there and sometimes that feeling doesn't conform to a jury quotient."

"Mr. Ford," Gloria said with a condescending laugh in her voice, "we've consulted over 3,000 civil cases. Our success record stands at 85%. It's hard to argue with a record like that. I would add that a large number of that 15% who lost did so because they didn't take our advice. Now, these are the jurors." She pointed to the easel. "Your concern should be plotting strategy on how you're going to make sure they're still standing at the end of the day tomorrow."

"Ms. Fisher," Kurt smiled, looking down at the table and resting both palms on it, not two feet from Gloria Fisher's seat. He stared her squarely in the face and lowered his voice to a more intimate tone. "Just so we don't misunderstand one another, I am the lead attorney and you are the consultant. You make suggestions. I make decisions. Is that clear?"

The Core held their collective breaths awaiting her response.

"Suit yourself, Mr. Ford." Gloria Fisher stared back at Kurt trying to size him up. Perhaps she had misjudged him. Maybe he wasn't as pliable as she had first concluded.

23

Day two of jury selection saw more press and more gawkers outside the federal building. Security had been beefed up to meet the demand. Jurors parked at a specially designated parking lot behind the building with a short walk, out of view of anyone but court personnel. They showed the temporary ID cards that had been given to them, emptied their pockets for the metal detector, and showed their handbags to security. Once they had redeposited their belongings into their pockets or closed their handbags, they picked up their numbered pins then followed the wide, marble, spiral staircase up to the second floor courtroom.

Gloria Fisher and her three assistants stood in the hallway outside the door and watched each of them enter. Their numbered lapel pins corresponded to the new list issued by the clerk reflecting the dismissed jurors and the reshuffling of the deck by the computer. The four consultants jotted notes beside each number, things like whether or not they seemed alert or if they were open and cheery or serious. The two consultants for the plaintiffs stood on the other side of the hallway, clipboards in hand. They, too, were sizing up the prospects.

After all the jurors were present, the deputy opened the doors for the same press and the same consultants who attended the day before. The attorneys emerged from the wings and went directly to their seats. Kurt tried not to look at Gloria, but it was difficult. She was burning a hole right through him. Jonathan Sagar sneaked in and sat on the back row. He had heard about the confrontation. Gloria, quite naturally, had tattled, but Jonathan had chosen not to intervene. Kurt was right, Sagar determined. He was the lead attorney and everyone working on the case needed to respect that. The last thing Sagar wanted to do was undermine his authority.

The bailiff announced Judge Kincaid with the traditional pageantry. Kincaid thanked the jurors once again for coming and explained what would happen. The attorneys from both sides would talk with them, possibly ask them questions, and give them a chance to ask a few of their own. He cautioned them that the speeches they would hear from both sides were not testimony and should not be interpreted as such.

Kelly Morris stood up before the assembled multitude of 69 jurors and introduced herself. Before she got too far into details about the case she wanted to know something. "How many of you think homosexuals are born that way? Let me see a show of hands." About a quarter of them raised their hands. She asked them to keep their hands up while she looked back over her shoulder at Norm and Rex and their jury consultants. They were putting checks beside numbers on the juror list. About two-thirds of the raised hands were women. When she got the nod, she thanked the jurors and moved on to the next question. "How many of you think it's a learned behavior?" Another twenty or so raised their hands, mostly men. All of the attorneys and consultants for both sides made checks on their lists. "How many of you aren't sure?" Thirty-one, a plurality, raised their hands.

Kelly explained to the jurors that their decision in this case would determine the destiny of human beings forever. She wanted to make sure they grasped the gravity of their task. She tried to assess each juror as did Norm, Rex, and their two consultants. The last thing they wanted was a juror who thought altering someone's genes was no big deal, or, worse yet, had no idea what a gene was. She asked if any of them had gay relatives. Several raised their hands. She probed their relationships with their gay relatives. Three had gay sons. She asked those parents if they would've changed the fact that their son was gay had they been given the chance. All three said yes. Rex put an X by Jurors 5, 24, and 32. The others with gay relatives were more unsure. One had a gay uncle she was especially fond of, though she wasn't fond of the fact he was gay. That was a dangerous juror. She could fall for the defense, but she could just as easily fall for the plaintiffs' contention that his homosexuality was a large part of who he was. Rex put a question mark beside Juror number forty-three. The other two had lesbian aunts. Neither of them seemed to be too troubled by it.

Kelly spent the next hour probing and prodding and digging into the minds and personalities of the sixty-nine. By the time she was finished, she had all of her questions answered and about half of Kurt's. Kurt's sheet had been carefully prepared, a cooperative effort, or so it was described by Gloria Fisher, between The Core and the consultants from VDI. Everyone had a copy, including Jonathan Sagar who prepared to follow along from the back row. One question came to Kurt during the brainstorming session that he chose not to reveal. It was an obvious question that everyone had overlooked, but it needed to be asked. He held it out because he wanted there to be no mistake in Jonathan's mind that *he* had thought of it.

Kurt introduced himself to the jurors. He didn't tell them he was gay. It seemed awkward to do so. Besides, he wanted an honest discussion on the subject. He began his questioning with the only one not on the prepared and agreed upon sheet. "Have you or any of your family members ever had a genetic defect?" Gloria Fisher frantically scanned the prepared list looking for the question. Several hands went up and Kurt listened to their stories. One man with a Down syndrome daughter. Another man had a son with multiple sclerosis. One woman was, herself, color blind. Kurt's colleagues made notes as did the plaintiffs' attorneys. He then asked the jurors to play his speculative game. "How many of you would change color blindness if you could even if there was some risk involved?"

Kelly Morris rose. "Objection, Your Honor."

"State your objection," Kincaid said.

"It's too close to the circumstances of this case."

"Your Honor," Kurt interjected, "it's imperative that we judge the temperament of potential jurors before we select them. If a juror is completely hostile to our client, we have a right to know."

Kincaid nodded slightly. "Objection overruled."

"A show of hands, please." Kurt resumed, "how many of you would change color blindness if you could even if there was some risk involved?"

Thirty-two of the sixty-nine raised their hands. Gloria Fisher begrudgingly made note of the thirty-two. Jonathan Sagar smiled broadly.

Kurt Ford went through the rest of his prepared questions. How many have ever watched the TV show *Modern Family*? How many have bumper stickers on their cars? What do those bumper stickers say? How many have ever participated in a public protest? What did you protest? Judge Kincaid was bound and determined to finish this process by the close of business. Kurt ended his questioning, and Kincaid recessed for lunch. He ordered the jurors to return in exactly one hour.

Kurt waited for the elevator and checked his watch. He didn't want to be late for the afternoon session. He rattled off a short list of restaurants in his head trying to decide which one was most likely to get him in and out in under an hour. His thought process was shattered by the annoying voice he had come to recognize as Gloria Fisher's.

"That question wasn't agreed upon by me," she fired at Kurt from behind.

Kurt turned to face her. "Oh, hello, Gloria," he said, completely ignoring her protest.

"That was dangerous, Kurt, and you know it. You could blow this case before it starts with stunts like that. Now, I don't know what your problem is—"

"My problem is you." He tried to contain his anger. The elevator opened behind him. He ignored it. "As I explained to you before," he pointed first to himself then to Gloria, "lead attorney, consultant." He reached behind him and stopped the closing door of the elevator then backed in.

She turned her nose up. "If you screw up this case, it won't be because of me."

Kurt pushed his floor and smiled as the elevator doors closed between them.

The afternoon session was a high-stakes game of 'Let's Make A Deal.' The sixty-nine jurors were safely locked away at the other end of the federal building. The doors to the courtroom were closed to everyone except the dickering attorneys. Judge Kincaid firmly laid down the ground rules. He would allow each side ten peremptory challenges, or strikes as the lawyers referred to them. An attorney could use a strike to ditch a juror for absolutely no reason. They would start with the plaintiffs' attorney and take turns until both sides had agreed to the first twelve jurors.

The bench recognized Kelly Morris. She immediately spent one of her ten strikes on the very first juror, one of the thirty-two who indicated they would change color blindness. Those jurors became known as Kurt Ford's 'Hypothetical 32.'

Juror number two had not been among the thirty-two. "The plaintiffs accept juror number two," Kelly announced.

"Defense?" Kincaid waited.

"The defense accepts number two."

Juror number three was a walking example of the defense's Perfect Juror. Gloria's JQ rated him a 95 out of 100. Even in spite of her scientific data, Kurt liked him. The defense held its collective breaths. With nine strikes left, they hoped Kelly wouldn't squander another one this early in the game.

"The plaintiffs accept juror number three."

Kurt kept his poker face. "Likewise."

Number four was agreed upon as well. Then came juror number five. The plaintiffs hated her. She was one of those who had a gay son, but, interestingly enough, she was not one of the 'Hypothetical 32.' Even though she didn't appear open to a genetic correction, she was a religious fundamentalist. Not good for an organization like GALLANT. But the defense didn't like her, either. She was not someone they wanted listening to the likes of Norm Woodruff. This is when the game took nerves of steel. Kelly needed to save her strikes. She wanted to clear out as much of Kurt's 'Hypothetical 32' as she could. Kurt was certain she couldn't allow this dangerous woman on the jury. Kelly was about to find out what her opponent was made of.

"The plaintiffs accept juror number five." She looked over at Kurt and smiled.

Kurt was blind-sided. It was a given she would strike her. Why wouldn't she? Now he was confronted with a dilemma. Juror number five was as religious as anyone they saw in the questionnaires. She attended church at least three times a week and had a 'very favorable' impression of the CWO. Could Norm Woodruff convince her that altering someone's genes was the devil's work? Kurt couldn't take that chance. He pulled the trigger. "The defense strikes juror number five."

The plaintiffs spent their remaining strikes on as many of Kurt Ford's 'Hypothetical 32' as they could. They struck jurors twenty-four and thirty-two, the other two parents of gay sons who were part of the 'Hypothetical 32.' The defense struck jurors number nine, thirteen, seventeen, eighteen, and jurors twenty-nine and thirty-four.

By the time both sides agreed on juror number thirty-five, it was all over. Of Kurt's 'Hypothetical 32,' five had made it on the jury. Kelly Morris was pleased with that accomplishment, although she admitted to herself that the bulk of them being back-loaded on the high end of the numbers certainly helped. The remainder of the sixty-nine were thanked for their indulgence and sent on their way. What was left were nine women and three men. Of the twelve, three were black, one was Hispanic, one was Asian, and the rest white. The jury was hailed in the press for its reflection of the diversity of the community, an accolade that would make any attorney nervous. The deputy escorted the twelve jurors back into the courtroom. Judge Kincaid looked down over his reading glasses and waited for the last one to take his seat.

"Ladies and gentlemen, we appreciate your patience over the past two days. This court has gone to great lengths to choose the best possible jury for this case and I must congratulate you on being chosen. We expect this trial to last no longer than two weeks during which time you will be excused from your jobs as prescribed by law. Also, under the law, this court will exercise its right to sequester the jury for the duration of the trial. I realize what a burden this is on you, but this court must do everything possible to preserve the integrity of the jury. For the length of the trial, you will not be allowed to have any contact with anyone outside this court including family and friends except for a brief phone call this evening. The bailiff will escort you in just a moment to make a phone call to have clothing, toiletries, and other essential items delivered to you here. You are not to discuss the nature of this case during that phone call. Suitable accommodations will be provided and all of your meals will be paid for. You are not to discuss this case among yourselves until instructed to do so. You are also urged to select a foreman as soon as possible. Any questions?"

There were none. A few of the jurors groaned as they were led from the courtroom. The attorneys packed their briefcases and filtered out of the room. The table was set. The players were in place. The biggest spectacle to ever hit Loveport — maybe the entire country — was set to begin.

24

Kurt Ford rubbed his temples after reading over his opening argument notes for the umpteenth time. He could almost do it in his sleep. The knock on the door of his office was a welcome break.

"Come in," he said, pouring another cup of coffee from the coffee maker on the credenza behind his desk. Sandra Spencer slunk into the room, all five feet ten inches of her. She had a wicked grin on her face. She silently eased into the chair in front of him and crossed her long, shapely legs.

"What's up, Spence?" Kurt asked suspiciously.

"Take a look at this." She pushed a piece of paper across the desk at him with a devious smile. "For the plaintiffs' first witness tomorrow, Dr. Bernstein." She sat back and locked her fingers together and watched Kurt absorb the morsel of information she had dug up.

He smirked. "Well, well, well. Great work, Spence."

Spence basked in the praise.

"As recently as 1973, eh?" Kurt said as he read on. "Bernstein has to know we'd find out about this, doesn't he?"

"You would think so," Spence said. "The question is, does Kelly Morris?"

"Oh, she will tomorrow." Kurt leaned back in his chair and continued to read the paper. "She will tomorrow."

Don Bissette sat at his desk pouring over the latest wire copy. He crammed a hamburger into his large mouth almost unconsciously while absorbing the latest news from the Loveport Trial. Just as he had predicted, the national press was brutal to Dr. Penrose. The op/ed pieces in the newspapers were blatant slams, but the stories moving on the wire were more insidious. It was obvious to a trained journalist like Bissette that the writers had already reached a conclusion even before the opening arguments.

The newly hired news director, Michael Thomas, made no bones about his regrets over sending Bissette to cover the Loveport news conference. Had he known the story was going to be so big, he would've sent his pet reporter whom he had brought with him from his last job. It's not that there was anything wrong with Bissette. Thomas just wanted to build the station in his own image and that meant destroying everything that had come before him, even if it was working. Bissette had the luxury of a long contract and barring some incident of moral turpitude, Thomas was going to have to live with it.

The phone on Bissette's desk rang. He casually picked it up, his eyes still glued to the newspaper. "Bissette," he barked with some burger still in his mouth. Bissette put the paper down with a start and straightened up in his chair. "Yes. What can I do for you?" He listened intently to the caller. "Well, yes." He extended his left arm out to expose his watch and checked the time. "I'm leaving here in about thirty minutes. I've got to do a live shot from the courthouse for the six o'clock cast." He listened for a moment then offered his assurance. "Listen, I will go to my grave with any information I have about you. I promise you. I don't care if they throw me in jail, I never reveal my sources." Bissette smiled and scrambled for a pen. "You bet!" He pulled a pad over with his free hand. "OK, shoot." He wrote a name down on the pad. "Uh, huh. Uh, huh. Really? Thank you. Hey, listen, I appreciate your making this call. If you have any other info just let me know."

Bissette hung up the phone and stared at the name on the pad. He would have to trust his source that the information was correct. There was no time to check it out. He didn't dare wait, not even until the late news. This was his chance at a scoop and he wasn't going to blow it. He hoped his instincts were right. He didn't much like this side of the business, trashing an otherwise innocent man, but there was too much on the line. The career clock was ticking loudly, a constant reminder that this might be his last chance to catapult himself out of a small market. He looked down at the name again. In less than an hour, the world would never be the same for Dr. Stanley Bernstein.

A jury can be an interesting microcosm of society. More times than not, baser instincts take over in the cramped confines of the jury room. A social hierarchy is established. The leaders and the followers are quickly distinguished one from another. True leaders are few and far between, but followers, like sheep, are always plentiful. Most just go along to get along.

As in real life, the leaders sometimes choose to be king makers instead of kings. Such was the case with John Banta, a successful businessman with a receding hairline, slight character lines in his face, and a golfer's tan. The rationale behind his nomination of Estelle Wooten to be foreman was purely self-serving. Estelle was an attractive, gray-haired, sixty-something woman. Handsome is how women like her were described. Banta thought she looked more at home baking cookies for her grandchildren than running a jury. She seemed to be the one juror most impressed by his intelligence. She had said as much. Banta was accustomed to getting his way. He had mixed emotions about his assignment to the case. He wasn't particularly thrilled to be there, but he had come to terms with his lot. He had learned long ago the only way to make the best of a situation was to take control of it. With Estelle Wooten's help, he planned to do just that.

Within the first thirty minutes, the personalities of each juror were coming sharply into focus. Dana Crockett was a young, professional woman, practical and calculated. Her good looks had been more of a hindrance than an asset and she constantly struggled to be taken seriously. She often went overboard in making her point just to make sure everyone knew she had plenty of sense. Much like she was doing in the jury room.

"We're going to need someone who's sharp and organized," Dana pointed out. "Someone who can assimilate all the information and keep us on track." She didn't want to come right out and challenge John Banta's candidate, but she didn't take Estelle for the aggressive type. Dana would've liked nothing better than to be foreman of that jury herself, though she would never be presumptuous enough to suggest it.

"Why don't you be the foreman?" Ron Dallas offered. Dana Crockett acted as if the idea had never crossed her mind. She pretended to be flattered and humbled.

Ron was jovial and good-natured. He liked harmony and abhorred confrontation, though he wasn't one to back down from a fight. He was born on the cusp of the civil rights movement, something which shaped his childhood. Not to the point of being militant and bitter, but of being keenly aware of his black heritage and his history. This was his first shot at jury duty and he took the responsibility very seriously. He was well aware there were just three blacks on the jury. Justified or not, he held no delusion that he could ever be foreman himself.

Denny Sullivan lacked the self-esteem to pursue the lead role, but he was very careful not to let his insecurities show. He was born and raised in a blue collar family and was proud of it. Not a lot of education, but he was quick to remind anyone who would listen that he was no idiot. He didn't care too much for people who rested on their diplomas and thought that was enough to get them through life. He fought every single day for what little he had. Denny had no compunction in busting someone's lip if he believed in something and he had no respect for anyone who did otherwise. Just by the fact that some fat cat like John Banta was backing her was enough to turn Denny off to Estelle Wooten. If Banta wanted her, there must be something wrong.

Some of the jurors had more patience than others. Harvey Goldstone poured himself a cup of coffee. Denny Sullivan thought how little Harvey needed another cup. The fact that Harvey never sat for more than two minutes made Denny nervous. To Harvey, time was money. He was one of those who had some lame excuse for getting out of jury duty, one that Judge Kincaid didn't buy. Harvey was still in shock that he was being sequestered. There was so much he had to do, so many places he'd rather be than sitting on a jury. He felt naked without his cell phone. He quickly assessed the situation and determined that John Banta wielded the most influence in the room. In the end, Harvey figured, Banta would get his way. To expedite things, Harvey planned to back Banta's horse.

As if he were her campaign manager, John Banta made a case, based on his limited knowledge of Estelle Wooten, as to why she would make the perfect foreman. She had kept the books for her husband's plumbing business for nearly forty years, so she was obviously organized. She had served on three previous juries, although she was never foreman, and she knew the intricacies of jury duty better than anyone at the table. It was certainly a disparate jury with unique individuals, but, in the end, the sheep went along with John Banta's nomination. They might each have had their own idea about who the foreman should be, but they weren't as determined and strong-willed as Banta. Besides, they liked Estelle Wooten. They figured her to be fair and conscientious, traits one needed to be foreman. Banta had no idea which way he would go on the case. All he knew was, when he *did* decide, he wanted someone in charge who he could manipulate. Little did he know, he had met his manipulative match in the demure Mrs. Estelle Wooten.

25

Kurt Ford hurriedly pulled the TV tray over his knees with one hand and flipped on the television remote with the other. He had rushed from the kitchen to catch the local news. Steam rose from his Lean Cuisine, which had become a staple as of late. He was just in time as the logo for WPCV News 3 flashed on the screen. There was no doubt what would be the top story.

"The nation awaits the opening day of testimony tomorrow in a trial that has split some of the most solid special interest groups right down the middle," the anchor began. "No issue before has ever been so divisive. Groups as diverse as the religious right and the gay rights advocates find themselves aligned for the first time ever on the issue of the gay gene. Demonstrators vie for the prime real estate outside the federal building downtown, but police forces have been beefed up and they are turning them away until tomorrow morning. Don Bissette is there live."

Bissette stood in front of the camera-hungry crowd that had gathered as police instructed them to move on. Demonstrators didn't waste the television opportunity, waving placards and shouting slogans behind Bissette as he filed his report.

"The battle lines are already being drawn here at the courthouse a good sixteen hours before the opening arguments." Bissette walked from the cordoned off area over to where the courthouse was in the background. "Just behind me is the site of all the action to come in this very emotional controversy where a jury of twelve, just chosen today, will listen to all the testimony then make, what has to be, a most difficult decision. The judge has put a pretty tight lid on the case, barring any of the parties involved from talking about it. However, News 3 has learned that the first witness to testify tomorrow for the plaintiffs in this case is the president of the American Psychiatric Association, Dr. Stanley Bernstein. According to sources close to the case, Dr. Bernstein's credibility is being called into question. Bernstein, who is married with two children, is alleged to be having an affair with a nineteen-year-old student at Georgetown University in Washington, D.C."

The angry call from Jonathan Sagar was not unexpected. All Kurt could do was keep repeating that he had no idea who leaked the information or even where the information had come from, for that matter. For the next hour, he and Jonathan plotted damage control. Kurt's stomach churned. He stuffed two Tums into his mouth. This was not the way he wanted to go into the opening day of testimony. He spent the rest of the evening pacing back and forth in front of his dresser mirror, practicing his opening argument, trying not to look at his note cards. At twelve-fifteen a.m., he was as ready as he would ever be. He crawled into bed and begged his mind to stop racing so his body could get some badly needed rest.

Jack Hawkins sat in a rented Chevy chain-smoking Vantage Menthols and peering out the window at the café across the street. A pair of binoculars and a beat up 35mm camera with a telephoto lens lay on the seat next to him atop a half-folded city map of Chapel Hill, North Carolina. Wadded-up empty fast food bags littered the floor of the passenger side. He yawned and extinguished another butt in the overflowing ashtray. His mark, Dr. Martin Whitaker, was in plain view having his breakfast at a table by the window. Hawkins took a sip of coffee from his drive-thru cup. He had been on more bizarre goose chases before, but he couldn't remember when. He had no idea who had hired him. He knew his client only by one name — Raven. He talked with Raven by phone, never in person. With the fiber optic phone lines, he couldn't tell if he was calling local or long-distance. His caller ID read 'Unknown.' He had no idea who Raven was and had no way of telling. Raven masked his voice with a Harmonizer, a piece of electronic equipment once used by radio stations and production houses to change the pitch and texture of the voice. The voice was low, almost guttural. It sounded like something from a B-horror movie. Although Hawkins knew fully that the voice on the other end was electronically altered, it still gave him the creeps.

Within two hours of their last conversation, he was at Reagan National wheels up heading for RDU International in Raleigh, North Carolina. As the plane climbed to cruising altitude, he had gazed upon the beautiful sight of the City of Monuments and all its lighted splendor. From high above it, the city looked much more symmetrical and planned than it did traversing its streets by car. The view was even more pleasant from his plush seat. He had asked for first class and Raven hadn't balked. As long as he got what Raven wanted, the money he spent to get it was inconsequential. So far he had been pleased by what Hawkins had managed to dig up. Just who was this Raven, Hawkins wondered. As long as he paid in cash, he didn't much care.

He was a bit nervous being in unfamiliar territory. He knew the streets of Washington and the suburbs of Virginia and Maryland like the back of his hand. He rarely knew his clients there either, but at least it made more sense. He was usually on the tail of some government official, trying to gather dirt for one of the parties. It didn't matter to Hawkins which one. He had the loyalty of a poker chip. The only politicians he was loyal to were dead presidents and Raven was coughing up more of them than he'd ever made in the District: $1,000 per day, a week in advance, plus expenses. Raven always took the information by phone. Any photographs and tangible evidence used to corroborate Hawkins' research were left in manila envelopes in a locker at Union Station to which Raven had sent him a key. Hawkins never staked out the locker to see who picked up his work. He wasn't about to do anything to upset the gravy train. Anyway, as thorough as Raven was, he was sure to have covered that detail as well. Hawkins had gathered dirt on some of the biggest names in Washington and never had the client been so mysterious. The mystery, however, did nothing to relieve the tedium of a stakeout. Hawkins yawned a cavernous yawn. He was bored, but at a grand a day, he could suffer through the boredom.

After about thirty minutes, he started to feel a bit uneasy. This wasn't like Washington. Chapel Hill was a small college town. A man just sitting in his car drew more curious looks, especially a chain-smoker. Hawkins got out of the car and walked over to the paper machine, dropped the coins in, and pulled out a USA Today. He walked over to a knee-high wall where students sat with open textbooks. He took a seat on the wall. His pudgy, middle-aged frame looked out of place among the young, bright-eyed coeds. He began to read the paper, ever conscious of Dr. Whitaker across the street. *Loveport Baby Trial Begins,* read the headline. In smaller bold print below it, *Judge Furious Over Pre-Trial Leak.* Hawkins read on. The name almost jumped up and slapped him in the face.

"Well, I'll be a son-of-a-bitch," he said to himself.

The leaked witness was Dr. Stanley Bernstein, the very man Hawkins had tailed and researched for a week in Washington. Every juicy morsel he had turned over to Raven was there in print, including Bernstein's secret rendezvous with a lovely, young psych major from Georgetown. Hawkins' heart raced. He was part of the biggest story in the country and didn't even know it. Now the mystery surrounding his employer began to make sense. He looked up from the paper just in time to see his mark pay the bill and leave the café. Dr. Martin Whitaker headed down the street on foot. Hawkins, a renewed bounce in his step, was in pursuit.

26

The old federal building downtown was awash in a sea of spectators, reporters, cameramen, satellite trucks, protestors, and street vendors. The pictures from the hovering helicopters on the networks looked more like Woodstock than a trial scene. The circumference of the courthouse was roped off, taking in an entire city block. The dark, deserted street resembled a moat around the federal building. Below the police tape were metal barricades which looked like bicycle parking racks. Only those with press passes or official courthouse credentials were allowed inside. The perimeter of the secured area was lined with people twenty deep or more hoping to catch a glimpse of one of the key players. Opportunists on both sides of the issue held placards and chanted. A young college kid with green spiked hair and rings through his ears, nose, and tongue held a homemade sign which read 'TOLERANCE NOT GENOCIDE.' A grandmotherly-type with bifocals and a purse hanging from her wrist stood next to him holding another placard reading 'EUGENICS DIED WITH HITLER.' They argued with a man carrying a sign reading 'CURE THE QUEERS.' People shoved and shouted while the police — standing two feet apart on the safe side of the barricade — tried to maintain order. It was an absolute zoo. Hot dog vendors, who normally catered to the courthouse lunch crowd, were doing a land-office business. In the midst of the chaos, a religious group calmly lit candles, locked arms, and sang hymns. Television reporters did their trial coverage stand-ups with the federal building and the bedlam as the backdrop.

The jurors arrived by bus with a full police escort. The large touring coach with dark windows approached the courthouse from the rear to shield the jurors from as much of the spectacle as possible. Sheriff's deputies, assisted by federal agents, kept a watchful eye and the jurors disembarked and filed inside. They were escorted to the jury holding room where donuts, bagels, and coffee awaited those who hadn't taken advantage of the free breakfast at the hotel. They sat in the jury room, reading the magazines and newspapers provided for them by the taxpayers with any reference to the trial surgically cut out. Harvey Goldstone observed to no one in particular that it must be one hell of a big trial. Practically the only thing left of the newspaper was the sports section. None of the magazines had covers.

Estelle Wooten chose not to read but waited patiently with her hands in her lap. She was proud to be doing her civic duty and could hardly wait for the trial to begin. She made small talk with John Banta who seemed never to be too far away.

The start of the day's proceedings was delayed by a particularly brutal conference inside the judge's chambers. Judge Kincaid called the lead attorneys in to read them the riot act. After Kincaid finished his harangue, Kelly Morris took her turn at ranting and raving. She was livid. Eleanor Henson, the court reporter, tried desperately to keep up with her.

"Your Honor, I call for a mistrial," Kelly finally insisted.

"Denied," Kincaid said. "Although the information reported is embarrassing to the witness, it doesn't diminish his credentials as an expert witness. The jury's been sequestered so there's no chance of contamination."

"Your Honor, that's not the point. The defendants clearly violated your own gag order."

"Miss Morris, you heard the counselor. He denies any knowledge of the leak and I have no reason not to believe him." Kincaid turned to Kurt Ford. "Mr. Ford, I do believe that leak came from somewhere inside your organization and I expect you to put a stop to it! Do you understand?"

"Yes, sir. I can assure you that we will, Your Honor, and swift and severe action will be taken if we find someone with our firm is responsible. I talked at length with Mr. Sagar last night and he's as outraged as you are about this. He doesn't tolerate this kind of conduct in his firm."

That seemed to assuage Judge Kincaid, but Kelly Morris was nowhere close to satisfaction. She muttered something under her breath and shook her head.

"Ms. Morris?" Kincaid said.

"Your Honor, Dr. Bernstein is scheduled to testify today and now he wants to back out."

Judge Kincaid leaned back in his chair.

She asked, "What am I supposed to tell him?"

"You can assure Dr. Bernstein that no information about his personal life will be admissible in court. Questions will be limited to his professional expertise and its bearing on this case." He turned to Kurt. "Is that clear, Mr. Ford?"

"Yes, sir."

"Now, let me reiterate what I said before." The finger of Kincaid's free hand emerged from his robe and he pointed it at the two attorneys. "There will be no more leaks in this case, from either side. I'm holding both of you responsible. Understood?"

They both nodded nervously.

"I'm not above hauling that reporter's ass in here, uh, strike that, Mrs. Henson," he instructed the court reporter. "I'm not above bringing that reporter before this court and holding him in contempt if he doesn't reveal his sources. You make sure your people know that if this happens again, I *will* get to the bottom of it."

The interior of the courthouse bore no resemblance to the confusion outside. Once past the encampment of media personnel and hysterical throngs, one found a virtual oasis. More accurately, it was like the eye of a hurricane. The major networks, wire services, and newspapers were issued permanent press passes to the press section while the other passes were rotated among the vast number of out-of-town press who drew numbers and waited their turn. Against his better judgment, Kincaid had relented and honored Kelly Morris' request for cameras in the courtroom. Kincaid rationalized that daily exposure of the trial might relieve some of the enormous pressure which had built up around the case. The networks would take their feed from two pool cameras stationed inside the courtroom and controlled by Judge Kincaid. One was situated directly behind the jurors so the people watching at home could see exactly what the jurors were seeing. The other was positioned in the rear of the room in the middle. It would zoom in to catch the judge and a close-up shot of the witness stand. The cameraman locked the pan so the camera wouldn't veer too far to the right and expose the faces of the jurors.

Through his connections at the courthouse, Don Bissette from WPCV News 3 had managed to snag one of the permanent passes and staked out his territory on the front row of the press area. Dr. Penrose entered from the rear of the courtroom and made his way up the center aisle. Don Bissette tried to catch Penrose's eye as he took his seat in the front row just behind the defense table. Penrose searched the crowd for the Andrews, the couple at the epicenter of this whole controversy. He didn't see them and didn't really expect to. He had discouraged it, actually, just as he had discouraged his own family from attending. Kurt Ford entered from a side door, filling Bill Dumaine in on the action in the judge's chambers as they walked. Sandra Spence and Vince Tordella followed silently behind. The huge crowd took them all by surprise. The Core nervously took their places at the defense table. The four lawyers were followed by two paralegals who lugged in armfuls of files and then plopped them on the table. Several more young paralegals with note pads and pens in hand sat on the front row on either side of Penrose except for the places to his immediate right and left. The seat to his right was reserved for Roy Kirsch of Loveport Medical Center. Dr. Kirsch whispered something to Penrose that Bissette strained to make out as Kirsch took his seat beside his prized geneticist. Dr. Baxten was already in place on the other side of Penrose. Not one to engage in small talk, he sat silently, watching the various officers of the court take their respective places. Jonathan Sagar sat with his arms crossed next to his old friend.

On the opposite side of the room, Greg Wently and Jon Carroll made their way to the plaintiffs' table and took their seats with Kelly Morris, Rex Randle, and Norm Woodruff. Kelly huddled with her clients to bring them up to speed. A couple of paralegals from Woodruff's office took seats on the front row directly behind the plaintiffs' table. Dr. Lucius Gaylord was offered a seat at the plaintiffs' table, but chose the front row behind the railing instead. He chatted nervously with an aide from the CWO. Greg Wently had never had a face-to-face encounter with the famous Dr. Gaylord. He seemed smaller in person than he appeared on TV. Not nearly as menacing as Greg would have thought.

The courtroom was full but comfortably so. Judge Kincaid had taken great care to ensure that the audience wasn't packed in like sardines. He loathed a media circus and did his part to retain some semblance of a normal trial, if that was even remotely possible. A clerk's assistant entered the courtroom and headed for the press section. She whispered something to Don Bissette. He looked up at her in disbelief then was escorted from the room by a sheriff's deputy, by order of Judge Kincaid.

The bailiff led the jury into the courtroom and oversaw their seating in the jury box. The gallery murmured to one another, sizing up each of the twelve, one-by-one. The jury consultants watched them even closer. The bailiff quieted the crowd with his announcement. "All rise! U.S. District Court will now come to order. The Honorable Seamus Kincaid presiding."

Judge Kincaid seemed to emerge from the paneling in the front of the courtroom. His red flame of hair burned against the black background of his robe. He confidently strode to the bench and took his seat.

"Be seated," he instructed into the microphone then nodded to the clerk. Monica Lawrence announced the case in a monotone voice.

"Gay And Lesbian Liberation And National Tolerance, et al. versus Loveport University Medical Center, Doe."

Judge Kincaid almost began when his attention was distracted by one of the paralegals behind the Loveport team whispering into a cellular phone.

"We'll have none of that in this courtroom," he barked to the petrified young girl. "No cell phones. If you've got more important business than the business of this court, then I suggest you leave now and attend to it." Seeing there were no takers, he began. He greeted the jurors with uncharacteristic cordiality. "Good morning, ladies and gentlemen. I trust you found your accommodations acceptable. If you're having any troubles, please let someone on my staff know and we'll take care of it."

The jurors all smiled in appreciation of His Honor's concern.

Judge Kincaid asked the jurors collectively by way of raised hand if they had been approached by anyone trying to influence them in any way. No hands went up. He asked them if they had discussed the case among themselves and, again, no one indicated in the affirmative. He warned them of the seriousness of jury tampering and instructed them to contact him immediately if an attempt were ever made. He then schooled them on the process, outlining their duties and what would be expected of them, asking if they understood. The jurors nodded.

"Have you elected a foreman?" Kincaid asked.

All eyes turned to Estelle Wooten on the front row, far left. Estelle stood proudly. Gloria Fisher checked her notes. Wooten had a JQ rating of 62, not very good, but it could've been worse. She scored a little high on the religious question. She attended at least once a week. She, however, was Presbyterian, a mark in her favor as far as Gloria was concerned. If she had to be religious, it was one of the more liberal denominations, she reasoned. Kelly Morris breathed a sigh of relief. Estelle was not one of the 'Hypothetical 32.' As long as that disaster had been averted, she didn't care if Bozo the Clown was the foreman.

"Now then, is the plaintiff ready with an opening statement?" He looked down on Kelly Morris.

"Yes, Your Honor." She pushed herself away from the table and walked around to the podium. Her colorful African Mutusi-print dress stood out among the drab blue suits like a blooming flower against the desert floor. The camera at the back of the room followed her first, then the jury camera picked her up as she turned to address the jurors. She took a moment to arrange her index cards. Every eye in the courtroom was trained on her. The jurors sat attentively. The reporters watched with pens poised on pads.

"Ladies and gentlemen, we intend to prove conclusively to this court that the procedure Loveport University Medical Center intends to perform on the Loveport Baby is unnecessary for the health and well-being of that child and, in fact, is dangerous. We believe this procedure is prohibited under U.S. Code Title 42, Chapter 6A, Subchapter III governing fetal research under the Department of Health and Human Services. Section 289g, paragraph (a) states: 'The Secretary may not conduct or support any research or experimentation in the United States, or in any other country, on a living human fetus for whom viability has not been ascertained unless the research or experimentation (1) may enhance the well-being or meet the health needs of the fetus or enhance the probability of its survival to viability; or (2) will pose no added risk of suffering, injury, or death to the fetus, and the purpose of the research or experimentation is the development of important biomedical knowledge which cannot be obtained by other means.' This statute applies to all government agencies and while Loveport doesn't fall under that direct jurisdiction, we believe the same standards should apply. First of all, you need to understand that this procedure *is* experimental. It's never been attempted on a human being before. We will prove that not only is this procedure experimental, but it doesn't meet either of the criteria set forth in Title 42 for experimental research, namely it doesn't enhance the well-being of the fetus," she counted with her finger, "and it poses an added risk of suffering, injury, or death. Furthermore, we will prove that because homosexuality is predetermined genetically, it is no more a genetic defect than being left-handed or," she glanced up at the carrot-top judge and smiled, "being red-headed. Ladies and gentlemen, we believe not only will this procedure be detrimental to the Loveport Baby, but it will throw open the doors of genetic tampering that might never again be closed. Once this technology is allowed to be utilized by parents, it will be impossible to stop it."

She went into great detail describing the discrimination against homosexuals. Her review of documented cases of physical violence against gays was explicit. Some jurors squirmed in their seats at the graphic depictions. Her plan was to construct a pattern in the jury's mind, to demonstrate an escalation of hatred against gays which was now culminating in their very annihilation through the Penrose Project.

"If Dr. Penrose's procedure is allowed to go forward," Kelly Morris cried out, "it will be the ultimate act of discrimination! It's bad enough that this man obviously has an aversion to homosexuals. Now that aversion has manifested itself in the science of their destruction!"

The jury was enthralled as Kelly's wild eyes met theirs. Homes and offices across the country fell silent as people dropped what they were doing and gathered around television sets. Even Judge Kincaid, who ordinarily fought off boredom throughout opening arguments, found himself hanging on every word like a page-turning suspense novel. Every cause, every belief, everything she held sacred was summoned from deep inside her for this one and only chance to make a lasting first impression.

"Ladies and gentlemen, we intend to prove that this horrible procedure is not only unethical," she concluded emphatically, "but it violates the fundamental civil rights of the Loveport Baby *and* future generations of homosexual men and women. Quite simply, this procedure *must* not be allowed to proceed." She returned to her seat. Judge Kincaid jotted notes on a pad.

"Does the Guardian wish to make an opening statement?" Kincaid inquired.

"Indeed, we do," Norm Woodruff said. He rose to address the court. His style was a marked contrast to that of Kelly Morris. Where she was factual and professional, he was folksy and charming. Where she was impassioned and borderline hysterical, he was downright theatrical. Shock value was his oldest and truest weapon in the courtroom. In this case, he intended to bring it all down to a personal level. Everyone on the jury could relate to parental instincts of protection for his or her child. It was Norm Woodruff's aim to bring that into such clear focus that the jury could almost taste it.

"Ladies and gentlemen, as legal guardians for this child — this boy — we intend to assert *his* rights in this case."

Norm came out from behind the podium. The pool cameraman behind the jury box had grown accustomed to Kelly Morris' static presentation. He scrambled to unlock the pan then followed Norm as he walked.

"There are going to be all sorts of experts paraded in front of you," Norm continued. "Some will be more convincing than others, but, in the long run, only one thing counts and that's what's best for this boy." Woodruff moved in closer and rested his right foot on the bottom rail of the jury box. "He's not here to defend himself. He's counting on us to do the right thing *for* him, to protect him."

Norm was on the move again. The camera followed. "Now, we agree with Ms. Morris that this procedure is dangerous and we intend to bolster that argument, but we also intend to challenge the very research done by Dr. Penrose and his colleagues at Loveport. I've listened to the talk shows on the radio and the TV. I've seen the news reports. People seem to be taking his conclusions at face value that a single gene — one single, solitary gene — is responsible for one's sexual orientation. We intend to prove that there are all sorts of factors which determine that. The notion of one gene, one all-powerful gene, as the only factor is complete lunacy. Experts in the field will tell this court that there are myriad variables which come into play in determining such a complex thing as one's sexual orientation. Do genes have an impact? Perhaps. To what extent? The fact is, ladies and gentlemen, we just don't know and I don't intend to stand idly by while Dr. Penrose experiments on *my* client. Basically, that's all this is, as Ms. Morris said, an experiment. It's one thing to experiment on someone of legal age who, of sound mind, signs a consent form. It's quite another to subject a young, innocent, defenseless little soul to an unproven, unsafe, and untested experiment." He paused as he walked in front of the jury box, hands locked behind his back like an officer reviewing his troops. "What's best for the boy?" he asked dramatically. "That's the only question we need to concern ourselves with. Really, nothing else matters. No advances in science, no Nobel Prizes, no political agendas. What's best for the boy?" He lingered a moment for effect then softly repeated. "What's best for the boy? Thank you."

Judge Kincaid jotted a few more notes. Upon finishing, he looked over at the defendant's table awaiting their opening argument. Kurt Ford stepped forward, placing his note cards on the podium. He felt the enormous pressure of the jury, of the press, of the cameras, but he felt the most pressure from Jonathan Sagar. He recalled standing in that very spot with no one else in the room. Even then, the pressure was stifling. Now it was almost asphyxiating. He tried to block all of it out of his mind and concentrate on the task at hand.

"Ladies and gentlemen, contrary to what the distinguished counselor representing the legal guardians in this case stated, there is overwhelming and conclusive proof that the gay gene exists and can be corrected. We intend to lay that proof before this court. We will also prove that Dr. Penrose is one of the most respected scientists in his field. Colleagues throughout the world of genetics stand in awe of his accomplishments and his contributions to this vital discipline. Dr. Penrose is not some genetics cowboy armed with a secret weapon to eradicate homosexuals. His work is born of compassion and a desire to contribute, in a positive way, to the betterment of mankind. Dr. Penrose is a family man with a wife and two teenage children, not some mad recluse bent on using technology to an evil end."

Kurt moved out from behind the security of the podium, a move which made him uncomfortable but, he knew, would make him seem more at ease in front of the jury. He took care not to stray too far from his notes on the podium.

"There are three questions that will be determined in this trial. Does the condition of the child warrant correcting the defective gene? What is the risk? And does the end result justify it? We will prove to you that, first of all, the risk is minimal. Secondly, we will prove to you that the end result is something that not only warrants correcting, but it's something these parents owe their young son. Mr. Woodruff asked you the question: what's best for the boy? That's a very good question, and you know what? I don't have an answer for you." Jonathan Sagar shifted nervously in his seat. "What's best for this boy is not my decision to make. Only his parents can answer it. You see, that's what this basically boils down to. Parental rights. Parental rights mean parental choices. What school will this young boy attend or what clothes will this young boy wear or what will he be exposed to on television. Those are parental choices stemming from parental rights to make those choices. To undermine that is to undermine the most basic of rights in this country. No, Dr. Penrose doesn't have the right to make that choice. Neither does Mr. Woodruff nor do you or I. The only people who have that right are the parents. And given the information that their son will be born a homosexual, this boy's parents have chosen to spare him that torture. Thanks to Dr. Penrose, this couple and millions of couples like them to follow will be able to, at last, spare their children the pain and the suffering of growing up gay. As much as the plaintiffs in this case would like you to believe it, homosexuality is not normal. We have finally advanced to a point in medicine where we know that homosexuality is a genetic condition which is now treatable yet there are those who would stand in the way of treatment. Why? It's purely selfish, ladies and gentlemen. It's because *they* can't be treated. At this point, there's nothing science can do for them, so they'd rather that no one benefit from Dr. Penrose's incredible discovery. As the old saying goes, misery loves company, and these people want to spread their misery to another generation. A generation that doesn't deserve it!"

Kurt walked back to the podium and shifted his note cards. He stared at the top card for a moment then looked up at the jury. "I'd like to quote from a document we're all familiar with. In the Declaration of Independence, our founding fathers maintained that each of us has an inalienable right to 'life, liberty and the pursuit of happiness.' The reality, ladies and gentlemen, is that for a homosexual, it's hard to pursue happiness when you're ridiculed; when you have no chance of leading a normal life; when you're afraid to tell your own family who you really are. Liberty?" he scoffed, almost under his breath. "Gays still aren't at liberty to work wherever they please. They're not at liberty to live wherever they please, so, in short, it's certainly not the life our forefathers envisioned. What Dr. Penrose has discovered is a way out." Kurt slowly scanned the jury, meeting each eye. "That's right, a way out. A procedure to save future generations from the ridicule, the discrimination. We will prove to this court that the procedure is not only safe but it's also humane."

Kurt hesitated before he made his next statement. The same anguish he felt when Jonathan Sagar first named him lead attorney came surging back. He felt like a whore. In a way, he was. It wasn't that he was ashamed of what he was about to announce to the jury. He was ashamed that he was using it as one of his many cards in the deck, dealt to sway their thinking, dealt to garner their sympathy.

"When I tell you of the pain of being gay, I know what I'm talking about. I," he proclaimed, "am a homosexual."

Some of the jurors looked at him with surprise. Others looked puzzled as if to ask, so what? He felt silly for even bringing it up, but it was out there. Kelly started to rise to object, but before she could leave her seat, Norm Woodruff grabbed her arm. He pulled her ear close to his lips.

"Let him go," Norm urged quietly in her ear.

"But his personal experiences are irrelevant," Kelly almost shouted in a whisper through clenched teeth.

"I know that, but in this case, we might just give him enough rope to hang himself."

Kelly thought about it a moment. Perhaps Norm was right. She relaxed a bit. She listened to Kurt's sob story, reserving her right to object.

"As a homosexual, I can tell you that there are many of us who have dreamed of this moment. We've longed for the day when medicine would be able to put a stop to our plight. Being gay is not who I am. It's what I suffer through. Thanks to Dr. Penrose, countless children will never have to suffer through it again. As that great document states, the Loveport Baby has the inalienable right to life, liberty, and the pursuit of happiness. Through Dr. Penrose's miracle breakthrough, and with your help, he will. Thank you."

There was a slight murmur in the courtroom which was quelled by a menacing gaze from the bench. Judge Kincaid made some final notes to himself, checked his watch, then looked down over his courtroom.

"We'll take a break for lunch. This court stands in recess until two p.m." Judge Kincaid whacked the gavel once and left the courtroom.

27

The talking heads on the cable news channels jumped into action the moment the court recessed. Expert guests were eager to voice their opinions on the opening arguments. Those with preconceived positions on the issue eloquently defended their sides as well as the attorneys who represented those points of view.

Kelly Morris was criticized mostly because of her failure to break the chains of the podium. She got high marks for her passion and articulation of her message, but it was the general consensus from the pundits that she would have been more effective had she engaged the jury a little more. She was also chastised for her attire, criticism which came from the female commentators. Unless a male was completely outlandish, his dress or hairstyle rarely got any notice from the news media.

Kurt Ford was both slammed and praised for his admission to being gay. Supporters of the Penrose Project spoke of his courage to share that intimate facet of his life with the jury while taking the chance that it might backfire. Critics of the project called Kurt's confession nothing more than a cheap ploy to garner the sympathy of the jury. It opened wide the doors of criticism that the defense team had pushed Kurt into the limelight simply because he was gay. To his detractors, Kurt would have to go the extra mile in proving he was worthy of such extraordinary responsibility. Other than the bombshell that he dropped, both sides agreed that Kurt's opening argument held little substance, only a promise of things to come.

Like him or not, the greatest accolades from both sides were reserved for Norm Woodruff. He was down-to-earth without being too casual. He spoke on the jury's level without pandering. Despite the agenda either side had coming into the trial, Norm had made a compelling argument. He contended the most important factor was focusing on the best interest of the unborn child. Both sides agreed his contention was almost irrefutable.

After a long midday break, Judge Kincaid gaveled court back into session.

"Ms. Morris, you may call your first witness."

"The plaintiffs call Dr. Stanley Bernstein."

Dr. Bernstein, well-tanned, dressed smartly in a gray suit with a yellow tie, stood up from the crowd in the courtroom. His gait suggested a man of confidence, a successful man. He took the stand, tucked his tie inside his coat, placed his hand on the Bible, and took the oath.

"Dr. Bernstein, if you would for the court, give us your title," Kelly Morris said.

"Certainly. I'm Dr. Stanley Bernstein. I'm president of the American Psychiatric Association."

"Dr. Bernstein, are you gay?"

The doctor smiled slightly. "No, I am not. I have a wife and three children."

"The reason I asked is because I want this court to understand that you have no axe to grind when it comes to the issue of homosexuality. Is that correct?"

"That is correct."

"Have you had the opportunity to study this issue to any degree?"

"Indeed, I have. A colleague of mine, Dr. Webster, and I have done extensive research into this area. In fact, we have just released the results of our study which will be published next week in The American Psychiatric Journal," he stated proudly.

"And what conclusions did you draw?"

"We came to the same conclusion that the American Psychiatric Association has maintained for many years."

"And that is?"

"That homosexuality is not a mental disorder. That it is, in fact, as much a part of who that person is as heterosexuality is to someone straight. In other words, it's a natural condition and not some deviant behavior that needs to be changed through therapy."

Kelly Morris took two steps back to her table and picked up a photocopy of an article. "Dr. Bernstein, I'm going to read a passage from a statement on homosexuality released in 1994 by the American Psychological Association. In that statement they said, and I quote, 'The research on homosexuality is very clear. Homosexuality is neither mental illness nor moral depravity. It is simply the way a minority of our population expresses human love and sexuality. Study after study documents the mental health of gay men and lesbians. Studies of judgment, stability, reliability, and social and vocational adaptiveness all show that gay men and lesbians function every bit as well as heterosexuals. Research findings suggest that efforts to repair homosexuals are nothing more than social prejudice garbed in psychological accouterments.' Do you agree or disagree with that assessment?"

"I totally agree. And if I may add?"

"Please."

"Our research found that not only are homosexuals perfectly normal in every sense of the word, but efforts to change them, whether that be through psychotherapy or medically, for instance, through the introduction of more testosterone to their systems, are quite detrimental to the individual."

"Thank you, Dr. Bernstein. No further questions, Your Honor."

Judge Kincaid looked to Kurt Ford who decisively approached the witness stand. "Dr. Bernstein, you say you're president of the American Psychiatric Association?"

"That's correct."

"And you're thoroughly convinced in your mind that the Association's position on homosexuality is 100 percent correct?"

"I am," he answered cautiously.

"Absolutely? Without a doubt?"

"Without a doubt."

"I see," Kurt ran his fingers through his hair as he read over the sheet of paper in his hand. He then looked up at the doctor with a quizzical expression. "Do you have any expertise in genetics, Dr. Bernstein?"

The doctor hesitated, "If you mean am I well-read on the subject then yes, I would have to say that—"

"That's not what I mean, Dr. Bernstein. Let me be more specific. Do you have any degrees that would qualify you to do genetic research?"

"Objection, Your Honor," Kelly Morris said. "We've established Dr. Bernstein's area of expertise. Mr. Ford is attempting to embarrass the witness."

Kurt smiled at Kelly's attempt to distract him. "I'm not trying to embarrass the witness, Your Honor. I'm trying to demonstrate the boundaries of that expertise so the court might decide whether or not he's qualified to answer the questions fully."

Judge Kincaid paused a moment. "Objection overruled. Proceed, Mr. Ford."

"Dr. Bernstein, do you have any degrees that would qualify you to do genetic research?"

"No," he answered reluctantly.

"Then the scope of your study only included data you gathered from a psychiatric or psychological viewpoint. Is that correct?

"That's correct."

"No genetic research was used in your study. Is that correct?"

"Correct."

"So staying within your area of expertise, it's your judgment that homosexuality is normal and that's the official position of the American Psychiatric Association?"

"That's right."

"Dr. Bernstein, have you ever heard of a publication entitled the

'Diagnostic and Statistical Manual of Psychiatric Disorders?'"

Dr. Bernstein looked pale. He swallowed hard. "Yes, I have and I know—"

"I'm looking at a copy of this publication from 1973. Do you know whether or not homosexuality is included in this manual?"

Dr. Bernstein hesitated. "Back then, I believe it was."

"It was indeed, Dr. Bernstein. The American Psychiatric Association, the organization of which you are president, as recently as 1973 classified homosexuality as a sexual deviation, a mental illness. Is that correct?" Kurt walked back toward the defense table.

"That's right," Dr. Bernstein said under his breath.

Kurt swiveled to face the witness and cocked his ear. "I'm sorry, doctor. I couldn't hear you."

"I said, that's right," Bernstein snapped. "But you have to understand that the policy prior to 1973 was a mistake."

"A mistake? A mistake, Dr. Bernstein? Since around the turn of last century until 1973, the conventional wisdom was that homosexuality was a mental illness. That's some mistake, wouldn't you agree, Dr. Bernstein?"

"It was an error that was corrected," Bernstein said. "When we had more data, more understanding of homosexuality, our official position was changed accordingly."

"Is that to say the psychiatric community is capable of making mistakes?"

"Well, certainly, but we made great strides in those seventy-three years. There were some major breakthroughs, some great discoveries."

"Then tell me, Dr. Bernstein, how do we know that your recent study and the policy of the APA, without considering one shred of genetic evidence, by your own admission, won't be found to be a *mistake* in light of Dr. Penrose's discovery?"

Dr. Bernstein stared vacantly at Kurt Ford. He had no answer.

"Nothing further, Your Honor."

28

After Jack Hawkins had tailed Dr. Martin Whitaker to his classroom at the University of North Carolina, there was little else to do but snoop around town for any tidbit he might dig up. It would be hours before Whitaker emerged from the campus and resumed his private life. It was then that Hawkins might find a crumb to collect and feed Raven. He turned down Franklin Street and parallel parked his rental car. What in the world could I possibly find on the head of the psych department, he wondered. His background check had turned up nothing, not even a speeding ticket. His credit check was unblemished. Whitaker lived alone, so adultery, the staple of the dirty tricks business, was out. Hawkins feared if he returned to Washington empty-handed, Raven would look elsewhere for information.

He pulled on his Vantage Menthol while he strolled by the various shops and restaurants which lined Franklin Street. Then something caught his eye. In the display window of the book store was one of Whitaker's books. Hawkins extinguished his smoke and stepped inside. He was informed by the clerk that the book he spied was one of four by Whitaker. Hawkins bought them all then carried his package back to the rental car. He had seven hours to kill. He settled in for some intensely boring reading.

The large empty sanctuary of Peachtree Grove Baptist Church lay silent. The pews, which normally sat better than a thousand, seemed to swallow the image of Dr. Lucius Gaylord. Inconspicuously tucked away in the corners, the television cameras, which carried his message to the masses each Sunday, were covered. The pulpit from which he'd preached a multitude of sermons was bare, cold, quiet, of no help in solving the mystery that occupied his mind these interminable days and sleepless nights. He sat about a third of the way back looking up at the huge, wooden cross on the wall behind the pulpit. He concentrated on that cross and all it stood for and searched his soul for the answers to his questions. Could the Bible be wrong? Was homosexuality really an abomination as it said, or was that merely the opinion of men, somehow filtered into the translations and passed down as the Word of God? His heart ached. He couldn't seem to get past this very troubling contradiction. Why would his loving God make a creature with such an affliction as homosexuality then condemn him for acting as he was created? It made no sense. His mind relived the Sundays when he preached God's damnation for homosexuality. His vitriolic words replayed in his mind. His personal distaste sharpened the rhetoric and cut deeper than necessary. Homosexuality was wrong. He was sure of it. Everything about it disgusted him. He had tried to keep the focus on the sin and not the sinner, but sometimes, his aversion to the act drove him to personal attacks. Now he tried to imagine just what the sinner was going through. If God made them homosexuals, weren't they more to be pitied than condemned? Were they the modern-day lepers whom the Church had cast into the outer darkness? Dr. Gaylord bowed his head and prayed for guidance. If he was successful in stopping Dr. Penrose from going forward with his procedure, which he felt in his heart was the right course of action, he would surely have to deal with the alternative. He might also have to confront the reality that he had been wrong all along, a prospect for which he was not prepared.

The hotel into which the plaintiffs' legal team had been booked was the oldest in Loveport. The three-story eighteenth-century hotel was a personal favorite of Norm Woodruff, a spot where he and his late wife had vacationed on several occasions. Norm, dressed in khakis and a golf shirt, descended the grand staircase and took a right into the familiar small, dimly-lit bar. As he approached the bartender, he noticed Kelly Morris sitting all alone in a dark corner by the window in the almost empty room. She sat with a full glass of Chardonnay on the table, her forehead rested in her hand. Norm approached cautiously.

"Mind if I join you?"

Kelly looked up a bit startled, shook her head then returned her face to her hand.

"Come on," Norm encouraged. "It's not that bad."

"Damn! I should've known he'd go there." Kelly Morris was still beating herself up over the shellacking she took when Kurt Ford exposed the American Psychiatric Association's change in policy on homosexuality.

"Come on, it's just the first day," Norm said. "I don't think he did that much damage, anyway. The point is the psychiatric community has evolved past believing that homosexuality is a mental illness. That's all the jury will take away from that witness. Who cares what they used to think. This is their position now."

"Do you believe it?"

"Do I believe what?"

"Do you believe homosexuality is a mental illness?"

"What I believe isn't important," Norm hedged. "It's what the jury believes based on the evidence presented and, let me tell you, you presented the evidence. Forget it. Shake it off. If I were you, I'd bask in the glory of your opening argument. Now *that* was impressive. Your passion was incredible. That goes a long way with the jury, believe me."

Kelly seemed to perk up a bit. "You weren't too bad yourself. I'd never seen you work before. You really have a way of connecting with a jury."

"Well, as the late, great George Burns once said, 'The key to success in this business is sincerity and once you've learned to fake that, you've got it made.'"

Kelly chuckled uncharacteristically. A server approached the table. "Can I get you something from the bar, sir?" she asked.

"Yes, a whiskey sour, please."

She turned and left to fill his order, and Norm helped himself to the peanuts on the table. Kelly smiled deviously. "Would Dr. Gaylord approve?" she asked.

"Let me tell you, the good doctor would probably join me after a day like today." He popped another peanut into his mouth from his fist.

Kelly smiled and took a sip of her wine. "Thanks," she said softly.

"For what?," he asked over crunches of peanuts.

"For pulling me out of my funk. I guess I tend to overreact sometimes."

"Yeah, I noticed."

Kelly looked down. "I'm sorry about jumping you the other day," she said, looking up. "I was out of line."

"Forget it." The waitress returned with Norm's drink and placed it on a cocktail napkin in front of him. He thanked her and she left. "You seem to take this cause of GALLANT's very seriously." He took a sip of his drink.

The smile left her face. "This is the second great struggle of my lifetime. I was too young to participate in the first. I don't intend to miss the second."

"Do you really equate the gay rights movement with the civil rights movement?"

Kelly became immediately defensive. She opened her mouth to speak.

"I'm not trying to start an argument," Norm insisted. "I'm asking because I'm seriously curious."

Kelly seemed to accept that. "I see them as equal, yes."

"I don't understand how that can be," Norm said. "Black people in this country were treated like second-class citizens or worse. They weren't allowed to live where whites lived. In many parts of the South, they weren't even allowed to use the same bathroom as whites or drink from the same water fountains. That's nothing like any discrimination gay people have had to endure."

"Look, gay people have been ostracized, beaten, even murdered just because they're gay. I think they've earned a place at the table of the oppressed. But I guess I shouldn't expect a white heterosexual man to understand hardship and suffering."

Norm tried to keep a lid on his temper. He took a long sip of his drink. "What did your parents do for a living?"

"Mine?"

"Yeah."

"My father's parents were sharecroppers in rural Georgia. I'm talking about dirt poor. My grandfather was determined that his sons would have a better life than he'd had. My dad was the oldest of four boys and as soon as Daddy was born, Grandpa started putting away money for his college education. His 'ticket' as Grandpa used to call it. As much as he tried to save, Grandpa and Grandma just couldn't seem to put away a dime before some emergency would come up and they'd be back down to nothing. But Grandpa was bound and determined that his boys would get their ticket somehow, some way. So, he made sure they hit the books. No sports, no girls, no nothing before their studies were done. My father says Grandpa was so strict he used to hate him for it. It was only after he was grown that he came to realize that Grandpa knew the only way those boys were going to school was on a scholarship because he sure couldn't afford to send them. Grandpa's persistence paid off when my dad was accepted to Albany State. Back then the choices for a black man were slim, even slimmer for a black woman." Kelly smiled, remembering her father telling the story. "Lord, Daddy says that was the happiest he had ever seen his father, the day he got that 'ticket' in the mail. Daddy went on to graduate then was accepted into law school. After law school, he came back home and practiced in a little firm in Atlanta until he retired a few years ago. He met my mother at Albany State. They fell in love, dated most of their undergrad years. Got married his first year of law school. She had a teacher's degree and went to work to pay his way through law school. She taught school until my older sister was born, then she stayed home to raise the two of us." Kelly took another sip of her Chardonnay. "You asked me a simple question and here I've rambled on and on."

"No, that's fine. I enjoyed hearing it." Norm lifted his glass to his lips and finished off the last of his whiskey sour. "You must be proud of your father for how far he came in such a short time."

"I am." Kelly's mood was upbeat again. "How about your folks?" she asked, trying not to be so self-absorbed.

"Aw, you really don't want to hear about them."

"I do," Kelly smiled. "I really do."

Norm looked at her for a moment and assessed her sincerity. Satisfied there was an ample amount to justify his opening up, he began. "My father was a truck driver. A long hauler. He drove the route from Atlanta to Dallas round trip about once a week. It was a straight shot down I-20. He'd made the trip dozens of times. When you drive the same route over and over, you start to pick out your favorite spots to stop, or eat, or sleep. You know. One of my dad's favorites was a truck stop just outside of Shreveport. He used to eat there quite often, refuel, even stopped to sleep there on occasion. Now, understand, my dad was no choir boy. He wasn't a bad guy, really, he was what was referred to in Georgia as white trash. Like a lot of truckers who spend long, lonely nights on the road, he was subject to the sins of the flesh. Late one rainy night in October, he pulled into that little truck stop in Louisiana and no sooner had he set the brake than a young lady was tapping on his door. Well, being the 'gentleman' my father was," Norm rolled his eyes, "he opened the door and she climbed in. Turned out she was a business girl, if you know what I mean. Now, it was cold out there in the October night and ole Dad didn't want to see her freeze to death, so he decided to listen to her sales pitch. She made him a proposition. He counter-offered, as any good Woodruff would do, and a price was agreed upon."

Kelly laughed. She had never heard such a tawdry tryst couched quite that way.

"Anyway, the business transaction was consummated, and the young lady showed herself to the door. He made the same trip dozens of times over the next year and every once in a while, when he was feeling lonesome, he'd pull in hoping that sweet, young thing was working the beat, but he never saw her. Then one day he happened to be low on fuel about the time he hit Shreveport. He was getting hungry anyway, so he decided to pull into that little truck stop. He walked inside, sat down, ordered his meal. He had long since given up on seeing that young lady again. Before his food came, a woman came busting through the door ranting and raving and asking him where the hell he'd been for the past year. My father was, naturally, taken aback. It was her. He'd gone out of his way to find her. Then she ran out of the restaurant and returned a minute later with a baby seat and a diaper bag and screamed, 'I can't take this anymore,' and left. My father looked down into that seat and he said it was like looking in a mirror. There was no doubt about it. That kid was his."

Kelly's face was filled with pity. "And that kid was you?"

Norm nodded. "I was a long hauler at three-months-old."

"What about your mother?"

"We never heard from or saw her again and it was probably best. My father was sorry enough. No sense in compounding the problem."

"That's incredibly sad. She just left you with your father? What did he do?"

Norm popped another peanut in his mouth. "Well," he continued as he chewed, "dear ole Dad took me home with him. Now, obviously I couldn't ride along each week while my father drove a truck, so during the week I stayed with an aunt who didn't much care for children and then with my father, who didn't want me, on the weekend."

"That must've been awful."

"Actually, it really lit a fire under me. I figured out real soon that if I screwed around in this life, I'd end up just like these people I was living with. Some kind of motivation, huh? Unlike your daddy, mine didn't give a crap about college. In fact, he didn't trust anyone with more than a high school education. So, I made good grades, kept my nose clean, and got accepted to the University of Georgia. I applied for financial aid and got some deferred loans. I worked at a pizza joint slinging beers to pay my expenses in college. Then I got into law school and started working part-time for a law firm. I ended up accepting a job with them when I got out and eventually made partner, and here I am."

Kelly took another sip of wine. "You make it sound so simple."

Norm turned serious. "I don't mean to. It was anything but. I hear people talking about the 'good old days' and I just laugh. There was nothing good about 'em. It was hard work just surviving. It seemed like an eternity before I ever got out of there."

"How in the world *did* you?"

"You've heard the old saying necessity is the mother of invention?" Norm leaned back in his chair. "Well, poverty and desperation are the parents of ambition. It doesn't take very long, walking around among the rotting humanity, before you can no longer stand the stench. And, let me tell you, if the day ever comes that you stop smelling it, you've become part of the rot." Norm pushed himself away from the table and pulled out several bills. "I apologize for leaving the mood in worse shape than I found it."

Kelly watched him as he laid the bills down next to his empty glass. "I can't imagine the childhood you went through," she confessed.

"I guess I shouldn't expect a lawyer's daughter to understand 'hardship and suffering.'"

Kelly looked down, embarrassed at hearing her own words thrown back at her.

"See you in the morning," he said then turned and headed off to the solitude of his room.

"A slam dunk for the defense today in the Loveport Baby trial," Duncan Reynolds gladly announced to the *The Pulse's* audience. "What was supposed to be a star witness for the plaintiffs turned into a witness, essentially, testifying for the defense. Dr. Stanley Bernstein, president of the American Psychiatric Association, admitted today that, up until 1973, his own organization regarded homosexuality as a mental illness."

"Big deal," Betty Duvall fired back. "That was 1973, Duncan. A lot's changed since then. Look at all of the advances we've made. Duncan, do you realize that in 1973, if a child was diagnosed with leukemia, his chance of survival was about five percent? Today, his chance of survival is better than eighty percent. As the old cigarette ad went, we've come a long way, baby. You can't fault the psychiatric community. Just look at the advances we've made since 1973. My God, computers, cell phones—"

"Don't forget the gay gene," Duncan added with a chuckle. "Come on, Betty. You're not willing to admit that if the shrinks were wrong once, they might be wrong again."

"No. What I'm saying is psychiatry is evolving. Dr. Penrose is *devolving*. He needs to get a clue. This is the twenty-first century. Just because he doesn't like something doesn't make it evil."

29

As soon as Dr. Penrose and Lauren slowed to turn into their driveway, the swarm was upon them. Hysterical faces screamed inaudible questions through every window. The scene so terrified Lauren that she had to look away. Once past the mob, they pulled under the portico and exited their vehicle while the sea of cameras and lights and reporters threatened to spill over the curb and into their yard. Several policemen now stood guard at the edge of the lawn to keep the overzealous press in check. Penrose was past the point of being cordial. He was beyond saying 'no comment.' He wrapped a protective arm around his wife and headed for the door. Once inside, he locked every lock and fastened the chain as if preparing for a full-scale assault. They both retreated to his office.

"Good Lord, Clark. We can't go on like this," Lauren said peering past the curtain at the hoard of reporters camped out in front of their house. "They've been out there for weeks now and they're not going anywhere until you give them what they want."

"They're not going anywhere regardless of what I tell them. You know I can't talk to the press."

"Look, Karen and Brandon can hardly make it out of here to go to school," she said still leaning with one knee on the sofa in Penrose's office looking out the window. "Every time I leave, they're on me like a swarm of bees." She closed the curtain.

"I know, I know." Penrose walked over to the desk and picked up the phone and punched in the number. "Yes, Dr. Penrose here. Dr. Kirsch, please." He held his hand over the mouthpiece and looked over at Lauren, talking in hushed tones. "Kirsch has to do something. This has *got* to end."

Lauren turned to look back out the window.

As soon as Kirsch picked up the phone, Penrose started in on him. "Roy, we've got to do something. These reporters have been living in my front yard for weeks and we just can't take it anymore."

"I know it's annoyin', Clark, but we need y'all to put up with it just a little while longer," Kirsch pleaded.

"What do you expect us to do in the meantime? We're prisoners inside our own home."

"I know what you must be goin' through. At least the press being there twenty-four hours a day provides a measure of protection."

"Protection? From what?"

Lauren's attention whipped from the scene outside to the telephone conversation. "What's he talking about?"

Penrose stuck a finger in his ear to block her out.

"There have been some death threats from some gay rights extremists," Kirsch explained.

"What?"

"Well, what'd you expect? You thought this was gonna be a cakewalk? You knew this was gonna be controversial when you started. We talked about that in my office, remember?"

"I knew it was going to be controversial, but I guess I didn't know just *how* controversial. What about my family?"

"The police don't feel these threats are anything to take too seriously. Just some kooks takin' advantage of the moment. They've got a couple of officers assigned to your house. But if you'd feel safer, we'll move y'all someplace where the press won't find you."

"I don't know, Roy. I don't want to be run out of my own house."

"Suit yourself. Hang in there, partner."

Penrose returned the phone to the cradle.

"Who do we need protection from?" Lauren demanded.

Penrose looked up from the desk. "It's nothing. Just some nuts trying to scare me off the project," he said casually, running both hands up over his face and down the back of his head.

"Nothing? Clark, if we're being threatened, I think I have a right to know!"

"It's nothing, I said!" Penrose slammed his fist on the desk.

Lauren's eyes filled with tears. "I don't know if I can handle all this," she whispered, trying to fight back the tears.

He rose from his seat, walked around the desk, and pulled her close. "I'm sorry," he said quietly. "I know this is tough on you, too. We have to do something to relieve the pressure. Roy has offered to put us up at a hotel until the trial's over, even beyond if necessary. We probably should take him up on it."

"I'm not going to let these people run me out of my own house," Lauren insisted. "Just, please, give them what they want and make them go away."

Penrose cradled her in his arms like a child. He hoped his protective embrace would comfort her at least through another day.

Everyone associated with the Loveport trial was assembled in the conference room of CC&D. Kurt Ford, who called the meeting on behalf of Jonathan Sagar, sat to the right of the head which remained vacant. The early forecast for the office called for a storm moving in from the direction of Sagar's office. One of the secretaries caught a glimpse of Sagar before he locked himself in his office with instructions to hold all calls. He was not happy. Kurt vouched for the secretary. The usual banter, typical just prior to a meeting, was replaced with cold silence.

The conference door bolted open. The storm had arrived. Jonathan Sagar didn't bother sitting down. He was too agitated. He just glared at the group from over the top of the high-back chair.

"Somebody's talking to the press." His eyes were on fire. "I don't know who and I don't know why, but your actions could jeopardize this case. I'm only going to say this once." When he paused, the muscles in his jaw bulged. His lips pursed together and his nostrils flared. "If anybody in this firm is guilty of violating that gag order, you will be fired immediately, and I will personally turn you over to Judge Kincaid to face contempt charges! This kind of conduct will not be tolerated!" He turned on his heels and left, shoving the chair aside. It spun round and round as the stunned staff all took a collective gulp.

It was five p.m. on the nose when the phone rang in Jack Hawkins' modest Washington office. He picked it up midway through the first ring. He knew exactly who it was. Raven called him every day at five to check his progress.

"I've got another name for you," the eerie electronic voice informed him.

Hawkins squinted as the smoke from the cigarette in his mouth burned his eyes. He held the phone on his shoulder with his head, steadied the pad with his left hand, and wrote with his right. "OK. Shoot."

"Dr. Frank Bomar," the distorted voice told him. "He's a pediatric surgeon at Children's Hospital in Philadelphia."

"You know anything about him?"

"That's what I'm paying you for," Raven said. "We don't have much time."

"I'm on it."

"Do you have anything on Whitaker for us yet?"

"It's all in the locker at the station," Hawkins said.

"Excellent. Someone will retrieve it this evening. Your expenses for your North Carolina trip and an advance for your next case will be in the locker by morning. Don't check it before seven a.m. tomorrow."

"Understood."

Raven hung up.

Kurt Ford was pouring over the next day's witness roster and fine-tuning his cross-examination long after the office had closed. Even though it was after hours, the office buzzed like it was ten in the morning. Paralegals, secretaries, and lawyers scurried throughout the entire eleventh floor, piecing together this very complex case. Bill Dumaine knocked on the door frame of Kurt's open door.

"Got a minute?" he asked.

Kurt stretched his arms then rubbed his eyes, happy to get a momentary break from the grueling work. "Sure. Have a seat."

"I know we're working at a war time urgency around here, but I need to take a quick trip back home to Michigan."

Kurt knew Dumaine wouldn't leave unless it was something very important. "Everything OK?"

"Yeah. Yeah, everything's fine. There's just something that I have to take care of. Something I should've done a long time ago."

"Hey, look, we've been working pretty hard. You need at least one day off. Sure, that's fine. When did you want to go?"

"Well, we're not scheduled for court this coming Monday. I can get a connecting flight that gets me up there Sunday afternoon. I'll come back Monday."

"Sure," Kurt said. "Go ahead."

"I, uh. I also want you to know that I was impressed with you in court today. I mean, you were cool as a cucumber when you nailed that shrink to the wall. Did you see his face when you asked him if it was possible his organization had made a mistake? He didn't know what in the hell to say!"

Kurt stared back at him with a cynical face. He didn't trust him, especially a Bill Dumaine bearing compliments. "We'll get a chance to see how cool *you* are tomorrow," Kurt said.

"What do you mean?"

"Tomorrow it's you up there."

"Me? Why me?" Dumaine was almost panicked.

"Dr. Proctor's on the stand. Proctor's your boy. You've researched him. You know all about him. Only makes sense you should cross-examine him."

Dumaine smiled nervously. "You don't have to do this. This is a big case and you're the man. You cross him."

"And jeopardize the case? Not a chance. Jonathan's always taught me that one of the tricks to being a good lead attorney is knowing everyone else's strong suits. You're a talented attorney."

Dumaine shifted from one foot to the other. "I'll try to live up to the hype."

30

Estelle Wooten had become sort of a den mother to the jury. Anyone with problems naturally gravitated to her for a sympathetic ear. Her job as foreman had been augmented to include troubleshooter, quartermaster, and nursemaid. Anything the jurors needed from the outside world, any complaint they had, Estelle was the one asked to handle it. Ordinarily one would grow tired of holding the hands of eleven other grown-ups but Estelle reveled in it. Her newfound authority gave her a feeling of importance the likes of which she'd never known.

Estelle and the other jurors waited in the jury box for the day's proceedings to begin. There was a lot more down time than she ever imagined. In the movies, it seemed to flow so quickly, so succinctly. In reality, it was incredibly laborious. The wheels of justice did, indeed, turn slowly. She sat there observing the players and trying to figure out who had the biggest ego. It must be the judge, she decided. The judgeship was the closest thing the country had to an absolute monarchy. The robe, the title, the pomp that surrounded his every move in the courtroom. Everyone was required to stand in his presence and address him as 'Your Honor.' What he said was the last word. Anyone who questioned it or showed him any disrespect could be held in contempt and thrown in jail. He was the all-powerful king of the courtroom. Estelle studied Judge Kincaid's face. She interpreted his smiles to the jury as condescending and patronizing, like he was addressing a group of kindergartners. Estelle could only imagine what the pompous windbag thought of her being named foreman. He passed judgment not only on the cases which came before him, but, Estelle figured, on everyone upon whom his steeling gaze was cast. But there was someone else in that courtroom who could challenge the judge's grip of absolute dominion. The only other person there who came close to wielding as much power as he, she thought, was the foreman. She planned not to squander this rare opportunity.

"Please state your name for the court, sir," Norm Woodruff instructed the bespectacled little man with the bow tie on the witness stand.

"My name is Dr. Evan Proctor," he answered obediently.

"Dr. Proctor, what is your title?"

"I am a professor emeritus from the Harvard Biological Laboratories."

"And you've had some experience with genetics?"

"Extensive experience. I've written three books and countless published articles on the subject."

"You also sit on the board of the American Society of Genetic Ethicists, is that right?"

"I do."

"What is the ASGE's position on the Penrose Project?"

"The board voted unanimously some time ago that it would be fundamentally unethical to take the technology of discovering a gay gene and use that knowledge to alter a person's sexual orientation from homosexual to heterosexual, or vice versa, for that matter."

"I see," Norm replied as he tugged on his chin. "Is Dr. Penrose a member of the ASGE?"

"Yes, he is."

"And he's aware of the policy of the ASGE?"

"I should say so. Dr. Penrose was one of the few geneticists who wrote letters disagreeing with the board's decision."

"On what grounds?"

"On the grounds that he believed homosexuality to be a disease."

There was a murmur in the courtroom. Norm made sure he didn't continue until it had died down. He wanted the jury to get the full impact. The judge banged the gavel once and restored order.

"A *disease*. He used that exact word, disease?"

"Yes, he did."

"Do you believe homosexuality to be a disease, Dr. Proctor?"

"Of course not," he smirked. "No doctor worth his salt believes that."

Kurt Ford came out of his seat. "Objection, Your Honor. The doctor isn't stating fact, just his view of doctors who don't share his opinion."

"Sustained," Judge Kincaid ordered. "Dr. Proctor, you will stick to answering the questions, not speculating on other principals or witnesses in this case unless asked directly to do so."

"Yes, Your Honor," Dr. Proctor answered timidly.

"As a geneticist yourself," Norm continued, "are you familiar with Dr. Penrose's experiments?"

"Yes. I have followed them quite closely, well, as closely as one can. He's been very secretive about them. But I have friends inside Loveport who have shared information with me from time to time. I also made it a point to read his full report since all this went public."

"Knowing what you know about Dr. Penrose's gene therapy experiments, would you say it's safe to try this gene-altering procedure on humans?"

"I should say not."

"And why not?"

"I believe much more research needs to be done. I mean, he's only performed this procedure on one orangutan and a handful of dogs. What's even more disturbing is one of the dogs died."

An audible gasp swept through the courtroom.

"One of the dogs in Dr. Penrose's experiment died?" Norm asked, confirming the ugly revelation.

Kurt Ford whipped around to Penrose in a panic. "Is that true?" he whispered firmly, leaning back over the railing.

"Yes, but it had nothing to do with my experiments," Penrose whispered in frustration.

Kurt didn't know all the details and he didn't have time to learn them now. What he *did* know was that he couldn't let this line of questioning continue. They had just been torpedoed and they were taking on water. Kurt quickly twisted forward in his seat. "Your Honor, may I approach the bench, please?"

Norm was stopped in mid-sentence. "Your Honor, I'm not through questioning the witness."

"Your Honor, this line of questioning may be irrelevant to the case. I would like a moment to discuss it, please."

Judge Kincaid, who was as intrigued as anyone by the latest revelation, pondered the situation for a moment. "Both attorneys approach the bench," he instructed.

Kurt Ford was frantic as he whispered up to the judge. "Your Honor, the death of this dog had nothing to do with my client's experiments."

"What else could it have been?" Norm countered.

"There's a very logical explanation."

"Well, what is it?" Kincaid asked.

Kurt glanced back at Penrose. "I need some time to talk with my client."

"Your Honor, he's just trying to derail this testimony," Norm insisted. "He doesn't have an explanation. He's just trying to buy some time, to stall so he can think up an excuse."

Kurt was beet-red in the face with anger. He leered at Norm then looked back up at Kincaid. "Your Honor, my client tells me the death of this dog had nothing to do with his experiments. The court owes us a little time to explain why the dog died."

"All right, both of you just calm down," Judge Kincaid ordered. He looked at his watch. "It's getting pretty close to lunchtime anyway." He leaned back up and addressed the courtroom. "This court stands in recess until two o'clock." He banged the gavel once and exited to the judge's chambers.

The lunchroom at the courthouse had been declared off limits to anyone but court personnel by order of Judge Kincaid so Kurt Ford was allowed to speak with his client without the glare of camera lights and the pestering of reporters. "All right. Tell me about the dog." He hated surprises.

"The dog Proctor is talking about didn't die because of any experiment we did. She *did* die while she was pregnant with the gene-altered fetus and we, of course, feared it might have been associated with the gene therapy. We did an autopsy and found she had a rare canine blood disease, totally unrelated to anything we did."

"Why didn't you tell me about this?" Kurt was visibly irritated.

"Because it had nothing to do with our experiments and would only put doubt in someone's mind about the safety of our project."

"Well, now the doubt's in that jury's mind!" He glanced around the cafeteria then lowered his voice. "If I'd known about this before the big surprise this morning," Kurt lectured through clenched teeth, "I could've diffused it before it blew up in our faces."

The two men sat in silence for a moment while Kurt calmed down.

"Do you have proof of this blood disease?" Kurt asked.

"Absolutely. It's in my file back at the lab. Carol can pull it for you right now."

"Great." Ford grabbed his cell phone from his briefcase and dialed up the office.

"Janet, this is Kurt. Call Pam Dixon. She's somewhere in the vicinity of the federal building. Have her run by Dr. Penrose's lab at Loveport and pick up a file from his lab assistant. Her name is Carol Boyce. Have her bring it back to me here at the courthouse within the next forty-five minutes. Thanks." He punched the 'end' button on the phone.

"Any other surprises that I need to know about?" Kurt had a tinge of sarcasm in his voice.

Kurt hurried down the hallway of the courthouse. He had called for the meeting in the judge's chambers. Also present were Kelly Morris, Norm Woodruff, Rex Randle, and Eleanor Henson, the court reporter. The judge looked over the file from Penrose's lab.

"Your Honor, the questioning into this area is inappropriate and irrelevant," Kurt insisted. "The dog in question died of a rare blood disease. It had nothing to do with Dr. Penrose's experiments."

"How do we know that?" Norm asked. "We're going on Dr. Penrose's word. For all we know he's trying to cover up the fact that his experiment went awry."

"Dr. Penrose's honesty is beyond reproach," Kurt shot back. "Motion to suppress, Your Honor."

"Denied," Judge Kincaid answered without hesitation. "The death of this dog may or may not have anything to do with Dr. Penrose's experiments, but I think it's certainly relevant and should be hashed out in the courtroom."

"I request a twenty-four-hour delay," Kurt pleaded.

"Denied," he said as quickly as the first time. "As for Dr. Penrose's integrity, he'll get a chance to defend himself when he takes the stand. Now, let's not keep everyone waiting any longer. Shall we?" Kincaid motioned toward the door with his robed arm.

"Dr. Proctor," Norm began as court resumed, "you say that one of the dogs on which Dr. Penrose was experimenting died?"

"That's right," Dr. Proctor said smugly.

"Had Dr. Penrose performed his so-called gene-altering experiment on the fetus this dog was carrying?"

"Yes. From what I read in the report, one of the puppies this dog was carrying tested positive for the gay gene."

"As a geneticist, any chance the experiment which Dr. Penrose was conducting had anything to do with the death of this dog?"

"Objection!" Kurt shouted. "The witness is speculating."

Norm jumped to his defense. "The witness is a doctor, Your Honor. He's fully qualified to answer any question regarding the risk of experiments."

"Objection overruled."

"Dr. Proctor, any chance Dr. Penrose's experiments killed that dog?"

"Well, sure. Anytime you experiment with gene-therapy it's hard to tell what might happen. That's why we do experiments on lab animals before we dare try these procedures on humans."

"Do you know how many of these dogs Dr. Penrose experimented on?"

Dr. Proctor thought for a moment. "As I recall, his published study stated there were six dogs."

"Six dogs," Norm seized on the number. "Let's see now. That means it's possible that something went seriously wrong in better than 15% of these experiments?"

"That's correct."

"In your estimation as a scientist, in a controlled environment like the lab, are those pretty good odds?"

"Those are lousy odds," Proctor said. "It would be one thing if Dr. Penrose had learned from the death of the dog and corrected accordingly, but there's no such indication in his papers."

"Objection, Your Honor! The witness is speculating again," Kurt insisted.

"Overruled!"

"No more questions." Norm returned to his seat. Kelly gave him a squeeze of congratulations on his arm, out of sight of the judge.

Bill Dumaine was a bit nervous. It was difficult enough that this was such a high-profile case and this was his first day at cross-examination, but to have this hitch to contend with was almost too much. His whole list of prepared questions would have to take a back seat until they could put out this fire. He was shooting from the hip.

"Dr. Proctor, are you familiar with a canine disease by the name of

Primary Autoimmune Hemolytic Anemia?"

"Vaguely, yes."

"And what are the symptoms of this disease? Do you know?" Dumaine prodded.

"I'm a geneticist, not a veterinarian."

"I understand. I'll tell you. Primary AIHA destroys the animal's red blood cells for no apparent reason. The symptoms include possibly pale gums, maybe red or orange-brown urine, but the animal might look normal. As a geneticist, there's a good chance you wouldn't know Primary AIHA if you saw it. Is that true?"

"Well, I'm not sure."

"Dr. Proctor, you just stated that you didn't even know the symptoms, so if the symptoms were not apparent, isn't it safe to say that you wouldn't recognize the disease?"

"I guess that would be true."

"The dog in question, the one that died during Dr. Penrose's experiment, were you aware this dog had Primary AIHA?"

"No, I was not."

"Oh, yeah," Dumaine confirmed, "Dr. Penrose and a veterinarian performed an autopsy. Here's the report, right here." He held up the file for the jury to see. "Did you read the autopsy report, Dr. Proctor?"

"No, I did not."

"You didn't read the autopsy report, yet you speculate before this court on what might have killed that dog?"

Proctor said nothing.

"In all of your years in genetic research, Dr. Proctor, have you ever heard of a genetic experiment causing this disease?"

"Oh, well, as I stated before, there are so many unknowns when it comes to genetics. We're just starting to scratch the surface, really."

"You didn't answer the question, Dr. Proctor. The question was: in all of your years in genetic research, have you ever heard of a genetic experiment causing this disease?"

Dr. Proctor was slow to answer. He looked up at the judge hoping Kincaid would intervene and not make him answer the question. Dumaine waited impatiently, his eyebrows raised, his arms outstretched as if waiting to catch the answer in his hands.

"No," Proctor answered curtly, "but we really—"

"Thank you. You see, Dr. Penrose and the vet conducting the autopsy," he looked at the file for the name, "Dr. Zucker, both concluded that the death of this dog was totally unrelated to Dr. Penrose's experiments and, in fact, this whole dog business is a red herring."

Dr. Proctor stared at him expressionless.

"Let's talk ethics, Dr. Proctor. You've stated for this court that you sit on the board for the American Society of Genetic Ethicists."

"That's right."

"Ethically, has the board ever found it appropriate to alter a gene?"

"Certainly. If there is a genetic defect, the board whole-heartedly endorses a procedure to correct it."

"I see. Dr. Proctor, how would a condition qualify for your endorsement?"

"I'm not sure I follow."

"What are the criteria set forth as cause for altering a gene?"

"I suppose it depends on the individual situation."

"Well, for instance, a genetic disorder of some kind would qualify, correct?"

"Yes."

"Dr. Proctor, would you consider homosexuality a disorder?"

"Absolutely not," he replied, almost laughing.

Dumaine grabbed a dictionary from the defendant's table and opened it to a book-marked page. "I'm reading now from Webster's New World Dictionary. Disorder — an upset of normal function." He closed the book. "An upset of normal function," he repeated. "Biologically speaking, what is the normal function of the act of sexual intercourse?"

Dr. Proctor shifted in his seat. "Well, um, any number of things. To bring pleasure."

"*Biologically* speaking, Dr. Proctor. And I'll remind you, you're under oath."

"Biologically speaking, I would say the basic function is to procreate."

"It would be fair to say that since the act of homosexuality cannot fulfill that basic function that it deviates somewhat from the normal function of sexual intercourse?"

"Well, uh, as I stated, the sexual act is also used to bring pleasure."

Dumaine hammered home. "We're not talking about bringing pleasure, Dr. Proctor, we're talking about the basic function of sexual intercourse and homosexual sex does not meet the requirements of that basic function. Is that correct?"

"I suppose so."

"Going back to Webster's definition, I'll read it to you again," he offered as he flipped the dictionary open. "Disorder — an upset of normal function. In homosexuality, the normal function — in this case procreation — has been upset; therefore, it fits the definition of a disorder. Is that correct?"

Dr. Proctor felt defeated. "I suppose so, in this particular case, but—"

"Then it would stand to reason if your organization, the ASGE, endorses altering genes in the case of a genetic disorder, then it would endorse the Penrose Project." Dumaine walked back to the table and set the dictionary down allowing his line of reasoning to sink in with the jury. After a moment, he turned back to the witness stand. "It seems you find yourself at odds with your own organization, Dr. Proctor." He looked at the jury then up at the judge. "Nothing more, Your Honor."

31

Don Bissette sat alone at his computer. The newsroom was buzzing with people scurrying about in preparation for the next newscast. Bissette typed feverishly trying to meet his deadline. The phone on his desk rang. He almost ignored it then decided to pick it up, hardly missing a beat on the keyboard. He stopped everything. He glanced around the room then lowered his voice. Bissette scrambled for a pen and pad and started writing. He dared not enter the information on his keyboard. Someone could've been tapped into it. He was taking no chances. Another witness. More dirty laundry. Bissette probed deeper, but the line went dead.

Bissette sat for a moment and contemplated taking the information to Michael Thomas, his news director. After all, his boss had received a fierce dressing down by the judge, heat which he promptly passed along to Bissette. Another unauthorized story over their air, and it was hard to say what might happen. Bissette hoped the station would go to bat for his First Amendment rights, but Thomas was a weasel. He had been a gopher for a large New York affiliate, gotten blown out but managed to parlay that brief brush with excellence into one news director's job after another. He dropped names and talked about the good old days in the big city until management finally figured him out and he would be sent packing to play the same game in a new market. Bissette imagined in a place like New York the news director would stand up for him. He certainly couldn't count on Thomas. Thomas was too spineless. Anyway, the story could wait. It would have its best impact if released at just the right time. Bissette had time to decide if it was worth the risk. He tucked the details in his shirt pocket and returned to the keyboard.

"Dammit!" Kelly's angst was drowned out by the din of the crowded bar. She and Norm sat at a small two-top trying to sort through the events of the day. Kelly had been in the same position for ten minutes, hands locked behind her head and staring down at a cheeseburger she hadn't even touched. Norm was more than halfway through his.

"Come on," he consoled between bites. "We gave it our best shot. We gave 'em a left hook and we knocked 'em down. They managed to get back on their feet and take a few jabs at us. That's not to say they won the round." Kelly didn't move. "We wounded 'em. That's all we could hope to do. We knew they'd rebut the dog thing. We just didn't think they'd recover so fast. Eat up. Your burger's getting cold," Norm instructed like a concerned father. He took another bite of his.

Kelly finally looked up. "It's not so much the dog thing. I knew we'd only get limited mileage out of that. It's their incredible comeback after that. Pummeling Dr. Proctor with the 'disorder' definition. Aw, it was brutal."

"You're not looking at the big picture. That was today. Tomorrow things could turn completely around. You can't relive each day over and over. We have to plan the next day's strategy."

"I know that." Kelly returned her eyes to her plate.

Norm chewed as he took a moment to examine her closely. "There's something else, isn't it?"

Kelly's eyes met his just for a moment, long enough to catch him peering into her soul. She felt so transparent.

"Kelly, listen to me." He moved closer. "You've got to be sure of yourself when you go back in there tomorrow. A jury can smell the uncertainty."

"I'm not sure of anything anymore," she shot back.

Norm backed off.

"Look, Dumaine not only got to Dr. Proctor today," she confessed, "he got to me, too. Tell me he didn't make a lot of sense to you."

"Hey, hey," Norm comforted, "this is not a black and white issue we're dealing with. There's a lot of gray area. Sometimes we're going to venture into that gray area and we're gonna find ourselves lost in it, but we have to be able to find our way out and back to our side."

"Do you ever wonder if we're doing the right thing?" Kelly asked, hoping for an honest answer.

"No," Norm responded emphatically. He chewed another bite of his burger. "Don't allow the other side to take your focus off the ball. Whether or not homosexuality is a disorder is not the issue. The issue is a doctor shouldn't make that determination. Neither should parents. If the child were severely deformed, then, yeah, it should probably be helped. Even if homosexuality is clinically a disorder, that doesn't mean it has to be changed. That jury's going to decide that the condition of homosexuality does not warrant being changed. Regardless of anyone's opinion of gays, it's indisputable that they certainly are quite capable of functioning perfectly well in society. Look at all the gay friends you have. Do they need changing?"

Norm's decisiveness helped to put Kelly somewhat at ease. They both turned their attention to the televisions spaced throughout the bar that, simultaneously, were broadcasting the nightly network news.

"Good evening," the anchor greeted after the fancy graphics of the show open. "We're going to begin tonight with an incredible story of courage in a remote section of the Sierra Nevada mountain range in eastern California."

Kelly and Norm looked at one another, confused. It was strange. Since the whole Loveport issue hit, it had taken center stage on the network news every evening. Now another story had knocked it from its perch?

"A young boy has overcome incredible odds and the elements," the anchor continued, "and he has man's best friend to thank. Cynthia Dunn has the story."

The reporter was wrapped in a thick, powder-blue parka with a white fur fringe. Her backdrop was the snow-capped mountains of

Sierra Nevada. Her warm breath plumed like smoke from a chimney in the cold air as she reported the dramatic story. "Twelve-year-old Jason Roth, missing for three days and feared dead, was found alive around one o'clock local time this afternoon as rescuers followed the barking of his golden retriever, Scout. As our viewers watched the story unfold live this afternoon, rescuers took a tip from a hunter who said he heard a dog frantically barking this morning. That was just after noon eastern time today." The report cut to aerial footage of the mountain range, the camera zooming in on the rescue team fanning out across the mountainside. "Just a couple of hours later, happy rescue personnel found young Jason lying under a pile of leaves with Scout on top to keep him warm. Apparently, the boy had been out hiking, got lost, then fell down a ravine breaking his leg. Tired and hungry, but aside from the broken leg, OK, Jason recounted the story of how his trusted friend saved his life."

The lost hiker gushed with the news of how Scout had kept him warm by night and searched for help by day, each time coming back to his master. Scout sat proudly at Jason's side, wagging his tail and hamming it up for the cameras while Jason recounted the ordeal.

"An incredible story of a boy and his trusted friend, a golden retriever named Scout, who never let him down. Cynthia Dunn, reporting from Sierra Nevada."

"Ironically," the anchor set up the next story, "the trial between Loveport University Medical Center and the gay rights organization GALLANT and the NCRA centered on a dog today. In a dramatic turn of events, a witness, Dr. Evan Proctor, a professor emeritus from the Harvard Biological Laboratories, he's the gentleman in the bow tie," the anchor pointed out from the video on the screen, "claimed one of Dr. Clark Penrose's experiments in gene therapy left a lab dog dead. The Loveport attorneys were quick with the damage control maintaining the dog died of a rare canine disease totally unrelated to the experiments. Still, the incident has cast a large shadow of doubt over whether a gene-altering procedure is safe for humans. Sam Brock with that story from the federal courthouse in Loveport."

A photograph of an adorable golden retriever, identical to the canine hero of the lead story, filled the screen as the reporter explained. "No, it's not Scout the wonder dog. It's Sandy, the experimental dog. This is one of the dogs whose supposedly gay puppy was experimented on in utero by Dr. Penrose of Loveport University. Dr. Evan Proctor, a geneticist himself and a board member of the American Society of Genetic Ethicists, testified today that this golden retriever, one of Dr. Penrose's lab dogs, died shortly after the gene-altering procedure, bringing into question the safety of the procedure."

The story cut to courtroom video. The reporter's voiceover told what happened leading up to the new revelation of the dog. Then, they went to a replay of a snippet of Dr. Proctor's testimony.

"I mean, he's only performed this procedure on one orangutan and a handful of dogs," Dr. Proctor said. "What's even more disturbing is one of the dogs died."

An audible gasp swept through the courtroom.

"One of the dogs in Dr. Penrose's experiment died?" Norm asked.

Reporter Sam Brock was back on screen. He played up the reaction to the dog's death and Kurt's frantic attempt to stop the testimony but failed to mention the name of the disease that killed the dog or that the autopsy report concluded it was unrelated to the experiment. Brock wrapped up the story then relinquished the screen to the anchor back in New York.

"In a moment, today's other news including reaction to America's latest hero, a dog named Scout." The bumper music and video dissolved into an advertisement for the latest cold relief.

Norm smiled a devilish grin, cocked his head, and held up his half-empty glass of Coke. "To Scout," he toasted.

Kelly smiled and touched her glass to Norm's. "To Scout." She then proceeded to devour her stone-cold cheeseburger.

"Unbelievable," Duncan Reynolds began the day's edition of *The Pulse*. "Of all the testimony that came out of the Loveport Baby trial today and the news media focus on a stupid dog. And how ironic that the dog that died — not from Dr. Penrose's experiment but from Primary AIHA, I might add — looks exactly like Scout, the hero in the rescue story that knocked the trial out for the lead story. I'll tell you what else is unbelievable. Almost all of the networks dropped the courtroom coverage of the trial to cover this stupid dog story."

Betty Duvall looked at Duncan with feigned hurt. "You're calling Scout a 'stupid dog.' That's what's wrong with you conservatives. No compassion." Duncan threw his hands up. "And don't tell me you think young twelve-year-old Jason Roth is part of some conspiracy to sway public opinion to the side of the plaintiff."

Duncan was incredulous. "Of course I don't, but, Betty, come on. Even *you* have to admit that the liberal-leaning news media used this story against the defendants."

"I'm not willing to admit any such thing. There was a breaking story and they covered it. It's a heart-warming story."

"How about the autopsy report? Not one network news broadcast mentioned that the autopsy report concluded Dr. Penrose's experiment had nothing to do with the death of that dog."

"That's because Dr. Penrose conducted the autopsy!"

"Dr. Penrose *and* a veterinarian, Betty! The networks conveniently left that little tidbit out."

"Nearly every one of us has had a dog like Sandy. If it weren't for Dr. Penrose, Sandy would still be alive."

Duncan's frustration level rose to the point of boiling over. "Not to mention the testimony the networks missed when they went to chase the rescue team! Dr. Proctor, the same guy who brought up this whole dog thing, finally had to admit that homosexuality was, by definition, a disorder and that the ASGE was in contradiction with itself over its policy toward gene altering when it comes to the gay gene! Not one mention of that on the news!"

"Didn't you ever own a dog, Duncan?"

"What?"

32

Kurt Ford steered his car as Bill Dumaine tried to reason with him. "It's not important. I'm telling you, the only thing that matters is what happens in that courtroom. Who gives a rat's ass how the media twist it?"

"I do!" Kurt fired back. "It's not the coverage. It's the fact that they didn't respond to the facts. All they cared about was that damn dog. If that's all they cared about, then that's all that jury cared about." He rested his elbow on the door and rubbed his aching head. They sat waiting for the traffic cop to signal them through the wall of people surrounding the courthouse.

"Come on, man." Dumaine stoked him up. "Give the jury a little more credit than that. If they're as inept as the news media we never stood a chance in the first place."

They pulled up to the front of the courthouse and eased forward toward the parking garage. While they waited to be cleared through, they observed the media circus. The same curiosity seekers and protesters were gathered, but their numbers had increased. Kurt Ford caught a glimpse of the placards being waved. They were all basically the same as before with one addition. In bold letters above a drawing of a golden retriever were the words 'REMEMBER SANDY.' Kurt shook his head, and the police officer motioned them into the garage.

Don Bissette did his stand-up in front of the federal building bringing the morning TV audience up-to-date on the trial. He recapped the events of the day before, concentrating not so much on the dog issue, but the defense's rebuttal to it. He went into great detail about the autopsy report that concluded the dog's death had nothing to do with Dr. Penrose's experiment.

Then, another bombshell. Bissette revealed that his sources close to the trial told him a prominent author would be testifying at the day's proceedings. His name was Dr. Martin Whitaker, a psychologist. His sources also told him that Dr. Whitaker had been sued for malpractice fifteen years earlier. He had been experimenting with something he called 'rebellion therapy,' a technique he had developed to help troubled youth, based on his days in theater during which he practiced Method Acting. During the course of the therapy, he encouraged his patients, who were minors, to act out their rebellion during his sessions. He played the part of the authority figure, whether it be a parent or a teacher. He prompted his patients to express their anger, to 'act through it' as he liked to say. Whitaker would videotape the kids then go over the tape with them. The theory was that when they saw themselves in the midst of their anger, they would be more objective and would have something tangible to deal with. It was much like taping a golfer's swing then letting him step back and see what he was doing wrong. Whitaker had even set up a stage, complete with props, in hopes of making the scene more realistic. It apparently became too real for one fifteen-year-old boy whose 'rebellion therapy' spilled over into real life. After one of Dr. Whitaker's sessions, he went home and emptied a revolver into his father's chest. The mother sued. Dr. Whitaker settled out of court for an undisclosed sum.

By the time Kurt and Bill parked the car, the story had spread through the building like wildfire. A clerk's assistant grabbed Kurt as soon as he entered the building and escorted him to the judge's chambers where a seething Judge Kincaid sat waiting. Kelly Morris sat with her legs crossed, agitatedly rocking her foot up and down as she stared at the floor. The fact that the court reporter was also there told Kurt something was seriously amiss.

"I thought you were going to plug the leak, Mr. Ford!" Kurt had never seen anyone as angry as Judge Kincaid.

"I did, Your Honor. I mean, we never found a leak in our office, but Mr. Sagar made it clear that he would fire anyone caught leaking and turn them over to you." He looked first at Kelly then back at the judge. "What's happened?"

"Oh, don't play innocent, Kurt," Kelly shouted. "You know damn well what's happened!"

"Miss Morris! If you don't mind," Kincaid interrupted, "I'll handle this. That reporter, Don Bissette, just leaked another witness, Dr. Whitaker. He also said a 'source close to the trial' had told him Dr. Whitaker was sued for malpractice some years back and settled out of court."

"Your Honor, I can assure you, I didn't leak anything to Bissette or anybody else. What motive would I have?"

"To intimidate this witness," Kelly answered, "and send a message to any other plaintiff's witness that if they testify in this trial, their personal life is subject to be broadcast all over the news."

"Look, I'll admit that we knew about the malpractice suit, but the leaks are not coming from my law firm, Your Honor! We have nothing to gain by leaking!"

"Mr. Ford, I'm going to hold Mr. Bissette in contempt. Maybe with the prospect of jail time staring him in the face he might be in the mood to help us get to the bottom of this. In the meantime, I'm suppressing the evidence of Dr. Whitaker's malpractice suit."

"But, Your Honor, that evidence is clearly relevant. It calls his credibility into question!"

"Mr. Ford," Kincaid shouted, "you are about two inches away from a mistrial! Unless you want to push this case over the edge, I suggest you back off! Dr. Whitaker's malpractice suit is inadmissible! Is that clear?"

Kurt didn't back down. "The defense requests to know on what grounds."

"Federal Rule of Evidence 403, Mr. Ford." Kincaid whipped the reading glasses on his face and read from the large law book on his desk. "Relevant evidence may be excluded if its probative value is substantially outweighed by the danger of unfair prejudice, confusion of the issues, or misleading the jury." He snatched the glasses from his nose and glared at Kurt.

Kurt slumped down in the seat in a huff. "Thank you, Your Honor."

"Today's proceedings will be delayed until two o'clock. In the meantime, I suggest you do more plugging, Mr. Ford."

In the short drive from the federal building back to the office, Kurt's rage had grown, not subsided. Someone was gumming up the works and he was convinced he knew who. Jonathan Sagar had heard about the morning report and was eager to debrief his lead attorney.

"It *has* to be him," Kurt insisted. "He was the one who told us about Whitaker's malpractice suit to start with."

"Proof, son. That's what we need. Not conjecture. That's a serious offense you're accusing him of. Without proof, I can't go confronting him with an accusation like that. Contempt of court and witness intimidation. Those are very serious charges."

Kurt was frustrated. He was positive his suspicions would be born out, but he also knew Sagar was right. He had to have something concrete before he opened his mouth or the repercussions would be serious.

"I have all I can handle as it is," Kurt pleaded. "I can't afford to waste precious resources trying to track down proof. Can't you at least have him shut down?"

Sagar laughed at the suggestion. "You *are* joking, aren't you? Of all the people involved in this trial, who's going to have the guts to try and shut him down?"

Don Bissette entered the newsroom the way he always entered, from the employees parking lot in the back of the building. He approached his desk, and the room went silent. All eyes were on him. Obviously, he had been the topic of discussion and, from the looks of his co-workers, that discussion had not been favorable. Michael Thomas, his news director, burst from his office. The top button of his dress shirt was unbuttoned and his tie was loose. His fat head was crimson. He didn't wait until he made it across the vast room to Bissette's cubicle to begin shouting.

"Bissette, you son-of-a-bitch! I warned you about those leaks." His chubby index finger repeatedly stabbed the air. Bissette tried to ignore him, but it was futile. Thomas was up in his face, the sausage-like finger poking his chest. "You're history, pal. There's a sheriff's deputy waiting in the lobby with a warrant for your arrest."

Bissette looked at him with dismay. "What did you tell him?"

"What'd I tell him?" Thomas laughed in his face. "I told him as soon as you got here, he could lock you up."

"Did you call our lawyers?"

Thomas couldn't believe it. Bissette obviously didn't understand. He wasn't even going to dignify that question with an answer. "Don't bother packing your things. I'll have somebody send 'em to you in jail, you pompous ass!"

"You're firing me?" In all his vanity, Bissette somehow thought the station would come to his defense and protect his Constitutional rights. No such luck. Thomas punched his ticket as the deputy cuffed him and hauled him away.

33

By the time court reconvened in the afternoon, tempers had calmed, and the attorneys could get back down to the business at hand. The jury was in its place, the judge had been announced, and Rex Randle called his first witness of the trial.

Dr. Frank Bomar was a pediatric surgeon from the Children's Hospital of Philadelphia, the best in his field. Rex had used him before in a trial against a couple he defended who had been stripped of their child by Social Services because of abuse. With the help of Dr. Bomar, Rex was able to prove that what looked like abuse was actually a rare medical condition that needed treatment. If Bomar hadn't been so instrumental in his winning the case, Rex probably wouldn't have put up with him. For starters, he was afraid to fly. Rex's office had to spend over an hour on the phone setting up connecting trains that worked with Bomar's schedule then had to, at the good doctor's insistence, meet him at the station and drive him to his hotel. He had a special diet that any hotel in which he stayed would have to accommodate. That took more of Rex's precious time finding one that would cooperate. Then there were the constant calls at home. My hotel doesn't carry the magazines I want, he whined. The TV doesn't carry the channels I want. It was like baby-sitting a spoiled two-year-old. Now, finally, Dr. Bomar was being sworn in.

Rex put him through the usual exercise of name, position, and credentials to establish his expertise. He made sure to point out some of the groundbreaking procedures the doctor had developed and perfected at the premier pediatric facility in the country. Any he left out, Dr. Bomar was quick to fill in.

"Dr. Bomar," Rex asked, "what criteria do you set for determining a candidate for in utero surgery?"

"We must first determine the ailment of the fetus and the chances we have of saving it. All that, of course, is weighed against the current health condition of the mother and whether or not she's physically able to undergo such a procedure."

"When you say 'ailment' I assume there are some you regard as more serious than others?"

"Of course."

"Multiple sclerosis, spina bifida?" Rex asked. "These are diseases you would deem serious enough to risk in utero surgery?"

"Yes, you see, these are life-threatening illnesses. If we could correct these in utero, given the general good health of the mother, we would recommend to the parents that the procedure be done."

"On a scale of one to ten, ten being the most serious, how serious would you rank a fetus being diagnosed as homosexual?"

Bomar thought for a moment. "Oh, I don't know. It certainly isn't life-threatening. I would even go so far to say the quality of life of this person would not be diminished. I'd give it a one on your scale."

"A one. Can we gather from your answer that you wouldn't recommend an in utero procedure for a fetus diagnosed as homosexual?"

"You might certainly gather that. I would no more consider that risk than I would changing the baby's eye color, if that were possible."

"This is not a procedure, even if it were available, that you would be performing at your facility in Philadelphia, the country's most renowned facility of its kind?"

"That's correct."

"Thank you, Dr. Bomar."

Norm Woodruff buttoned his coat and rounded the table. He was taking advantage of this opportunity to question Dr. Bomar to ask him one simple question. One he hoped would resonate with the jury.

"Dr. Bomar, you're a father. Is that right?"

"Yes I am."

"If the Loveport Baby were your child and you were having to make a decision about his safety, would you approve the procedure proposed by Dr. Penrose and Loveport?"

"No, I would not."

"No more questions, Your Honor."

Kurt Ford sat for a moment before he approached the witness gingerly. He was the kind of witness Kurt hated to cross-examine. Bomar was an experienced witness and, undoubtedly, a master of his field. However, Kurt knew that much of what had just passed for expert testimony was unadulterated personal opinion. The difficulty was demonstrating that without appearing to impugn his integrity. Kurt knew the jurors respected this man, and his goal would not be furthered by trashing Dr. Bomar. Still, Bomar looked at him with suspicion as he approached the podium.

"Dr. Bomar, you talked about MS and other diseases you deemed serious enough to warrant an in utero procedure. Let me ask you about another condition. Color blindness. Would you advise a couple to undergo in utero surgery to correct a fetus that was color blind?"

Bomar thought for moment then answered. "That's a hard one to call. I guess it would depend on the other conditions, you know, the health of the mother and so on."

"Would there be any situation, say, when the mother was completely healthy and there were no other extenuating circumstances that you would correct color blindness in utero?"

"Yes. If there were no other problems."

"But Dr. Bomar, color blindness is not a life-threatening disease, the criterion you mentioned in deciding such a matter."

"It's a serious enough condition to affect the quality of life. It can cause all sorts of difficulties in life and I would have no problem in recommending its correction."

"Multiple sclerosis is not considered a fatal disease."

"Well, it can certainly shorten one's lifespan."

"Yes, doctor, by about six years, but that's not life-threatening."

"But we're talking quality of life here. MS certainly can diminish quality of life."

"Let me make sure I understand. You're saying if a condition affects quality of life, then you would consider the in utero procedure to correct it."

"Um, yes," he said almost noncommittally.

"Would it be safe to say that there is a degree of subjectivity in making this type of decision?"

"To a certain degree, I suppose that's so."

"Depending on what attributes one finds objectionable, different people would prioritize differently?"

"I suppose."

"It would stand to reason that determination may vary from doctor to doctor."

"Um, I suppose."

"No more questions, Your Honor."

Kurt returned to his seat and quickly assessed the jury hoping his point had hit its mark. From their looks, he was not confident that it had. Judge Kincaid made notes.

Kelly Morris called her last witness. The famous Dr. Martin Whitaker had been on every TV talk show in the country. Whitaker, head of the psych department at the University of North Carolina, had just written a book on the subject of how to deal with gay family members. The book was called 'Cast No Stone,' an obvious reference to the Biblical passage John 8:7 which says: 'Let him that is without sin among you first cast the stone at her.' Kelly Morris ran him through her typical drill of how homosexuality was not a genetic defect, believing the old adage that you remember best what you hear the most. Kurt had decided that, in light of the leak, he would leave this witness alone. He couldn't shake the nagging feeling, though, that the jury deserved to know this man had no credibility, but he dared not go there. Kelly finished her questioning, and Judge Kincaid asked Kurt if he would like to cross-exam the witness. To the judge's surprise, and almost to Kurt's, he answered yes. Dumaine looked at him with bewilderment. Kurt approached the witness stand. Kincaid shot him a warning eye.

"Dr. Whitaker, have you ever been in private practice?" He was shooting from the hip like some drunk cowboy. Kelly sat ready to object at even a hint of the malpractice suit.

"Yes."

"Have you ever had patients who were homosexuals?"

"Oh, yes."

"Were any of their emotional or psychological problems related to their homosexuality?"

"Yes, quite a few."

"What kinds of problems?"

"Well, most of my gay patients suffer from anxiety over telling their family the truth. Others suffer from an identity problem resulting from never really coming to terms with who they are. Many, especially those who have come out of the closet, have been harassed and have suffered quite serious emotional problems because of it."

"Would it be accurate to say that their sexual orientation was at the root of their problem?"

"Well, I think it would be more accurate to say that being *harassed* for their sexual orientation is at the root of their problem."

"I see."

Dr. Whitaker quickly added, "Much like blacks were harassed for their skin color. It wasn't their fault they were black, just as Dr. Penrose has proven that it's not a homosexual's fault if he's gay."

Kurt froze. He had violated the sacred lawyer's creed. Never ask a question unless you know the answer. A few steps further down this line of questioning and he was dead. Dumaine tried not to show his astonishment to the jury. Norm, Rex, and Kelly exchanged satisfying glances. Kurt's mind raced down each possible avenue of escape, hitting a brick wall each time. He didn't dare suggest at this point that a genetic change would solve the problem. Not after Whitaker had brought up the 'black thing.' He surely didn't want to link the two and most certainly didn't want to suggest that black people would be better off if they had their genes altered to be white. He did what any smart attorney would do at a time like this. "No further questions, Your Honor."

"Redirect, Ms. Morris?" Judge Kincaid inquired.

She looked over at Kurt Ford and smiled. "No, Your Honor."

"Anymore witnesses for the plaintiff?"

"No, Your Honor. The plaintiffs rest."

Dumaine nudged his partner. Kurt Ford slowly rose from his funk. "Your Honor, I move for a dismissal based on the fact that the plaintiffs failed to make their case." His heart wasn't in it.

"Motion denied," Kincaid said without hesitation. "Tuesday morning at nine the defense presents its case. Until then, have a good weekend. This court stands in recess." Bang! went the gavel, and Judge Kincaid was gone. Once the last juror was escorted from the room, Kurt buried his face in his hands. What a stupid move, he thought. What a stupid, idiotic move. Why couldn't he just leave well enough alone?

Karen Penrose passed the media encampment and entered the family home the same manner in which she had entered each day since her father dropped the bomb. She slammed the front door and headed for the stairs. This time, her father was waiting. He exited his study and stood at the bottom of the steps. The afternoon sun was sliced by the living room blinds, which scattered light up the otherwise dark stairway.

"Karen." His voice stopped her in her tracks, but she wouldn't turn to face him. "We have to talk."

"There's nothing to talk about," she answered acidly then proceeded up the stairs.

"Karen, I'm your father."

She didn't stop.

"Karen, I love you," he said desperately.

She whipped around, fighting back the tears. "Don't say that to me. Don't you *dare* say that to me!" A sliver of sunlight shone on her glistening green eyes.

Penrose didn't know how to reach her. Why was all of this tormenting her so? "Karen, I..." He had no idea what to say.

"Are you that blind, Dad?"

Penrose returned a puzzled look.

"Where's Brandon?" Her eyes darted about the house.

"He's at a friend's house."

"You really don't see it, do you?" she continued.

"I don't understand."

"You've been so busy working on your *project*. You've been so self-absorbed that you haven't even seen it and it's been right under your nose the whole time."

It was obvious to Karen that her father hadn't the faintest idea what she was talking about. She took a couple of steps down the stairs. "Brandon, Dad."

"What about Brandon?" Penrose asked.

She laughed out of pain, turning her head as the tears streamed down her cheeks. After a second, she managed to compose herself. She wiped her cheek then locked eyes with Penrose once more. "He's always been the perfect son. He wants to be a doctor just like you. He always wants to make you proud, to be exactly the person that you want him to be."

"Look, Karen if you think I've been too hard on Brandon, I can assure you I've never pushed him to do anything that he—"

Karen calmly interrupted, "Brandon's gay."

Penrose just stood there as the words reverberated down the steps and round and round in his head. He felt as though he had been socked in the stomach, his very breath knocked out of him. He felt his knees start to buckle. He stared back at Karen hoping she would tell him that she was only joking, but she wasn't. He felt his way to a chair in the living room just a few feet away and collapsed in it.

Karen had been waiting for this confrontation since she first learned of her father's project. She had dreamed of knocking the wind out of the old man with her news. Now that it was done, she felt as though she was going to be sick. She turned and ran sobbing up the stairs to her room.

Penrose sat in his state of confusion with a million thoughts racing through his mind. First and foremost, what had this whole project done to his son? How it must make him feel. The pain he must be going through. In all his research, in all the imagined scenarios, it never dawned on Penrose that this could ever happen to *him*.

Lauren quietly emerged from the kitchen and knelt down beside the chair. Penrose was startled.

"Did you hear what . . ." He couldn't finish the sentence.

"I heard," she confirmed. "I already knew."

He quickly looked up in surprise. "You knew? Why didn't you tell me?"

"It wasn't my place to tell you," she said, looking up the stairway. "It wasn't Karen's either. That was Brandon's decision. Clark, he's been agonizing over whether or not he should tell you."

"How long have you known?" Penrose asked.

"Not long. He came to me shortly after your announcement of the project, but I've suspected it for some time. My guess is you have too. You just never wanted to admit it to yourself."

Penrose looked back at her as she gently rubbed his hand. There was a lot of truth in what she said. Deep down in his subconscious were latent thoughts of the unthinkable, that his own son, his own flesh and blood could be gay. Perhaps that's why he had pursued this project so fervently.

But there really was a gay gene. He had found it himself. He had run the countless tests. He had done the experiments. He really could change it. Now, the big question nagged at his soul. Should he? Everything was different. There was an entirely new question, one that was so personal, so incredibly distressing that no parent should ever have to answer it. If given the chance to go back in time, would he change his own son?

34

Rex Randle, Kelly Morris, and Norm Woodruff sat in the ornate dining room of their hotel and enjoyed a cup of coffee after an early dinner. Their view out the window overlooked the small town square of Loveport. The cobblestone streets had been closed to traffic years before. Tourists strolled around the historic square, window shopping in the quaint shops. The marble statue of a Confederate general on horseback was the centerpiece of the square with four Civil War cannons standing guard. The church bell atop the centuries-old church at the opposite side of the square struck seven.

Rex looked at his watch and dabbed the corner of his mouth with his napkin. "I better get going. My plane leaves in two hours."

Norm stood to shake his hand before Rex headed back to Atlanta.

"I'm sorry I won't be with you on Tuesday," Rex said. "If I could change this appointment, I would, but it's been set up for months. Knock 'em dead for me."

"We plan to," Kelly said. "Have a safe trip. We'll see you in a couple of days."

"See ya, Rex. Watch for us on TV," Norm joked.

Rex laughed, dropped his napkin on the table, and left. The house lights dimmed as the restaurant prepared for the dinner rush. A server came by each table lighting the small lanterns which sat in the middle.

"Can I buy you a drink?" Norm offered.

"No, thanks."

"Hope you don't mind if I do."

"No, go right ahead."

Kelly seemed to be preoccupied with something. Norm put in an order for a whiskey sour and sat back, staring out the window at the passing people. Each time she was alone with Norm, it was always the same. There was so much tension at first, as if it were actually sitting in a chair at the table with them, but once they started talking, she felt like she'd known him her whole life. She looked at him as he looked out the window.

"How do you feel about things?" she finally said.

"About what things?"

"You know, about how the trial's going."

"After today? Great. We ought to put a little something extra in Dr. Whitaker's check."

The waitress brought his drink. He took it from her hand, not waiting for her to set it on the table, and thanked her.

"No kidding," Kelly agreed. "I don't know why *we* didn't think of that angle. It sure shut Kurt Ford down. How do you think the jury took it?"

"Well, between Dr. Whitaker saying it and Ford's reaction to it, I'd say it had a huge impact."

"So, you agree that there are similarities between the gay and the black struggles?"

"Oh, we're not gonna do this again, are we?" Norm said lightheartedly.

"Now, come on," Kelly said then laughed slightly. "You said it had a huge impact."

"I said it had a huge impact on the jury."

"But not on you."

He took a sip. "Look, you've gotta understand, I'm not sure I buy this whole gay gene stuff to start with." Norm couldn't believe he was getting dragged into another argument.

"You wouldn't understand," she said. "White privilege."

"My dear, you have the biggest chip on your shoulder I believe I've ever seen." He laughed out loud. "This persecution complex you've got. Don't you ever shut it off? I mean, my God, don't you ever think about the wonderful things in life? Relax. Enjoy the scenery."

"You see, that's how desensitized you are as a white man," Kelly said.

Norm rolled his eyes and took a drink.

"What do you see out that window?" she asked.

Norm squinted his eyes a bit to see. "I see a bunch of tourists on a lazy evening, window shopping in a beautiful little town after a nice, quiet supper."

Kelly pointed. "You see that huge antiques mall across the square?"

"Yeah."

"What do you think that used to be?"

"Oh, I don't know. Looks like probably stables or something."

"I read the plaque on the side of the building. That used to be where they auctioned off slaves. You see the statue of the man on horseback? That's a Confederate general who led thousands of boys into battle so the men in that building could continue doing what they were doing."

"What's your point?"

"My point is you're white, so you don't notice things like that. The Civil War, slavery, they don't mean anything to you because your ancestors weren't the ones being held in bondage. It's easy for you to just walk on by that antiques mall and accept it for what it is today, but it *means* something to people of color."

Norm leaned back in his chair and shook his head. "You know what your problem is? People aren't miserable enough for you."

Kelly waved Norm's comment off as if he'd said the sky was green.

"No, I mean it," he said. "For some untold reason you feel guilty if you're happy. You feel guilty being happy, so you don't think anybody else should be happy, especially a honky man like me." Norm shook his head again and took another sip.

"That's not true," Kelly said, though her voice wasn't very convincing.

"It's that cut and dried for you, isn't it? The war was over slavery."

"Of course it was over slavery," she said.

"That's your problem. Everything is so simple to you. The Civil War was over slavery. The white man's evil. Black folks are victims. Listen, I'm going to give you a little Woodruff history lesson," he said, crunching a piece of ice in his mouth. "My old man wasn't good for much, but he was good at keeping up with our lineage. He kept this old family Bible that listed all of our relatives. It had been passed down from generation to generation. My father moved down to Atlanta from Pennsylvania. Most of my people came from Washington County in the western part of the state. In fact, I've got quite a few relatives still up there. One of my ancestors, Seth Woodruff, worked on the family's small farm in Washington County. When the War Between the States broke out, he left a wife and a newborn baby boy to take up arms with his three brothers and join the Union army. They all were mustered into the 140th Pennsylvania Infantry Regiment on September 4th, 1862. Seth Woodruff's younger brother was killed at Gettysburg in July of 1863. The following year, he lost his two older brothers in the Battle of the Wilderness. He was mustered out in 1865 and came home to find that his mother had died from the devastation of losing three of her four boys to the war. He and his father and his wife and his young son struggled to rebuild the family farm which had been badly neglected. For the next three generations, the Woodruffs fought to recover what they had lost during the Civil War, each new one doing no better than the last. So, when you look at that old slave building over there — if you think the war was just over slavery — remember that my family, a bunch of white men, sacrificed three sons to free those slaves. Over 350,000 Union soldiers lost their lives in battle or to disease for the same cause. You want reparations? Let me tell you something, sister. The bill's been paid in blood."

There was an awkward pause as Norm looked out the window. Kelly cleared her throat. "I think I'll have that drink now."

Norm motioned to the waitress who promptly came to their side.

"Chardonnay?" he asked Kelly.

She nodded.

"Your house Chardonnay, please," Norm said.

The waitress left to fill the order.

"You want my honest opinion?" Norm asked.

"Do I have any choice?"

"I think you feel guilty."

"Guilty of what?"

"I think you grew up learning about your black history but soon realized that, as an attorney's daughter, you were as far removed from that history as I am."

"Don't be ridiculous."

"You feel guilty because so many people who look like you have suffered, but you never have, and now you want everyone else to share in your guilt."

Kelly straightened herself in her seat and looked down. "That's enough."

The waitress brought her drink. When she left, Norm leaned back in.

"Let me just say this," Norm said. "You were never a slave and I was never a slaveowner, so why should I be held responsible for the plight of black people?"

"Because white people have enjoyed a lifestyle in this country which African Americans have been locked out of for centuries. That's why we need affirmative action. That's why we need set-asides. To right the wrongs of the past."

Norm chuckled sarcastically. "A wise man once said, 'You don't right the wrongs of the past by wronging the people of the present.'"

Kelly took a gulp of her wine. "I wouldn't expect you to understand. You've never been followed by security at a dress shop just because you're black. You've never been pulled over by a cop who looks at you suspiciously and asks all sorts of intrusive questions just because you're driving a nice car and you're black."

Norm reached over and took Kelly's hand in his.

"What do you think you're doing?" she asked indignantly.

Norm looked down at her light-brown skin. Her hand was soft and dainty, the color of lightly-creamed coffee. He rubbed the top of her hand with his thumb. "Black? I think there may be some white blood coursing through your veins."

Kelly drew her hand back abruptly and rubbed it with her other, as if Norm had just bit her.

"Oh, my God," Norm said dramatically. "You're one of us." He chuckled a delighted laugh and raised his glass to his mouth. He could smell her perfume on his hand.

"Probably the result of one of my ancestors being raped by the massah." She finished off the glass of wine.

"Always have to put a positive spin on things, don't you?"

Kelly motioned for the waitress to bring her another glass of wine.

"Maybe you're a descendant of Sally Hemings," Norm suggested.

"Now, there's a prime example of hypocrisy. Here's Thomas Jefferson, president of the United States, a wealthy Virginia landowner. He claims he's opposed to slavery, but he won't give up his own slaves. World renown for his virtue, yet this powerful, white slave owner secretly uses a young, innocent slave girl for his sick sexploitation. Even fathers some children with her. She's good enough to lay, but she's not good enough to free."

"See, that's exactly what I'm talking about. You see Jefferson as this dirty old man lusting after this light-skinned slave and having his way with her against her wishes. I see a very dignified middle-aged man who had lost his wife, falling in love with a beautiful, young slave — the ultimate forbidden fruit. I'm convinced he was probably very much in love with her."

"In *love* with her?"

"Yes. Have you ever thought about what a huge risk Jefferson was taking with his love affair? Imagine the stigma of the day associated with having any kind of a relationship with a slave. A man of Jefferson's stature had the most to lose by acting on his feelings for Sally Hemings. He could never marry her. That was far too taboo. It was scandalous for him even to be seen with her in public outside of a slave/master relationship. So, he had to sneak around, rendezvous with her at secret places at the house. Maybe meet her miles out in the woods. Pretty romantic, if you think about it. He gave her as much of himself as he could. I think it's one of America's great love stories." Norm took a sip of the whiskey sour. "Spoken like a true male chauvinist honky pig, huh?"

Kelly burst into laughter. She took the last gulp of her wine and motioned to the waitress to bring another.

35

Penrose sat alone on a small hill overlooking the water. He listened to the distant sound of water lapping the dock below, of sailboat lines tapping their masts in the breeze, of the occasional seagull answering a call on the wing. This was Penrose's favorite spot in Loveport, a place where he came to think, especially at this time of day when the sun hung low in the sky. One of his few extravagances was his dream of someday building a nice, little home on that hill. It was a dream he relived over and over in his mind. A dream of getting away for good, leaving behind the pressures of his job for the serenity of the sea. Perhaps now was as good a time as any to do just that. Regardless of how the trial turned out, Penrose had made his mark on the world, for better or for worse. His place in medical history was set in stone. No matter what else he did, he would never live that down.

The thoughts that clouded his mind would not soon be cleared by the tranquility of his favorite thinking spot. He tried to take on the multitude of feelings one by one, but they came at him as if they were shot from a gun. He sifted through his emotions and there was one that stuck out. He was mad. Mad at himself for not seeing Brandon for who he really was. Mad at himself for being so wrapped up in himself and his work that he didn't stop to think what it might be doing to his own son. The low rumble of thunder in the distance sent the birds scurrying for the trees. Penrose pulled his coat's collar up around his face, bracing himself from the cool gust of wind, which whipped across the barren hilltop. He could see clearly in his mind the moment he first laid eyes on Brandon. He had delivered countless babies during his career, but there was nothing to compare with seeing his own take his first breath. Barely a minute old, Penrose had held him gently in his arms and tenderly kissed him on the forehead. Like a video, he replayed Brandon's first steps and the look in his eyes when he first mastered tying his own shoes. Penrose relived Brandon's first soccer game and his first goal. His little chest swollen with pride as he ran to his father's arms after the game. He remembered the day he and Lauren put their baby boy on the school bus. How Brandon found his way to an open seat and they lost him among the other children. Just as Penrose had thought he had made it through the ritual without crying, his young son appeared in a window. Brandon looked back at them as the bus drove away and mustered a tentative wave goodbye. They both forced a smile and waved back as they felt their eyes fill with tears.

Had it not been for the rain, Penrose might have sat on that hill forever. It was just as well. The rain helped hide the tears that streamed down his cheeks. He pulled his jacket up over his head and headed back down the hill. Back to reality.

Duncan Reynolds had been eager all day to draw first blood in the daily debate. First, he had to set up the day's events for the audience of *The Pulse*. "In a bizarre twist to the Loveport Baby Trial, local television reporter, Don Bissette, was arrested today on contempt of court charges." He turned to Betty Duvall. "But, Betty, I tell you who they should've arrested and that's Dr. Frank Bomar for impersonating an expert witness. The defense ate his lunch today. Bomar's supposedly one of the premiere pediatric surgeons in the country. The defense got him to admit that he would perform an in utero procedure to correct *color blindness* when he wouldn't recommend correcting the gay gene. That's just incredible!"

"No, Duncan, what was incredible was the way Kurt Ford sewed up the case for the plaintiffs when he tried to cross examine the next witness. If somebody ought to be arrested for impersonation it's this kid for impersonating an attorney. He tried to match wits with the famous psychologist, Dr. Martin Whitaker, and soon found himself out of his league. Dr. Whitaker made the most salient point of the whole trial and that is being gay is as immutable as being black. No one chooses to be black, or white for that matter, and no one chooses to be gay. Instead of concentrating on changing the person who's gay, we should be concentrating on changing the people who bash them. The irony of it," Betty Duvall crowed to Duncan Reynolds and the nation, "is that Kurt Ford, the lead attorney for the defense, led the witness to bring it up! And it's a great point. Why would homosexuals anymore want to alter who they are than African Americans would? Take a cue from Black America, my gay friends out there. Stand up and be proud of who you are!"

The room was quiet save the slow tick tock tick tock of the grandfather clock in the corner. Penrose sat all alone in his wood-paneled study engulfed by the darkness except for the light emitted from the small, green-shaded bankers lamp on his desk. Sitting parallel to the desk, he stared out at nothing in particular and slowly rocked in the highback leather desk chair. He thought of nothing but his son. He thought of the plans he had for his son. A wedding, children, grandchildren for himself. Now it would never be. He thought back to when Lauren delivered Brandon. If he only had the knowledge, the power that he has now. Would he change things? Would he go back and risk changing who his son is, his very personality, just to prevent him from being *gay*? He tried to get used to the word, but he couldn't. He wondered if he ever would.

Two soft knocks and Brandon appeared in the doorway. He looked different. Penrose hated himself for feeling that way, but he just looked different. It was as if he hadn't really known him before now. He hurt for Brandon. More than anyone, Penrose knew his son hadn't chosen this for himself. He rose from his seat. Brandon closed the door behind him. His son came closer, and Penrose walked around the desk. The last thing he wanted was for this moment to appear to be an interrogation. There was a long, awkward pause, then Brandon spoke first.

"Dad, I'm sorry."

Penrose's eyes welled with tears. He grabbed his son and pulled him tightly to his chest. His head rested on his young son's shoulder as he sobbed uncontrollably. "You have nothing to be sorry for," he insisted through his tears.

Brandon cried, too. "I know how much this hurts you."

Penrose held his son's face in his hands. Tears streamed down both of their cheeks. "Brandon, listen to me. I love you. That love is unconditional. There's nothing you could say or do to change that. But I want you to understand one thing. You have nothing to feel guilty about. You have nothing to be sorry for or be ashamed of. I know you didn't choose to be this way." He still couldn't bring himself to say the word 'gay' when it came to his own son. "God knows, that's what my work's been all about," he said. His voice trembled. "That's what I've spent all these years trying to prove. I just never stopped to think how it would feel if it were my own son."

"All I ever wanted was to make you proud," Brandon said. The tears began to flow again.

Penrose held him tightly once more. "I *am* proud, son. I *am* proud. I'm proud of you because you're my son. Nothing can ever change that. Do you understand? You don't have to prove anything to me. You don't have to win my approval." Penrose smiled through his tears. "From the second you were born and I held you in my arms, I've loved you more than life itself."

They held each other, father and son, like they were seeing each other for the first time in years. The great chasm which had been created by Brandon's revelation closed in an instant. Nothing had changed, really. This was still his little boy. The same little boy whose tender forehead he had kissed just moments after his birth. The same little boy whose innocent eyes had looked to him for acceptance and love. A little boy onto whose shoulders he had unloaded a great burden. Now, Penrose decided, it was time to relieve that burden.

"I'm going to call Dr. Kirsch and cancel the project."

"No, you can't," Brandon shot back. "Dad, you *have* to go forward with this project."

Penrose was puzzled.

"Look, Dad. I know what I've gone through with this. You can't stop now."

Penrose was taken aback. He took a couple of steps away, thinking about what he just heard then turned back toward his son. "You mean you *approve* of what I'm doing?"

"Dad, no one was more excited over the news of your project than me."

"I don't understand."

"You think I *want* to be like this?"

Penrose let the words sink in.

"Dad, you *have* to win this case. You *have* to. Not for me but for the millions of unborn children who'll get a second chance at being normal. You were right from the beginning. This is a medical disorder just like any other disorder and you've found the cure. You *have* to share that cure with the world."

Penrose returned to his chair. He reflected on all that had been said and looked up at his son. Those eyes. They were the same eyes he saw squinting and peering the first moment of his young life. They were the same eyes that gazed upon him as if he were some hero, not just another dad. He knew those eyes as well as he knew his own. He loved those eyes. He trusted those eyes.

The hour was late and the bar bill was high. Norm Woodruff paid it with his American Express card then pondered what to do about his partner. Kelly Morris was drunk as a skunk. If her arguments made no sense before, they were now almost completely incomprehensible. She was talking non-stop. When Norm offered to help her to her room, she insisted she could make it under her own power.

"I'm not as think as you drunk I am," she mumbled.

They rose from the table. Kelly lost her balance and fell back into her seat.

"Easy there, girl."

Norm put an arm around her waist and helped her up. Halfway through the lobby, she stumbled. Norm caught her before she hit the floor and wrapped his arm around her waist again, this time throwing her arm over his shoulder.

"You're very sweet, do you know that?" she slurred while Norm pressed the up arrow by the elevator. "And I thought you were gonna be a real horse's ass."

"Flattery will get you nowhere."

"Nobody's ever been sweet to me. I jus wan you ta know that." Her head bobbed from side to side and front to back.

"Yes, well, thanks for the information."

How he hated trying to carry on a conversation with a drunk. The door to the elevator opened and Norm walked her in. He pressed their floor then leaned her up against the side.

"Where we goin'?" she asked.

"To your room."

"O-o-o. Naughty, naughty," she giggled.

The elevator opened to their floor. Norm resumed the position with his arm around her waist and walked her off the elevator and down the hall. Once in front of her room, he leaned her up against the wall and rummaged through her purse for her door pass as she mumbled incoherently. Upon finding it, he fumbled with the card while pulling her up again by the waist.

"Aren't you going to kiss me goodnight?" she asked.

She puckered her lips and closed her eyes. Her head began to bob again. Norm ignored her and continued to try and get the door opened. Kelly opened her eyes, her pupils dilating and contracting, trying to focus. She frowned, seemingly insulted by Norm's lack of action.

"What's the matter? Dr. Luscious Gaylord wouldn't approve of you kissin' a *black* girl?"

"That's *Lucius*."

"Oh, sure. My bad."

Norm got the door opened, let themselves into her room, and dumped her on the bed. She attempted a few words then was out cold. He stopped for a moment and took in the image of her lying there. She looked so much softer when she was asleep. Her face didn't have the strained look it wore during consciousness. Her dress was hiked up, revealing much more of her thin, brown legs than Norm had seen before. He reached down and gently pulled her dress back down below her knees. He picked up the phone beside Kelly's bed and dialed the front desk.

"Yes, I'm sorry to bother you, but I have a young lady up here who, well, who's had a little too much to drink. Could you send a female up here to help me get her ready for bed? Yes. Thank you. Oh, and she has to catch a flight tomorrow morning. Could you give her a wake-up call for, say, seven-thirty? Thanks."

Norm went into the bathroom and scrounged around in her toiletry bag until he found some aspirin. He emptied three into his hand, replaced the cap, and tossed the bottle back in the bag. He filled a glass half full with water and returned to the bed. Sitting down beside Kelly, he raised her upright. She came to, but barely.

"There you go, girl. Here, hold out your hand. Take these. You'll thank me in the morning."

Her eyes fluttered open and shut then open again and she held out her hand. He dropped the pills into it, and she threw them into her mouth. He handed her the water. She chugged it all then fell back onto the bed, asleep.

Norm searched the dresser for a nightgown. About the time he found one, there was a knock on the door. Norm opened the door and let the nice lady from the hotel in. He explained his dilemma, handed her the gown, then stepped out into the hallway. He fretted like an expectant father until the lady emerged. He tipped her handsomely and walked back into Kelly's room. There she lay, all snug beneath the covers. Her face looked beautiful against the pillow. She looked so tranquil, not the troubled face he saw each day. Norm leaned down, kissed her on the forehead, extinguished the bedside light, then slipped quietly out of the room.

The airplane touched down, and Bill Dumaine grabbed his jacket. It had been a little while since he'd lived up north, but he figured one thing probably hadn't changed. He could count on it being a good thirty degrees colder this time of year. He deplaned and headed straight for the car rental counter. He checked out a mid-size sedan for the day and headed out of the airport complex. The cold, gray skies seemed to weigh his mood down even lower. He had some making up to do and the sooner he did, the better he'd feel about himself.

He stopped by a flower shop. A nice bouquet would be appropriate after such a long separation. He hopped back into his car and headed out of the city. Even though he was heading to his home town, he wouldn't be paying a visit to his parents. It was not them with whom he needed to make amends. They didn't even know he was coming. Had they known, his mother would surely have insisted he stay for the night or at least for dinner. He hadn't the time for either. He wanted to make his apologies and get back to Loveport. There was much to do there, but this could wait no longer.

He saw the entrance up ahead. He hadn't been there in years. Everything looked the same. He turned in and hoped he could find the right place after all these years. He drove straight a little ways then took a left onto the small dirt road. A hundred yards or so then the first right. He pulled to a stop and placed the car in park and looked around to get his bearings. This looked like the right place. He looked out the window for a moment and took a deep breath. Grabbing the flowers from the seat, he got out, zipping his coat up tightly. He walked on the brown grass for about twenty feet and stopped. This was the place. He looked down at the headstone. The name 'Dumaine' was carved across the top. He stooped to one knee and closed his eyes. He prayed in silence for a moment then crossed himself. He braced himself with one hand on the headstone and gently laid the bunch of flowers on the ground.

"I'm so sorry," he tried to say but was unable to utter the words before he broke down and cried. The years of pent up emotion and guilt came gushing out and he made no attempt to hold it in. He dropped to both knees and wept.

36

Kurt Ford sat alone in Jonathan Sagar's office. The note had said he wanted to see him first thing in the morning. Sagar was not yet in, but his secretary ushered Ford into Mr. Sagar's empty office just as she was instructed. It seemed like eons before Kurt heard Sagar greeting his secretary in the outer office. Kurt's stomach churned. Sagar entered the office door behind Kurt and closed it without a greeting. Bad sign. He removed his suit coat and hung it on the coat rack then took his place behind his desk.

"You got scratched up pretty good yesterday, didn't you, son?" It was more of a statement of fact than a question.

Kurt nodded. "I'm sorry, Mr. Sagar. I got ambushed."

Sagar corrected him. "No, now, that was no ambush. That was carelessness on your part." Sagar felt sorry for the young man. "Look, I've been there. We've all been there. You feel like you're not contributing because you're not saying anything. You've got to resist that temptation to ask questions just to appear to be engaged. Sometimes there's no need for cross-examination. Sometimes there's nothing gained by asking the witness anything at all. Just let them go. Sometimes, like yesterday, you do more damage by going off on some fishing expedition. Especially with a witness like Whitaker. Hell, that man's seen more courtroom action than most trial lawyers. What do I keep telling you, son? Know your enemies. Know what they're capable of so you don't get caught with your pants down."

"I'm sorry, but the judge said I couldn't bring up Whitaker's malpractice suit to the jury because that Bissette character leaked it on the news. I didn't think that was fair."

"So you got frustrated and made a mistake."

"I blew it."

"You didn't blow it," Sagar lectured. "You got tripped up. The main reason I wanted to see you is to make sure you understand that it's done. It happened and it's over. You have to shake it off, son, or it'll haunt you for the rest of this trial and impede your judgment. It happened and you learned from it. Tomorrow's a brand new day. It's your turn to go on the offensive. Move on."

Sagar knew he couldn't beat Kurt up any more than he had already pummeled himself, and he had certainly suffered enough. Good advice and a pep talk from the coach was what he needed most and Kurt Ford appreciated it more than Sagar would ever know.

The Loveport trial had been delayed by a day while Judge Kincaid took care of an important matter. He intended to get to the bottom of the leaks before the end of the day. The courtroom at the federal building was cleared. No press. No spectators. No jury. Just Kincaid, the court reporter, two deputies, the clerk, Don Bissette, and his lawyer. Jerry Broder wasn't the most competent attorney available, but he was the most affordable. Since News 3 had cut him loose, that attribute sailed to number one on Bissette's list. Broder had never actually represented anyone on a contempt charge before, but he was confident he could handle it.

Judge Kincaid looked down on Bissette trying to contain his vexation. "Mr. Bissette, you've been charged with contempt of court for your blatant disregard for not only the gag order, but warnings to cease and desist from revealing classified trial information to the general public. Can you show cause why this court should *not* find you in contempt?"

"No, Your Honor," Bissette announced. Broder had advised his client not to further irk His Honor with lame excuses. Just take the medicine.

"Mr. Bissette, as you know, the Loveport trial is particularly sensitive for a variety of reasons. This court has attempted a certain decorum of silence in an effort to preserve its sanctity. That attempt has obviously failed. Your defying the order of this court is, indeed, serious, but the fact that someone associated with this trial, perhaps even an officer of the court, has broken its confidentiality is especially grievous. In light of the importance of discovering who is responsible for that infraction, this court is prepared to suspend your sentence on the condition that your source for this classified information be revealed."

Jerry Broder huddled with his client. He thought the judge might offer a deal and he had encouraged his client to accept it. Bissette had refused, but Broder gave it one last try before the judge imposed his sentence. After a brief discussion, Broder and Bissette once again faced Judge Kincaid and reluctantly gave his answer.

"Your Honor, my client refuses to reveal his source based on his First Amendment right to freedom of the press."

Kincaid was clearly annoyed. "Very well. The court sentences Donald Frederick Bissette to ninety days confinement." He banged the gavel and the deputy took the prisoner away.

The revelation that had just been dropped in his lap from one of the diggers had far-reaching implications. Kurt mulled it over and tried to think of any possible way it could hurt their case. He insisted on an immediate meeting with Penrose, just the two of them, without giving any details of the subject matter. Penrose agreed to see him right away at his lab.

Ford had never paid a visit to Dr. Penrose's famous lab. In fact, he couldn't remember ever visiting any scientist's lab. It looked like something from the set of Flubber. Junk, or what appeared to Kurt to be junk, was scattered everywhere. Books piled high on top of files on top of hi-tech equipment. Penrose had his hands stuck inside one of the pieces of equipment. He turned around and introduced Carol Boyce to Kurt. Penrose held his hands up like he was going into surgery. He apologized for not shaking Kurt's hand and proceeded to scrub up in the sink. Not wanting to be rude to Carol, Kurt made small talk for a brief moment before asking if he and the doctor could talk alone. Penrose suggested she grab a bite to eat, and Kurt waited for the door to close behind her.

"Why didn't you tell me?" Kurt asked pointedly.

Penrose rubbed his hands together under the hot water. "Why didn't I tell you *what*?"

"You know damn well what I'm talking about. I thought you weren't going to keep anymore secrets from me."

Penrose looked at him over his shoulder as he soaped up his hands. "You're going to have to do better than that."

"I'm talking about your son."

Penrose stopped washing his hands for a second then resumed. "What about my son?"

Kurt was in no mood to play games. He walked up behind Penrose. "He's gay."

Penrose closed his eyes. It hurt to hear it out loud, especially from someone he hardly knew. "So what?"

"So what? How long have you known?"

"Not long. A few days." He rinsed the soap from his hands.

Kurt backed off. He knew the freshness of the wound must still sting. He recalled the pain of telling his own parents. It was the most difficult time of his life. "I'm sorry." He offered Penrose a paper towel.

"Sorry?" He accepted the towel. "There's nothing to be sorry about. He is what he is as we all are. I accept him for who he is."

"That's very big of you."

Penrose wanted no praise.

"What does he think of your project?"

"He's very much in favor of it, believe it or not. He hates being gay. I know that may offend you, but he does. He's told me he wouldn't wish it on his worst enemy."

"I can relate to that," Kurt said.

"I was ready to pull the plug on the whole thing. I was ready to call Kirsch, Baxten, everyone and tell them I couldn't do it. Hell, the last thing I want to do is torture my own son with this bloody media dog and pony show, but he insisted I go forward. He says I owe it to future generations not to subject them to what he's gone through."

"That's pretty unselfish of him."

Penrose finished drying his hands and tossed the paper towel in the trash. "Yeah, it is, isn't it?" He walked back over to the table. It was obvious that talking about it made him uncomfortable. Kurt followed.

"We've got to put him on the stand."

Penrose turned to face him. "Absolutely not."

"Look, you don't understand. The effect he could have on our case is immeasurable."

Penrose rested both palms on the lab table and locked his elbows. Kurt noticed Penrose's jaw muscle flexing and his nostrils flaring. Kurt braced himself for impact. "I'm not going to drag my son into this, this mess and humiliate him in front of the whole world!" Penrose shouted at the table.

Kurt hesitated a moment before attempting to penetrate his anger. "Dr. Penrose, think about this. The media have portrayed you as some homophobe bent on ridding the world of homosexuals. The plaintiffs have painted you as uncaring, even sadistic. They've called you everything but a mad scientist. If we put Brandon on the stand and he tells the world that the 'evil' Dr. Penrose has a gay son then that throws their credibility into a tailspin. The man they've fashioned into Hitler personified is actually a compassionate physician and a loving father who knows firsthand the pain homosexuals endure and wants to do something to help them. It's the story that *has* to be told!"

Penrose continued to look down at the table. "I just can't do it!"

Kurt gently gripped his arm. Penrose looked up at him intently. "Dr. Penrose." He softened his voice. "Listen to me. I'm not a pessimist, but I *am* a realist. We've taken some pretty serious hits. There's a good possibility that we might not win." Penrose looked away. "If we don't win," Kurt continued, "there goes years and years of research. There goes your dream, something you've poured your life into. We're running out of time, Dr. Penrose. We *need* your son."

"You're the expert!" Penrose exploded. "You're the lead attorney! It's up to you to win this case, not me! Don't come in here looking to me for a way out! I told them you couldn't handle this job! They should've gone with somebody who could!"

Kurt didn't respond. He knew why Penrose was mad and it had little to do with him. He'd seen the same thing in his own father when he finally told him the truth. It was confusion, hurt, disappointment all tangled up together. Penrose had been simmering, ready to erupt, ever since he learned about his own son. Penrose continued to look down at the table. His harsh words still lingered in the air, yet he felt no obligation to take them back. He never looked up as Kurt turned and walked away.

37

Tuesday morning brought a new confidence in Kurt Ford. This was his day to drive the trial in his chosen direction. Jonathan Sagar shot him an encouraging smile from the front row. The sunlight filtered through the small gaps in the blinds of the federal courtroom. The usual faces took their usual places. Norm Woodruff took his seat at the plaintiffs' table and looked around for Kelly Morris. After a moment, she emerged from the side door and took her seat at the table.

"Well, you're looking mighty chipper this morning," Norm observed quietly. "Certainly more chipper than the last time I saw you."

"What happened the other night?" she asked in a whisper.

"Before or after you got knee-walking drunk?"

Kelly was a bit irked. "After."

"Let's see, I carried you to your room and poured you into your bed."

"But I woke up in my nightgown."

"Compliments of guest services, my dear."

"So…"

She didn't have to finish. Norm could tell where she was going.

"Miss Morris, I can assure you, I was a perfect gentleman."

Kelly smiled to herself and gave a sigh of relief. "And you let me wonder about that all weekend?"

Norm smiled and leaned back in his seat.

Judge Kincaid gaveled the court to order. Kurt called his first witness, Dr. Kent Garcia, program director for the Human Genome Project. Dr. Garcia was quite handsome with a dark complexion, black hair, and shiny, white teeth. He adjusted his five-foot-nine frame to the well-worn leather witness chair after being sworn in, and Kurt Ford approached the stand.

"Good morning, Dr. Garcia."

"Good morning."

"You are the program director for the Human Genome Project. Is that correct?"

"Yes, that's correct."

"For the court, Dr. Garcia, explain what the Human Genome Project is."

"Of course. First, it's important to know what a genome is." He had given this speech a million times. "A genome is all the DNA in an organism, including its genes. The Human Genome Project is a coordinated effort by the U.S. Department of Energy and the National Institutes of Health to identify all of the estimated 80,000 genes in human DNA. Furthermore, we are determining the sequences of the three billion chemical bases that make up human DNA, storing this information in databases, and developing tools for data analysis."

"Are you familiar with Dr. Clark Penrose?"

"Oh, yes, indeed. Dr. Penrose has been extremely helpful in mapping genes. As a matter of fact, he's mapped more genes than any other scientist or doctor in the country."

"Does the Human Genome Project have any ethical guidelines?"

"Yes. We do not condone the use of genetics, for example, to discriminate against someone or to deny someone health insurance because they might be predisposed to a certain disease. Things like that."

"Do you have any restrictions on gene therapy, Dr. Garcia?"

"That's a controversial area as you might imagine. We currently have an open dialogue going on about when it's appropriate to use genetic engineering."

"Meaning: there's no specific policy when it comes to the gay gene?"

"As I said, there are areas of controversy. That certainly is one of them, but we have no official policy against gene therapy when it comes to the gay gene."

"Dr. Garcia, let me ask your professional opinion. As a geneticist, do you have any problem with genetically altering the genes of a homosexual fetus?"

"Not at all. I happen to agree with Dr. Penrose's hypothesis that the gay gene in homosexuals is, if you will, defective. That being the case, I have no problem with correcting it."

"You've reviewed Dr. Penrose's notes from his experiments for the court. What is your conclusion as to the feasibility of the gene therapy Dr. Penrose has planned and, in your opinion, how risky would it be?"

"I think it's not only feasible, it's a logical next step in the work of a geneticist. I mean, what good is identifying a defective gene if you don't develop a way to correct it. There's no doubt that Dr. Penrose has located the gay gene, but the really incredible part is he's proven in his experiments that he can correct it. You have to understand what this discovery of Dr. Penrose's means to the world. Because of it, we've now leapt years beyond where we were just a few months ago. I'll put it to you this way. Three, maybe four, months ago, before Dr. Penrose's discovery, we were just getting the airplane off the ground. Dr. Penrose just landed on the moon."

His words obviously struck a chord with the jury.

"And the safety of the procedure?" Kurt asked.

"Keep in mind that we're not talking about a conventional operation in utero where the fetus actually goes under the knife. We're talking about a comparatively noninvasive procedure. It works much like an amniocentesis, which is pretty much a routine procedure. I'd put the risk factor at a little better than 1%."

"Thank you, Dr. Garcia."

Kurt Ford returned to his seat.

"Dr. Garcia," Kelly Morris began. "Did I hear you refer to being gay as a genetic defect?" she asked in disbelief.

"That's correct."

Kelly laughed incredulously. "A defect! Dr. Garcia, what constitutes a defect in your book?"

"I would say anything that goes against nature."

"Anything that goes against nature," Kelly repeated. "Do you think it's natural for a human being to be six-foot-eight?"

"I don't know about natural. It certainly isn't normal."

"And if it isn't normal, then it probably isn't natural. Correct?"

"Probably."

"What would be a normal height for a man, Dr. Garcia?"

"H-m-m, I'd say around five-foot-ten, somewhere in there would be about normal."

"Would five-foot-ten be a normal size for a professional basketball player?"

Dr. Garcia chuckled at the absurdity. "Of course not."

"Dr. Garcia, did you know the average height of the Chicago Bulls is six-foot-seven?"

"No, I did not."

"Dr. Garcia, how tall are you?"

Garcia started to answer, but Kelly jumped in. "Remember, you're under oath."

The gallery chuckled.

"About five-nine," he admitted.

"What you're saying is, to a short-heterosexual-no-basketball-playin'-white-guy, six-foot-seven ain't normal." The courtroom crowd burst into laughter.

"Objection!" Kurt complained.

"Withdrawn, Your Honor. The point I'm making is when it comes to deciding what's normal or natural, as far as sexual orientation is concerned, it strongly depends on who's making that determination. From the standpoint of a heterosexual male, homosexuality is not normal, but if your circle of friends is gay, it is. Oh, one more thing, Dr. Garcia. Would you endorse a procedure that would make one of those NBA players only five-foot-nine?"

The courtroom snickered.

"No, I would not."

"No more questions, Your Honor."

Judge Kincaid scribbled. Kurt took it as a bad sign.

"Redirect, Mr. Ford?" Kincaid asked.

Kurt started to rise, then Sagar's sage advice spoke to him. "No, Your Honor."

"Call your next witness."

"The defense calls Dr. Shannon Glasco."

Dr. Glasco was an attractive black woman of fifty. Her bright red suit and complimenting scarf were a welcome addition to the drab witness stand. She stood erect with perfect posture as she took the oath. Smoothing the skirt on the back of her legs, she took her seat. Kurt led her through the questioning, and she told the court she was a clinical psychologist from San Francisco. She had relocated to the city because of its large gay and lesbian population. She was particularly interested in helping them cope with their sexuality and their lives. She painted a picture of despondent souls trying to come to grips with who they are. Several had failed and had chosen to destroy themselves. Although many of them learned to love themselves, there still seemed to be a void. She had spent many years researching this and had coined a term for their problem: Progenitive Deficiency Syndrome. She explained that their homosexuality was in constant conflict with their instinct to procreate. In essence, there was a continual internal battle that could not be resolved. She admitted that it was not impossible for them to have families, but having a mate just to reproduce brought more complexity to an already difficult predicament. PDS had become a common term in psychological magazines and had become a particular favorite with the religious right wing. As much as she tried to distance herself from the politics of the issue, her name had become closely associated with the anti-gay movement. Kurt Ford was very much aware, but even with the baggage, he felt her work was too important to ignore. He stuck to the raw science of her study, venturing nowhere near supposition.

"Dr. Glasco, in your years of research, have you found a solution for PDS?"

"No, nothing has seemed to work. There are ways to mask the problem, but to actually solve it, we haven't been successful."

"Are you familiar with the Penrose Project?"

"Well, I, like everyone else, have just become familiar with it."

"What do you think of it?"

"I'm really excited about it."

"What has you so excited? I guess what I mean is why does this particular procedure excite you when nothing else has?"

"Because altering the gay gene gets to the root of the problem. You have to realize that the instinct to procreate is one of the strongest instincts we have. It's my opinion that correcting the gay gene is, indeed, far easier than suppressing a natural instinct to procreate."

"How many patients have you seen?"

"Oh, goodness. Thousands."

"Thousands of patients with Progenitive Deficiency Syndrome?"

"Yes."

"What does this mean to people with PDS?"

"Well, of course, the people who already suffer from it won't benefit from Dr. Penrose's procedure, but future generations will. In another couple of generations, we will see PDS eradicated."

"Thank you, Dr. Glasco."

Kurt relinquished the witness to the plaintiffs. Judge Kincaid asked if they cared to question the witness. Kelly Morris chose to cross-examine. She approached the podium with no notes and, like a commando in a foxhole, lobbed her bomb at the witness.

"Dr. Glasco, are you a member of the American Psychological Association?"

"Certainly." Dr. Glasco seemed offended that she would even ask.

"This so-called Progenitive Deficiency Syndrome that you've come up with, does the American Psychological Association recognize it as a legitimate condition?"

Dr. Glasco hesitated. "Uh, no. But—"

"Thank you, Dr. Glasco. No more questions."

"But I—"

"That'll be all, Dr. Glasco," Kelly insisted.

Dr. Glasco sat in frustration, looking at Judge Kincaid in bewilderment.

"Redirect, Mr. Ford?" Kincaid asked.

"Yes, Your Honor." Ford formulated the damage control as he rose to the podium. He knew there was a way out. He knew Dr. Glasco knew the way out, but he couldn't very well ask her in front of the judge and the jury. There was something she wanted to add, something that would explain why the APA hadn't endorsed her term Progenitive Deficiency Syndrome. Kurt was going to have to find that door himself.

He also had to take great care not to make the matter even worse. The debacle of the Whitaker testimony gnawed at him. He proceeded with caution. Her eyes were trying to tell him something, yet he had no idea what.

"Dr. Glasco, does the APA make a practice of recognizing psychological conditions like PDS?"

"Yes, they do."

If they do, Kurt thought, why hadn't they recognized hers? Could he have driven off the cliff this soon?

"I see." He swallowed hard then wet his lips with his tongue. "Is it common for a condition such as yours *not* to be officially recognized by the APA?" Come on, Doc. Help me out, here. Throw me a bone.

"It's a very rigorous and time-consuming process. The APA doesn't make endorsements of new theories lightly."

"So, they haven't rejected PDS." He stayed away from referring to it as a theory.

"Oh, absolutely not. Once a new discovery is made, it must undergo five years of scrutiny by the psychological community. I'm only eighteen months into that process. The discovery is debated at various forums, written about in numerous magazines, then the board takes the issue up after five years. So far, many influential colleagues of mine have endorsed PDS and we expect the APA to come onboard after the appropriate trial time."

Ford gave a sigh of relief. He had, at last, found the door. "So, the APA has far from rejected PDS. They are currently reviewing it for inclusion as a psychological condition."

"That's correct."

"No more questions, Your Honor."

Kurt returned to his seat and caught a glance from Jonathan Sagar. One side of his mouth was slightly raised to a grin with the corresponding eyebrow. Kurt took it as a compliment.

38

"If it were a fight, they would've stopped it," Betty Duvall asserted to the *The Pulse* audience. "Kelly Morris, the plaintiff attorney, made a brilliant point about what's considered normal. She used the analogy of the NBA to illustrate what may be a normal height to you and me is considered abnormal in professional basketball. I thought it was a great point and a great day for the plaintiffs."

"Let's not forget the second witness, Dr. Shannon Glasco," Duncan Reynolds reminded her. "She's coined a term for a condition she calls Progenitive Deficiency Syndrome."

"Sounds like what you conservatives call psychobabble to me," Betty contended.

Duncan laughed. "Actually, it's a natural condition in homosexuals where their instinct to procreate runs head-on into their urge for homosexual sex causing severe psychological problems. Dr. Glasco maintains that in order to solve the problem, you have to change either the instinct to procreate or the urge for homosexual sex. She contends that it's much easier to change the urge for homosexual sex."

"Only because Dr. Penrose has claimed to have discovered a 'cure.' If he'd developed some kind of instinct suppressant, then she'd probably go with that too. Look, the point is we fight instincts all the time. You men have the instinct to knock us women over the head and pull us back to the cave, but you don't."

Duncan said, "I don't know about the cave part but knocking you over the head is rather tempting about now."

Clark and Lauren Penrose sat in the kitchen and talked about the trial, their son, and their lives. How different things were from just a few weeks before. Everything seemed to be happening too fast, but it was out of their hands. They had expected controversy, but nothing like the firestorm that was now ablaze around the world. They had, at least, always been in control of their own home and now they had lost even that. What had come to be known as 'Camp Penrose' continued just outside their door. The reporters were there day and night. They had to have their telephone number changed. Every hour on radio and television, Penrose was praised as a genius one minute, vilified as a mad scientist the next.

Their conversation was interrupted by the sound of Karen's car pulling into the driveway. A key turned in the front door. The door opened then gently came to a close, not the usual slamming they'd come to expect over the past few weeks. Her footsteps dragged to the stairs and slowly plodded to the top. Once inside her bedroom, the door quietly latched shut.

"I think it's safe to have that conversation now," Lauren said.

Penrose softly knocked on the door. Hearing no response, he slowly turned the knob and opened the door. Karen sat cross-legged in the middle of her bed. Her cold, distant look did not betray the thoughts behind those blue eyes. Penrose proceeded with caution.

"Mind if I come in?"

"No," she answered faintly.

He stepped inside, closing the door behind him. He took a seat on the edge of the bed.

"I had a talk with Brandon."

"He told me." Her tone was noncommittal.

"Look, I know how you feel about everything, and I understand. It must be tough hearing all those awful things said about your old man and not knowing how to respond." He scratched behind his ear as he searched his mind for the right words. "This thing with Brandon, it's, well, it's put everything into a different perspective. For me, anyway. It's not that I wasn't aware of what homosexuals and parents of homosexuals went through, but now it's happened to me, you know. It's happened to us." Karen's icy exterior began to slowly melt. Penrose kept chipping away. "I don't love Brandon any less now that I know. In fact, I love him more. I feel bad for him. I wish I could help him, but I can't." He shook his head. "Isn't that ironic? I spend all my time coming up with a way to prevent homosexuality, and I can't even help my own son."

Karen's bottom lip twitched just a bit.

Penrose shifted on the bed and cleared his throat. "I want you to understand my motivation behind my work," he said tactfully. "When *you* look at the homosexual movement, you see it as a great civil rights cause. You see the marches, you see the demonstrations, you hear the speeches, you see the injustice. You see the millions and you sympathize with their plight. I see the same things, but I think of the millions more to come. I see a world that has loathed homosexuality for thousands of years and realize that they'll never achieve total acceptance. I also realize there's a biological reason for their condition and, as a scientist, I can use my education, my knowledge, my skills and help them."

"But these are loving and compassionate people," she said, looking for assurance from this man she loved and admired. She longed to believe he wasn't the monster he was made out to be. "All they want is to be accepted for who they are."

"I know that, honey, but if they're truly loving and compassionate, they would never wish their condition on another human being. Would they? I can't tell you how many letters I've gotten from homosexuals thanking me for, at last, breaking the cycle. As much as these friends of yours who are leading the charge against me would want you to think otherwise, there are millions of homosexuals who hate being gay. There are millions who, if given the chance, would become heterosexual today. You see, when you strip away the politics, when you strip away the hype that constantly surrounds this issue, you find a basic selfishness at the core of the movement against my procedure. My procedure won't affect those people, Karen. It will only save the millions who come after us from having to endure the same pain. Why would they oppose that? This isn't about the homosexuals who hate me. This is about the future generations of children to come. Did you know it was Brandon who persuaded me to see this thing through to the end?"

"I know," she said. "He told me."

"Brandon is a selfless young man. I'm very proud of him."

Karen started to cry. Penrose leaned over and held her close as she sobbed. The memories of his little girl flooded his head. He rocked her back and forth in his arms like he hadn't done in years. "Sh-h-h," he consoled. "It's going to be OK. Whatever that jury decides, it's going to be OK."

The plaintiffs' attorneys all gathered together over breakfast in the hotel restaurant. Rex Randle, fresh back from Atlanta, had watched the highlights of the trial on TV and was extremely encouraged. He and Norm were already at the table when Kelly came down and joined them.

"Your NBA thing with that Dr. Garcia was awesome!" Rex gushed, giving Kelly a high five.

"Yeah, but do you think Dr. Glasco did any damage?" she asked.

"That's my girl," Norm chimed in. "Always positive."

Rex said, "Glasco, smasco. That Progenitive Degenerative whatever crap went nowhere." He held his index finger and thumb close together. "You came that close to totally sinking that, too."

"Today it's Penrose," Kelly warned. "He's not going to be easy."

"Well, let me make it a little easier for you." Rex produced a file from his briefcase. "I got the information from the Election Commission like you asked." He handed the file to Kelly who promptly opened it. "Some pretty juicy stuff in there, too."

Kelly glanced over the information. "Very interesting. Very interesting, indeed. Here, take a look." She pushed the sheet over to Norm.

"Wow!" Norm exclaimed. "Good work, Rex."

"Anything on their other witness today?" Kelly asked.

"He's a damn good one, I know that much," Rex answered. "Dr. Harry Goodlum from the Centers For Disease Control. He's going to hammer home their 'disorder hypothesis.' He's a big gun. His word carries a lot of weight. If he's convincing, we'll have some mending to do."

"We'll assess any damage done after the fact," Kelly said. "I'll be addressing all of that again in my closing argument. Depending on how effective he is, I may have to ratchet my rebuttal up a couple of notches."

"Do we have all our bases covered?" Norm asked.

"We do," Kelly said, "unless they hit us with something unexpected. Other than that, I think we've done all we can do."

"All right," Rex said as he got up. "I've got some running around to do. See you in court."

Kelly and Norm both said goodbye to Rex, and they were back to the awkwardness.

After a moment, Kelly spoke, "Did I say 'thank you' for taking care of me the other night?"

"No, you didn't."

"Oh." She thought she had. "Well, thank you."

"Don't mention it."

"Listen, are you hanging around here this weekend or, uh, or what?"

"I figured I'd head back to Atlanta. Maybe fly back here Sunday night," Norm said.

"Why don't you stay here for the weekend. We can go to the beach on Saturday."

"Go to the beach? This time of year?"

"Yeah," she said. Her eyes sparkled.

"I don't know."

"Come on, Norm, we can take a picnic lunch. Get away from the trial for a little bit."

"Well . . ."

"Come on, Norm. It'll be fun. I really need some fun."

Norm looked at those chocolate eyes. It was hard to say no. "OK."

"Perfect," Kelly exclaimed. "We'll meet in the lobby at eleven a.m."

The mistake that led to his eventual demise was a foolish one. Jack Hawkins kicked himself for being so stupid. He tried to pay everything in cash, but there were some businesses that just wouldn't accept greenbacks. Because of one credit charge, his cash cow had been skewered. At the behest of Judge Kincaid, the FBI had descended upon Chapel Hill, North Carolina, like a swarm of locusts. They talked with everyone who Hawkins talked to and obtained a sketchy description. Their big break came during their interviews with the shopkeepers and clerks on Franklin Street, the main drag in the little college town. It seems Mr. Hawkins had visited a book store there and bought four of Martin Whitaker's books for research. The clerk remembered Hawkins distinctly because he had requested all of their Whitaker books in stock. She was able to describe him down to his socks. The agents figured whoever was snooping around Whitaker was the same guy who dug up the dirt on the other witnesses. He probably wasn't from Chapel Hill, so he had to have rented wheels somewhere. RDU International Airport wasn't that large. After a few stops at car rental desks, they hit pay dirt. Hawkins had paid the four-day rental by credit card.

The FBI walked out of Jack Hawkins' office with boxes of files, his answering machine, and his computer. There was little else to take but a desk and a chair. They combed through the trash cans, the underside of drawers, everywhere looking for a sign of Raven. Meanwhile, Hawkins sat at a nondescript table in one of the interrogation rooms inside the J.

Edgar Hoover building in Washington, D.C. His attorney sat close by as the two agents grilled him about his work.

"I swear to you, I never met this Raven character," he insisted. "I only talked to him over the phone."

"Do you have anymore tapes of your conversations with him?" one of the agents asked stone-faced.

"Just the one I gave you. The only reason I got that one is because my answering machine picked up before I did. It didn't cut off when I answered the phone, the piece of crap." He took a drag from his cigarette and stared at the floor.

"Mr. Hawkins, did you know that witness tampering was a federal offense?" the second agent asked, trying to intimidate the truth out of him.

"What witness tampering?" Hawkins acted as if he were offended. "I was just doing a job, working up a background check for my client. How am I supposed to know who these people are?"

"Don't you read the papers, watch TV?" the first agent asked. "This is the biggest story in the country."

Hawkins laughed. "Like I got time. This Raven character was keeping me pretty busy. I hardly had time to eat and sleep."

The agents looked at each other while Hawkins snuffed out his cigarette in the ash tray.

"Any further questions, gentlemen?" Hawkins' mouthpiece asked. "If not, we'd like to get out of here and get some sleep."

Technically, there was nothing illegal about tailing someone and interviewing their friends and associates. They decided Hawkins had spilled all he was going to spill. They confiscated the tape and let him go.

39

The day off that Judge Kincaid had given the trial, due to a conflict in his schedule, had given the defense some much needed time. Still, little could prepare them for the unexpected. Kurt Ford had called for the special meeting in the judge's chambers. Kelly noticed how stressed he looked, even more than was to be expected under the circumstances. He had taken a couple of serious body blows in court and had been pummeled in the press. Now he was forced to announce one more setback. No attorney likes to make last minute substitutions to their witness lineup, but Kurt Ford had no choice.

"Our last witness, Dr. Harry Goodlum, is not going to be able to make it," Kurt announced, almost in distress.

"You understand, Mr. Ford, that we cannot postpone this trial until your witness shows," Judge Kincaid informed him.

"I know, sir."

Kelly almost felt sorry for the poor guy. He seemed to have been counting on Dr. Goodlum to make his case. Now he was going to have to regroup.

"I'd like to request a substitution. I'd like to put a character witness in the place of Dr. Goodlum," Kurt requested.

Under the circumstances, Kelly had no problem with it. She was not without compassion. Moreover, Dr. Goodlum had been a worrisome witness for the plaintiffs. Kelly was glad to see him go. Kurt submitted the name of the character witness. Kelly approved and the issue was decided in a matter of minutes. As they were leaving the judge's chambers, Kelly's cell phone rang. She pulled the earring from her ear and answered it.

"Kelly Morris." She headed down to the small cloak room near the courtroom for some privacy.

"Hi, Kel. Where do we stand?" Greg Wently asked on the other end.

"I just left a meeting with the judge. Some minor details about defense witnesses. Where are you?"

"Still in Atlanta. We're coming in tomorrow. I wanted to take you to dinner, if you're available. I've hardly seen you since this trial started."

"Oh," Kelly fretted. "I'm having dinner with Norm."

"Yeah? Business or pleasure?" Greg teased.

"Get real. Business, of course. We're going over my closing argument."

"All right, then. What do you say we get together on Saturday? You can stay in town, can't you?"

Kelly was embarrassed to tell him she was picnicking with Norm. "I'm afraid I'm tied up Saturday, too."

Greg acted as though he were put out with her. "Hey, whose attorney are you, anyway? Won't you even meet with your own client?"

"If you've got official business to discuss, then I'll work you in. Otherwise, I'll have to see you on Sunday. We've gotta make sure we're ready for Monday's showdown."

"Fair enough. I'll see you Sunday. Love you."

"Love you."

Kelly returned the phone to her purse. It occurred to her she had just deceived her best friend — and her client — and she couldn't readily answer why. She would evaluate her feelings later. There was battle to be done in the courtroom.

The bailiff announced His Honor and Judge Kincaid took his usual perch on the bench. The jurors were all in place. Kurt Ford squirmed nervously. Kincaid shuffled the papers in front of him and cleared his throat.

"You may call your next witness, Mr. Ford."

"The Defense calls Dr. Clark Penrose."

Dr. Penrose was led to the witness stand where he was sworn in and seated. The weeks of silence would now be broken. The man at the epicenter of this controversy sat calmly and coolly. Every eyeball in the house was trained on him. The pool TV camera in the back of the room zoomed in on a headshot. All that could be heard was the creaking of the bailiff's leather holster against the wooden chair as he returned to his seat.

"Good morning, Dr. Penrose," Kurt greeted.

"Morning."

"Dr. Penrose, I won't embarrass you this morning by asking you to rattle off your credentials. For the record, I'll summarize your resume. Feel free to correct me," Kurt said, looking down at his notes. "You received your undergraduate degree from Duke University and your M.D. from Vanderbilt Medical School. You earned your Master of Science degree from Harvard School of Public Health. You've been recognized with numerous awards and honors including the Outstanding Investigator Award from the American Federation of Clinical Research and the John Snow Award from the American Public Association. You're a fellow of the American College of Physicians, the American College of Preventive Medicine, the American Association for Advancement of Science, and the Royal Society of Medicine. You've written more than 400 articles and two textbooks on genetics. You also have the distinction of having mapped more genes than any other doctor in the world for the Human Genome Project. Does all this sound correct?"

"Yes."

"You don't sound like Dr. Frankenstein to me."

A wave of laughter swept across the courtroom.

"Thank you." Dr. Penrose smiled slightly.

"Dr. Penrose, tell the court how you came to take up the search for the gay gene."

Penrose took a deep breath. "Well, it started, actually, out of my research into AIDS. We were intrigued that such a devastating disease was disproportionately brutal in the gay community. I set out to see if there was some genetic reason for it which led me to a more fundamental question: why are people homosexual to start with? I learned that there was surprisingly little research in the area of sexual orientation. I believed, and still believe, that research into this area might help us understand not only homosexuality, but a whole host of other genetically-based conditions."

"Such as?"

"Well, we found that in the same region as the gay gene are genes linked to other traits like color blindness and hemophilia. It only stands to reason that if we were successful in altering the gay gene, that we might have success with these other conditions."

Kurt Ford then invited Dr. Penrose to step down from the witness stand. He asked him to give the same presentation he gave in the law offices. Dr. Penrose used the overhead projector and the updated digital slides from Kurt's legal exhibits guy to explain his theory of the gay gene to the jury and how he came to discover it. As in his talk to the lawyers, Penrose was charming, affable, and obviously quite knowledgeable about his subject, just as Kurt had hoped he would be. After the presentation, Dr. Penrose reassumed his place on the witness stand.

"Dr. Penrose, how would you describe homosexuality in medical terms?"

"I believe, as do many of my colleagues, that homosexuality is a textbook example of a disorder."

"Define 'disorder' for the court."

"Basically it's an upset of normal function. In this case, the basic function of sexuality is to procreate. It stands to reason that anything that deviates from that function is a disorder. Sterility deviates from the basic function and we view it as a disorder and try to correct it. Erectile dysfunction is also viewed as a disorder. We try to correct it."

"What was your goal when you set out to find the origins of sexual orientation?"

"My goal was to find what we believed was the most likely cause and that was a gay gene."

"Then what?"

"As a doctor and a scientist, it's only logical that if we ever found the gay gene, we would develop a way to correct it."

"You never had this grand scheme to wipe out all the homosexuals?"

"Absolutely not. Let me make this point very clear. We do not yet have the technology to alter the gay genes of humans after they're born. The immune system is too developed by the time of birth to allow the enzyme we developed to work. There's no 'grand scheme,' as you put it, to change the homosexuals who are alive today. Furthermore, that's something individuals would have to decide for themselves if such a procedure were ever developed. Nobody would be forcing anyone to do anything. What this particular procedure of ours does is give the parents the choice to decide if they want their child to be homosexual or heterosexual."

"I see." Kurt Ford pulled at his bottom lip as he phrased the next question in his mind. "The couple, Dr. Penrose, the parents of the Loveport Baby, do they have any other children?"

"Yes, they have two teenage children."

"Either of them gay that you know of?"

"Not that we know of. The mother's brother is gay, which makes sense. As I pointed out in the presentation, we've learned the gay gene is passed down through the mother, so if a woman has a gay sibling, that increases the chance that her son will be gay. Naturally, it doesn't always mean the child will be gay, but his chances are increased somewhat."

"Have you talked with this couple at any length about their decision?"

"We talked at great length. I broke the news to them and laid out all of the options."

"Which were?"

"Well, they could opt for termination, which they ruled out immediately. They could go with the procedure or they could simply do nothing."

"They ruled out abortion?"

"Yes."

"They were unwilling to take the life of this fetus?"

"That's correct."

"And they chose the procedure?"

"Yes."

"Did they tell you why?"

"Oh, yes. We had a long discussion about her brother."

"The gay brother."

"Yes, and she had seen the torment he had undergone. She couldn't bear to put her own son through that, so they decided on the procedure."

"And they feel like they're doing the right thing?"

"Oh, absolutely. They feel like they're giving their son a chance at a normal life, a chance to marry and have children. They have no misgivings about their decision at all."

"Thank you, Dr. Penrose. Nothing further, Your Honor."

Judge Kincaid asked, "Does the plaintiff wish to cross-examine?" knowing the answer.

Kelly Morris was already around the table. "Yes, Your Honor. Dr. Penrose, you obviously support the right of a parent to change the genes of their fetus if the child is going to be gay. What if a couple wanted to make their straight baby gay? Would you support such a move?"

"No."

"Oh? And why not?"

"As I explained earlier, the basic function of sexuality is to procreate. Changing a straight fetus to a gay fetus would not accomplish the goals of nature."

"The goals of nature," she mocked. "You talk about us as if we're animals."

"Well, we are, technically," Penrose glibly responded.

"But we are human beings, Dr. Penrose. We have the ability to choose and sometimes our choices are against nature. For example, there are many couples who choose not to have children. Are you saying that we should force them to have children so they conform to the 'goals of nature'?"

"Of course not, but—"

"Men and women every single day undergo operations so they cannot reproduce. Should we deny them this procedure because it goes against the 'goals of nature?'" Her volume increased with each question.

"No."

"I guess condom manufacturers and birth control makers should close up shop today because what they're doing doesn't conform to your so-called 'goals of nature.' Is that what you want, Dr. Penrose?" she shouted.

"No!" he shouted back.

Kurt Ford moved to the edge of his seat. Dr. Penrose was agitated and there was no telling what he'd say.

Kelly took a deep breath. "Dr. Penrose, is it true that your research team worked around the clock to find a suitable couple for your procedure?"

"Yes."

"Why the urgency?"

"Because the director, Dr. Kirsch, had given me a limited amount of time before he was going to have to go public with what we had discovered."

"So what if he went public?"

"I'm not naive, Ms. Morris. I knew once the discovery was made public, it would be quite controversial, therefore, making it more difficult to find a willing couple."

"I see. Is it true that the period of time you searched for a suitable couple with a homosexual fetus was referred to in your lab as 'Gay Watch?'" she asked with contempt.

The courtroom burst into laughter. She cocked her head toward the gallery but kept her eyes on Penrose, never cracking a smile. She obviously hadn't meant her question to be funny. Dr. Penrose stared at the floor while Judge Kincaid restored order to the courtroom.

"Is that true, Dr. Penrose?"

"I believe one of our lab technicians dubbed the process as such, but it was only done to help relieve the pressure. It certainly wasn't official, by any means.

"Dr. Penrose, do you have a political ulterior motive for wanting to alter the gay gene?"

"That's ridiculous!"

"A simple 'yes' or 'no' will do."

"No."

"Are you a Republican or a Democrat?"

"Objection!" Kurt Ford came out of his seat. "The witness' political affiliation is irrelevant, Your Honor."

Kelly hurried her small frame toward the bench. "I'm trying to establish motive, Your Honor."

"Overruled."

Kelly turned back to the witness. "Republican or Democrat, Dr. Penrose?"

"I'm an Independent," Penrose asserted.

"Is that a fact? According to records down at the Election Commission, you voted in the Republican primary five times out of the last five primaries."

Dr. Penrose didn't protest the allegation.

"Isn't it true, Dr. Penrose, that you've given somewhere in the neighborhood of $40,000 over the past ten years to various conservative organizations and candidates including the American Conservative Union, the Competitive Enterprise Institute, GOPAC, a Republican congressman, and two Republican senators?!"

"That's true, but—"

"And many of these organizations have anti-gay agendas and, in some cases, have been downright hostile to the gay rights movement. Isn't that right?"

"Quite frankly, I don't—"

"Dr. Penrose," her volume increased, "the fact is, you *do* have a political agenda and it has manifested itself in your work!"

"Objection!" Kurt shouted at the top of his lungs trying to overpower Kelly Morris' shrill tirade. "Your Honor, please let the witness respond to these wild accusations!"

"Sustained!" Judge Kincaid was exasperated. "Ms. Morris, you are badgering this witness. You will lower your voice in my courtroom and, for God's sake, let him answer the questions!"

"I apologize, Your Honor." Kelly regained her composure.

"Dr. Penrose," the judge instructed. "If you would like, you may respond to Ms. Morris."

Penrose wasn't sure where to start. "Well, there's a lot of territory to cover there. As for my party affiliation, I do consider myself an Independent. The reason I've voted Republican for the last few years is because the Democrats haven't shown a propensity for coming to the aid of us doctors lately." The courtroom laughed, but Penrose was indignant. "That's why I've felt compelled over the years to give a little of my resources to those candidates and organizations I felt had my best interests at heart. I never checked their position on the gay issue and, quite frankly, I don't care. But if a man can't vote his conscience and give his money where he wants to without his work coming into question, I don't know what this country has come to."

Regardless of Penrose's rebuttal, Kelly had made her point. The seed had been planted in the jury's mind and that's all she could hope to accomplish. "No more questions." Kelly returned to her seat.

"Any redirect?" Kincaid asked.

Kurt took a glance at the jury to take their temperature. He wondered if Kelly Morris' reckless but bold attempt had hit its mark.

"No, Your Honor."

Judge Kincaid looked at his watch. "The court stands in recess for lunch. Two hours."

Sabrina Andrews stared out the window of their spacious den with the TV remote dangling from her hand. The screen was freshly black. She thought about her son. No matter what happened, she had decided he must never know. The spectacle which she had seen unfolding before her over the last few weeks must never be attributed to him. No matter what the outcome, that was a burden no one should ever have to bear. She second-guessed herself. That was only natural after watching every minute of the trial. At times, the plaintiffs could be as convincing as the defense. And to think the attorney who had been assigned to represent her son was on the opposing side, trying to stop them from doing what they felt was best for their son. She didn't even know her own son yet and his court-appointed representative was at odds with her in a court of law. She felt robbed. Robbed of the normality of bringing another child into the world. She also felt betrayed, that some other entity with its own motives and its own agenda would claim to represent her own child against her. What right did they have? She gently rubbed her stomach. In reality, what right did she have? Was it her place as a parent to take so drastic a measure as to undo what nature had done? Or, was it her obligation to correct what nature was unable to correct itself? Dr. Penrose had just testified that she and her husband were positive they were doing the right thing. He was just going on what they had told him. He couldn't know what it really felt like to make that decision. No one could.

She looked at the clock on the wall. Tom wouldn't be home for another five hours. She counted down the seconds each day. Together, they could lean on one another. She shuddered to think how it would be if she had to go it alone. She feared her self-doubt would surely consume her. She looked over at the telephone and tried to resist the temptation of calling him at work again at the risk of becoming a nuisance. If she were lucky, he would call her before too long to check on her. Perhaps he needed reassurance as much as she did.

It seemed her mind ran the same track every day. An emotional roller coaster of extremely high peaks and equally low valleys. First, she felt good in their decision, knowing that they were saving their son from a life of extreme difficulty. Then the doubt began to creep in and she would plunge so far so quickly that she would almost become nauseous. Once she had thoroughly depressed herself, she would rationalize that it was out of her hands, regardless of what decision they made. The issue would be decided with or without them. Her hopes would begin to climb, if only ever so slightly. Her mind would then finally focus on her brother. She had seen firsthand the misery his homosexuality had brought him. He had swung from guilt and shame to righteous indignation throughout his thirty-four years, but she had never seen him come to a rest on contentment. Whoever he was, he didn't much care for himself. Just as she reached the summit of comfort in her justification, her mind was off on the roller coaster ride again. She feared the endless cycle might never stop, even after this nightmare was over.

40

After lunch, Judge Kincaid reconvened the court. The attorneys settled back into their seats. The bailiff closed the back doors and the pool television cameras came to life. Kelly Morris figured the afternoon to be a mere formality. A character witness, especially this one, should carry little weight with the jury. He was too close to Dr. Penrose to be considered credible.

"You may call your next witness, Mr. Ford," Kincaid instructed.

"The defense calls Brandon Penrose to the stand."

The courtroom murmured as young Brandon was escorted down the center aisle. He paused beside the front row where his parents and sister sat. His eyes met his father's. Penrose gave him wink. Brandon proceeded on to the witness stand. His thick, black hair was neatly combed over. He wore a blue blazer with a red tie, which gave him the image of a prep school student. As he was sworn in, Norm leaned over to Kelly.

"Are you gonna cross-examine the kid?" Norm asked.

"What's the use?" she whispered. "He's a character witness for his old man. You think I can get him to say anything bad about his own father? Anyway, he was a last minute substitution. He's a pinch-hitter."

Norm shrugged in agreement then leaned back up to catch Kurt Ford asking his first question.

"Brandon, you're Dr. Penrose's only son. Is that right?"

"Yes, sir," he answered nervously.

"And you're how old?"

"Sixteen."

"Sixteen, huh? Brandon, in your sixteen years, have you ever known your father to be homophobic?"

"No, sir."

"And how do you know Dr. Penrose is not homophobic?"

Brandon paused for a moment and looked at his father. Kurt smiled and gave him a slight nod to let him know this was the time. Brandon hesitated, taking one more look at his father then back to Kurt. He swallowed hard. "Because, uh. Because I'm gay."

The entire courtroom broke into chatter. Reporters vigorously wrote in their note pads. Kelly Morris' mouth dropped open. Judge Kincaid pounded the gavel. She looked at Norm and Rex in disbelief. They'd been had.

"Ladies and gentlemen, let's have order, please." Judge Kincaid demanded.

When the commotion died down, Kurt resumed. "You are gay?" Kurt confirmed.

"Yes, sir."

"When you first told your father, how did he react? Was he angry? Was he embarrassed? Was he sad?"

"He wasn't angry. I thought he would be, but he wasn't. I guess he was sad but not because I was gay."

"Then, why was he sad?"

"He was sad because he thought he had hurt me."

"He thought he had hurt you? How so?"

"He thought his efforts to find this gay gene and correct it had hurt me."

"Had they?"

"No," he answered as if that were a stupid question.

"Why not?"

"Do you think I like being like this? I mean, for the longest time, I didn't understand what was wrong with me. When I started to understand, I tried to hide it. The only person I told was my sister. In fact, she was the one who finally told my parents because she thought I was suicidal. I hated myself."

"You hated yourself to the point of considering killing yourself?"

"Yes, sir."

Lauren reached for her husband's hand.

"You said 'hated,' past tense. You don't hate yourself anymore?"

"No, sir."

"When did that change?"

"Well, when…" Brandon's eyes welled up with tears. Dr. Penrose covered his own eyes with his hand for a moment then wiped the tears. Blinking a couple of times, he looked back up at his son baring his soul. Lauren squeezed his hand tightly.

"It's OK, Brandon," Kurt consoled. He grabbed a box of tissues from the defendant's table and set them on the witness stand.

"It all changed," Brandon began again, "when I talked with my father about it. I told him I was sorry." He could no longer hold back the tears. He paused after every few words to wipe the tears with the tissue. "He grabbed me and held me tight and he told me that I had nothing to be sorry for. I told him I knew how much this must hurt him, but he seemed surprised that I said that." Brandon sniffed and pressed the tissue to his cheek.

"What do you mean, surprised?"

"Well, he held my face in his hands. Boy, he was crying," he nervously laughed through his sobbing. "He said, 'Brandon, listen to me. I love you. That love is unconditional. There's nothing you could say or do to change that.' He also said that I had nothing to be sorry for or be ashamed of." He grabbed another tissue from the box. Judge Kincaid sat there stone-faced. Several jurors wiped tears from their eyes.

"What else did he tell you?" Kurt pressed.

"He said that he knew more than anyone that I didn't choose to be this way. He said that's what he'd spent all these years trying to prove. I told him that all I ever wanted was to make him proud." The tears began to flow again. "He held me tight again and said 'I *am* proud, son. I *am* proud.' He said he was proud of me just because I was his son." Kurt stood there trying to hold back his own tears. Those were the very words he longed to hear from his own father. "He told me nothing could ever change that. He said I didn't have to win his approval, that he had loved me since the day I was born."

Soft sobs echoed throughout the chamber. Given how close to home this was for Kurt, he could hardly proceed, but he knew he must.

"Brandon, you said he thought his work at Loveport would hurt you?"

"Yes, sir. He wanted to call the whole project off, but I insisted he go forward with it."

"*You* insisted. Why?"

"Because I really believe what he's doing is right. I mean, look at me. You think I *want* to be like this?" His words quietly stabbed Kurt like a knife. He closed his eyes for a brief moment to absorb the pain. Brandon continued, "If my dad can save one child the pain I've been through, it'll be worth it."

Kurt looked at him for a moment. Dare he go any further? He felt he had put the boy through enough. He decided there was nothing left to say. He returned to the defense table and sat down.

Judge Kincaid, apparently unaffected by the testimony, looked cautiously at Kelly Morris who was, herself, wiping away tears from the corners of her eyes. "Cross-examination, Ms. Morris?"

Kelly looked at Norm then Rex then back up at the judge. All eyes of the jury were on her. She wondered how effective Brandon's testimony had been. A couple of the women jurors dotted the corners of their eyes with tissue. Kelly hesitated to inflict anymore damage by appearing insensitive to Brandon's pain, but there was one point she yearned to make.

Judge Kincaid was growing impatient. "Ms. Morris. Cross-examination?"

"Yes, Your Honor." Kelly slowly rose from her seat and approached the witness stand. She cleared her throat and looked tenderly up at Dr. Penrose's son. "Brandon, just for clarification of the record, how long has your father known you were gay?"

Brandon looked over at Kurt then back at Kelly. "About a week."

"About a week," Kelly repeated. "That's all?"

"Yes, ma'am."

"So, it was well after this trial began that your father learned the truth?"

"Yes, ma'am."

"And it was after the trial had begun that your father wanted to, as you said, call the whole project off?"

"Yes, ma'am."

"No more questions, Your Honor."

Judge Kincaid watched as Kelly returned to her seat. "Redirect, Mr. Ford?"

"No, Your Honor."

"You may step down, son," Kincaid instructed Brandon. Once he was back in his seat, Kincaid refocused his gaze on the defense table. "Any more witnesses, Mr. Ford?"

"No, Your Honor. The defense rests."

"In that case, this court will reconvene Monday morning at ten o'clock for closing arguments. Court stands in recess. Ms. Morris. Mr. Ford. I would like to see you in my chambers."

Kurt closed his briefcase wondering what kind of trouble he was in this time. He would rather have been flogged than endure another tongue-lashing from Judge Kincaid. He felt like a twelve-year-old in the principal's office. Kelly sat there in silence. She glared at Kurt, her crossed leg vibrating rapidly. Playing Penrose's gay son was way below the belt. It was a nasty trick meant only to yank the heartstrings of the jury. And after Kurt had played her like a harp with that sob story of his final witness canceling. It happened that way sometimes when trials got dirty, but this was different. It wasn't just Brandon Penrose. It was the inexcusable leaks. It was the way they were trying to intimidate her witnesses. Apparently, with Don Bissette behind bars they hadn't found anyone else sleazy enough to leak to, but it didn't matter. They'd done their damage. All of her witnesses were called. There was no one left to intimidate.

"We're closing in on the leak," Kincaid bluffed. "The Feds picked up a small-time private eye from Washington who'd been doing the legwork for the leaker." Kelly seemed to come back to life at the news. Perhaps there would be justice after all. Kincaid carefully watched Kurt's reaction. "We think we know who it is." Kurt looked as interested in finding out as Kelly. Could it be he was being kept out of the loop so he wouldn't be compromised?

"Who is it?" Kelly leaned forward.

"Well, we don't know exactly yet." Kelly sank back into her seat. "Whoever was paying this private detective was disguising his voice. He went by the name Raven. The FBI has a tape of him. It's only a matter of time before they find him."

"Somebody calling themselves Raven? That's all they know?" Kelly was disgusted. Couldn't the FBI do better than that?

"They know all about him," Kincaid assured her. It was as much for Kurt's benefit as hers. If he *did* know who the leaker was and thought federal agents were on his trail, he might get nervous and do something reckless.

"One more day of testimony," Kincaid reminded them. "I trust we can put this little sideshow behind us and concentrate on the business of the court."

The two attorneys nodded and were dismissed.

41

It had been quite a stressful ordeal, but now there was light at the end of the tunnel. The day's testimony had ended earlier than anticipated. There was plenty of time left in the afternoon to work on his closing argument, but Kurt Ford put it on the back burner. Dumaine, despite his acute homophobia, had turned out to be quite an asset to the defense. Kurt felt it appropriate to buy his co-counsel a drink. Dumaine accepted the invitation and the two drove about a mile away from the courthouse to a little tavern.

The bartender and several waitresses readied themselves for the inevitable onslaught of working stiffs that would stream through their door at five o'clock. For now, the bar was empty except for a middle-age man who sat mesmerized in front of the poker machine. Kurt and Bill took two seats at the far end of the bar.

"What can I get you gentlemen?" the bartender asked, laying two cardboard coasters on the bar in front of them. Kurt deferred to Dumaine.

"I'll have a Honey Brown. Long-neck, please."

"I'll have the same." Kurt made it easy. "That was one helluva trial," he said a bit nervously. This was one of the few times the two had ever actually been alone together. The one which stood out in both of their minds was the big blowup in the conference room.

"Yeah, it was," Dumaine agreed. "How do you feel about it?"

"I thought we did very well. It's hard to read that jury, though. I could never tell if I was really getting through to them."

The bartender brought the beers. Kurt held his up to toast.

"Here's to a happy verdict," Kurt offered. Dumaine touched his bottle to Kurt's, and they both took a big gulp.

"Penrose's kid," Dumaine said. "Man, that was powerful testimony."

"Very powerful." Kurt stared straight ahead at the assorted liquor bottles that lined the wall.

After an uncomfortable moment, Dumaine broke the silence. "There's, uh, something I have to say."

Kurt felt another apology attempt coming and tried to deflect it. "Bill, please. You don't have to—"

"No, I have to. For me." He was very serious. Kurt shut up and let him talk. "Did I ever tell you about my brother?" Dumaine asked.

This is an odd apology, Kurt thought. He shook his head.

Dumaine took another big gulp and continued to stare straight ahead. "My younger brother, Tom. Man, when we were growing up, he was always into something. My parents never really knew what to do with him. He was as wild and adventurous as I was serious, but we were as close as two brothers could be. Our differences seemed to be what kept us so close. I guess I really wanted to be a little more like him and, if the truth were known, he wanted to be a little more like me. 'Here come the Dumaine Brothers,' people used to say. I really knew they were talking about Tom because, man, he was trouble." Dumaine chuckled and took another sip of beer. "You never could tie that guy down. I mean, he was into everything, but he never seemed to be going anywhere. Just going. You know what I mean?

Kurt smiled politely.

"I went off to college. A couple of years later, Tom graduated from high school. Barely. It wasn't that he wasn't smart," Dumaine added quickly, "it was that he was just too busy with other things to ever buckle down and study. Instead of going to college, he got a job at a furniture store delivering furniture. My mom and dad were disappointed, of course, but what could they do? This was Tom, man. They couldn't make him go to college. That was when we seemed to lose touch. We began to not have anything in common. He had his friends. I had mine in college. His friends seemed to be the screwy type, you know, just plain weird. They had dyed hair, all different colors, earrings, nose rings, tongue studs, you name it. People would see Tommy out with these folks and they'd run into me and they'd say, 'Man, Tommy is really hanging out with a strange crowd.' So, I tried not to come home too much because it only made it more obvious that we were drifting apart. Plus, I didn't want to hear all these stories about Tommy, and I didn't feel like it was my place to tell him who his friends could be. Then I got into law school and that drove an even deeper wedge between us.

"One of those rare weekends when I was home from school, Tommy called to make sure I was there because he wanted to get together. I hadn't seen him in months. I opened the door and I hardly recognized him. I mean, he looked awful. He sat down in the den with Mom and Dad and me and just blurted it out. 'Mom, Dad, Bill,' he called us each by name, 'I have AIDS.'" Dumaine's eyes filled with tears. He stared straight ahead. Kurt was stunned. This was the very last thing he ever expected to hear. He didn't know what to say. Dumaine took another sip then laughed nervously. "Well, you can imagine my mother's reaction. She fell to pieces. Crying. Wailing, actually. She grabbed Tommy and hugged him like she'd never let him go. I remember my father just sat there with this dumb expression on his face like 'what have you gotten into this time, Tom.' Then my dad, who has the finesse of a foghorn, said, 'I thought only queers got AIDS.' Tommy looked back at him and said, 'Dad, don't you get it? I'm gay.' It didn't seem to faze Mom. Hell, nothing could be worse than the news she just got, right? She just kept hugging and crying. But Dad? Dad didn't say a word. His expression never changed from that dumb look. He just got up and walked out of the room. He never saw Tommy again. I guess the only bond stronger than a father and his son is a man and his prejudices." Dumaine's voice cracked, but he quickly wrestled his emotions under control. Tears trickled down Kurt's cheeks. He couldn't look at him.

"Me? I was mad, I mean really pissed," Dumaine continued. "I never believed Tommy was gay. Not my brother, oh no." He leaned back on his stool and took a long sip from his bottle. "I mean, we were thick as thieves. The Dumaine Brothers. There's no way he was gay. I blamed the crowd he was hanging out with. Here was this lost soul and they had taken advantage of him, brainwashed him. I hated those bastards." He downed another gulp of beer and clenched his fist. His jaw tightened. "I thought, 'Those faggot bastards had done this to my little brother.'

"The next two months were the longest two months of my life. Tom, of course, got progressively worse. I visited him in the hospital but was afraid to touch him." Dumaine's voice cracked again. The tears streamed down his cheek. He looked over at Kurt. "Can you imagine that? I wouldn't even touch my own brother. There he was lying there dying. My little Tommy. And I treated him like a freak." He looked back at the shelves of liquor in front of him. "Then he was gone. Just twenty-one years old and he was gone. And I was pissed. I hated what those people had done to my brother. I still didn't believe he was gay. I mean, why would he choose a lifestyle like that on his own, right? Those deviants had to have turned him into one of them. From then on, any time I saw a homosexual on TV, my blood boiled. I'd see news clips of gay pride parades and want to mow them all down. They had taken my little brother."

The hatred showed on Dumaine's face. He clinched his teeth and tore at the label on his beer. Kurt had never felt so uncomfortable.

"And then came this case," Dumaine began again. "When we had that fight in the conference room, something you said hit me like a baseball bat. You asked me why anyone would choose to be gay. It didn't really come together until Dr. Penrose spoke to us. I sat there in the dark, looking at those images on the screen, listening to him speak and choking back the tears. Everything he said made sense. The gene being passed from the mother's side. The chance of being gay increasing if you had a maternal uncle who was gay. We had an uncle. Michael was his name. He never married, and there were always whispers that he was gay. The whole family treated him like shit, ostracized him. Everybody except Tommy. It all started to make sense. I got home that night and all the pieces of the puzzle fit together. Tommy, my own brother, really *was* gay. It wasn't anybody else's fault. Hell, it wasn't Tommy's fault. He was gay, but none of us were understanding enough for him to feel like he could come and tell us until it was too late. The really sad part is all Tommy saw of me near the end was this angry brother who was ashamed of him, who wouldn't go near him. You know, I was so mad. I was so concerned about how it all affected *me*. I didn't think about a lot of things back then. I just tried to block it all out. At least he had Mom. She stayed by his side night and day. She wasn't concerned about the stigma or the shame or anything else. All she knew was her son was dying, and if she could help it, he wouldn't die alone. My father never set foot in that hospital. People would ask him about his son and he'd say he only had one and he was doing just fine. You know, the worst part is, I never told him how much I loved him. Then he was gone and it was too late. It was too late." He broke down and quietly sobbed, his face buried in his hands.

Kurt held both hands around his beer, his head hung low. He was not at all prepared for what he just heard. To think he was expecting an apology. He was ashamed now for thinking he even deserved one. No one should have to endure what Dumaine had gone through, Kurt thought. No matter how insensitive and callous he had been, Dumaine didn't deserve this. Kurt mustered the courage to glance over at him. He hesitated then reached over and gently squeezed his shoulder.

"Without a doubt, the most poignant testimony in this trial, Betty," Duncan Reynolds began the night's broadcast of *The Pulse*.

"If you call exploiting a sixteen-year-old boy poignant then, I guess," Betty Duvall countered.

"Exploiting? You liberals are incredible! The plaintiffs crucified Dr. Penrose, trying to make him out to be some mad scientist. I think having his son testify that he, himself, is gay was the perfect way to burst their balloon. I mean, how homophobic can he be if his own son is gay?"

"I don't think the jury's going to buy it," Betty said. "Penrose was working on that project for years. He just found out in the last week that his own son was gay, and he still didn't back down from this horrible procedure. All that shows is he puts his work ahead of his own family, something I don't think is going to be lost on that jury."

It was a sunny Saturday, about sixty-five degrees. Norm Woodruff, in his khakis and golf shirt, sat on a borrowed blanket from the hotel room. The rhythm of the ocean waves was soothing. He munched on an apple and watched the seagulls play. Hardly anyone else thought it sensible to go out on the beach this time of year. Kelly Morris, in a casual dress, lay face down on the blanket. She had hardly said a word all day.

"Working on your tan?" Norm asked dryly.

"Very funny," she mumbled.

"You can't sulk all day." He took another bite of the apple. "By the way, wasn't this your idea?"

He got no response.

"Come on." He playfully whacked her on the backside.

Kelly flew to her feet. "Don't you dare touch me there," she said only half-serious.

"So, sue me for sexual harassment." He looked up at her with one eye shut. She stood there, her silhouette against the sky, as if she were waiting for an apology. "Sit down. You're in my sun."

Realizing she wasn't going to get one, Kelly sat down cross-legged beside him. "How do you do it?"

"How do I do what?"

"How do you not let your work eat at you?"

"Simple. I've got more important things in my life than work."

"Oh, yeah? Like what?"

"Like my son."

"I didn't know you had a son."

"Yep, Ben. He's twenty this year. He's a University of Georgia man, just like his old man."

"Do you see him much?"

"Are you kidding? He comes home just to wash clothes, raid the pantry, and beg for a little more money, then he heads back to Athens. He's a typical college kid."

"Is he going to be a lawyer like his dad?"

"I don't think he has any idea what he wants to be." Norm threw the apple core down the beach and watched the seagulls dive for it.

"I was lucky in that regard." Kelly lay down on her back and covered her eyes from the sun. "I knew from the time I was a little girl that I wanted to be a lawyer. It's funny. Back in those days, the profession was regarded as noble. Nowadays, with all the sleazy lawyers advertising on TV and the ones who'll sue anybody to make a buck, we rank just below used car salesmen. It's nice you have things that are more important to you than being a lawyer. I guess that's my problem. *This* is the most important thing to me."

"There's nothing in your life that's more important?"

"Maybe some real close friends, but even that's debatable. Being an attorney is who I am. Although, I must admit, it hasn't always been pretty. I've been asked to do some seedy things, believe me. I represent those who can't afford a lawyer. A lot of these folks are good people, salt of the earth type folks. Some are just plain rotten. I had one guy try to pay me in crack cocaine."

"You're kidding!" Norm laughed.

"No. And the funny thing is I'd just gotten him off on a drug charge. I really believed he was innocent, too," she said sadly. "That was a real eye opener. I've seen attorneys sell their souls for a lot less than a couple of rocks of crack. But, you know what? No matter what the consequences, I'd like to think I'd never do anything to dishonor my profession." She looked up at Norm. "Does that sound corny?"

"No, not at all. That's quite an admirable trait. I agree. If I can't win with honor, I'd rather not win at all." He closed his eyes and clasped the bridge of his nose with his thumb and forefinger as if trying to remember. "Let's see. Bear with me, now. It's been a few years.

> *There is reward for those who dare, for those who dare and do:*
> *Who face the dark inevitable, who fall and know no shame;*
> *Upon their banner triumph sits and in the horn they blew,*
> *Naught's lost if honor be not lost, defeat is but a name.*

Kelly smiled up at him. "Madison Cawein. The Man In Gray."

"Very good," Norm said. "I'm impressed. Brown University did a first-class job."

Kelly turned on her side and smiled broadly. "Actually, my father used to recite that one."

"Oh, now I'm sounding like your father. Thanks."

Kelly snickered and looked out at the ocean. They both pondered the words of the poet for a moment. Then Norm broke the silence.

"Your dad did tell you Cawein wrote that for a reunion of Confederate veterans, right?"

"You made that up," she said.

"I swear." He laughed at the irony.

"I don't care. It makes me think of my dad."

"They're gonna take your PC card away," Norm teased. "I'm curious, how did you hook up with GALLANT?"

Kelly sat up and retrieved an apple from the picnic basket. "Well,

Greg and I have been friends for a long time. We marched together in gay rights parades all over — New York, San Francisco, you name it. When he started GALLANT, they didn't have a lot of money, but they needed a lawyer. He knew I lived in Atlanta, and he also knew I would work cheap for causes I believe in. He, Jon, and I got together and I guided them through the legal maze of getting started and here we are." She bit a small chunk out of the apple.

"Greg and Jon are old friends of yours?"

"Greg is," She finished the bite of apple. "I don't really know Jon that well. To be honest, I think he's kind of jealous of me. I know that sounds weird, but I think he feels threatened by me for some reason. But Greg and I are best friends. This may be a stereotype, but you know how gay men are. It's like having a girlfriend. We gossip. We talk about awful clothes people are wearing. We go to sad movies together and cry. He's just always there for me and I'm there for him. I'd do anything in the world for him."

Norm leaned back on his elbows. He envied Kelly for her close relationships. Norm had friends, too, but no one really close. No one in whom he could really confide. No one with whom he could share his dreams and his fears. He had a friend like that once, but she had died long ago. He had given up hope of ever finding anyone like her.

42

The scene outside the federal courthouse in Loveport was indescribable. This was the crescendo of the biggest event in the country and everyone wanted to be a part of it. Kelly Morris, Kurt Ford, Judge Kincaid, and, to a lesser degree, Norm Woodruff and Bill Dumaine were household names, instant celebrities. Each time one of their cars moved anywhere near the courthouse, they were mobbed by reporters and protesters and curiosity seekers.

Kelly, Norm, and Rex Randle carpooled together from the hotel. Norm pulled their rental car up to the police checkpoint and the mob was nearly out of control. Policemen on horseback patrolled the perimeter on the street along with a walking patrol two men thick. Police in riot gear stood their ground on the sidewalk in front of the courthouse, the last line of defense in case all hell broke loose. Kelly looked out her window in horror at the hysterical horde which directed its myriad emotions at them. There were placards of every description and people of all walks of life, each with a decided opinion. They seemed to almost slobber, screaming their message at the car. It was close to impossible to tell friend from foe.

"This makes the OJ trial look like a day in the park." Norm rolled down the window to show his ID to the policeman.

When his window came down, the shouts and chants were more distinct. They could hear the vitriolic venom directed, personally, at each one of them among the shouts of adulation and support. Policemen locked arms to make sure the angry rabble didn't break through. Camera crews were literally falling all over each other trying to get pictures of the plaintiffs team and the reaction to them. There was little doubt in their minds that if the mob somehow broke loose, they would surely tear them apart like wild animals. The checkpoint officer quickly checked their IDs then flagged them through. Once out of their car in the underground garage, they could still hear the bedlam in the distance. They hurried to the elevator and the inner sanctum of serenity.

Kurt Ford and Bill Dumaine pulled up to the checkpoint not two minutes after Norm's car had been cleared. The same crowd released a torrent of obscenities and veneration down upon them. Police pushed the multitude back. They were cleared and proceeded to the parking garage. They could both see and hear the crowd through the windows of the hallway leading to the back steps to the courtroom.

"If we lose, I don't wanna face them," Dumaine said off-handedly.

"No matter what the outcome, I don't wanna face them," Kurt joked.

They showed their identification to the sheriff's deputy at the top of the steps and were allowed into one of the small vestibules just off the courtroom floor. Like two performers standing just off stage, they psyched themselves up for the big show.

"You ready?" Dumaine asked.

"As ready as I'll ever be," Kurt said. His stomach was full of butterflies. He popped a Tums tablet in his mouth and reached for the doorknob. He opened the door and the TV camera in the back of the courtroom locked on him and followed the two attorneys to their table. Kurt checked his watch. It was straight up ten o'clock. He watched as the jurors were shown into the jury box. They quietly made their way to their seats and sat, patiently waiting for court to begin.

Both Jon Carroll and Greg Wently joined Kelly, Norm, and Rex at the plaintiffs' table. Rex and Norm whispered to one another while Kelly took the last precious moments to review her note cards.

"All Rise! Oyez, oyez, oyez. Court is now in session. The Honorable

Seamus Kincaid presiding!" the bailiff announced.

Judge Kincaid entered and took his seat. Everyone then took theirs.

"Are the plaintiffs ready for closing arguments?" Kincaid asked.

"Yes, Your Honor," Kelly answered.

"Please, proceed."

She approached the podium and cleared her throat to speak. It hit her that this was not only the climax of the trial but her last chance to win this jury over. The gravity of the moment washed over her. The very future of homosexuals hung in the balance. She felt every ounce of the tremendous pressure. All eyes in the courtroom were on her. She studied the jury. They all looked eager to hear her thoughts, open to her persuasion. No folded arms. No distant looks. Victory is mine to seize, she thought, if only she had what it took to seize it. She took a deep breath and began.

"Ladies and gentlemen, we're not here today to stand in the way of progress. Heaven knows, it's progress that has brought us to this place. To the point where those people among us who were once thought of as odd or different are now beginning to be accepted into our society for who they are and the contributions they have made to it."

She nervously took a sip of water. "If you've ever taken a trip to Italy, you're surely familiar with the works of Michelangelo. Even if you've never seen them in person, you're aware that Michelangelo was one of the most wonderfully prolific artists of all time. His paintings and sculptures and works of art grace museums and churches around the world. His style set the standard for those who followed. Even today, young artists and sculptors study his works hoping to capture at least a glimmer of inspiration for their own craft. His contributions to the world of art now belong to the ages, yet if Michelangelo had been born today, it might be quite different. You see, Michelangelo was gay. Gay was not only *what* he was, it was *who* he was. However, if Michelangelo's mother had been afforded the opportunity that Dr. Penrose and Loveport University would like to afford all mothers, we would never have had the beautiful paintings of The Sistine Chapel. There would not be any such thing as the Venus de Milo."

She took a couple of steps out from behind the lectern, looking down and tapping the tips of her fingers together as she thought. "You know, over the years, there's been some speculation that liberal arts in general have been made up of a large number of gay people, so my colleagues and I decided to do a little research. The best estimates today are that somewhere between five percent and ten percent of the population is made up of gays. When you look into fields such as opera, ballet, symphonic music, and other liberal arts or creative fields such as television and motion pictures and popular music, the number of gay people is much higher. Our best estimate was somewhere around thirty percent or better and that's just from the admitted gays. The actual number could be far greater. Why is that? Are they gay because they are creative?" She turned slowly to the courtroom assemblage then back again to the jury. "Or are they creative because they're gay? Ask any creative gay person and they'll tell you that their homosexuality and their creativity are so intertwined that it would be impossible to separate them. Many experts in the field of psychology believe the same thing, as you've heard them testify before this court.

"Down through history, we have dealt with megalomaniacs who have sought a master race. Hitler was just one example. A man who, through his own demented logic, summarily eradicated six million people from the face of the earth merely because he determined them inferior. If we lose here in this place in history, where will it end? Think about it. Where will it end?" She paused a moment for the thought to sink in, then her volume increased with her rhythm as the next lines hit them like a barrage of gunfire. "Today it's homosexuals. Tomorrow it could be redheaded babies or brown-eyed babies or left-handed babies or any other attribute one might find distasteful. Do we want cafeteria-style babies whose attributes are chosen and pieced together, picking and choosing the type of build here, the hair color there, piecing together a human being like Frankenstein's monster?"

She stopped right in front of the jury box. The camera over their shoulders zoomed in on her face. She looked at each juror individually and brought her tone of voice down to almost a whisper. "If we lose this case here today, there won't be another holocaust like we knew before. People won't be rounded up and shipped off to die. These victims might never even know what happened to them." Her volume increased. "But history, ladies and gentlemen, history will know! History will remember! And it will be history's great loss! We might never again be fortunate enough to know the future Michelangelos of the world. Once this genie is out of the bottle, there's no putting it back. Once the Penrose Project is put into practice for the first time, we will have reached the point of no return."

She walked to the podium. "My goal in this trial has not been to persuade you to accept homosexuality as an agreeable lifestyle. My goal has not been to persuade you to embrace the homosexual community. My goal has been to enlighten you as to where this could all lead. I believe that allowing man to play God and altering someone's genetic makeup before they are born is not only dangerous, it's just plain wrong. We, as human beings, don't have that right," she said, scanning the jurors, "and I hope you'll have the foresight to stop it here today. Thank you."

She picked up her note cards from the podium and returned to the plaintiffs' table. She took her seat and gave a sigh of relief. Rex Randle leaned over and casually whispered in her ear. "You nailed it," he observed as the jury refocused its attention on the next attorney.

Norm Woodruff knew that first impressions were crucial but not nearly as important as the last impression. He wanted to make sure his words echoed in the jurors' heads as they made their decision. He bypassed the lectern completely and approached the jury box.

"Ladies and gentlemen, my client could not be here today," he began matter-of-factly. "My client doesn't have the luxury of choosing his lawyers or speaking for himself. My client is the unborn child known now throughout the world as the Loveport Baby. He and countless others like him to follow are counting on my colleagues and me to put a stop to a scientific experiment gone awry before it has a chance to do any further damage."

Norm took a few steps in front of the jury then turned to address them again. "In recent years we've seen science fiction become science fact. The horrors of cloning, depicted in books and movies for years, have now come to fruition. There was a popular movie out a few years back starring Gregory Peck called 'Boys From Brazil.' Maybe you saw it. It was a fantasy about Dr. Josef Mengele, who was one of Hitler's most brutal butchers, escaping to Brazil after the war with a sample of the Fuhrer's DNA. He proceeded to clone little Hitlers around the world then control the environment of these young boys by killing off their fathers, just as Hitler's father had died when he was a young boy. Today when most people think of cloning, they think of Dolly the sheep, the first animal ever cloned. Seems innocent enough, doesn't it? The agricultural benefits from this technology are quite apparent. But, imagine that technology in the hands of a Dr. Mengele. Fortunately, the leaders of the world have come together in agreement that this can never be allowed to proceed to the human level. They realize how quickly these seemingly innocent intentions can turn evil. The same foresight needs to be applied in this case. Now, I'm not, by any stretch of the imagination, comparing Dr. Penrose to some demented Nazi. I'm worried about the scientists to come who might use his procedure for evil. I'm sure Dr. Penrose thinks what he's doing is right, but Dr. Penrose has failed to figure one person into this equation. My client. What right does he have to decide who my client will become? Perhaps down the road this will lead to being able to change not only his sexual orientation but his sex. Think about it. An argument could be made that it's still a man's world therefore the humane thing to do would be to transform the child from a female to a male. Whatever the change, Dr. Penrose does not have the right to force that on my client who is not able to defend himself here today."

Norm spread his hands out and leaned forward on the railing of the jury box. "Ladies and gentlemen, my client has a right to the same thing as any other child. My client has the right to be born into this world just as God intended and to make his way through his life knowing that he wasn't genetically altered like some freak from a science fiction novel. On behalf of my client, I implore you to stop this experiment-gone-awry where it stands and spare him and countless more unborn children the suffering that embarking down this slippery slope will surely bring. And I thank you."

Judge Kincaid made a few notes then looked down at Kurt Ford over his reading glasses.

"Mr. Ford," Kincaid said.

Kurt glanced back over the railing at Dr. Penrose before stepping out from behind the defense table. This was it. The courtroom sat perfectly still, awaiting his words. His heart pounded. He felt the sweat as it broke out on his skull. He wet his dry mouth with a sip of water, trying to ignore the multitude of eyes that quite nearly stared him off balance. His audience was the jury. He attempted to block everyone else in the room out of his sight and out of his mind, to focus his complete attention on swaying that jury. He walked up about fifteen feet from the jury box and began.

"Ladies and gentlemen, in his closing argument this morning, the attorney for the legal guardian, Mr. Woodruff," he motioned to Norm Woodruff, "spoke to you about an unborn child. An unborn child whom we've all come to know as the Loveport Baby. Mr. Woodruff comes to this courtroom purportedly in defense of this unborn child's civil rights, an admirable assignment he's taken, I might add. Admirable but misguided. I, too, believe this child has inalienable rights. This child has a right to grow up like every other child. This child has a right to, at some point in his life, have children of his own if he so chooses. This child has a right not to be tormented, not to be confused about who he is. This child has a right to two loving parents who will nurture him and take care of him and provide for him and, yes, protect him. You see, my colleagues and I not only represent Loveport University and Dr. Penrose, we represent the parents of that little child. Two loving parents who already have children of their own. Loving parents who have nurtured, agonized over, and dedicated their lives to raising the best possible children they know how. And now, before this little boy even begins his life, these fine parents are thinking of his well-being. Thinking of what will be best for him as he goes through life. Thinking about how this little guy will fit into society. Now, I know perhaps society should be a little more tolerant of homosexuality." His tone became serious. "But the cold, hard reality is society is not. So, what are these parents to do? Dedicate their lives to changing society? An insurmountable task, no doubt. No, you see, what they have chosen to do is to not subject their son to that life of rejection, that life of pain. What they have chosen is to spare their own flesh and blood the torment he will surely endure if the present course is followed. Mr. Woodruff asked the question: what is best for this child? Isn't it fundamental that these loving parents decide what's best for their child? And that last part is key in this trial. *Their* child. Not the Christian Way Organization, not Big Brother, not even Loveport and Dr. Penrose. The *parents* should have the right to choose what's best for *their* child."

Kurt paused to gather his thoughts for his next point. "Miss Morris talked earlier about a theory of hers. She talked about Michelangelo and all he gave to this world and you won't find any argument from me. However, the theory that he was gay is still very much in dispute by historians. And I do take issue with her assertion that even if he was gay that his homosexuality made him great. For every great gay figure in history, I can name for you dozens who were not. For every

Michelangelo, there were countless Rembrandts and Renoirs. Many in the gay community would want you to believe that Michelangelo was gay and that's symptomatic of what this whole trial has been about, theory versus fact. I want you, ladies and gentlemen, to understand something this morning. The life of a homosexual is not a life to be envied. They refer to homosexuals as gays, but that's misleading because, let me tell you, most homosexuals are not happy with their sexuality. Believe me, it's not a life to be coveted. It's not easy on the individual and it's not easy on his family. There is, often times, a guilt and a sadness and a general lack of understanding between that individual and his family that's too painful to put into words. Most of the homosexuals I know would become heterosexuals today if it were possible, but it's not. Unfortunately it's not because, you see, once we're placed on this earth it's too late. It's too late to stop the ridicule. It's too late to stop the deprecation. It's too late to stop the pain. But it's not too late for this little baby because this little baby boy has loving, caring parents who want desperately to spare him that life of pain and humiliation."

He looked at the jury, searching for a sign he was getting through. They gave nothing away. "During the course of this trial, the defense has proven, beyond a shadow of a doubt, basically two things." He held his hands out in front of him and counted them off with his fingers. "One: that the genetic defect that causes homosexuality is no different from any of the other genetic defects that cause a whole host of other conditions and disorders from Down syndrome to spina bifida. And two: we have demonstrated to you that this family not only has a right to go forward with Dr. Penrose's procedure, they have an *obligation* to do so.

"Ladies and gentlemen, you've heard a litany of excuses from the plaintiff's lawyers in this case as to why this medical procedure should be stopped. Even with their last gasp here today, they have equated Dr. Penrose to some of the darkest figures in history. Fear-mongering!" he shouted. The startled jurors jumped. "Fear-mongering is the only hope they have. It's a tactic taken when there's no factual argument to stand on. One of the questions you're going to be asked to decide is the question of risk. How risky is this procedure? You want to hear some facts? Your chances of developing a mental disorder this year are twenty-five times greater than something happening to that child during the procedure. Twenty-five times! You have about the same chance of going to prison this year as this baby has coming to any harm during this procedure. In fact, your chances are about thirteen times greater that you'll hire a sleazy lawyer this year." The jurors' stone faces broke into smiles. "The figures I just quoted for you are actual statistics, facts, proof. I urge you to wade through the hypotheses and speculations. I ask that you disregard the irrelevancies and the fear-mongering. Look at the facts. Look at the facts and look at this case for what it truly is. The basic right of two loving parents to make an extremely difficult medical decision as to what's best for their own child *without* any outside interference from their government. That's what this whole case boils down to. Parental choice," he almost whispered. "Parental responsibility. There are those who would take that away. There are those who already suffer from this genetic disorder we know as homosexuality. The sad fact is those who are already afflicted are trying to force their plight on an unborn child because for them, you see, it's too late. Well, it's only too late for this unborn baby boy if *you* say it is. The future of this child and the many children to follow is in your hands. Thank you."

Kurt returned to his seat. The stress drained from his entire body. Jonathan Sagar gave him an approving wink.

Judge Kincaid reviewed the documents in front of him through his glasses, shifting his head as he alternated his attention from the papers down to Monica Lawrence then back to the papers again. She took the papers one-by-one from Kincaid, his chin dipping each time as he peered over the reading glasses to look at the clerk then jutting upward as he looked down through the glasses. When he was satisfied, he handed down the last of the documents to Ms. Lawrence and turned to the jury, removing the glasses altogether.

"Ladies and gentlemen, we now turn this matter over to you. Let me remind you of what your duty requires of you. You are to first determine if the present condition of this fetus warrants the procedure in question that would correct that condition. If you decide the condition does not warrant correcting, then your job is done and you must notify this court that you've reached a decision. If you come to a unanimous decision that the condition *does* warrant changing, you will then need to determine the risk involved in this procedure. Having determined that, you are to decide the second question of fact, which is whether the outcome of this procedure justifies that risk. Keep in mind this is a building block approach. You will need to assess the evidence and testimony to determine the first question with unanimous consent before moving on to the second. Please feel free to have the foreman contact the clerk's office if there's anything at all you don't understand about the case or your duties. I've issued detailed instructions for deliberations which will be given to you in the jury room. Good luck."

Clark Penrose did what he normally did when he was anxious about something. He blocked out the problem by immersing himself in his work. He had dismissed Carol Boyce for the day. She was preoccupied with the pending verdict and was of little use to him anyway. He checked various equipment around the room, referring back to his notes and jotting down new ones. The voice from the doorway startled him.

"Dr. Penrose?"

He whipped around. Standing there was the last person in the entire world he would expect to see in his lab.

"Dr. Gaylord?" Penrose had never met him in person. Only his image on television and a glimpse across the courtroom. Could it actually be him?

Lucius Gaylord obsequiously took a couple of slow steps toward him with his hand extended. "It's nice to finally meet you, Dr. Penrose. I hope you don't mind my barging in like this."

Penrose was stupefied. He accepted Gaylord's handshake. "No, that's quite all right." His first reaction was hostility, but he sensed Dr. Gaylord was not there on a malevolent mission. He decided to reserve judgment until he determined just what that mission was.

"I know you're probably not too fond of me and I can understand that," Gaylord said. He looked down at the floor, fishing for the right words. "I want you to know that I've never held anything against you. My criticism has been over your procedure, not you personally. But I didn't come here to talk about that."

Penrose was stumped. What else would he be there to talk about?

"May I sit down?" Gaylord asked.

"By all means." Penrose cleared books and papers from a stool and offered it to Dr. Gaylord. He then pulled one up for himself.

"Dr. Penrose, I know you've been a scientist all your adult life. That's the way your mind works. That's the way you've been trained to think. And I've been a preacher all *my* adult life. In the time I've been preaching, it seems that me and science have been at odds more than a few times," he chuckled. "Evolution versus Creationism. Miracles versus scientific explanation. You know. But now." He shook his head. "Well, now I have a problem which I can't seem to resolve. It's important to me that I come to some kind of closure with this problem. I've prayed about it and, quite frankly, I feel like I've been led to you. I know it may sound strange, but you're probably the most qualified person I know of to help me with this problem."

Penrose couldn't imagine what kind of problem a man like Lucius Gaylord could have that would require his help, but he was willing to try. "What seems to have you stumped?"

Gaylord cleared his throat and adjusted his tie. "Well, I live my life by the Word. Whatever problems life throws me, I'm always able to find comfort in the Bible. But on this issue of homosexuality, there's something that I just can't reconcile. If your study is correct, and I must admit that you've laid out a very convincing argument for it. If you're right, that homosexuality is genetic, then why would God make someone that way then condemn their conduct in the Bible?"

Penrose tugged at his chin. That was a very interesting question. He got up from the stool and walked over to a table across the room. Walking always seemed to help him assemble his thoughts. "First of all, there's probably something that you don't realize." He turned around. "Science and religion are not mutually exclusive."

Gaylord thought about it a moment. He had been on the defensive for so long that the proposition of science and religion being on the same side seemed somehow foreign to him.

"I've never been one to set out to try and disprove the Word of God," Penrose explained. "Nor have I been one to try to prove it. I merely follow my work where it leads. In fact, my work has led me to wrestle with the very question that brought you here."

Gaylord listened intently.

Dr. Penrose returned to his stool and rested one arm casually on the lab table. "You know, we humans are probably genetically predisposed to do a lot of things. We all have our weaknesses to overcome. Alcoholism, for example. It's widely believed that it's a genetic disorder. Not all of us are going to become alcoholics, but for those who do, we don't simply condone the behavior just because they can't help themselves, do we? Indeed not. We try to get them help. We try to save them from a destructive lifestyle. The same could be said for homosexuality. It's a destructive behavior if not physically, it certainly is theologically and can be emotionally, as well. And like homosexuality, the Bible admonishes getting drunk with no instruction on how to treat the alcoholic."

Gaylord nodded in agreement. He hadn't really thought about it that way. "So, what you're saying is it's one thing to be genetically predisposed to behave a certain way, but it's another to act on that predisposition."

"Precisely," Penrose said. "There are scientists who believe that some people are predisposed even to murder. How about child molesters? There are those who believe they're genetically predisposed to that behavior. The question we have to ask ourselves is does that excuse the behavior? That's a completely subjective call. Is homosexuality a sin if that's the way you're wired? I don't know."

"Interesting." Gaylord contemplated everything Dr. Penrose had just said. "Very interesting. Well, I won't keep you from your work." Gaylord lifted himself from his perch and shook Penrose's hand once again then turned to leave. "Dr. Penrose," Gaylord hesitated at the door, "thank you."

Penrose smiled warmly. "Glad I could be of service."

The irony was not lost on Dr. Gaylord. Ordinarily, one sought comfort and refuge from the confusion of science in the Scriptures. In this instance, it was theology that had sought comfort and refuge in science. Dr. Gaylord left not only feeling better about his nagging question, but he felt completely different about Clark Penrose.

43

The jury seemed to be stuck in a rut. They had deliberated for hours with little progress. They were all exhausted and wanted to start fresh after a good night's sleep, but Estelle Wooten was eager to take charge and move the deliberations forward. As the other jurors poured themselves coffee, munched on snacks, and made small talk, she became increasingly impatient.

"Come on, now. Let's not prolong this. Let's get back to work!" She clapped her hands together like a football coach. The others turned to look at her. She had seemed like such a sweet lady until she got a little power. Most were sorry they had voted for her. Some wondered if there was a jury version of a mutiny. They had been sitting all day. They wanted to stretch their legs, clear the cobwebs of the trial for a moment. Estelle sat with her chin in her palm, restlessly rapping her finger tips on the table top. Succumbing to the pressure, the jurors reluctantly took their seats.

Estelle reread aloud the questions they were to decide while everyone followed along. She finished then asked if anyone had any questions. There were none.

"Let's review the testimony from the witnesses."

"Why don't we just vote on the first question and see where we are?" John Banta grumbled.

"No!" Estelle snapped. "The judge says to review the testimony *before* we vote."

There were no other challenges to her authority. They went over the plaintiffs' witnesses first. Dr. Evan Proctor's testimony got the most attention because of his revelation that one of Dr. Penrose's lab dogs had died. They pored over the veterinarian's autopsy report and decided it was satisfactory evidence. The death had nothing to do with Penrose's genetic experiments.

Dr. Whitaker's testimony resonated with the three black jurors. They related to his statement that gays were harassed and discriminated against like blacks. The three were quite vocal to that injustice. Ron Dallas emerged as a spokesman for the three.

"Look, I don't want to overstate the obvious here," he said, "but if you're not black, you're clueless when it comes to discrimination."

"That's right. Amen," the other two black jurors echoed.

"I mean, you may have seen it before, but until you've *lived* it, man, it just isn't the same."

"But being homosexual is not the same as being black," argued Denny Sullivan, one of the white males on the jury. "The plaintiffs may argue that it's an immutable trait, but you can choose not to engage in homosexual sex. You can't choose your skin color."

"But isn't it the defense that's arguing that homosexuality is an immutable trait?" asked Dana Crockett. Several others nodded in agreement. "I mean, they're the ones trying to convince us that this condition is so ingrained that they have to change it genetically to save the child." She leaned back in her chair, thrilled with herself for making such an intelligent point.

Harvey Goldstone got up and served himself another cup of coffee. "Damn," he complained. "This is getting too complicated. Let's just vote on the first question of fact, for crying out loud."

"Now, hold on," Estelle Wooten ordered. "Let's not make this harder than it actually is. We're on the right track. The first question we need to answer is whether the present accepted condition of the fetus is one deemed necessary of correcting. Stay focused on that question until we get past it."

They reviewed the remaining plaintiff witnesses and argued the first question, giving each juror time enough to ask questions or voice opinions. It was a spirited debate and took up better than an hour. After a short break, they reviewed the defense witnesses' testimony. Kelly Morris had struck a nerve with her challenge to the standards of normality. Her point was driven home with the NBA analogy. Equally compelling was Dr. Glasco's Progenitive Deficiency Syndrome argument, asserting that gays were in constant conflict with their natural instincts to procreate. It certainly bolstered the argument that being homosexual went against nature. But the defense witness who got the most attention was Brandon Penrose. The arguments were heated on both sides.

"This kid is the personification of the argument in favor of the procedure," John Banta argued. "He hates being gay."

"He hates disappointing his father is more like it," Dana Crockett shot back. "We can't seriously consider his testimony. He's too biased."

"He may be biased," Harvey Goldstone interjected, "but he was compelling. I gotta tell ya, I'm not gay, but I came as close to understanding how it feels to be gay when that kid was on the stand as I ever will."

The other jurors nodded. All twelve agreed they were moved by his testimony. If nothing else, Brandon Penrose evaporated the plaintiffs' contention that Dr. Penrose was on some kind of mission to exterminate homosexuals. The jurors found Dr. Penrose to be quite credible and conscientious even if they had misgivings about his project.

Inevitably, each juror weighed not only the courtroom testimony but their own personal experiences with homosexuals in their own lives to determine the first question of fact.

At last, they were ready for the first vote on the first question of fact: was the present accepted condition of this fetus one deemed necessary of correcting? Estelle suggested a secret ballot. That would alleviate some of the peer pressure. The others agreed. The ballots were cast and passed to the foreman. Estelle deliberately counted the votes then counted them again to make sure. The vote was seven to five. The twelve groaned. They had a very long way to go.

"The jury is still deliberating at this hour," Duncan Reynolds announced to the national audience of *The Pulse*. "In my mind, that doesn't bode well for the plaintiffs."

"How do you figure?" Betty Duvall asked.

"Just common sense. The jury was to determine two things." He counted them off on his fingers. "First, if the condition of the fetus warranted changing. If not, their job was done. If they thought the condition of the fetus warranted changing, they were to determine the risk factor. They've been in there two days now. Surely they're past the first question and the second one is a slam dunk for the defense."

"Oh, come on, Duncan. Have you ever been on a jury?" Betty asked.

"No, I haven't," Duncan admitted. He looked away from Betty's gaze.

"And it shows." She used her expertise as an attorney to let Duncan know he was in over his head. "It's not a simple matter of getting back to the jury room and voting. They have to study hours and hours of testimony and discuss every detail. It's quite possible they haven't even gotten past the first question yet. As for the second being a slam dunk for the defense, I strongly disagree. Determining a condition is one thing. Taking a risk in correcting it is another. You know, you people on the right are so homophobic you think being gay is such a horrible condition. I've gotta tell you that gay people are just as, quote 'normal,' as straight people. Why do you people insist on changing everybody who's different from you?"

The two jury consultants joined Rex Randle, Norm Woodruff, and Kelly Morris in Norm's office for some eleventh-hour analysis of the jurors. Even the experts had to admit it was too close to call. By their count, three could go with the defense. Two of the jurors, they were confident, maybe a third, could go their way. At least half of the jurors were impossible to call. It would all depend on how the first vote went. Verdicts, by and large, go with the majority if there's a split on the first vote. Depending on how strong the majority, they could beat the others down in a matter of minutes or it could take days. There was just no way of telling who that first vote would favor.

The conversation eventually drifted to the leaks and what effect they would have on the outcome, if any. Who was this Raven character? Had the leaks done any real damage? Certainly the jury wasn't affected. They had never heard Don Bissette's reports.

"You know, something that keeps bugging me, I really don't understand why they took that chance," Rex said, referring to the defense. "They ran a strong risk of causing a mistrial. I mean, Kincaid came real close to calling one. With a mistrial, there would've been no way to put together another trial before the mother had the baby. Once that happened, whether or not the case was ever decided after the birth, they would've lost a distinct advantage."

"Yeah," Kelly added. "The injunction would've remained in effect so Penrose wouldn't have been able to proceed and the child would be born gay." She frowned as she thought about the whole scenario.

"See," Rex said, "it just doesn't make sense."

Something came over Kelly. "Please excuse me." Kelly turned toward the door.

"You OK?" Norm asked.

Kelly turned to face him. She looked sick to her stomach. Her eyes were red-rimmed. "I'll be fine," she said.

"I'll walk you to your car," Norm offered.

"No!" Kelly exclaimed then lowered her voice. "No, thank you," she said more calmly. "I'll call you later."

Penrose flicked on the radio for his evening commute. He hadn't received any official calls all day, so he surmised the jury had not yet made up its mind. Just to be sure, he listened intently to the news. He had tried to keep his mind on his work but with the verdict hanging over him it was hard to concentrate on anything else. He didn't go straight home. There was something he wanted to take care of before it was too late. He made one stop then drove his Buick out of town, among the well-manicured lawns of the suburbs of the upper-middle class. Kids played in their yards, trying to squeeze out every last drop of sunshine left in the day. He checked the address on his sheet of paper against the one on the brick-enclosed mailbox and turned into the aggregate driveway. The two-story French colonial sat a good distance from the curb. Penrose put the car in park and grabbed the long white box on the front seat. He pressed the doorbell and waited for the occupants to greet him.

The front door opened and Tom Andrews, wearing a nervous smile, gave him a hearty welcome. Hearing who was at their door, Sabrina popped up from the den sofa where she'd been following the news, anxiously awaiting word on the verdict. She was considerably larger than when Penrose last saw her. She gave Penrose a hug, invited him in, and offered him a glass of iced tea. He accepted.

"I just wanted to stop by and say thanks to both of you." Penrose handed Sabrina the box of twelve champagne-colored roses. "There's one for every juror," he joked. "I hope it brings us luck."

Sabrina thanked him and gave him another hug. He wanted to let them know how much he appreciated what they had gone through. It was important to him that he did so before the verdict. If the verdict went their way, it would be easy to drop by with roses to celebrate. This way, his sincerity wouldn't be questioned.

"I realize how traumatic this all has been for both of you. I want you to know how much I appreciate your enduring it all."

The Andrews didn't know what to say. It had been quite an ordeal. Much more than Dr. Penrose could ever fathom. However, they knew

Dr. Penrose had gone through an emotional wrenching finding out his own son was gay, something from which he was trying to spare them. Penrose addressed his next statement more to Sabrina.

"Look, I know you're concerned about the procedure. Everything will be just fine," he assured her.

"I know," she answered, trying desperately to hide her doubt.

"I also want you to know that if we lose this case. If your boy is born as he is now." He hesitated a long moment. "Well, that will be just fine, too."

Sabrina looked up, almost shocked by his candor. She reached for his hand and squeezed it softly.

Penrose took a sip of tea. "Have you picked out a name for the baby yet?" He asked, more as a chance to change the subject than real interest.

Tom and Sabrina looked at each other a bit embarrassed.

"We gave it a lot of thought," Tom admitted. "This is a very special baby."

Penrose nodded.

"We're naming him Clark," Sabrina announced.

Penrose was speechless. He fumbled for an awkward moment as the Andrews smiled back at him. Then he raised his glass of tea. "To Clark," he toasted. "May the Lord and life bring him happiness."

Kelly's mind raced as she drove, putting all the pieces together. She arrived at the offices of GALLANT, parked the car, and ran up the steps. Her heart raced to find Greg and Jon still there. Greg greeted her at the door and invited her in. She brushed past him. Immediately he knew something was wrong. Her glance was cold. Jon Carroll was sitting in Greg's office. He hopped up as Kelly entered the room and welcomed her with an energetic hello. Kelly ignored him. Jon looked curiously at Greg for a clue.

Kelly took a deep breath then began. "It really took me a while to piece it all together." She paced slowly around the room and tugged on her upper lip.

Greg and Jon exchanged puzzled looks.

"Jonathan Sagar's reputation for playing every card in the deck," she said, "is legendary in lawyers' circles. We knew Kurt Ford was assigned the case because he was gay. We knew that homophobe, Dumaine, was attached to him to keep him from going too far afield. When we learned there were leaks, it didn't surprise me that Sagar would pull something like that, you know, to get the upper hand. But something kept nagging at me. In reality, what did he have to gain? The jury was already chosen and sequestered when the first leak occurred. The judge didn't allow the jury to hear the leaked information. All along he ran the risk of a mistrial, which would've meant the injunction would remain in place and the procedure would not have been performed. That could give other groups enough time to mobilize and swing the momentum in our direction making it difficult to win the case. Jonathan Sagar is not that dumb. The next logical question was who would benefit?"

Greg walked back around behind his desk as he listened. He took a seat and leaned back in his chair. Jon joined Greg at his side.

Kelly continued with her theory. "Then I remembered something you said, Greg, when you were making the decision to bring the CWO onboard. You said, 'This isn't some test to see if GALLANT has principles. This is all out war.' That stuck in the back of my mind. Then it finally dawned on me." She looked long and hard at Greg. "It's you." It almost made her sick to say it. "You're Raven."

Greg looked down trying to cast aside her gaze. Jon looked down at Greg, waiting for his response.

"And the graffiti on your door," Kelly continued. "That was more of your handiwork."

Greg was solemn. "Is that what you believe?" He looked hurt that Kelly would accuse him of such a thing.

"Oh, come on, Greg. Don't play coy with me! You jeopardized our whole case because you didn't think I could get the job done!"

"Come on, Kel. Get real! Do you actually think we can win this one?"

"That's not the point!" she screamed back at him. "There are more important things than winning. Things like honor and doing what's right and working within the system."

Greg laughed. "The system?" He rose from the desk. "The system?" He stabbed the air with his index finger. "To hell with the system! What did the system ever do for us? Nothing!" He slammed his fist on his desk. "Not a damn thing!" He lowered his head and grunted a single chuckle then looked back up at his old friend and attorney. "You just don't get it, do you, Kel? It's not the process that's important. It's the goal line that's important. Winning," he said through clinched teeth. "That's *all* that matters."

Kelly said calmly, "We'll win." Restraint turned to anger. "We'll win because we have the truth on our side, not because we tried to intimidate witnesses, for God's sake. We'll win because we're right and they're wrong and if you don't believe that, you have no business in this movement."

"The stakes are too high, Kelly," Jon added. "We can't risk losing this one."

Kelly turned to face him. The anger and hurt tore at her heart. "You wanna talk about risk? You wanna talk about risk? What about the risk of the FBI tracing this whole thing back to you? What about risking *my* reputation and integrity? I would be implicated as well! You had no right to do that!"

"So, what are you going to do?" Jon asked. "You're so sure we had something to do with it. You're convinced we're guilty. What happens now?"

Kelly hesitated before answering. "You've forced me to do something that I never thought I'd do."

The two men's faces filled with concern.

"There's no easy way out of this for me. As an officer of the court, I'm duty-bound to tell Judge Kincaid all about this. But I believe so strongly in this cause that I've fought for all this time that I'm not going to let you ruin it for all of the people who've been counting on me. If I win this case, it'll be a win with dishonor and that's something I'll have to live with for the rest of my life."

Greg almost spoke but didn't.

"Consider this my notice." She turned to leave. "After this trial is over, find yourself another attorney."

"Kel!" Greg yelled after her.

She opened the office door and slammed it behind her.

Jon fell to his chair and covered his face. Greg simply stood there in silence, his face still solemn, never giving away his emotions.

Kelly Morris' stomach churned as she took the ramp to the interstate. She cried and wiped the tears so that she could see to drive. She was oblivious to the nighttime traffic, considering all that had just transpired. She had lost her best friend and her biggest client in an instant. She had also committed herself to an ethical compromise from which she might never recover. Why was she doing it? Was it for her friendship with Greg? That was surely over and he, obviously, wasn't the friend she thought he was. That alone ripped her heart apart. If not for friendship, why was she so willing to surrender her principles? She was compromising herself for one reason: the cause. She had thrown her complete self into the struggle, so much so that she would do anything to protect it. Even if that meant become an accessory to a felony. She was also compromising the profession she had dreamt of joining since she could remember. A profession she had vowed never to dishonor.

Her brow was damp with perspiration. Her mouth was dry. She veered sharply to the right and slammed on the brakes. Blue smoke rolled from her tires until the car came to a rest on the shoulder of the interstate. In one movement, she unlatched her seatbelt and opened the door. A passing car's horn blared as she rounded the door and headed toward the front of the vehicle. The lights of her own automobile blinded her, and she cried and groped her way around the front and over to the passenger side. Her right hand found the front quarter panel of the car, and she steadied herself. Vehicles passing close by at high rates of speed caused her car to shake. The hurt and the compromise and the feeling of betrayal all erupted together deep inside her stomach and spewed out of her mouth onto the dark pavement at her feet. The first eruption was followed quickly by another. Kelly raised up and screamed out into the darkness.

44

All of the parties had been summoned back to the federal courthouse. Speculation ran rampant as to what a four-day deliberation meant. The talking heads on both sides of the issue were claiming victory. By the time Dr. Penrose arrived, the throng had again descended. The numbers were staggering. Policemen on horseback walked the perimeter of the crowd making sure no one entered the restricted area. The protestors with their placards and their chants were in full force. The television crews clamored for position. The circus was back in town. Better than an hour passed before all the necessary parties were in place.

Inside, the courtroom was instructed to rise then went silent except for the gentle swishing of the robe and the creaking of the leather chair as Judge Seamus Kincaid took his seat. Penrose sat expressionless. The whole ordeal seemed to pass in slow motion. It was as if Judge Kincaid purposely wanted to torture them. Kurt Ford was rather like a duck, calm and cool from the waste up, but underneath the table, both legs shook almost violently. Bill Dumaine sat next to him, back stiff, elbows on the armrest, like he was sitting at attention — or strapped in the electric chair. The judge looked over the courtroom. Satisfied everyone was in attendance, he began.

"Bring in the jury," he instructed the deputy.

One by one they slowly made their way into the large wooden box. Kurt looked at each one hoping something would betray their secret, but there was nothing. None of the twelve would meet the eyes of any attorney in the room. They either looked down or looked at the judge or stared straight ahead at nothing at all. Gloria Fisher, the jury consultant from VDI, studied Estelle Wooten's body language. She looked for a nervous twitch, a stray glance, anything. There was nothing. Kelly Morris had positioned herself on the inside seat closest to the defense table with Norm and Rex as buffers from her soon-to-be former clients. She kept her eye on the prize that transcended their tragic relationship.

Kincaid addressed the jurors. "Has this jury reached a verdict?"

Estelle Wooten stood. "We have, Your Honor."

"Is the verdict unanimous?"

"It is."

She handed the folded piece of paper to the bailiff who walked it over to the judge. Kincaid placed his reading glasses on his nose and unfolded the paper. He read for several moments then refolded the paper and handed it back to the bailiff who returned it to Mrs. Wooten.

"Madame Foreman, you and the rest of the jurors were charged with the task of deciding two questions of fact. First, is the present condition of this fetus necessary of correcting? Second, in light of any risk this procedure might pose to the life and/or health of this fetus or the mother, does the benefit of this corrective procedure outweigh the risk? How does the jury find?"

Kelly Morris locked arms with Norm Woodruff. She nervously bit her bottom lip. Rex closed his eyes as if concentrating would make the decision go their way. Norm Woodruff stared at the foreman's mouth. Kurt's legs continued to vibrate. Dumaine retained his rigid posture. Dr. Penrose clasped his hands together and rested his mouth on his thumbs.

"On both questions of fact, Your Honor, we, the jury, find in favor of the defendant."

"Yes!" Dr. Penrose exclaimed under his breath. Gasps were heard followed by a few sobs. The courtroom erupted into chaos and confusion. Reporters sprinted to the exits in an attempt to file their story first. It was like hearing the results on election night with the opposing camps in the same room. From person to person, emotions ranged from distress and anguish to sheer euphoria.

The victorious attorneys tried to remain dignified, but it was impossible. This one was too big. Dumaine and Ford popped up out of their seats in excitement. Kurt turned to Dumaine and offered his hand. Dumaine looked at it for moment then completely ignored it. Instead, he grabbed Kurt, threw his huge arms around him and hugged him tightly. Kurt slowly reached up and returned the hug, his eyes filled with tears.

Kelly couldn't believe her ears, covering them as if that would make the verdict go away. Rex buried his face in his hands. Norm tried to hold back his disappointment. He placed a fatherly arm around Kelly's shoulders.

Kurt turned to Dr. Penrose with a vigorous handshake and congratulations, barely heard over the noise and commotion. He moved on to Drs. Kirsch and Baxten, then his boss. Jonathan Sagar could hardly contain his happiness. Not only had his client won, but he had been vindicated. He had made the right choice in young Kurt Ford. He grasped Kurt's hand tightly and shook it firmly. His eyes told Kurt everything.

Lauren, Karen, and Brandon fought their way through the crowd to Dr. Penrose and embraced him. Penrose cried tears of joy and relief as his family nearly smothered him with hugs and kisses. Greg Wently and Jon Carroll remained seated, holding hands as tears streamed down their faces. Lucius Gaylord quietly turned and exited the courtroom, the celebration continuing around him. Reporters shouted for a statement, but he simply ignored them. Norm looked over his shoulder at where his client had been sitting. Seeing he was gone, Norm glanced around the courtroom, but there was no trace of Dr. Gaylord. Norm redirected his attention to the bench.

Judge Kincaid observed the maelstrom like an eagle observing his prey from his perch. After a few moments, he decided it was time to turn the disorder into order. Three loud cracks of the gavel seemed to have no effect on the boisterous crowd. Three more, twice as loud, and he got their attention. The crowd settled down and the attorneys took their seats.

"Do the plaintiffs wish the jury polled?" Kincaid asked.

There's no use belaboring the point, Kelly thought. They had all heard the verdict. Why have to sit there and listen to twelve people confirm it? "No, Your Honor," Kelly answered.

"Very well. Having ruled in favor of the defendant," he announced, "this court hereby dissolves the injunction issued against Loveport University and its Medical Research Facility. The procedure may continue as planned. Court is adjourned."

This time, a cheer rang out in the courtroom. The celebration returned to its previous fevered pitch. Kelly Morris shoved files into her overstuffed briefcase. Never acknowledging Greg or Jon, she deliberately pushed her way past them and exited out the side door. Rex and Norm lingered, offering condolences to the devastated men and puzzled looks as Kelly walked away. Kurt and Bill shook hands and exchanged hugs with total strangers, making their way down the center aisle and out to meet with the press. Dr. Roy Kirsch was already there. Facing a bank of microphones, he hailed the wonder boy of Loveport, the inimitable Dr. Penrose.

Norm offered his apologies, excusing himself from Rex, Greg, and Jon. He headed out the side door through which Kelly had just exited. He found her standing in the vestibule, her back to the door, as if she were waiting for Norm to come after her.

"You all right?" Norm asked.

Kelly turned to face him. Tears streamed down her cheeks.

His heart broke for her. "Oh, Kelly," Norm consoled. He knew how much this case meant to her. He knew how much of herself she had thrown into the cause. "It's going to be fine."

He pulled her close to his chest. Her briefcase dropped to the floor. She grabbed Norm tightly and sobbed out loud. He held her for a long moment.

"We gave it our best shot," Norm reassured her. "There's nothing else we could've done."

"I know that." Kelly's voice was muffled against Norm's suit coat. She placed her hands on his chest and looked up at him. "That's not why I'm crying."

Norm looked down at her face. It was obvious her hurt went deeper than just the loss of a trial. Her spirit seemed to be shattered.

"Last night," she confessed, "I found out who Raven was."

Norm held her shoulders and looked at her suspiciously but said nothing.

"It dawned on me when you and Rex and I were talking about who had the most to lose by intimidating witnesses." She wiped her eyes and nose with a tissue. "I drove to Greg's office and I confronted him. Norm, Greg is Raven."

"Did he actually tell you that?"

"He didn't have to. I pieced it all together and when I told him I knew, he didn't deny it." She began to cry again. "Norm, I knew who was intimidating those witnesses. I knew and I said nothing. I was legally obligated to go to Kincaid, but I didn't."

Norm pulled her close again. His mind raced. Right then and there, he knew what he had to do.

"I thought we would win," Kelly said, looking up at Norm again. "I really thought we'd win. I thought that if we could just pull this thing out, I would worry about rationalizing what I'd done later. I figured the end would justify the means. I knew it ran contrary to everything inside me, but I believed so much in what we were doing that I allowed the lure of a victory to overpower me. And now look," she cried. "I've lost my best friend. I've lost the case. And now I've lost my honor. I threw away everything that ever mattered to me, and for what? For nothing. For absolutely nothing." She clung to Norm as tightly as she could.

"You didn't throw away anything," Norm responded almost coldly. "If you had followed your instincts, you would've damaged an innocent man."

Kelly stopped crying and peered up at Norm with a confounded look. "What are you talking about?"

"I'm talking about Greg. If you'd turned him into Kincaid, you would've turned in an innocent man."

"What are you talking about. Greg—"

"Greg's not Raven, Kelly," Norm said.

"Greg's not Raven? How do you know?"

"I know because…" He had to force the words out of his mouth. "Because I'm Raven."

"What?" she asked in almost a whisper. "No, it's not true." She couldn't believe it. She wouldn't believe it.

Norm dropped his arms to his side. "I'm sorry," he said.

Kelly pushed herself away from his chest. She backed up, shaking her head slightly. Norm stared back at her, trying to hold his composure. She knelt to pick up her briefcase, her eyes still affixed to his, holding out hope that he would tell her it was all just some sort of joke.

"*Naught's lost if honor be not lost, defeat is but a name,*" Kelly recited. The tears streamed down her cheeks. "You didn't mean a word of it, did you?"

Norm said nothing. He merely stared back at her, praying for the agonizing moment to end. Kelly took one long last look at him then turned quickly and hurried out the exit into the hallway. Norm simply stood there staring at the door. He knew he would never see her again. As that reality sunk in, the door behind him opened. He glanced over his shoulder to find Greg and Jon standing behind him.

"Is she gone?" Greg asked.

Norm nodded slightly. His eyes remained glued to the door, half because he didn't want them to see the tears running down his cheeks and half because he wanted to indelibly burn her image into his mind.

"What did she say?" Greg asked.

"She was crushed, naturally. She really believed in you and your self-indulgent cause," Norm said virulently. "Why, I can't imagine. You're lucky. If I'd known this morning what I know now, I would've turned you both in to Judge Kincaid" His voice was laced with disgust. "Instead, you forced Kelly to compromise herself while you two just stood by and watched."

"We never asked her to compromise herself," Greg defended.

"You were her friends," Norm shot back, still too angry to face them. "You could've salvaged her integrity, but you'd rather save yourselves. She deserved better than that."

Neither Greg nor Jon offered up an excuse. Any they could've mustered would have been unsatisfactory to Norm.

"I told her I was Raven," Norm announced.

They looked at each other in confusion. "You did that for us?" Jon asked. "Why?"

"I didn't do it for you, you pathetic little bastards." He turned to face them. "I did it for Kelly. You forced her to choose between a profession she loved more than life itself and a cause she believed in with all her heart. She felt a responsibility to the people who had worked so hard for that cause, an obligation not to let them down. So much so that she would sacrifice her own integrity to win for them. You stripped her of the one thing that mattered most to her. You robbed her of her honor." He looked at Greg and then Jon. "I just gave it back."

EPILOGUE

It had been months since the verdict, and things had almost returned to normal around Loveport. With the exception of the pestering media wanting to know when the Loveport baby was going to be born or if he had already been born, the attention had subsided. 'Camp Penrose' had long since been dismantled and life at home was back to normal. Penrose smiled at the tiny TV on his office desk. The network's newest reporter was doing a stand-up in front of an official-looking Washington office building. Don Bissette, out of jail and living his dream, was reporting to the entire nation about the latest FDA investigation into the poultry industry. After watching the two-minute piece, Dr. Penrose finished up his paperwork, grabbed his coat, and turned off the lights of his office.

On his way out, he paused in front of the baby nursery window. The nurses went about the task of changing diapers and taking temperatures. Excited family and friends pressed their noses against the window pointing and cooing at the sleeping wonders. Penrose lingered on each small face. Some cried, while others yawned. Their tiny hands all looked alike. Their scrunched-up faces so resembled one another, yet each was completely different. These young lives were starting with a clean slate. No mistakes. No bungled choices. His eyes sought out the blue card on the bassinet and found the name 'Andrews.' There, the little baby lay sleeping, no different from any of the rest. No different, except for his contentment in not knowing what would have been.

CPSIA information can be obtained at www.ICGtesting.com
Printed in the USA
LVOW11*1543211215

467398LV00005B/25/P